ASCENDANT

By Craig Alanson

Table Of Contents

CHAPTER ONE

"Oh, this can be nothing but trouble," Bodric declared with a grimace. "Koren, best you stay in the barn."

Bodric had heard it first, while he was standing on the floor of the barn, and his son Koren was above in the hayloft, wrestling a bale of hay down for the cows to eat. It was a familiar though infrequent sound; the slow clopping of horse hooves, and the creaking, banging noise of wagons, slowly making their way up the narrow, rutted dirt road that led to the Bladewell's door. And only to the Bladewell's door, for their farm was at the end of the road, beyond which lay only the uninhabited forest that was the Duke's hunting reserve. One wagon, unexpected, was unusual enough at their isolated farmstead. More than one wagon? Such a thing had not happened in all the years Bodric had lived there. He told Koren to hold the hay bale a moment, and stuck his head outside the barn to see who was approaching.

Since there was no good reason for a caravan of wagons to come all the way up the hill from the village, on the lonely, axle-breaking, wheel-splintering dead-end road to nowhere, it must be for a bad reason. A reason he could guess.

"Pa? What's trouble? What is it?" Koren did not want to hear of any trouble on this of all days, his thirteenth birthday. The one day of the year when he was allowed to sleep late, so late that the sun had peaked over the low hills to the east and sent the golden rays of morning into his bedroom window, before he had swung his feet onto the floor. So late that the chickens, sheep and cows in the barnyard, even the deer lingering at the edge of the wheat field, and the crows strutting around the cornfield, wondered why Koren was not yet out of bed. So late, that Koren had been sore from laying in bed that long, so late that by the time he had finally rolled out of bed when his mother called, he was more tired than if he'd gotten up in the pre-dawn darkness like he did every other day of the year. This day there would not be the usual oatmeal or eggs for breakfast, his mother was making batter for hotcakes, and soon he would be sitting down to enjoy a giant stack of light, fluffy hotcakes, layered with fresh butter, and swimming in a lake of maple syrup the family had made from their trees that very spring-

"Koren?" His father interrupted Koren's hungry day dream. "You listening to me? Stay here. Right here." Bodric stuck his head out the barn door, and spat on the ground in disgust. It was the county sheriff on a horse, leading several other horses, and at least a half dozen wagons that Bodric could see, strung out along the road, all headed toward the Bodric's front door. This could not be good. For his neighbors to leave their own farms early in the morning, and ride all the way up the rough road from the village center, must be something serious. Not every farmer in the poor village of Crebbs Ford could afford to own a horse, so many had crowded into their neighbor's wagons for the uncomfortable trip, and they all seemed to be staring and pointing at

Bodric, as he stood outside the barn. He didn't wave to his neighbors. Arriving unannounced, in large numbers, and led by the sheriff, was not neighborly behavior.

"Pa!" Koren called from the hayloft, having crawled on hands and knees to lean out the loft door. "It's the sheriff! Are they calling up the militia?" He asked excitedly. There were rumors that the royal army had suffered yet another defeat, and if the orcs were bold enough, raiding parties could sweep down from their mountain lairs to the north. At thirteen, Koren was almost old enough to join the annual militia training that was held in the village square every winter, and he was looking forward to practicing with the militia, even if it was only with wooden swords and pikes. Sometimes, the militia practiced archery, since only a handful of farmers had ever held a real sword, but everyone hunted. And Koren never missed with an arrow, he couldn't wait to show the village boys, and perhaps some girls, his skill with a bow.

"I see it's the sheriff, and if they were calling up the militia, they would have sounded the big horn at the Golden Trout. You finish feeding the animals, then clean out the stalls, and, and you fix that fencepost. Don't come to the house until I call you."

"But, Pa," Koren protested, having heard the wagons, and burning to know what was going on outside the barn, "what-"

"Never you mind what's going on, boy, get your chores done." Bodric said gruffly, troubled by what he thought the sheriff's visit meant.

And then he recognized the miller, perched on the seat of his wagon with his two boys, and he knew exactly what it meant, and his heart fell in his chest.

And Koren saw the miller at the same time. "Pa," his voice sounded strangled, "I'm sorry. I didn't mean to-"

"You didn't do anything, son, and you don't listen to any foolish talk, either. Mind your chores." He said in a tone that invited no reply.

Bodric strode across the field, fists clenched at his sides, until he was no more than a few feet from the sheriff, who had gotten off his horse and was standing with his own hands up in a peaceful gesture. Peaceful or not, the sheriff had a sword strapped to his waist, and a dagger tucked into his belt.

"You had to do this on my boy's birthday?" Bodric snapped angrily to the sheriff.

"Bodric, let's you and me talk inside-"

Ignoring the sheriff, Bodric strode toward the miller's wagon, shaking his fist. "I'm not paying a single coin to fix your mill, you thief! If you'd put any money toward keeping your equipment in proper order, it wouldn't have-"

The miller shouted louder, drowning out the farmer, his face beet red, standing up in the wagon. "There was nothing wrong with my mill! Your son is a-"

"Enough!" The sheriff stepped in front of Bodric, blocking the way, rocking back awkwardly on his heels to keep the bigger man from moving forward. "Bodric, we need to talk about this *in-side*. And you," the sheriff pointed sternly at the miller, "sit down and keep you mouth shut. Uh!" He rested one hand on the grip of sword for emphasis. "Not one word from you."

-"jinx!" The miller finished, but he sat down sulkily, and said no more.

Bodric opened his mouth to speak, when the sheriff leaned close and said in a low voice. "Do you really want to do this out here, good sir?" The sheriff glanced back at the villagers, who were all standing up in their wagons, or sitting tall in the saddle, anxious to see what the sheriff would do. "I'm here to *protect* you from these idiots."

Bodric closed his mouth, grinding his teeth while he considered whether to let pride, or good sense, win out. The crowd suddenly began muttering under their breath, some fearfully making hex signs with their fingers, toward the barn. Bodric turned his head to see Koren standing outside the barn door, hands clasped in front of him, his lower lip quivering as if he were about to burst into tears. With a gesture, Bodric shooed his son back into the barn and, his shoulders slumped, stepped back. "Sheriff, come inside my house, we can talk there."

In the Bladewell's cozy kitchen, which was more than warm because the stove was fired on a warm spring morning, the sheriff of Crickdon County was wishing he hadn't worn his official uniform, which included a leather jacket. A leather jacket which trapped heat and made sweat trickle down his back, sticking his shirt to his back. He also wished the villagers hadn't insisted on riding to the Bladewell's farm quite so early in the morning, for he had skipped breakfast and was hungry, and seeing a bowl of hotcake batter, with crocks of syrup, fresh butter and jam, was making his stomach growl.

He also felt rather ridiculous, sitting in the kitchen of the Bladewells, a family he knew fairly well, while wearing his official uniform, including a sword. The sheriff regretted bringing the sword inside this peaceful house, but as he had brought the sword with him, he couldn't simply leave it leaning outside the front door. He knew the Bladewells fairly well, having dealt with them occasionally on business for the Baron, and always on good terms. Knew them, and respected them, for Bodric and Amalie Bladewell had turned the stony, weed-choked soil of the poor-yielding farm they had bought into the finest piece of farmland in the county. Their fields grew more grain, their cows gave more milk, their pigs grew faster, their chickens laid more and larger eggs. Compared to other farmers in Crebbs Ford, the Bladewells were prosperous, and the sheriff knew that caused resentment in some people. Despite his admiration for the hard-working family, the sheriff ignored his growling stomach and his personal feelings on the subject, and did the job his distant cousin the Baron paid him for.

"My apologies, Mistress Bladewell," the sheriff said as he unstrapped his sword and set it down on the table beside the door, "for bringing a weapon into your home."

Amalie stood stiffly in her kitchen, torn between the obligations of a good host to a guest, and the obvious fact that the sheriff was not in her kitchen as a guest. She had been about to crack eggs to make Koren's birthday cake when, glancing out the window, she had seen the sheriff leading a line of people up the drive to her door. The eggs sat, untouched, on the table by the stove, and her apron was draped over a chair. Amalie did not want to appear before the sheriff, on his official business, while wearing an old apron with flour and hotcake batter on it. Every year, the Bladewells gave a plump smoked ham to the sheriff, and he accepted the gift gratefully. "We know you, Tom Mallow, you've sat at our table and enjoyed your fill of my cooking. There is no need for apologies, unless you've come here to do us harm." She squeezed her husband's hand, and he nodded to her.

"I came here to-"

"We know why you're here, sheriff." Bodric interrupted. "And I told you, we're not paying a single coin to fix that mill."

"I didn't-"

Bodric continued as if the sheriff hadn't spoken. "Our boy wasn't even inside the mill that day, did he tell you that? Wasn't near the miller's broken-down old gears."

"Bodric, I'm not here to collect money." The sheriff managed to say while Bodric caught his breath.

Husband and wife shared a surprised look. Amalie felt a chill down her spine. The family could not afford to fix the water mill's equipment, and despite whatever lies the miller had told, Koren hadn't done anything. A demand for money was at least understandable. And if not to demand money, why had the sheriff, and what looked to be half the village, come to the Bladewell's farm? "He's not asking for money to fix the mill?"

The sheriff shook his head. "The Baron has advanced funds to repair the mill, and is bringing in a skilled work crew from Norville to get the job done by the end of summer, before the harvest."

"That sounds expensive." Bodric observed warily.

"The Baron knows that without the mill, people in this village can't pay their taxes, and the Baron will still owe his taxes to the Duke, so…"

Bodric nodded. Sheriff Tom Mallow had been friendly, having grown up in Crebbs Ford before his distant cousin the Baron appointed Tom as county sheriff, but that friendliness was based on the Bladewell's paying their taxes in full, and on time. Other families in Crebbs Ford, and throughout Crickdon County, did not find the sheriff friendly at all. Not when he was taking away the grain they needed to survive the winter, or taking cows, pigs or chickens the family needed. Or even bringing in men of the Baron's guard, to help the sheriff force a poor family off their land, when the family had been unable to pay their taxes. Bodric and Amalie's had bought their farm land at auction, after the previous owners had lost their property to the Baron for failing to pay taxes. Amalie still vividly remembered the look the unfortunate family had given her, as they rode their wagon down the road, away from the land that had failed them. "If you're not here for money, then why?" Amalie asked, pointing vaguely out the window toward the people lined up along their road.

"To protect you, for one." The sheriff answered unhappily.

"Protect us?" Bodric angrily squeezed his wife's hand without realizing what he was doing. "From our neighbors?" He asked, astonished. Like any small village or town, some people could be petty or even mean-spirited, but Bodric had never known anyone to be violent, unless they had too much of their home-made drink. And he couldn't imagine so many of his neighbors drinking that much so early in the morning.

"Bodric, Amalie, people are scared." The sheriff said quietly.

"Scared?" It was Amalie's turn to grip her husband's hand tightly.

"Scared enough to call for a priest, or a wizard, to do something about Koren. The miller has people terrified, he's been sitting in the Golden Trout every night, whipping people into a frenzy, and Mistress Pettifogger has been helping him by providing free beer." The sheriff made a disgusted face, as much at the innkeeper's stupid behavior, as the poor quality of the inn's beer.

"Afraid of my boy?" Amalie gasped

"Superstitious idiots." Bodric grumbled.

"Idiots they may be, but there was talk of people coming up here with torches, and burning you out. They want you to leave."

"Leave?" Amalie nervously twirled around her finger the blue ribbon that tied back her dark hair. "Bodric's family has farmed land around Crebbs Ford for three generations. And Koren is not dangerous! He's just a boy, barely thirteen. I'll certainly not have the likes of Pricella Pettifogger," Amalie waggled her finger toward the kitchen window, "chase me away from my home."

Pricella, wife of the town's innkeeper, was a thin, unpleasant woman, who always had a disapproving look on her face, like she smelled something bad, and it must be *you*. The only time people ever saw Pricella smile was when she was trying to curry favor with the Baron or his family. Some people said that avoiding Pricella is why the Baron never visited Crebbs Ford anymore. Not that the Baron ever spent much time in such a small, poor village, the Baron being busy doing important Baron things, like ruling all of Crickdon County. As long as the people of Crebbs Ford paid their taxes when the Baron's sheriff came to collect at harvest time, the Baron could not have cared less what his subjects did in the tiny, poor village of Crebbs Ford. The only time the Baron passed through Crebbs Ford these days was in his four-horse carriage, on his way to visit the Duke. And the Baron would likely have avoided Crebbs Ford entirely, if not for the fact that the bridge in the village was the only way across the river for twenty five miles in either direction. Older folk in the village joked that they could remember when the Baron's carriage was pulled by only two horses, before the Baron grew so fat! Such things were not, of course, ever said outside of one's own home, the Baron being very vain about his appearance.

It was the Baron's total lack of interest in the goings-on of the inhabitants of Crebbs Ford that left Tom Pettifogger, owner of the Golden Trout Inn and the wealthiest man among the poor people of Crebbs Ford, the leader of the village. And since Tom had no interest in acting as mayor, and more than anything wanted to keep his wife busy so she would not have time to nag him to death, Pricella was left in charge of the day-to-day goings-on around Crebbs Ford.

The source of the Pettifogger's dispute with the Bladewells happened back around Koren's eighth birthday, when his father brought him into the common room of the Golden Trout, after they had sold a cow for what Bodric felt was a more than fair price. Bodric was in a very jolly mood, so he had decided to celebrate with a cold mug of beer in the common room of the Golden Trout. Koren was sitting with his father while Bodric sipped beer, told stories, laughed, and discussed the weather with other farmers, when Koren decided he wanted to try this 'beer' that all the men were so eager to drink. His father had gotten up from the table, to play a game of darts, and left his half-full mug of beer behind. No one was watching Koren, in the dark corner of the common room. One sip, that's all, just one little sip, he told himself. But the stoneware mug was heavy, and at first he didn't tilt it enough to make the beer close enough to sip. Then he tipped it too far, and got a mouthful.

Just at the moment Koren's eyes flew open wide in surprise and he choked on the bitter brew, the giant wooden vat in the back room of the Golden Trout burst open, and two hundred gallons of what Tom Pettifogger claimed was the best beer in Crickdon County came crashing through the door into the common room, washing away tables, chairs and customers alike. Now, whether Tom Pettifogger's beer was the best brew in the county as he claimed, or, as some of his customers grumbled, was stale swill not fit for horses to drink, was in dispute. Not in dispute was Tom and Pricella's shock and anger, and also not in dispute, as far as the Pettifoggers were concerned, was who was to blame: Koren.

The Great Beer Flood wasn't the first time that Koren had been present during an unfortunate incident in Crebbs Ford. In fact, Koren had a reputation as-

A *jinx.*

There is no nice way to say it. Koren was considered to be a jinx. A *bad*-luck charm. Strange things simply seemed to happen when Koren was around. Bad things, unfortunate things. Not that anyone ever saw Koren actually *do* anything to make bad things happen, they simply happened. And always when young Koren was involved.

The first couple times bad things happened around Koren, people laughed and said Bodric needed to be careful about that boy. But when the blacksmith's forge roared into a fire so hot it caused a white-hot pillar of flame to shoot up through the roof of the shed, at the exact moment young Koren yelped from burning his hand on a hot poker, people began not so much to talk, as to grumble. Began to mutter under their breath, to give Koren odd, unfriendly glances, and to wonder if, in fact, Koren really was indeed a jinx. Even sensible adults began to wonder if Koren was somehow cursed with bad luck.

So, when the Pettifoggers loudly banished Bodric and his boy from their inn after the Great Beer Flood, no one in the village stood up for the boy. No one could say for sure that Koren wasn't a jinx, now, could they? When Pricella tried to make Bodric pay for the damages, well, people said she had gone a bit too far, and most townsfolk took Bodric's side when he told Pricella exactly what he thought of her, the Golden Trout, and their sour, flat beer. After all, what Bodric said was what pretty much everyone in Crebbs Ford had wanted to say for years. Behind Pricella's back, of course.

Relations between the Bladewells and the other families in Crebbs Ford were strained for years after that, with half the townsfolk saying Koren was a menace, half saying there was no such thing as a jinx, and half saying, well, there might be something to this talk about a jinx. There were *three* halves because some people changed their minds about Koren, depending on the day, or the weather, or what they ate for breakfast. Truth was, most people in Crebbs Ford, and all of Crickdon County, were poor farmers, scraping out a living on land they rented from the Baron, and could not afford bad things to strike them or their family. Life was hard enough without a jinx making things worse. A lame horse, a broken plow, a hailstorm wiping out a field of crops, almost anything could spell disaster for a family already on the edge of poverty. And some people resented that the Bladewells owned their land, and their home was one of the best pieces of farmland in the entire county.

It was most unfortunate, therefore, that Bodric took Koren with him to the grain mill, a couple weeks before Koren's thirteenth birthday. That mill, along with the bridge across the river, were the only reasons for the village of Crebbs Ford to exist. Although no one particularly liked the miller, and his boys were bullies, the miller was grudgingly honest and his prices for grinding grain were mostly fair, and the closest other mill was a full day's journey along the river to the west.

When they arrived at the mill that fateful morning, Bodric left Koren to tend to the wagon, and get water for their horse. Koren carefully put wooden blocks under the wagon's wheels, unhitched the horse, and led the horse to the millrace stream to drink. The miller's two boys, seeing a chance for a bit of mischief, crawled over to the wagon and slipped the blocks from under the wheels. They were trying to hide in the tall grass and keep from laughing out loud, when they noticed that the wagon was rolling the wrong way. Rolling straight for their father's mill!

What the miller's sons should have done was to stop the wagon, but because they were cowardly bullies, they lay still and hoped they could blame it on Koren.

When Koren saw the wagon rolling toward the mill, he shouted in alarm, which caused the horse to bolt away. Koren ran after the wagon as fast as his legs could carry him, and grasped onto the tailgate, digging his heels into the dirt and trying to pull the wagon to a halt. The wagon was far too heavy for the boy, it dragged him with it as it rolled straight for the door of the mill. Koren swung his legs up, planted his heels in the dirt road, closed his eyes and gave one mighty heave with all his strength-

And the wagon did *stop*, at the same moment that the great waterwheel of the mill also *stopped*, causing the machinery inside the mill to break, shatter and fly around inside the stone building. Bodric and the miller ran out of the mill, holding their arms over their heads, and flung themselves flat on the ground, while the waterwheel jerked back to life, sending more large pieces of machinery flying about.

The miller's boys ran up to their father, blaming Koren for the wagon almost crashing into the mill, but the miller did not care about any stupid wagon. His mill! His precious mill was ruined! Ruined, and he might not have it fixed in time for the autumn harvest that year! What a disaster for the miller, and for the farmers of Crebbs Ford, who now had no place to take their grain for grinding!

The miller was sputtering with anger, pulling out tufts of his beard and yelling words that Koren's mother had told him were *very bad* things to say. And saying bad things about Koren, that it was all Koren's fault, that the boy was a jinx. Bodric shouted back that if the miller had taken proper care of his clunky machinery, it would not have broken. Both men were red-faced from shouting. They almost came to blows before Bodric told Koren to catch the horse, hitch it to the wagon, they would be leaving. Good riddance, said the miller, and don't come back, ever!

The Bladewells could bring their grain to some other mill in the future, he would not be grinding it for them, ever again!

The miller went to the Golden Trout Inn that evening to drown his sorrows in a mug of beer, and the more he drank, the louder and more angry he became. Something would have to be done about that Koren Bladewell boy, something soon, he declared to anyone who would listen. Among the farmers in the common room of the Golden Trout that night, he found an agreeable audience. The news that the village's only mill might not be available to grind their grain, with crops planted and harvest time approaching, spelled disaster for everyone in Crebbs Ford, not just for the miller. Koren was a menace, a danger to poor, honest, hard-working people who could not afford any more bad luck in their lives. When Pricella Pettifogger announced that it was time for action, not more talk, about Koren, no one spoke against her. When Pricella spoke to the sheriff of Crickdon County, and explained how much trouble Koren had caused, the sheriff knew his employer the Baron would care about only two things. First, that tax payments from Crebbs Ford might be reduced, or delayed, because there was no local mill to grind the farmer's grain. And second, that Pricella Pettifogger was very upset and worked up about the issue of Koren Bladewell, and that she was very likely to be pestering the Baron until he did something about it. The problem with tax payments was serious, for the Baron had to pay his taxes to the Duke, whether the Baron had collected taxes from his subjects or not. But the sheriff remembered the last time Pricella had pestered the Baron about something; the woman had been so persistent, and so annoying, that the Baron had taken to riding far out of his way to avoid going through Crebbs Ford, and had even begun to dread reading his mail, lest he find yet another strident message from Mistress Pettifogger. So the sheriff was not sure the Baron would care about the taxes, as much as caring about keeping Pricella from pestering him again. What the sheriff did know for certain was that the Baron expected his sheriff to take care of problems in the county. Which is why the sheriff rode directly to the Baron's castle, explained the problem, and suggested a solution. A solution the Baron liked, liked very much indeed. The morning of Koren's thirteenth birthday, the sheriff met a group of scared and angry people from the village who were assembled at the Golden Trout, and led them to ride slowly up the lane to the Bladewell's farm.

Bodric released his wife's hand, and put his hands on her shoulders, pulling her against him. "You can tell those people outside, that we'll not leave our home because ignorant fools are scared of a silly superstition." He spoke through clenched teeth, his jaw set in defiance. "It's going to be all right, honey. We're staying right here. Plain and simple."

The sheriff shifted his feet uncomfortably. "It's not that simple." He pulled a scroll from a pocket, and laid it on the kitchen table. "This has gone beyond the Pettifoggers, or the miller. My lord the Baron has declared your son banished."

"Banished?!" The Bladewells shouted together.

"And he's offered a fair price for your land," the sheriff continued, pulling another scroll from his pocket, "a more than fair price. Even generous."

"This is outrageous! The Baron-"

"Who is your liege lord, I caution you, Mister Bladewell," the sheriff said quickly, with one finger held up for emphasis. "It would not do to speak ill of the Baron in front of his sheriff, I remind you."

Bodric fumed, but held his tongue from saying what he felt about the Baron. "We will fight this," he said weakly, feeling he had to say something. "We can appeal to his grace the Duchess."

The sheriff shook his head sadly. "Bodric, yes, you can appeal to the Duchess, at the assize court next winter, if you travel to the castle. By that time, if you haven't taken the Baron's offer, he will force you off your land," the sheriff didn't need to mention that it would be he and his men carrying out the Baron's orders, "and sell your land at auction. And I can tell you, good sir, the Baron will make sure he is the only bidder at the auction, and you will be the poorer for it. I know him, he'll do it. Do you think the Duchess will side with you, over the Baron, who is cousin to the Duchess' husband?"

Bodric founds his hands were shaking as he held his wife, and she looked up at him with tears in her eyes. His own eyes stung, but he was determined not to show that to the sheriff. "This can't be happening, not to us. How can our neighbors, people we've known for years, be afraid of our boy? He's a good boy!"

"There have been odd things going on around Koren, for years now," the sheriff said gently.

"Odd? Rumors and silly stories-"

"Enough to scare people." The sheriff interrupted.

Amalie wiped the tears from her eyes; she wasn't sad or shocked, she was angry. "I didn't hear people complaining when Koren helped harvest their crops over the years. Or when Koren nursed Redding's cow back to health. That animal was near death's door, and Koren stayed by its side, day and night, and now it's scampering around the field like a calf! Strange things happen all the time 'round here, was it Koren's fault when that twister storm tore up the Rendell's barn? Or when the flood last year knocked out the bridge? Or when lightning stuck the blacksmith shop? Were all those Koren's fault?"

"Amalie, Bodric, I can't dispute that Koren has been a good boy; hard-working, always ready to help people. Maybe there's something strange about him, maybe there's not, maybe it's all superstitious stories. All I can say is that my master, the Baron, has declared your son banished, and he has until Midsummers day to leave the county. The two of you don't have to leave-"

"We're not sending our son away!" Mother and father said in unison.

Not knowing what else to say, for everything that could be said had been, the sheriff pointed at the scrolls on the table, tapping them emphatically with a finger. "You have been officially notified of our liege lord the Baron's declaration of banishment, and of his offer to purchase your property. I am going outside to calm people down, and get them off your land. I'll be back here next week, by myself, and you can tell me your decision then. Until then, I suggest you stay out of the village."

So it was that, the week before Midsummer's Day, the Bladewell family loaded the few possessions they hadn't already sold into their wagon, and started down the narrow, rutted lane into the tiny village of Crebbs Ford. Bodric had sold the farm, and all their animals except the horse, to the Baron. The sheriff, who had delivered the Baron's money, waved to Bodric as the wagon passed, but the sheriff wasn't smiling, and neither were the Bladewells. The sheriff wasn't smiling, because he felt sorry for the Bladewells; it had been the sheriff's idea for the Baron to send them into exile. The legal term was *banished*, but *exiled* sounded better, as if the Bladewells had a choice at all. And technically, the Bladewell family had not been exiled, only their thirteen year old son. Another reason the sheriff was not smiling was that he knew the Baron had likely paid too much for the Bladewell's farm. The amount of money the Baron had paid to the Bladewells was based on the amount of crops and animals the farm produced under the hard work of the Bladewell family. But the Baron had, foolishly, granted the farm to his youngest son, so the boy could 'learn the practice of farming and animal husbandry'. The lazy boy didn't know anything about farming, was apparently allergic to hard work, and was going to fail as a farmer. And the sheriff knew the Baron would not be happy when the most productive farm in the county fell into disrepair, and the sheriff would get the blame. So, he waved to the Bladewells that morning, and no one was smiling.

Bodric had to drive the wagon through the village, for the east road was the only way across the bridge. It was early yet, most people were either still in bed, or tending to chores around their farms. The few people they met fell into two groups; those who glared at them as if to say good riddance, and those who avoided their eyes or pretended to be sad the Bladewells were leaving. A mile down the lane, they passed by the farm of Bodric's brother Ander, who was pretending to fix a fence post, as an excuse to be out by the road. "Ander," Bodric said with a nod toward his brother, and he brought the wagon to a halt.

"Morning, Bodric." Ander responded uncomfortably. "So, you're leaving then? I hear the Baron gave you a good price."

"That's between me and the Baron." Bodric said bitterly. "Yes, we're leaving, as if you didn't know that. You're not going to say you wish I would stay?"

Ander looked down at his shoes. "I have a family too, Bodric. And you can't say your boy hasn't been around every time something bad happens around here."

"You should be ashamed of yourself, Ander Bladewell." Amalie snapped. "Superstitious foolishness! Koren is a good boy. Do you forget about the time Koren nursed your horse back to health, when you'd given up? Was *that* bad luck for you? Bodric, we're not wanted here, let's move on, before I lose my temper and say something uncharitable."

Bodric tapped the reigns and the horse pulled the wagon away, without another word to his brother. It had been Ander's betrayal that made Bodric decide to move; he did not care what the Pettifoggers, or the miller, or anyone else in the town thought. But when Bodric had looked out his front door that fateful morning, to see that his own brother Ander had joined the people seeking Koren to be banished, Bodric had not known what to say. His own brother wanted him banished from the town. Koren's mother and father had argued late into that night, before wearily deciding to sell the farm, and make the long journey to a distant village where one of Amalie's relatives lived. There, they could buy another farm, and get a fresh start.

First, though, they had to get through Crebbs Ford. Their route through the village was mostly quiet, until they passed by the mill, with its broken waterwheel. The miller's sons came out to jeer at the Bladewells, and then they were joined by other boys; bullies who saw that none of the adults in the village would step forward to defend the Bladewells. The family kept the wagon moving, and ignored the insults, but then the bullies began throwing clods of dirt, and other things. An over-ripe pepper splattered against the wagon next to Koren, then a boy threw a large potato at Koren's head. Quick as a flash, Koren caught it out of the air, and drew his arm back to throw the potato, when Bodric caught his arm. "Don't waste good food, son. You tuck that in the back of the wagon, and we'll eat it tonight." The wagon went around a sharp turn in the road, rumbled up the cobblestones onto the bridge, and they left the village of Crebbs Ford behind forever.

That first night, camped beside the road, Koren had to admit his father was right, the potato was good, and almost big enough to feed the whole family. For a moment, in front of a crackling fire, camped out under the stars, Koren could almost pretend he was on a fishing trip, and they would return home in the morning.

In the morning, they did not return home, and Koren awoke with a back stiff from sleeping on the ground beneath the wagon. His parents had spent the night in the back of the wagon, using what little cushioning they had to comfort their older bones. Koren got the morning fire started, and brought a pail of water to his mother to boil for the breakfast oats. "I didn't notice it last evening," Bodric declared, "but I believe this land used to be an orchard. Koren, come with me, we'll see if we can find some plums."

The tangled, overgrown trees indeed used to be an orchard, although it was hard to tell from the road. Most of the trees were apple, with fruit not yet ripe enough to pick. Plums, though, were to be found here and there, with most of that fruit already laying rotting on the ground. Bodric kept a wary eye out for bears, for such an abundance of fruit would surely draw animals to feast, and some trees bore telltale claw marks. A bear, Bodric warned his son, was bad enough, but a bear drunk on fermented fruit was a true danger!

Father and son wrestled their way through the overgrown branches to find ripe plums that hadn't fallen, and as always, Koren somehow knew just where to find the best fruit. Soon Bodric stayed on the ground while Koren handed plums down to him. For a moment, just a moment, clambering around tree limbs, with warm morning sunlight filtering through the leaves, the air scented with ripe plums, Koren could almost forget that they would not be bringing the fruit home, that he wasn't picking from trees in their own orchard.

"You saw the old stone wall under all that brush, as we got here?" Bodric observed. "This must have been someone's farm. A long time ago, looks like."

"Why would anyone abandon a good farm like this?" Koren asked, puzzled. The plum, apple and peach trees were terribly overgrown, what must at one time have been a wheat or corn field was a meadow full of bushes and sapling trees, but when Koren had kicked over a rock, he had seen rick black soil.

Bodric shook his head. "Could be anything. Sickness, accident, no children to take over working the land, taxes. Or the owner wanted too much rent. I wonder if our Baron owns this land." Bodric said with a grimace. "A spot of bad luck, that's all it takes, to knock a family off their land." Intent on picking plums, and talking halfway to himself, Bodric wasn't paying attention to what he'd said to his son.

Koren's ears burned with shame. A spot of bad luck, like having a jinx for a son. "I'm sorry I caused problems for you and mother."

"Oh." Bodric realized what he'd said, and that he couldn't take back, or explain away his words. "I didn't mean - it's not your fault, Koren. Don't worry on it."

"Am I a jinx?" Koren asked, knowing his father would tell him the plain truth whether he wanted to or not. Bodric was that way.

"Koren, I don't rightly know." Bodric said after a pause. "Strange things seem to happen when you're around, that's the truth, I can't deny it." When the mill's waterwheel broke because it *stopped* for no reason, Bodric had been as frightened as the miller. "If you're a jinx sometimes, well, you've been good luck, too, good luck for us, for sure. And you nursed old mister Redding's cow back to health, when he'd given up on it, right? Don't know what you did, but that old cow was back up, and giving milk in a fortnight."

Koren nodded. He had helped out when old mister Redding needed an extra hand on his farm, and when Redding's only cow had fallen down in her stall, glassy-eyed and moaning, Koren had convinced the man to let him try saving the animal. The poor old cow had lain on her side, muscles twitching, burning up with fever, and taking neither food nor water. Koren had stayed there for two days and nights, stroking the animal, and the twitching stopped, and the moaning went away, and when he spooned sugared water into the cow's mouth, it licked it up. If Koren left the cow's side, it moaned in pain, so he stayed right there, keeping a hand touching its hide, and draping an arm over the cow when he caught a few minutes of sleep. Mister Redding had been so grateful, he had given that cow's next calf to Koren.

Koren had always been especially good with animals. The Bladewell's chickens laid more and bigger eggs, their cows gave more milk, their sheep's wool was thick and grew quickly. Jealous neighbors grumbled that the soil under the Bladewell's farm was very rich, so of course their crops and animals were healthy and productive. Bodric's back, which ached from the hard labor of picking stones out of the soil, and spreading manure as fertilizer, would deny the soil there was anything special before he bought the land. "You weren't around when that hailstorm wiped out a whole field of the Pritchert's wheat, that weren't no jinx. Nor the flood that knocked supports from under the bridge, nor the forest fire a couple years back that sent sparks onto the roof of the Golden Trout and almost burnt the place to the ground. I didn't hear old sour face Pricella Pettifogger mention that, when she came to complain about you, now did she?" Bodric said with a wink.

Koren couldn't help a quick grin.

"Don't you worry on what people think about you, Koren. If you're a jinx, well, there must be a lot of jinxes around, seeing as how so many bad things happen. You hold your head up, and don't get to feeling bad about yourself. It don't do any good to be sitting around moping about how bad you got it in life, there's always somebody got it worse." Bodric held a perfectly ripe plum up to his nose and inhaled the sweet scent. "Let's get these back to your mother, she'll be well pleased."

A couple days later, in the afternoon, the family stopped outside of a village. Koren would wait in the woods, while his parents went into the town to buy supplies, and get directions. Koren was ashamed to see his own parents considered that their son was a jinx, they wanted to keep him away from any possible trouble by keeping him out of towns along the way. "It's not that we think you're going to jinx anything, Koren," his father said while he avoided looking his son in the eye, "but, well, you see, we can't afford to have any incidents, while we're on the road." They would be back before dark, they assured Koren, he was to stay in the woods and out of sight. And out of trouble.

Koren watched from the woods as the wagon rolled out of sight down the road, then he kept himself busy picking an entire hat full of wild berries. His mother would be pleased to have fresh berries when she returned. Having stripped the raspberry bushes of ripe fruit, he began looking for wild roots, the way his father taught him. He found and dug up a fair-sized pile of wild carrots when he noticed it was growing dark, and his parents hadn't returned. Koren carefully crept back to the road, and watched for his parents, until the light faded in the western sky, and stars began to twinkle. When it grew so dark he could barely see his hand in front of his face, he made his way back to the clearing where he had left his pack, and soon got a fire going. When his parents returned, they would see his fire from the road.

The stars winked out one by one as the sky filled with clouds, and rain began to fall. Koren rigged up a tarp to sit under, and tended to the fire as big heavy raindrops popped and hissed when they fell onto the fire. He sat up long into the night, jumping at every sound in the forest around him. Finally, he could not keep his eyes open, and he fell asleep under the tarp. In the morning, the fire was cold, and there was still no sign of his parents. Mindful of his parents' warning to keep off the road, Koren walked in the woods parallel to the road, until he came over the crest of a small hill, and could see the town stretched out in the valley below. It looked much like Crebbs Ford; a few buildings clustered together along a road near a river, surrounded by farm fields. Koren noticed that some of the buildings had brightly colored flags, and Koren realized with a start that the next day was the Midsummer's Day celebration. There was no sign of his parent's wagon. The rain had stopped and the sun came out, which lifted Koren's dark spirits. After sitting on a log and pondering what to do for a full hour, Koren stashed his pack behind a tree, and made his way across a field into the town. Pushing aside a tangle of pricker bushes, he stepped out onto the road.

The keeper of the town's inn wiped his flour-covered hands on his apron, and stepped out the side door of the inn, to where he had several pies cooling on a window ledge. Anticipating a crowd in town for the Midsummer's Day festival, he had baked twice as many pies as usual, and carefully selected the fruit to put into each pie. The innkeeper was, then, outraged to see one of his pies was missing! Missing! Gone! Stolen! And he knew who had stolen his precious sweets, there was a trouble-making group of boys around the village, boys who had not enough chores to keep them busy around their farms. With a bellow of rage, the innkeeper flung open the gate of the inn's yard, and charged out into the road. The first person he saw was a boy with dark curly hair, standing in the road with his back to the inn.

Koren spun around in alarm when the innkeeper shouted at him. "You there, boy! Don't you run away from me!" The innkeeper shouted, and of course what Koren did was run, run fast as he could. The innkeeper shouted for people to stop the boy, Koren ducked when a man tried to grab him, ducked again, rolled on the ground, scurried to his feet, and plunged through the pricker bushes and off the road. He pelted his way across the field, and had gone only a few strides, when he stumbled into a brush-choked ditch he hadn't seen, stumbled and fell into the muddy bottom of the ditch. Men crashed through the bushes, cursing as thorns tore at their skin and clothing.

Koren lay still in the ditch, hidden under bushes. He could see men's boots at the edge of the ditch, and he recognized the innkeeper's voice. "Where did that boy get to?"

"I can't see him." Another man said. "This is far enough for me. Look, I've ruined this shirt, my wife won't be pleased."

"We have to catch that boy!" The innkeeper said. "We have to nip this in the bud, I tell you. If we let that sort into our town-"

"Yes, yes," said another man impatiently. "Nip it in the bud, that's what you always say. Well, we've chased him away."

The men grumbled as they carefully made their way back through the bushes, until only the innkeeper's boots were visible. "I'll thrash you if I ever catch you, boy!" The innkeeper shouted as he shook his fist at the field. "Decent folk don't want your kind around. You stay out of our town, you hear me? Nothing but trouble, you are! Nobody wants you around." Huffing and puffing from shouting, the innkeeper stood still for a long minute, before crashing through the bushes back onto the road.

Koren lay still, barely breathing, in the ditch, until he was sure the men had gone. Slowly, he crawled through the mud along the bottom of the ditch, climbing out of the ditch only when he reached the edge of the field. Keeping low in the woods, he made his way back up to retrieve his pack, and sat on the log again to decide what to do next.

His hands were shaking with shock. He had never been to, whatever this village was called. He had only been out of Crebbs Ford a dozen times in his life, and never so far. Yet, somehow, even here, in this village, several long days' journey from Crebbs Ford, people knew about the awful jinx Koren Bladewell! Knew that Koren Bladewell was trouble, a jinx, and wanted to keep him out of their town. They chased him out of town, before he could even say hello. Had the Baron sent word, around Crickdon County, to warn people about Koren, perhaps all of Winterthur province was on the lookout for Koren the Jinx. There would be no place he could go. No town that would not have heard of him by the time he got there, or would hear about him shortly after he arrived. The boy who causes trouble. Good riddance to him.

Koren sat on the log until the sun was directly above him, and sliding down toward the western horizon. He still needed to find his parents. Perhaps he should go back to where they left him? Yes, that was the best idea. He climbed down the hill and cautiously walked out onto the road, the town was around a curve, unseen behind him. Koren trudged miserably down the road, past several farms. No one noticed the lonely boy passing by, until he came upon another boy, around his age, sitting on a stump, eating what looked like a blueberry pie. Koren's stomach grumbled with hunger, he hadn't had anything to eat since noon the day before. "Hey," said the boy, "what cha doin?"

"Nothing." Koren said defensively. "That looks like a good pie."

"It is, and it's mine." The boy hugged the half-eaten, stolen pie to his chest. "My ma made it for me." He lied as he ate another mouthful of stolen pie, the blueberry juice running down his chin. "I'm Roddy. You're not from around here, are you?"

"No. Did you see a wagon come into town, yesterday afternoon?" Koren asked hopefully. This boy, apparently, didn't know what a terrible menace Koren was.

"Big man, red hair, and a lady with straight dark hair? Yeah, they came by yesterday, then back this way again. What's it to you?"

"When did they come back, out of town?" Koren asked excitedly.

Roddy squinted warily. "An hour or so before dark. Why?"

"But, but I didn't see them on the road." Koren sputtered.

Roddy shrugged. "There's a fork in the road, half a mile up thataway, maybe they went the other way last night."

"But, they wouldn't, they wouldn't *leave* me." Koren's head spun, he leaned against a fencepost.

Roddy's eyes opened wide. When he caused more than the usual amount of trouble around the village, his parents sometimes threatened to toss him out of the house. Until he met Koren, it never occurred to Roddy that some parents actually did abandon their children. "Your ma and pa? They just up and leave you here?"

"I don't," Koren had trouble breathing, "I don't know. They couldn't. They wouldn't do that. Not my parents."

"Maybe," Roddy said fearfully, with a guilty glance at the stolen pie. "You cause them a lot of trouble, or something?"

"No." Koren grumbled, his head spinning. "Maybe. Yes."

"Huh." Suddenly, Roddy didn't feel like eating the other half of the pie. He shouldn't have stolen it from the innkeeper. "Hey, do you want the rest of this pie?" Giving the pie to a hungry person would, in Roddy's mind, make up for having stolen it in the first place.

Roddy held the pie out, and Koren took it without looking at it. "Why would they leave me here?"

"You got folks 'round Tinsdale? That's our town."

"No, we're from-" Koren decided not to tell Roddy where he was from, lest the boy figure out who Koren was, and tell his parents.

"Hey, listen, maybe your folks-" Roddy paused as a man's voice drifted across the field. "Uh-oh, that's my pa, I'm supposed to be doing chores. You, hey, good luck to you. And don't tell nobody who gave you the pie." Roddy hopped down off the stump and ran across the field, determined now to do his chores the way his pa wanted.

Koren looked at the pie in his hands, looked at the lonely road stretched out in front of him, and began walking, eating the pie as he went along, without enjoying or even tasting it. When he arrived at the fork in the road, he saw the previous night's rain had washed away any trace of wagon tracks. Feeling completely miserable, Koren sat with his back to the signpost, and used a handful of grass to wipe the pie plate clean. His parents would not have abandoned him, even if he had caused them so much trouble that they had been chased out of their home. There must be some kind of mistake.

Yes, that was it, a mistake, a misunderstanding. Why, even now, his parents were probably searching the woods where he was supposed to be waiting!

With hope renewed, Koren propped the pie plate up against the signpost, and hurried back down the road, headed for the clearing where he had spent the wet, lonely night. He had run no more than a quarter of a mile when he saw a tall merchant's carriage, accompanied by three armed guards on horseback. "Clear the road, boy!" The driver shouted, and Koren stumbled off the side of the road. Koren took off his hat. "Please, sir, have you seen a wagon, with a man and a woman, on this road?"

"No," replied the driver, "not a soul since the morning, not on this road."

One of the guards pulled his horse to a stop next to Koren. "You looking for someone, boy?" The guard asked in a low voice. Koren noticed the guard had his hand on his sword, and was looking warily into the woods even as he spoke.

"Yes, sir, my parents, sir."

"Guard! Leave that stupid boy to himself and get back to your post!" The merchant shouted as he leaned out the window of the closed carriage. "I don't pay you to talk to strange brats on the road."

The guard looked at Koren, shrugged, and tossed him a pair of copper coins. "Sorry. Good luck to you, boy."

The guard spurred his horse onward to catch up with the carriage, and then Koren was alone again. He sat down on the side of the road, staring at the two copper coins. The coins were silent; they could not explain what had happened, or tell him what to do.

It was growing dark by the time Koren picked himself up off the road. His parents had indeed abandoned him, just as Roddy said. He was too much trouble to bother with. The last straw, for his parents, must have been when they discovered that even people in the distant village of Tinsdale knew about their son about Koren the jinx, and wanted to keep him away. As long as Koren was with them, his parents could not have any sort of decent life anywhere in the whole province, perhaps even the kingdom, they must have realized. And so, on their way out of Tinsdale, they had turned the wagon south, instead of coming back for their trouble-causing son.

It was all his fault, Koren knew. If only he could find his parents again, he would promise not to cause any trouble ever again. If only he could find them.

But how? He didn't know where his mother's relative lived. And he needed to stay out of towns, anyway. He needed to go back to the fork in the road, take the turn his parents had made, and hope to catch up to them. If he walked steadily, without taking time to sleep, he could catch up to his parents, he knew he could! Koren brushed some of the dirt off his pants, wiped a tear out of his eye, and set off the way he had come, never looking back.

The decision to follow the fork in the road, instead of going back to the clearing in the woods where his parents had told him to wait, made all the difference in the rest of Koren's life. If he had continued down the road another mile, he may have noticed ruts gouged into the embankment, where someone had pushed a wagon off the road. He may have followed the faint tracks, mostly washed away by the rain, and found the wagon, in the woods, covered under a pile of brush. He may have seen bandits' arrows stuck in the side of the wagon. He may have noticed angry red traces of blood on the side of the wagon, the wagon which now lay empty, stripped of everything valuable.

Koren never saw the tracks, never saw the wagon. He reached the fork in the road as night fell, screwed up his courage, and walked forward in the darkness, hopelessly hoping to catch up to the wagon.

CHAPTER TWO

Thirteen (and nearly a quarter) year old Ariana Trehayme rummaged through the wardrobe cabinet, pushing aside jackets, skirts, robes, and selected a white dress. She bit her lip as she studied the dress, then put it back. It was nice, but too simple. Three other white dresses also failed her inspection, all either too plain or too fancy, until she found a dress with half-length sleeves, just enough lace, and beads that sparkled like tiny diamonds. Ariana held the dress up in front of her, and faced the mirror. She thought the sparkling beads nicely set off her rather pale green eyes. The curls of her auburn hair fell around her shoulders and over her eyes, she tossed her head to get the hair out of the way.

"Now what are you doing here, young lady?" Asked an older woman as she swept into Ariana's bed chambers, which was a suite of rooms which took up one whole wing of Duke Yarron's castle. Although the duke's wife, who usually occupied these bed chambers, probably thought the rooms were opulent, the cold gray stone and white plaster walls of the old castle were rather dreary compared to the Trehayme's royal palace in Linden, where crown princess Ariana lived. The woman was a maid named Nurelka, and she had an armful of clothes weighing her down. Older, to young Ariana, meant that Nurelka was the ripe old age of thirty seven, which clearly was impossibly, unimaginably ancient. Nurelka's own children were now grown and living on their own, but the woman had been a nanny, and now a maid, to Ariana since she was a baby. Nurelka had short black hair, a kind, roundish face, and a perpetually worried expression when she was around Ariana.

"Trying on gowns," Ariana said with a slight frown as she twirled in front of the mirror, making her cascading curls of hair swing around, "the duchess brought a whole trunkful of clothes in for me yesterday. Mother wants me to dress up for this stupid dinner tonight. I'm going to be queen, and command an army, I should be talking maps and defense strategy with Yarron's captains, not attending boring dinners."

"Your mother thinks this dinner is important. Why do you want to look at maps and talk about war anyway? Your mother doesn't do that."

"My mother wasn't raised to be queen, her parents never expected to do anything but marry a rich man. No one ever thought she would be Regent." The Lady Carlana Trehayme was a loving mother, and, in the opinion of her daughter the crown princess, a frustrating disappointment as Regent. Until Ariana became queen on her sixteenth birthday, her mother would exercise power in Ariana's name as the Regent of Tarador, although exercising mostly meant her mother timidly did nothing, while Tarador's allies became fearful, and the power of her enemy grew. "Someone needs to think about defending Tarador, since my mother is too afraid to do anything about it."

Nurelka knew Ariana disapproved of the way her mother was handling her Regency, so she changed the subject. "That dress is beautiful." Nurelka she said, setting her clothes down over the back of a chair.

Ariana stood still in front of the mirror, smoothing the gown so it lay properly against her. "This would be a beautiful wedding gown."

"And why are you thinking about wedding dresses?" Nurelka shook her head in mock amazement, "Is there a young man you have in mind? Perhaps Mark Yarron?"

"Oh, he's so *dull*." Ariana hung the dress back up, no longer in the mood for playing dress-up. The purpose of Ariana getting out of the palace to visit Duke Yarron and his family, in their home of LeVanne province, was for her to get to know the Dukes and Duchesses who would be her vassals, when she became queen of Tarador. Since the snow had melted off the roads in the springtime of the year, she had visited Duke Romero in Winterthur, Duchess Portiss in Anchulz, Duke Magnico in Rellanon, and now Duke Yarron in LeVanne. All were allies, or at least not active rivals, of the ruling Trehayme family. All were unfailingly polite and gracious hosts. All had seen to the crown princess' every need and desire. And all had tried to subtly point out how smart, how handsome, how strong, and how responsible their eligible sons were. Whether those sons were aged twenty two or ten, as long as they weren't already married, could walk without tripping over their own feet, and could manage not to be completely tongue-tied around the lovely young crown princess, none of their parents had missed an opportunity to push their sons at Ariana, in case she showed any interest.

She hadn't, not yet. Some of the boys were cute enough. Now, after being constantly on the road, and away from the palace that was her home, all she wanted to do was go home. "Does my mother really expect me to choose a husband now? I'm not even fourteen. I haven't even *kissed* a boy yet!"

Nurelka looked away, out the window, so the young princess wouldn't see her suppress a laugh. "You had better not choose a husband now! Your mother expects you to show interest in all of these boys, to string them and their parents along, give them hope, and keep them guessing. Until you're sixteen and you get your crown, you and your mother are at the mercy of the Regency Council," the dukes and duchesses who ruled the seven provinces of Tarador, "and your mother needs leverage over that pack of scheming jackals, until you're safely on the throne."

"They're not all jackals." Ariana sniffed. "The Yarrons have been allies of the Trehaymes for centuries."

"And the Magnicos you can also count on, in a pinch." The Magnicos had inherited Rellanon province from the Trehaymes, when the Trehaymes had taken over the throne of Tarador. "That's two out of seven provinces. The others are either against you, or would go against you, if it bettered their own positions. Your mother needs to worry about this now, and you need to pay attention, if you want that throne waiting for you in a couple years." When Ariana's father, Adric Trehayme, had been killed in battle eight years ago, he had only one child, five year old Ariana. Her mother Carlana had been chosen to serve as Regent, and rule Tarador in Ariana's name, until Ariana was old enough to become queen. Adric's brother had more interest in drinking wine and racing horses than ruling Tarador, and the seven dukes and duchesses of the Regency council had all wanted power for themselves. No duke or duchess wanted to support a rival for power, so Carlana had been a compromise to serve as Regent, a compromise agreed to because the dukes and duchesses thought Carlana was weak, and easily controlled. Since the day she was elected Regent, Carlana had one goal: to ensure her daughter assumed the throne on her sixteenth birthday. To do that, Carlana and her daughter needed to strengthen bonds with their allies, and keep their rivals off balance.

Ariana sighed. She knew all this. Her mother reminded her about it, almost every day. "Nurry," Ariana said, reverting to the name she had called her maid as a little girl, "today, all I want to do is ride down the river and have a picnic. It's the one thing I've wanted to do since we got here. Even if I have to go with Yarron's brats."

"Then let's get you dressed properly. You can't go out in the woods in your nightgown." Nurelka pointed to the clothing that lay over the back of the chair.

Ariana hugged her arms tightly around herself. "It's chilly out there, why can't I wear pants, like the boys all do? I saw some girls wearing pants yesterday."

"Those were peasant girls were harvesting potatoes in the fields, and only some of the youngest of them were wearing pants. You don't work on a farm, you're a princess, and princesses don't wear pants."

"When I'm queen, I'm going to declare that all women can wear pants, if they want to." Ariana said stubbornly, and picked out a woolen dress to wear.

"When you are queen, you can wear soldier's armor, and a fruit basket on your head, and everyone will think you've gone mad."

Ariana laughed at the thought of such an absurd outfit. "This dress will be warm enough, and good for riding." Ariana had wanted to ride a boat down the river, where they would meet her guards, have a picnic lunch, and ride horses back. It was a beautiful autumn morning, chilly, but promising to become sunny and warm. Soon enough, she would be back at the palace, stuck inside for the winter. One nice thing about being a princess was being able to order her guards around. It almost made up for having to wear dresses.

Koren woke when a large drop of dew fell from the tip of a leaf, right onto his nose. He yawned and stretched and rose wearily to his feet, stretching his cold and stiff muscles. It was chilly that morning, and the trees were tinged bright red and orange as the leaves began to turn color, summer was certainly over. A mist covered the ground in the forest, gathering thick in the low pockets of land. And the forest, in summertime filled with a chorus of insects buzzing, birds signing and little frogs peeping to each other in spring-fed ponds, was silent. Too silent? He sat still, listening intently, for he knew birds stopped singing sometimes if danger were near. Quietly, slowly, he climbed the two lower branches of the tree he'd been sleeping under and looked around. These weren't his woods he'd been camping in, these weren't anyone's woods, that he could tell, he had explored for miles and found nothing but old campsites. The forest was a true wilderness. He pulled his only jacket tightly around him, shivering, blowing on his hands to warm his stiff fingers before he made his way back to the ground. Today, he needed to find straw or dried moss, to stuff inside his jacket and pants to keep him warm, before winter arrived.

Using dry leaves that he'd kept inside his jacket overnight, Koren started a fire, blowing gently on the flickering flames to make it burn hot and clean, carefully adding twigs and then small sticks. Smoke and steam would drift through and above the woods and let anyone around know where Koren was, and he didn't want anyone finding him. Especially, he didn't want anyone sneaking up on him, for not all the dangers in the wilderness walked on four legs.

As he warmed his fingers, Koren looked around the woods, at the sheltered spot where he'd been camping. With summer gone and winter approaching, he needed to think about building a real shelter where he could survive the cold. These woods had plenty of game, the river had plenty of fish, and Koren hadn't seen any people around. No, not this place, he decided, he would keep walking south for another couple weeks. South meant warmer temperatures, if his mother was right about that sort of thing, she was from somewhere in the south of Tarador. Yes, south for two or three weeks, then he needed to find or build a shelter. He had been out in winter cold overnight before, while hunting with his father, but they had always been able to wait for good weather, and the warmth of home had never been no more than a day or two away. But this winter, he would be at the mercy of the weather, with only his wits to keep him alive until springtime.

Where would he go? It didn't matter, as long as it was toward the south. He didn't have any particular place to go, he'd given up trying to find his parents. That first night that he'd traveled alone, he came to a crossroads, where the roads went in four directions. Wagon tracks led every which way, leaving no clue to where his parents had gone. Not more than two miles further south was another crossroads, where three roads went south, across three bridges over the river. His parents had been clever, Koren had to admit, they had abandoned him at the best possible location, so that he had no chance of following them. And his parents had left him his pack, which had knives, fishing hooks, and other supplies that should be enough for any farm boy to survive in the wilderness. Koren had gone from being shocked, to sad, to angry, to grudging acceptance at his fate. His parents were gone. They had given him a chance to survive on his own, now his future was up to him, and only him. As his father had said, however bad Koren's lot in life, someone out there had it worse.

Not knowing where else to go from the first crossroads, he had walked steadily in a generally southerly direction, trying to stay ahead of the changing seasons, keeping away from towns, and out of sight as much as possible. Once, when he was very hungry, he had snuck onto a farm and stolen a handful of eggs, but as he sat down to eat them, he considered the children who likely lived on the farm. The missing eggs would not go unnoticed, and the children would get into trouble with their parents. Koren lost his appetite thinking that he might cause some other boy or girl to be abandoned by their parents, so he returned to the farm before daylight and put the eggs back. Since then, he lived on plants he found in the forest, and fishing and trapping provided just enough food. His pack contained his meager supply of possessions; two knives, fish hooks and twine, flint for starting fires, a length of rope, a small tarp, a thin sweater and a jacket. Koren was not terribly worried about being able to survive in the forest, except for during the winter. No child grew up on a farm in Winterthur province, boy or girl, without knowing how to hunt and fish, how to make clothing out of deer hide, to make a bow and arrows, how to find plants and roots to eat.

For this morning, he had a few wild potatoes and carrots that he'd found the day before. With a fire started, he huddled next to it for warmth while he roasted the vegetables for breakfast. When the carrots and potatoes were roasted soft, he munched on them, watching the small fire burn down. Koren stood up abruptly, kicking dirt into the fire to put it out without any smoke. Fires reminded him of home, a fire glowing on the hearth in their cozy kitchen, warming the house on a cold day, with a pot of stew hung over the flames, and his mother stirring and sprinkling in seasonings. Fires reminded him of home, and he now didn't have a home, or a family, so he didn't want to be reminded. When the fire was safely out, he ate a roasted potato while he made his way through the forest. It was time to check on the trap he'd placed in the river, to see if any fish had been caught during the night.

He hopped on rocks out into the river, to where he had set the trap. It was in a good place, for just downstream, the river picked up speed as it fell through a series of rapids, the strong current should push fish into his trap. Success! He would eat well that day, he thought hungrily. There were three fat fish swimming in the trap, Koren quickly lowered the upstream gate so the fish could not get out. With one of his knives, he sharpened the end of a stick, and held it like a spear, waiting for a fish to swim close-

Voices startled him, and he crouched down behind a rock. Sound traveled far across water. He heard deep voices, more than one man, and a higher sound, a girl? What were they doing, here in the wilderness? Koren had not seen a single person for three weeks, and he had been camping in these very woods for eight days. He tucked his knife into his belt, used the spear for a balance, and leaped across rocks back to the shore, to hide behind bushes on the riverbank.

A small boat floated into view, such a boat Koren had never seen before. It was no more than twenty feet long, narrow, brightly painted, with the carved head of a dragon on the front. A man paddled at the front, and two more men used paddles at the rear, in between were two boys and a girl, roughly his age. The men were armed with bows and short swords, and the children were wearing brightly colored clothes the likes of which Koren had never seen. Even the Baron of Crickdon County could scarcely afford such fine clothing.

Where was the boat going? Surely the man in the bow could see the rapids ahead? He did. The man called out, and the boat turned, steering for a gravel bank just upstream from Koren. Koren had a moment of panic, his pack was hanging from a tree, near where the boat was headed. Everything Koren owned was in that pack! He needed to crawl through the bushes over to-

Koren never finished that thought. The strange boat was almost ashore, the man in the front had laid down his paddle and swung a leg over the side to get out, when there was a blood-freezing roar, and the largest bear Koren had ever seen burst out the woods and crashed into the boat. Before anyone could react, the boat flipped over, spilling everyone out, the two men in the back were trapped underneath, the two boys were flung onto the gravel bank, the girl was tossed out to land with a splash in the river, and the man in front was knocked to fall face-first into the water.

The bear stepped back, momentarily confused, then focused on the girl, and bounded over the upturned boat. The man who had been in the front of the boat rolled to his feet, and tried to draw his sword, but the bear swatted him with his great paw, and the man was flung onto the shore, his sword flying away into the river.

Koren expected the girl to scream as the bear reared up in front of her. Instead she reached down to the river bottom, picked up a smooth stone, and threw it to hit the bear square on the nose! The bear stopped in its tracks and covered its now-bloody nose with a paw, the girl lost her balance, and stumbled backward to hit her head on a rock. She slumped on her back, her face barely above the water.

The bear shook its head, dropped its paw away from its nose, and rose up on its back paws to stand over the girl, its front claws glinting like daggers in the sunlight.

Koren's feet were splashing into the river before he knew what he was doing. He shouted something at the bear, holding one hand, palm outward toward the great beast, his other hand reaching for the girl. To his great surprise, the bear was *pushed* violently backwards, it rolled to sit on its haunches in the river, swinging its front paws around like

its face were being attacked by a swarm of bees. The bear roared again, splashed back to the shore, crashed head-first into a tree, as if it were blinded, and disappeared into the forest, bellowing as it went along.

Koren was so surprised to still be alive that he fell right on his butt into the chilly river, up to his waist. The two guards who had been under the boat were now standing near the boat, looking dazed but holding their swords with grim determination. Koren turned to look for the girl, she had lost her grip on the rock and was drifting helplessly into the current, her head barely above the water, one arm waving weakly. As she drifted by, she and Koren locked eyes for a split second.

They were the most beautiful eyes Koren had ever seen, ever imagined, a striking pale green that drew him in. How a moment could last a lifetime, Koren didn't know, but in that moment, time stood still, and he was lost.

Help me, her eyes pleaded.

"Boy! You, boy! Get away!" One of the men warned, as he splashed unsteadily into the river. Koren knew the man would not reach the girl in time, she was already being spun around as the river gathered force to rush through the rapids. Koren hauled himself to his feet, and saw that his only chance to catch the girl was to leap from one rock to the next until he was right at the first rapid, he might be able to jump in and hang onto the girl as she was swept by. He jumped wildly from rock to rock, his feet skidding and slipping, bruising his knees and knuckles as he steadied himself from falling. Just as he reached the last rock, he saw the girl plunged under the water. Koren took a deep breath as he launched himself into the air.

Somehow, Koren found the girl under the water, and held onto her. Held onto the girl, thinking of nothing else but clutching her to him as they were carried along, plunging down one rapid after another. When he could, he held the girl's face up so she could breathe, even so they both swallowed water and choked as he struggled to stay afloat. His body was battered as he was bashed against rocks by the tremendous, unrelenting force of the water. Atop one swell of water, just before they plunged down over a fall, Koren saw a relatively still pool to the right, and *willed* the water to sweep him in that direction. As they fell, he kicked his feet with all his might, before the swirling water spun him upside down, and he swallowed a mouthful of water. Koren gagged and almost lost his grip on the girl as he spat out water. He needed air. Desperately, he twisted to lift his head out of the water.

And found they were floating in a pool, a backwater where the current lazily spun around. The girl coughed, spitting out water. Koren swung his legs down and found he could stand on a rock, with the last of his strength he waded onto a wide, flat rock near the riverbank and pulled the girl to flop down next to him. The girl rolled onto her side, coughing and choking out water. "Help!" Koren managed to cry, between breaths.

When he could move again, he reached out for the girl, she was dazed, her eyes open but unfocused. Her dress was torn, her arms and legs covered with bruises. Koren tried to stand, and found his own limbs so battered and cold that he could barely control his hands and feet. Blood seeped from cuts and scrapes all over him, his already rough pants and shirt now ripped in so many places he could never patch them together again.

Koren was startled by the faint scratching sounds of something, or someone, trying to move quietly through the woods along the riverbank. And there was another, louder sound, further away but drawing closer. Men's voices, shouting, and what Koren thought were horses making their way through the woods at high speed.

The bushes along the shore above his head parted, and a man stepped out, followed by three more men. They were the type of men his parents warned against, hard-looking, carrying swords and knives, wicked grins on their faces. "What have we here? A rich girl, looks like, and her servant? I bet her parents would pay a pretty price to have their daughter back, in one piece, huh, boys?"

Bandits! It was Koren's bad luck to stumble across woods that bandits were using as a hideout. Truly his life was jinxed! Koren rose unsteadily to his feet and pulled a knife from his belt. "Stay away from her." He said in a voice hoarse from choking on water. He had never fought with a knife before, but it was a good blade, dwarf-made, and everyone knew dwarves were the finest metalworkers in the land.

"What? The lady's pet has a sting? Forget her, boy, drop that knife and we'll give you a share of the ransom money. More than you'd earn in a lifetime, I think."

"Hurry up about it, Togan, we've got company coming." One of the other bandits said, as the sound of men and horses crashing through the woods grew louder.

The man called Togan eased down the steep bank to stand on the rock on front of Koren. "I'll not say it again, boy, stand aside. There's no need for-" Togan struck, moving his knife in a slashing motion toward Koren's face, expecting the boy would flinch and back away. Instead, Koren's own hand came up faster than he could see, and his knife cut Togan's wrist, forcing the bandit to drop the knife.

"Argh!" Togan held his bloody wrist with his other hand. Koren found his ears burning red at the bad words Togan was screaming, in front of a girl.

"Don't curse in front of a lady, mister." Koren scolded the man.

"What?" The other bandits stared open-mouthed at Koren, as if they'd just discovered he had two heads. Who was this idiot boy? What kind of person cared about being polite, when attacked by bandits?

"Kill him!" Togan growled, as he tried to scramble backwards up the riverbank. One of the other bandits grasped Togan's shirt collar and pulled to help the wounded man up, but Togan slipped and fell heavily onto the rock. "Help me up." Togan ordered, as the sounds of men and horses crashing their way through the underbrush was now very loud, and Koren could see bushes swaying along the riverbank as the horses knocked them aside in their haste.

"Too late. Good luck to you, Togan." Said the bandit who had been trying to help Togan, and at that, the other bandits melted back into the woods.

"Ungrateful scum! I'll get you for this!" Togan shouted after his disloyal fellow criminals. "And you!" The bandit picked up his knife with his one good hand. "Forget the girl, I'm going to kill you."

"I don't think so." Koren said, keeping himself between Togan and the girl, his knife ready. For some reason he couldn't explain, with the knife in his hand, he wasn't afraid, not one bit. Men on horseback burst out of the woods, and a half-dozen men slid off their saddles, drawing swords or fitting arrows to bowstrings. Koren was about to say he was glad to see the men, when their leader, a tall man wearing a tunic emblazoned with a golden dragon, shouted at his men. "Bandits! Seize them both! Kill them if they move!"

Koren's heart fell. There he was, standing over the girl, a knife in his hand, just like Togan the bandit. Of course the soldiers thought he, too, was a bandit. If he were captured, Togan would likely confirm that Koren was indeed a bandit, and Koren would be thrown into a dungeon, or hanged. Koren glanced behind him at the river. He would rather take his chances in the rapids than be captured by these men.

The leader of the soldiers saw Koren looking at the river, and knew what he was thinking. "Don't you move, boy. I'll shoot you if I must." The man scrambled down the riverbank.

Just then, the girl moaned, and raised a hand to her face. It was enough of a distraction for Koren to spin around, leap onto a rock, and throw himself into the river. He almost made it, but the soldiers were experienced and disciplined, and one of the men put an arrow into Koren's left shoulder. Shocked by the searing pain, Koren dropped his knife, and fell headfirst into the foaming rapids.

"Find him!" The leader ordered, and two of his men climbed out on rocks into the river, but Koren could not be seen. The wounded boy had been swept under, likely to drown, if the arrow hadn't killed him.

Koren was barely aware of something gently rocking him side to side. There was a bright light above him, he blinked and it hurt to look at the light. He hurt all over, especially his head and his left shoulder. The rocking motion was making his shoulder hurt even more, pain, which made him grit his teeth and tears to run down his face. The shock was giving him chills, chills not caused just by the cold river water. To protect his left shoulder, he rolled to his right, and almost breathed in a mouthful of water.

He was laying on his back, in shallow water near a riverbank, below the last of the rapids. The current was rocking him side to side. Somehow he had survived the trip through the raging waters. How far he had been pulled down the river, he did not know. The bright light above him was the noonday sun. This part of the river was wide and calm, with only a few ripples on the surface to show how fast the current was moving. It was quiet and peaceful, except for-

Horses. Again the sound of men and horses. They were hunting him, they would never stop hunting him. The soldiers would never believe Koren had only wanted to help the girl, after all, they had seen with their own eyes that he was a bandit, hadn't they? He rolled onto his knees in the shallow water, and used his right arm to push himself to his feet. He could barely stand; the pain in his left shoulder was making him sick to his stomach. He felt with his right hand, and discovered part of the arrow shaft still stuck out from his shoulder. He needed to get it out, somehow. Later.

Horses splashed into the water on the other side of the river, and men shouted something to him. With eyes that could not focus properly, Koren looked back at the men, then turned and stumbled, tripping over his own feet, into the forest. The forest would protect him; give him a place to hide, to wait, hidden, until the soldiers tired of looking for him and went away.

He had not walked far when he heard horses splashing through the shallow water on his side of the river, they had swum across. He could see men climbing back onto their horses, spreading out to search for him.

His life was so unfair. Cursed to be a jinx. Exiled from his village. Abandoned by his parents. Forced out of every village in the land. And now, hunted as a bandit. What did it matter if he died now? Without the supplies in his pack, and with an arrowhead in his shoulder, he wouldn't last long in the wilderness anyway. Good riddance to you, Koren Bladewell, the world said to him, good riddance to the jinx, the world is better off without you. Koren stopped, and faced the approaching soldiers, his back to a tree. The arrow shaft brushed against the tree, and Koren's knees buckled with the overwhelming wave of pain. As the soldiers rode up to circle him, he pitched forward onto the ground, and the world slipped away.

Lord Paedris Don Salva de La Murta, master wizard and counselor to the throne of Tarador, looked down with dismay at the hem of his purple robe, which was dark and wet from trailing in the river. Certainly, Paedris would have preferred to simply wear pants, much more practical attire for tramping about in the woods. Being a wizard, however, indeed, the official court wizard of the land, he had to wear robes, because that is what people expected. Half the power of being a wizard was merely looking like a wizard; if Paedris dressed like a farmer then he might have to turn a couple people into toads to get some respect. Not that he would, or even could, turn people into toads; the threat was enough. He lifted his robe out of the water, and then dropped it, as he realized he looked like what women did with their dresses when stepping over a puddle. Perhaps he could get his robes shortened? He must speak with the royal tailor when he returned to the castle.

"Lord Salva?" A soldier called out from the riverbank.

"Yes?" Asked Paedris, without looking up from the river. Paedris had mostly black hair, gone grey at the temples, and he wore his hair long, like most men did, although Paedris did not tie his hair back out of the way soldiers did. A mustache and a short, pointy black beard added to the wizard's dignity. "What is it?"

The soldier held up a worn pack. "I found this in the woods, it could belong to the boy. Doesn't look like the sort of thing bandits would carry."

"Very well." Paedris said, and carefully stepped from one rock to another with long strides, back onto the riverbank. The soldier, one of the royal guards, was one of the men who had been in the back of the boat when it was attacked by the bear. The guard who had been in the front of the boat was on his way back to the Duke's castle. Paedris had examined the man, he would have an impressive scar on his chest from where the bear's claws had raked him, but otherwise should recover fully. "Tell me again, from the beginning."

The soldier related how they had been on a picnic trip for the children, silly, really, but that is what the princess wanted, and all had been well until the bear charged out of the woods, with no warning.

"And you say the boy held his hand out, like this, and the bear fell over backwards?" For Paedris, that gesture, harm held straight, palm open, was part of a warding spell. Powerful magic, that was.

"Yes, my lord. The bear was on its hind legs; the boy must have startled it. Although it did seem as if the bear were *flung* backwards, almost, instead of falling. Then, the bear swatted at its face, as though it were being attacked by bees, and it turned around and ran back into the woods. It seemed to be blind, Lord wizard."

"Curious. Most curious." Paedris closed his eyes and *felt* for the lingering power which permeated the area, the water, the rocks, the trees. The power was raw, uncontrolled, and frighteningly strong. The air fairly crackled with connection to the spirit realm. Stronger than any power Paedris had ever felt before, certainly stronger than any magic he had been able to handle himself. And there was something else, separate, something right at the edge of his senses, something sour, and dark, and evil. That power he recognized, and he feared. "Consider this. A bear, a wild animal that should only be looking to survive in the wilderness, for no good reason attacks a boat full of armed guards, and charges straight for Ariana. Of all the people in the boat, it concentrates on her. Then, this terrible beast that knocked aside three well-armed royal guards-"

"Forgive me, Lord Salva, but it was hardly a fair fight-"

"Never interrupt a wizard when he is thinking!" Paedris roared, using the tiniest bit of magic to add emphasis to his words.

The soldier fell to one knee and bowed his head. "Forgive me, my lord."

"Forgiven. You accounted very well for yourself. This was no ordinary bear; you faced a dark and foul magic, and faced it bravely. Now, where was I?" Being mildly absent-minded did seem to be typical of wizards. "Ah, yes. So, this terrible, magic-spelled beast is then scared away by a boy, a young boy, all by himself. This boy who rescued Ariana from a bear, and a raging river *and* a gang of bandits. Not bad for a morning's work, eh? I shall need to speak with this boy, as soon as possible."

"I, uh, I beg to remind you, my lord, the boy was shot. By mistake. And he was almost drowned. Our captain fears he will not survive the day."

"Oh," Paedris said with a smile and a twinkle in his eye, "I think the court wizard of Tarador may be able to do something about that."

CHAPTER THREE

"How is the boy?" Carlana asked quietly as she leaned into the doorway.

Paedris rose from the chair beside Koren's bed, the wizard had sat with the boy through the night. "He will live." Paedris said simply. "The wound was not deep, the arrow hit his shoulder blade, and I healed it as best I could. He did lose a lot of blood; I recommend he drink a broth of beef and vegetables when he awakens. For now, he is in a deep healing sleep."

"Very well." Carlana didn't need her court wizard to tell her the best remedy to recover from blood loss. She looked out into the hallway, and gestured to dismiss her maids. "Who is he?"

"I don't know, we don't even know his name. From his clothing and the pack we found, I would say he is a peasant, but that doesn't answer what he was doing alone in the woods. The guards searched the woods and found a camp site, the boy had been living there for a week or more."

"Hmmmm. This boy, and a pack of bandits have been using Duke Yarron's private hunting reserve as their campgrounds, for more than a week?" Carlana asked with a twinkle in her eye. "I think the Duke's sheriff is going to have much to explain."

Paedris did not care about whether people were poaching on the duke's lands. "There is one thing of which we must speak. I don't know who this boy is, or where he came from, but he is a wizard, the most powerful wizard I have ever known."

"What? You are sure?" Carlana bit her lip. She saw the look in her wizard's eyes. *Fear.*

Paedris was afraid, afraid of this boy.

"There can be no mistake about it. He stopped that bear, without having any idea how he did it. The fact that the Wizards Council knew nothing of this boy, right here in our midst, is deeply troubling!"

"You didn't know about him?" Carlana frowned. The boy had saved her daughter, three times in one morning. By rights, she should at least grant the boy a knighthood and a hundred acres of land somewhere. A thought popped into her head, she put one hand over her mouth, the other over her heart, and stepped away from the bed. "Acedor! If the Wizard's Council did not know about him, could he-"

"No, no!" Paedris dismissed the idea with a wave of his hand. "There is no trace of the foul magics our enemy uses to confound us. He has *not* come from Acedor, I'm certain of it. When the boy wakes, I will talk to him, learn where he came from, and what he knows of magic. Until then, we let him rest."

Koren awoke to the sound of voices, women's voices. He lay very still, and cracked opened one eye just wide enough to see where he was. In a bed, a big, soft bed, with his head resting on a real pillow! Beyond the bed, the room appeared to be large, and through an open window, he could see flags flying in the breeze, and soldiers standing on top of a thick stone wall. He must be in a castle, somewhere. Koren had never seen a real castle; the only one around Crebbs Ford was the small building that was home to the Baron of Crickdon County. What was he doing in-

Soldiers. He remembered being captured by soldiers.

"-can't believe everything the high and mighty tell you, Mathilda, why, I heard the little scamp was living in the Duke's own private hunting reserve, he was, poaching deer and scooping up all the fish. Don't know as how the Sheriff didn't find him first, he's supposed to be patrolling those woods. And you know, Duke Yarron don't take kindly to poachers. No, he doesn't."

"*I* heard that poaching be the least of his worries." Said another woman's voice. "Found him with a pack of bandits, the guards did, and he led them on a merry chase before they captured him. Likely he was trying to kidnap poor Ariana, so you can talk all you want about him being a scamp, I say he's a menace, pure and simple. Wouldn't turn my back on him, I wouldn't, no matter how young he is."

Koren could hear two women; he was laying on his side, with his back to them.

"Well, the wizard will have the truth out of him, sure enough. In here all night with the boy, conjuring up demons, or whatnot it is wizards do. Gives me the creeps, it does, and the sooner that wizard is out of here and back to the palace, the happier I'll be."

"It gives me the creeps just to be in here, where he was working his foul magic. Finish folding those sheets, Mathilda, and let's be rid of here. Fancy letting this boy sleep in here! Should be in the dungeon, he should. They'll hang him soon enough."

There were rustling sounds, and shoes scuffing across a floor, and a door opening and closing with a solid thunking sound. Koren remained still for a good minute, until he was certain the women had gone, before he opened both eyes. His head was spinning. Duke Yarron? He didn't know that name, so he must not be in his home Winterthur province. Whoever this Duke Yarron was, he apparently considered Koren to be a poacher. And a bandit. And a kidnapper.

Koren raised his head from the pillow and looked around the room. It was the most fabulous place he had ever imagined. The ceiling had to be twelve feet high, and the room was bigger than the entire common room at the Golden Trout Inn in Crebbs Ford. Bigger even than many barns in his hometown. There were pictures in gold-plated frames, large wall hangings, and an enormous fireplace at the far end of the room, over which was a crest, a red fox on a field of white. A large, fancy carved desk was up against the outside wall, Koren could see scuff marks on the stone floor where the desk had been pushed to make room for the bed he lay in.

Why was he in such a place? Were the Duke's dungeons full? Surely the Duke didn't treat all poachers, bandits and kidnappers by giving them a soft bed to lay in.

A chill ran up Koren's spine. The women said something about a wizard, working foul magic on him? Koren abruptly sat upright in bed, his stomach churning with fear. What had the wizard done to him?! Koren had never met a wizard, all he knew about wizards were the fearful stories told around Crebbs Ford. He pulled up the covers, he still had his own feet, and they worked. So he had not been turned into a pig, or a toad. The shoulder where the arrow had hit him was sore; he felt with his right hand and was surprised not to find a bandage there. Of course, if the Duke was planning to throw him in a dungeon and then hang him as a bandit, why bother bandaging the wound?

He needed to escape, now, before those women came back. Or the wizard returned. Slowly, because his shoulder was sore, he swung his legs over the side of the bed, and stood up. He was dressed in some sort of white gown that was too big, it draped on the floor. Over the back of a chair next to the bed were black pants and a gray shirt, in a size that could fit him. He pulled the gown off, and caught a glimpse of himself in a mirror. Surprised, he saw that his left shoulder, where the arrow had been, was unmarked; there was not even a scar. Only a redness, like a rash, remained. How had he healed so quickly? Had the wizard done this? And why?

Answers to his questions could wait, he needed to escape somehow. He crept quietly over to the door, and put his ear to it. There were men's voices, talking low. Guards outside the door. He could not escape that way. Next to the fireplace was another door, Koren pulled and pushed, and found it firmly locked. That left only the window. Watching the soldiers atop the stone wall outside to make sure they were not looking at the window, Koren looked out quickly. There was a ledge below the window, just wide enough for him to stand on, and the wall was built of rough stone, for his hands to grip. It was a long way down to the courtyard below. Beyond the thick wall where the soldiers patrolled, there were the buildings of a large town, surrounded by farm fields.

Koren pulled himself back from the window, trying to think what he should do. The sun was high in the sky, so the ledge below the window was in deep shadow, perhaps the soldiers would not see him. The soldiers were there to look outward, not in toward the castle, weren't they? If he could get to the roof, perhaps he could find a way down to the ground. Once outside the castle and out into the farmland, he could crawl into a haystack and sleep there, the hay would keep him warm through the night. Beyond that, Koren did not know what he would do. Without his knife and the other things in his precious, lost pack, he could not survive in the wilderness.

He would go. Anything was better than being hanged.

The only way Koren was able to inch his way along the ledge, gripping the stone wall as tightly as he could, was to keep his eyes closed. His fingers cramped from the strain of holding onto cracks in the stone wall, and his hands became slick with sweat. He inched along, pressing himself against the rough stone wall, until he felt his left foot touch the edge of the roof. Carefully, he crawled onto the roof and lay flat on the hard stone tiles, his whole body shaking with relief.

When he was able to open his eyes, he was alarmed to see that the roof was only a dozen feet wide, and there were no windows in the flat stone wall facing him. The stone roof tiles were old, worn and flaking away in places, and many of them were slippery with a coating of mold and moss. Koren crawled flat on his belly to the peak of the roof, but the other side was no better, and the sun shone directly on that side of the roof, making it impossible to hide.

Maybe if he crawled down to the edge of the roof, there would be a pipe, or a stone column or something he could use to climb down to the courtyard. There was no going back through the window, he would never be able to walk along that narrow ledge again, his arms and fingers were still trembling. The only way to see over the edge of the roof was to turn around and slide down on his belly, headfirst.

Koren froze. The roof seemed impossibly steep now that he was facing downward. Slowly, inch by inch, he slid along the roof, trying to ignore the butterflies in his stomach. Reaching the edge, he gathered up his courage and crept forward until his nose was over the edge, and he could see down.

Impossible. There was no pipe, no stone column. The roof ended in an overhang less than a foot wide, then a flat stone wall all the way down to the courtyard, four stories below.

Koren tried to slide back up, but his pants and shirt got snagged on the roof tiles, and a tile broke. It clattered along the roof and out into the air, Koren desperately reached for it and caught it between two fingers. There were people in the courtyard, a falling roof tile would have made people notice the boy on the roof, and then it would be straight to the dungeon for him. Carefully, he laid the broken tile on the roof next to him, and then found he could not move. Catching the tile had caused him to slide forward; his shoulders were almost over the edge of the roof. Another inch forward, and he would slide off the roof and fall. His fingers scrambled for a hold on the slippery tiles, without success. Koren closed his eyes, unable to look down.

"Hello over there!" Called a voice from the same window Koren had escaped through. Koren carefully opened one eye to look, and saw a tall, dark-haired man in a purple robe leaning out the window. "That looks very dangerous. What are you doing out on the roof? Be careful, or you'll fall off." The man asked as he stepped out the window onto the narrow ledge. Before Koren's disbelieving eyes, the man strolled casually along the narrow ledge, not holding onto the wall, with a small plate of pastries in one hand. When he reached the roof, the man stepped up onto the roof tiles, walked over to Koren, and scooped him up as if he were light as a feather. He carried Koren under his arm to the peak of the roof, set the boy down carefully, and lowered himself down next to Koren.

"It is a nice view up here." The man said. "But it seems like a lot of trouble to go through just to see the sights. Why, you have gotten your new clothes all dirty! You'll have to change into something presentable before you meet the Regent, of course. So, whatever made you climb out onto the roof? Your shoulder is still healing, it would not be good to have you undo all my hard work."

Koren could only stare open-mouthed at the man, his eyes almost popping out of his head. How could this man have walked along the ledge, and onto the roof, as if he were strolling down a country lane? "Sir, are you, are you a *wizard*?" Koren asked fearfully.

Paedris held up his right hand, palm open. A ball of flame appeared, floating above his hand. He winked at Koren, and the flame went out. "I'm terribly sorry, where are my manners today? I haven't introduced myself. I am Lord Paedris Don Salva de La Murta, chief wizard to the royal court of Tarador. I am the only wizard in the royal court, actually, but chief wizard sounds so much more impressive, don't you think?"

Koren nodded silently.

"And your name is?"

"K-Koren. Koren B-Bladewell. Sir. Of, of Crickdon County."

The wizard held out his hand to Koren, who shook it warily. "Pleased to meet you, Koren. Now, why were you out on the roof? Take a deep breath first, and calm yourself, I'd hate for you to roll off the roof now."

Koren didn't trust the wizard, who had likely pulled Koren out of danger so he could be thrown into the dungeon, which was the proper place for a poacher, bandit and kidnapper. "I heard two women talking when they thought I was asleep, Sir, they said I am a poacher, and that I was trying to kidnap that girl because I'm a bandit. I am *not* a bandit, and if this Duke didn't want me hunting in his private woods, he should have posted signs."

Koren had his arms crossed, and had such a look of determination on his young face that Paedris burst out laughing, and almost rolled off the roof himself.

"I don't think it is funny. Sir." Koren said indignantly.

"Posted signs! Ha ha!" Paedris said, wiping tears of laughter away from his eyes, "The Duke should have posted signs! Oh, I haven't laughed like that in a long time. Too long, I think. Thank you, Koren. And you are quite correct, if Duke Yarron wants to keep people out of his woods, he should post signs. I shall have to tell him that." The wizard's shoulders heaved as he chuckled.

"I'm not in trouble for poaching?"

"Trouble? Goodness, no, you're not in any trouble." Paedris considered the tray of pastries that he had balanced on his lap. "You must be hungry. I brought these sweets for you, but I find myself to be tempted. Especially by these," he picked up a fruit tart that was piled high with fresh whipped cream, "they are my favorite." The wizard took a large bite, and came away with his nose, mustache and beard covered with cream. He grinned at Koren, and looked so ridiculous that Koren had to laugh, despite his fear. "Here, take a pastry before I spill this off the roof."

Koren reached out carefully and took the smallest pastry on the tray. It had been so long since he'd eaten anything sweet, except for berries and wild apples. And the season for those was gone by. He bit into the cookie slowly, keeping a sharp eye on the wizard the whole time.

"Well, Koren Bladewell, I think you had better tell me how you came to be living in the wilderness by yourself. Where are your parents?"

Koren bit his lip while he tried to think of what to say, how much to tell. He couldn't lie to a wizard, from the stories Koren had heard about wizards, they were great and terrible, and fond of turning people into toads, or frogs. The truth tumbled out of Koren's mouth, he told the wizard of Crebbs Ford, and his family being banished from the village, his parents leaving him, and how he had made his way south, living in the wilderness, trying to stay ahead of the winter. "I'm not a bandit, sir, really I'm not, I was only trying to help that girl. Sir, I know I'm a jinx, and I don't want to be a danger to anyone, don't want to be any trouble, sir, I promise I won't be any trouble at all, so now that I'm better, I'll be on my way? Please, Sir?" Without his pack, he didn't know how he was going to survive, but it was best he got out of the castle before the Duke changed his mind. Or before there was an 'incident' in the castle, and the wizard realized what a dangerous jinx Koren was. Wizards, Koren was sure, knew all about jinxes. "Sir? Can I go now? I won't be any trouble, sir, I swear. Please, sir?"

It was the wizard's turn to stare in surprise. He needed a moment to catch up to Koren, the boy talked so fast that his words were a jumble. Paedris had never considered the possibility that this boy would not know about his own magical power! The boy had been exiled from his village, and abandoned by his parents, because they thought he was a jinx. Paedris knew the 'incidents' which caused people to think Koren was a jinx were actually signs of Koren's inability to control his magical power, the magical power the boy didn't even know he had! When the wagon was rolling toward the mill, Koren had willed the wagon to *stop*, and *stop* it did, along with everything else around him, including the unfortunate mill's water wheel. Until Koren learned to control his ability, he would be dangerous.

Paedris wished he could tell Koren why he wasn't a jinx. But he couldn't. No thirteen year old boy who knew he had immense magical power could resist using it, and Koren was far too young and untrained to control his immense power, not even with the help of a master wizard. Such a boy would be a constant target of Tarador's enemies; if they could not kidnap Koren, they would try to assassinate him. No, the only way to keep Koren safe was to hide his magical power from the world, even from Koren himself, until the boy was old enough to control his own power, and could protect himself from his enemies.

"Sir? Master wizard? Lord, uh, Murta?"

"Huh?" Paedris realized he had been silent for some time, contemplating what it meant that Koren didn't realize he was a wizard himself. "Oh, call me Paedris, please. Or, call me Lord Salva, when we're in public. La Murta is my home village, far away from here. Koren, you may leave here any time you like, but I think there has been a very great, a terrible misunderstanding. No one thinks you are a bandit, or a kidnapper, in fact, the room you were in was Duke Yarron's personal study, you are the Duke's honored guest in his castle. You are a *hero*. That girl you rescued is Ariana Trehayme, crown princess and heir to the throne of Tarador."

"P-princess?" Koren had heard the women say the name 'Ariana', but he never thought she was *the* Ariana. Even in tiny Crebbs Ford, people knew the name of their crown princess. "She is that Ariana?"

"Yes." Paedris nodded. "Whatever the people of, what did you call your village, Crab Ford? Whatever foolish thing they thought of you there, here you are a hero."

"But I'm a jinx." Koren sputtered, disbelieving his change of fortune.

"Bah!" The wizard snorted in disgust. "There is no such thing as a jinx, and don't you forget that. Trust me, wizards know about these things. You are not a jinx."

"I'm not a jinx?" Koren asked hopefully.

"No. Never have been. There is no such thing, it is a silly superstition."

"And I'm not in trouble?"

"Goodness, no, not at all."

"And the princess thinks I'm a *hero*?" Koren almost couldn't get the word out of his mouth, it sounded so strange.

"Quite so. I think you are a very brave young man. That was a rather large bear, and you faced it alone, unarmed?"

"It was a large bear, sir, and I, well, I couldn't think of anything else to do." Koren considered the wizard's words. Could his life truly be changing, for the better? "What will happen to me?" He asked in a whisper.

"Well, let me think." The wizard popped another fruit tart in his mouth. "There might be a feast in your honor, if you feel up to it. Listening to many tedious speeches, of course, that is the part of being a hero that never seems to make it into the legends. Then there will be much wearing of scratchy clothes that don't fit properly, and having to remember which fork to use at dinner-"

"There is more than one type of fork?" Koren asked, surprised. He was used to eating with a knife.

"Oh, yes, there are a frightfully large number of forks, all with their own purpose. And different types and sizes of knives and spoons, also, and you will have to know which type is proper to use, or it will cause an *immense* scandal. Later, when you have grown tired of being celebrated as a hero, you can come live with me in the royal castle, if you like. It just so happens that I am in need of an assistant at the moment. The pay isn't much, but-"

Koren's gasped in surprise. "I would be *paid*?" Who paid a boy to serve as an assistant? Most of the boys Koren knew of who served as apprentices earned no pay, and often a boy's parents had to pay to get their son such a position, to be trained in a trade such as blacksmithing.

"Er, well, yes. Would you be interested in such a position?" Paedris glanced sideways at Koren to see the boy's reaction. The only way to keep Koren safe was for Paedris to watch him constantly. "As my personal servant, as it were."

Koren's face fell for a moment. Being a *servant* was very different from being an *apprentice*. He would not be training to be a wizard. Still, Koren the unwanted farm boy, would be living in a castle and serving as the royal wizard's personal servant? And anyone working closely with a wizard must learn some magic, wouldn't they? He, Koren Bladewell, learning to use powerful magic? He came close to fainting and rolling off the roof. "I would have to ask-" Koren for a moment forgot that he didn't know where his parents were. What would they think now, their son a hero and soon to be living in a castle? "I mean, until I find my parents, I would like to be your servant, thank you very much, sir. Master Wizard, could you help me to find my parents?"

Paedris nodded very seriously. "I will certainly try to find your parents, young man, I promise you that. You, uh, to be my servant, and work in the royal castle, you will need to take an oath of loyalty to the crown."

Koren shrugged. "All right."

"That means renouncing your current loyalty to the Duchess of Winterthur, and your Baron, uh, whatever his name is."

Koren tilted his head in disbelief. "My loyalty to the Baron?"

"Yes."

"The baron who banished me, for being a jinx."

"Mm."

"Which, you say, I'm not."

The wizard shook his head. "Never have been."

"I think I will not have a problem renouncing my loyalty to Baron Fostlen." Koren said in a tone bordering on sarcasm, to a powerful wizard he'd just met.

"Nor the Duchess?" Paedris knew some peasants, deeply attached to the land and the tiny patch of the kingdom where they likely spent their entire lives, could be stubbornly loyal to royal people they had never met. "Your family could have appealed your banishment to the Duchess, if I understand the law here."

"Appeal to the Duchess, to rule against the Baron, who is first cousin to the Duchess' husband?" Koren said bitterly, echoing a sentiment his parents had expressed many times.

"Hmm. I rather see your point there. Unfortunately, Koren, loyalty most often flows only one way, uphill." The wizard pointed upward.

"What flows downhill?"

Paedris pursed his lips. "Something that smells bad. And comes out the back end of a horse, if you know what I mean. Now," the wizard rose to his feet, "I rather think we need to get you inside. You need to eat; I brought a delicious beef soup that is unfortunately cooling off next to your bed. And then you need to rest quietly, instead of scampering around the roof like a clumsy squirrel."

Koren looked glumly down the slippery roof tiles, from where he'd nearly fallen to his death. He'd never seen a clumsy squirrel, but then, any squirrel that was clumsy wouldn't live long enough to be seen by anyone.

"How is the boy?" Carlana asked quietly as the wizard came thru doorway, and shut the door behind him.

"Apparently, quite well, since he went out the window, trying to escape." Paedris said simply. The wizard strode to the window, looked outside, and pulled the heavy curtains shut, for privacy.

"Escape?" Carlana gasped in shock. "Did he fly?"

"What?" Paedris asked in surprise.

"What?"

"You asked if he flew out the window?"

"You said he was a wizard."

"Oh." Paedris was constantly surprised about the absurd things people thought wizards could do. "No, no, he didn't fly, he crawled out the window, and onto the roof. Almost fell off, if I hadn't been there."

Carlana gasped. She hated heights, was terrified of falling. "That's four stories off the ground! And the courtyard below is cobblestones. He would have been killed. Why was he trying to escape? Didn't he know he is an honored guest?"

"When he awoke, he heard a couple of the duke's foolish maids gossiping, and thought he was going to be thrown into a dungeon, and likely hanged, as a bandit who tried to kidnap Ariana."

"He *saved* my daughter!"

"Yes, and I told him not to pay attention to gossip. As regards his health, he is recovering well, and I fed him a broth of beef and vegetables."

"And some pastries, Lord Salva?" Carlana pointed with a sly smile to the streak of cream down the front of his robe.

"What?" The court wizard, his dignity injured, looked down in dismay. He had rinsed his face in the washbasin in Koren's room, but neglected to check his robe. "The pastries were, er, very tempting. For now, the boy is in a deep healing sleep."

"Very well." Carlana wearily pushed her reddish hair away from her face. "Who is this boy, this, wizard?" She added the last slowly.

"His name is Koren Bladewell, a farm boy from Crickdon." Paedris shook his head. "And, yes, a wizard."

"Hmm, Crickdon is in Winterthur province, not all that far to the northeast of here." Carlana pursed her lips in thought. "A peasant? Well, Ariana wants to grant him a knighthood, and I agree with the sentiment, but-"

"No knighthood! Calling any attention to this boy would be a terrible idea. There is a complication, which I had not considered. The boy has not had any training as a wizard, which is why I didn't know about him. This boy does not know he is a wizard!"

Carlana tilted her head quizzically. "He doesn't *know*? Are you sure he's a wizard?"

"Yes, yes, there can be no mistake about it. He stopped that bear, without having any idea how he did it. The- the very air, around where the bear attacked Ariana, was crackling with raw magical power, I could actually taste it, it leaves a metallic essence lingering, for a wizard's senses. Which reminds me, we need to start a rumor that I was with Ariana when that bear attacked. The amount of power Koren used is like ringing a bell heard far and wide to a wizard; the enemy cannot have failed to detect it. If the enemy learns I was not there, then Koren will become a focus of the enemy's attention. I cannot explain how the Wizards' Council knew nothing about this boy. He has had no training, that is certain, his power is raw, uncontrolled, a danger to himself and everyone around him. We have here a dilemma: the boy is now too old for another wizard to shape his power into something he can control, and he is still too young to control such power himself."

Carlana was still confused. "How could he *not know* he's a wizard? Your Council is supposed to identify wizards when they're very young."

"I believe the Council has sent wizards through this boy's home county, I can't explain how we could have missed this boy, especially a boy this powerful. As to how he could not know," Paedris shrugged, "strange things happened around him, and since no one thought he could be a wizard, the people in his village figured he was cursed with bad luck, that he is a jinx. In his last jinx accidents, he destroyed the village's only grain mill, and the baron of the county exiled him. Then, apparently, his parents became afraid of him, and abandoned him in the woods one night; he's not seen them since. That's why he was living alone in Yarron's hunting reserve, surviving on his own."

"His own parents abandoned him? That's terrible! If he doesn't realize his own power, is he dangerous?"

"I am afraid he is. I need to watch this boy, keep him close and watch him, until he is old enough to be trained. If the enemy were to learn of him, learn that we had a wizard of his power, untrained power, I believe the enemy would stop at nothing to capture him, and use him for their purposes. We cannot allow that to happen."

Carlana sighed. Paedris and her army captains were always telling her what a threat the enemy was, always urging her to strike first, before the enemy was ready for war. Carlana intended to do nothing that might endanger Tarador before Ariana took the throne. As Regent, she was a caretaker, and she would take care, and not be goaded into rash military actions. "What can we do?"

"I can cast a spell, to block the boy's ability to project magic. It will be temporary. But he won't be able to work magic, not until I know he is ready. Until then, we cannot let him know he is a wizard, lest he try to use his power, or tells others of his power."

Carlana rubbed her temples with her fingertips, and sat in the overstuffed chair beside the bed. The headache that often plagued her, from the enormous pressure of serving as Regent, was coming back. To hear that the boy who saved her daughter was a wizard, a powerful wizard, was the last thing she would have expected. "You're going to conceal his power from him? Deceive him?"

Paedris nodded gravely. "Magical power is far too great a temptation, for one so young. Do you know of any thirteen year old boy or girl, who would not use such power, if they knew it was within them? We cannot risk the enemy learning of Koren's immense power, until he can use it to defend himself."

The Regent let out a long breath. "Lord Salva, the Wizards' Council is responsible for this boy not being discovered. If he had been found when he was much younger, he would never have suffered being called a jinx by his neighbors. His family would not have been forced out of their home. His parents would not have abandoned him, they instead would have taken the bounty, and be living a life of luxury, while Koren served his apprenticeship as a wizard." The bounty, for any parents of a child discovered to be a wizard, was two hundred gold coins, plus another three hundred golds when the young wizard completed training and accepted service to Tarador. Five hundred gold coins is an unimaginable fortune for poor farmers, enough that they would never have to work for the rest of their lives.

"Instead, this boy has been cheated of the life he should have had, because the people responsible," she paused looked Paedris straight in the eye, "failed him." Carlana often disagreed with her court wizard, and sometimes she didn't quite trust any wizard, but she had never before questioned his, or the Council's, competence. "You are now going to compound the insult by deliberately misleading him?"

Lord Salva, who had been a master wizard for many years before Carlana became Regent, and never, until now, felt defensive about his abilities, was momentarily at a loss for words. Instead of stammering out nonsense, he nodded, and stroked his beard while he considered what to say. "I, certainly, understand your point, Your Highness, however, I do not see that there is anything else to be done, at this point. There is nothing for it but to continue to conceal the truth from him, for a few more years. I would like to take him to be my servant; I must keep a close eye on the boy. Is that acceptable, your Highness?"

Carlana hesitated. "You say the boy is dangerous, yet you wish to bring him to the royal castle with us? Isn't that inviting trouble?"

"Koren is *not* a jinx. As long as his power is blocked, there will be no further incidents, I can promise you that." Paedris needed to have a long, serious, and likely uncomfortable talk with Dragotil, the wizard who was assigned to Winterthur province. Dragotil was a wizard of no great power, and, Paedris feared, apparently no great concern for carrying out his duties. If Dragotil had been carrying out his responsibilities properly, he would have discovered Koren's power when the boy was a toddler. Perhaps it was time for Dragotil to be given another, less important task. "And now I must cheat him again, for I dare not tell him the truth, until he is old enough to begin controlling his power. As long as he is with me, there will be no jinx incidents around the boy."

"Then I agree he should become your servant, Lord Salva. Ariana already wants to invite the boy to come live with us in the palace." Ariana had so few true friends to play with. The Dukes who ruled Tarador's seven provinces all wanted Ariana to be friends with their own children, and none of them cared about Ariana the girl, only Ariana the crown princess. The reason they were now at the castle of Duke Yarron, of LeVanne province, was so Ariana could meet, and grow familiar with, the Dukes who would be her vassals when she became queen. Carlana was always anxious when they were away from the royal palace, even while guests of a strong ally like Duke Yarron. There was too much danger to be found wandering around Tarador, even without magic-charmed beasts seeking to feast on royal blood. Carlana was skeptical of her wizard's claim that the bear had been magically compelled by their enemy to attack her daughter; she thought it more likely the boat had interrupted the bear's fishing for its breakfast. Still, it would be good for her daughter to have a true friend, a friend who had already proven his loyalty and bravery. It was almost not possible to believe the boy was the powerful magical force Paedris claimed his to be. Yet, he had saved the crown princess, when the royal guards could not. "I shall have to think of a way to explain to my daughter why she can't grant this Koren a knighthood. I'm afraid she is quite taken with her rescuer." Carlana sighed. "Why is life so blasted complicated?"

"Life is-"

"Paedris, that was me complaining, it doesn't require an explanation." Carlana said irritably. She did not enjoy the responsibility of being Regent.

Paedris considered explaining things to a thirteen year old princess to be a trivial matter. "The question we should ask is, what does it mean, that we find a wizard of such power, in such a dark time of need? It cannot be a coincidence that this young man arrives in the same place, at the same time, as a creature sent by the enemy."

Carlana walked over to the window, gazing out across Duke Yarron's fields. "How long before the boy can travel? I wish to return to the palace as soon as possible, if the enemy has sent assassins to kill my daughter."

"He should be out of bed tomorrow, and if he can travel in a carriage, and he is careful not to exert himself, he could leave in the next day. I agree you should depart soon, but I will not be coming with you. I need to follow the trail of that bear, if I am able, and see where it leads. For an animal, a large bear, to be controlled by such a powerful a spell; there must have been a wizard somewhere with a few days' distance. I do not like the thought of an enemy wizard being in our territory."

"And then the bear rose up, like this," crown princess Ariana raised her arms over her head, her fingers curled like claws, "and it roared RAAAR!"

The girls seated on the floor around her squealed.

"But the boy wasn't scared at all. He stood right up in front of the bear, without even a knife in his hand, and that bear ran away!"

"Ooooh!" The girls exclaimed.

"He is the most bravest boy in the whole kingdom-"

"The most brave, or the bravest, Ariana, speak properly, please." Carlana admonished as she swept into the room. The other girls rose to their feet and curtsied to the Regent.

"Hello, Mother. The most brave, then. I shall grant him a knighthood!" Ariana, announced, excited. She picked up a hairbrush and gestured as if it were a sword.

Carlana acted quickly to stop her daughter's foolish plans. The last thing Paedris wanted was for anything to draw attention to the boy. "There will be no granting of knighthoods, at least not until you are queen, Ariana. And knights must be boys from good families. This boy is a commoner." She clapped her hands. "Time to go, girls, the princess needs to rest."

Ariana pouted as her friends hurried out the door. "I feel fine, mother, Paedris healed me. See, not even a scar." She pointed to her forehead, where only the faintest red bruise showed where she had bashed her head on a rock in the river. "I really can't make him a knight?"

"No," Carlana said, not being entirely truthful. There were exceptions for granting knighthoods to commoners, for bravery in battle. "Lord Salva has offered to accept the boy as his servant."

Ariana knew a job as servant to the royal wizard was something few commoner boys could hope for. "He will live in the castle with us, then?" She asked, excited.

"In the castle, yes, not with us in the palace. He would live in the wizard's tower. Don't get your hopes up, young lady."

Ariana thought for a moment. "If I can't grant him a knighthood, can I give him a medal for bravery, and a feast in his honor?"

"No medal, and no feast."

"No feast? But, but Mother! That's not fair!" Ariana sputtered.

Carlana sighed. "Ariana, try to think like the queen you will be, instead of like a girl. Lord Salva believes that bear was sent by the enemy to attack you. We can't let the enemy know they almost succeeded. As far as most people know, you went boating, and hit your head when you fell out of the boat. There will be no mention of this boy."

Ariana pouted, her lower lips stuck out. She'd been imagining a feast in his honor, with the boy wearing fine clothes, and him kneeling while she touched his shoulder with a sword, and named him Sir whatever-his-name the Brave. "It's not fair. He saved my life! Three times!"

"If you want to do something nice for him, perhaps you should consider whether it would be healthy for the him to let the enemy know who stopped that bear."

"Oooh." Ariana touched a finger to her lips. "I didn't think about that. The enemy would be angry with him."

"Yes they would, and that is never healthy for anyone. The best thing you can do for this boy is to let him remain unknown, and bring him to the castle, where he will be under our wizard's protection."

"If he lives with the wizard, where will his parents live?"

"Ariana, not all children are blessed to have parents who care for them." Carlana sat down facing her daughter, and took her hands in her own. While Koren's magical power must remain a secret, she should tell her daughter how the boy had come to be living in the woods alone. "Let me tell you about this Koren Bladewell boy-"

"I'm fine, truly I am, Lord Salva." Koren protested. "Look," he added as he balanced on one foot, "I feel fine. You healed me amazingly, sir." He was fairly itching to get out of the luxurious bedchamber; it looked like a beautiful day. Outside the window, he could hear children kicking a ball around, having fun in the fresh air. After spending months living outdoors, exposed to the elements and dreaming of shelter, he now couldn't wait to get outside again.

It was hard to believe it was only yesterday that the wizard has rescued him from the roof, and his life changed in ways Koren could scarcely have imagined. Koren didn't know whether to be disappointed, or relieved, that there would not be a feast in his honor; he had been very nervous about which fork to use. He'd seen a few people use forks, of course, at the Golden Trout Inn, but he, and most people he knew, ate with a knife. Perhaps the wizard had been joking, if wizards ever did that? Koren didn't want to take chances on that, Paedris still seemed great and terrible to him.

He was absolutely disappointed that he hadn't seen the princess again, and didn't dare to ask the wizard if he was ever going to see her again, for commoners didn't expect royalty to pay attention to them at all. When he closed his eyes, he could picture her face, that most beautiful face, even wet and terrified as she had been when their eyes met, that day she fell into the river. It was likely, Koren thought, that he would never see Ariana again, except from afar, if he was lucky to be in the castle as she was passing by. Still, how many farm boys from Crebbs Ford had ever met the future ruler of Tarador? Exactly one, he thought with at least some satisfaction.

Paedris hadn't told Koren, because Koren hadn't asked, that Ariana had been pestering the wizard, and her mother, because she wanted to see Koren. To thank him, personally. But mostly, truthfully, just to see the handsome young man who had saved her life. The wizard had firmly informed the princess, through her mother the Regent, that Koren needed to rest and recover fully, and that the princess should do that same. Not that Paedris expected the princess to listen to him, but she did listen to her mother.

"Mmm, yes, very impressive, young man." Paedris responded distractedly, glancing at Koren's balancing act while the wizard was measuring herbs for a potion. "You still need to heal, which I can tell by the simple fact that you slept nearly until noon today. This potion, will, hmm." The wizard held an herb bottle up to the window. "I haven't created this particular potion in several years. Koren, can you tell me what that books says, it is open to the page I need."

Koren walked over to the book, and was silent for a minute. The wizard looked over at him; the boy's lips were moving, and he was tracing words on the page with his fingertip. Paedris was embarrassed for the boy, who apparently could not read, and felt terrible that he had thoughtlessly put Koren on the spot. "The boy can't read." Paedris whispered to himself. He should have considered that many farm boys never learned to read! "Oh, don't bother, you don't need to-"

"It says one measure willow bark, two measures of, uh, does this say chamomile? I'm sorry, sir, this handwriting is *terrible*. Can you read this?"

Paedris scratched his head. "That *could* be chamomile, I think that's right. Darn it, I can't read my own handwriting." He chuckled ruefully.

"You wrote this, sir?" Koren exclaimed, surprised. Wizards had to write with their own hands, like everyone else? Koren had imagined pens dancing magically across the page by themselves, while the wizard cast spells, or whatever they did.

"A long time ago, apparently, but now I remember the formula. Which is good, because you're right, I can't read this either. You're handy with a pen, then?"

"I'm no scribe, sir, but I can write well enough, if you don't need anything fancy like prayer books have."

"Fancy is what I don't need. Plain, legible script is what's required." Then the wizard had an idea. "One thing you can do for me, when we get to the castle, is copy some of my old potion books, so they're more readable." By copying the potions, Koren would be learning them, which would be good training, without Koren knowing he was being trained. Paedris was pleased with himself for thinking ahead. "What about mathematics? Do you have any of that?"

Koren nodded proudly. "I can cast accounts, sir; count to a thousand, or more, if I think hard enough on it. Add, subtract, multiply and divide, though I haven't had much call to do anything with that, other than learning it." Everyone in Crebbs Ford knew that, if you couldn't figure numbers yourself, you were sure to get cheated by merchants, or grain millers. Reading may be considered an impractical luxury for many people in rural areas, but every farmer in Crebbs Ford knew how to reckon the value of their grain, or their animals.

"Oh, very good, very good." Koren would certainly be better than most of the servants Paedris had employed over the years. "For now, your job is to rest, and recover your strength, which is not full yet, whether you can stand on one leg, or none, for that matter. You will be leaving in the morning, with the Regent and the princess, to ride to Linden. When you get to the castle, wait for me in my tower, I shouldn't be long."

"You're not coming with us, sir?"

"No," Paedris said with a troubled shake of his head, "I fear that bear is only the tip of the danger we face, and I need to root it out now, rather than later."

"Why a bear, Lord Salva? Why a wild beast, why not a human assassin? That wouldn't have been simpler?" Duke Yarron asked quietly, slightly out of breath from climbing the steep slope. They were struggling up a ridge, through thick, tangled woods, stumbling and slipping over moss-covered rocks, banging their knees and shins, pulling themselves up by hanging onto trees and vines. The sky overhead hung low, gray clouds sodden with rain. It had rained several times throughout the day, the trees were still dripping water down onto Yarron's head, soaking his silver hair and beard. The Thrallren woods, at the eastern end of Duke Yarron's LeVanne province, were part of the border with Acedor. Elsewhere along the border, Yarron maintained troops, reinforced by part of the royal Taradoran army. But since the Thrallren woods were so thickly tangled, and the land was nothing but sharp ridges, deep gullies, and impassible dark woods, that Yarron only posted a few sheriffs there. He could not imagine an enemy invasion force coming through the Thrallren woods. Until now.

"Because," Paedris explained, "if Ariana had been killed by an assassin's blade, such an action would likely pull the Dukes together against our common enemy. But if she were simply killed by a wild beast, an accident in the wilderness, you and the other six Dukes would be fighting each other to control the throne. And that would leave us weak and divided, open for invasion."

"Ah." Yarron said simply. He had much to think about. The wizard was correct, the seven Dukedoms of Tarador could not agree on much, other than that they all wanted more power. And, almost as important, they all wanted to prevent the other six from gaining more power. Carlana was serving as Regent, not because she was qualified to rule Tarador in her daughter's name, but because the Dukes had been unable to agree on anyone else as Regent after her husband the king had died. "Ariana's father was my strongest ally, and my friend, I care for that girl as if she were my own daughter. For the enemy to attack her, on my land, while she is under my protection-"

"Halt!" Paedris called out in a loud hiss. "Halt, you up there!"

The three scouts ahead froze, turning around slowly. They waited for the wizard to make his way up to their position, offering hands to help him scramble over the last rock. "Thank you." Paedris huffed and puffed, catching his breath. He was very glad that he had switched his official purple robes for plain brown pants and a warm jacket. "There is a ward spell up ahead, between those two boulders." Paedris pointed to a pair of giant rocks, which had tumbled down the ridge long ago. They blocked the way above; the gap between them was the only way to the top of the ridge.

One of the scouts kneeled down, waving his hand over a place where moss had been flattened. "That is where the trail leads. The enemy's tracks go in that direction."

"And they knew we would follow the trail if we were tracking them. Stay here." Paedris approached the boulders, stopping just short of where the ward lay across the gap like an invisible spider web. The ward was powerful and somewhat crude, typical of the enemy's magics. He could not release the ward without alerting the enemy. What he could do is fool the ward, so it didn't react to troops passing through it. It was a simple matter for a master wizard; he waved to the scouts to him when it was done. "What lies beyond the top of this ridge?"

One of the scouts spoke. "I've only been here once, Lord Salva, but what I remember is a shallow gully, then another ridge, a bit lower than this ridge. Beyond that is a deep, wide gully, almost passes for a valley in these woods."

Duke Yarron held out a hand for his scouts to pull him up. "A valley? I am ashamed to say that, though these are my lands, I don't know this area. Is this valley a good spot for a raiding force to gather?"

The scout nodded. "It could be. You wish us to follow their tracks?"

Yarron looked to the court wizard for guidance. Paedris rubbed his beard while he considered what to do. "No. A ward here means the enemy must be close, close enough to hear if the ward is triggered. Go to the top of the next ridge, keep low, so you can see if the enemy has placed any pickets, but without revealing yourself. Duke, I propose we turn right just this side of the ridge top, and follow it north half a league. There, we will see if we can cross to the next ridge east of us, and see what lies in this valley beyond."

"Agreed." Yarron pointed to the sky. "We must make haste, the light will be failing us in a few hours."

"These old eyes are, I fear, not as good as they used to be. But even I can see a substantial force." Yarron whispered. The light was poor, the setting was almost hidden behind heavy clouds to the west, just a vaguely less dark part of the sky. It had started to rain again an hour ago, making everyone miserably cold and wet, if they weren't already. Yarron was lying in a squishy pool of cold, muddy water under an overhanging rock, peering down into a valley that was not as deep, or steep-sided, as most of the Thrallren woods. The enemy had been camped there long enough to have cut down trees, and build a partial fence along the valley floor. Camped on his land, treating it as if it were already their own! The enemy had chosen well, the valley lay less than ten leagues from the western edge of the woods, where some of the best farmland in LeVanne province lay. And an enemy who controlled that part of the province could cut the major roads to the south, which would make it difficult for reinforcement royal army troops to reach LeVanne in case of war.

"I count perhaps two hundred of the enemy, my lord." One of the scouts observed. "Men only, I don't see any orcs."

"The enemy rarely mixes men and orcs, they usually end up fighting each other sooner or later." Paedris observed. "Two hundred is a good estimate. And they have a wizard with them."

Yarron frowned. He had less than sixty men; twenty of his own, and forty troops of the royal army. All were cold, wet, and exhausted from the grueling trek through the woods. There had been no chance for hot food on the march, and since horses, and even mules, were unable to walk in the tangled mess of Thrallren, the men had been forced to carry all their weapons, food and gear on their backs. To set an example, even Duke

Yarron carried a backpack, something he had not done since he was a young boy. The problem was not that his men were not walking on fresh legs; the problem was that he had far too few men. Sound battle tactics usually called for an attacking force to outnumber the defenders by at least three to one. "Lord Salva?"

Paedris considered what to say, to persuade the Duke to attack the enemy force that had invaded his land. "I know your men are tired, Yarron."

Yarron shrugged, as much as he could in the confined space under the rock. "No battle was ever won except by a tired army. But I won't throw my men's lives away in a futile gesture."

"I believe I can even the odds. The enemy is also cold, wet and tired, they have likely been in these woods for a fortnight, and they haven't been allowed any fires for cooking or warmth. Their wizard is weary; keeping a concealment spell for so long is a terrible strain. Unless I am greatly mistaken, their wizard is no match for me." Yarron raised an eyebrow at that remark, so Paedris added "that is a fact, not a boast."

"You have a plan? We would have to cross open ground; I can see at least two sentries facing our direction. Lepto," Yarron asked his lead scout, "could your men take out those sentries, silently?"

Lepto shook his head. "No, my lord. They are behind a screen of brambles, very clever, for that would deflect any arrows, but they can see through it. They would surely see me and my men, before we could get to them."

"Lord Salva, unless you can do something about those sentries, and do so quietly, I think this attack is impossible. Then, there are barricades on the valley floor both north and south, blocking our path, and the valley walls east and west are too steep for my men to attack from there. Anything you do about their wizard will alert their soldiers."

Despite the cold, and his muddy, soaked clothing, and his empty belly, Paedris smiled. The Duke underestimated the power of a master wizard. "I have a plan. Let's get out from under this rock, and prepare."

The enemy wizard was well aware that the men under his command were cold, wet, tired and hungry, which did not make for alert sentries. The sentries were, therefore, relieved every hour, to keep their eyes, and ears, fresh. And to keep them awake. It would therefore have surprised the wizard from Acedor to see that the sentries at the north barricade were yawning, and barely able to keep their eyes open. The two men were very sleepy, sleepy, sleepy. Unusually, suddenly, terribly sleepy. Their wizard had placed wards around the area, how could an enemy approach without being detected? The sentries did not need to watch, they could sleep. Sleep. And so they did, without their wizard noticing anything wrong. Soon after, Lepto's scouts carefully moved the brambles aside, and had the two sleeping enemy sentries bound and gagged. But the scouts then retreated back to the north, which also would have surprised the enemy.

The ridge to the east of the valley was steep, especially at the top. At the top, there were many large rocks clinging to the slope, in many places held in place by other rocks. It started with a few pebbles slipping down the slope, then small rocks clinking against each other as they fell. Small rocks coming down the ridge was nothing new, the valley floor was littered with them. What was new, and would have alarmed the enemy if they had known, were the very large rocks that were swaying back and forth. The clatter of small rocks became a cascade, which now did cause the enemy below to look up in curiosity, but it was too late. One giant boulder, the size of a farmhouse, broke loose, and that started an avalanche. With a terrible roaring sound, rocks slid, tumbled, rolled and bounced down the slope, gaining speed as they fell.

Enemy troops, dulled by sleep, staggered out of their tents, fumbling for weapons. Officers were running around, shouting and kicking their men to get them to move, when the first boulder smashed into the barricade, crushing the logs like a pile of twigs.

While Paedris had shaken the rocks loose from the ridge, he had not been able to control where they fell, and most rolled down around the barricade, missing the main encampment. In the dust, darkness and confusion, the enemy wizard held his staff high, with an angry red glow from the tip of the staff illuminating the valley. He had sensed no magic. Was this merely an accident, a rockslide caused by the soggy ground being loosened by several days of rain? The wizard was still gathering his senses, to search for a hostile presence around the valley, when his mouth opened wide in terror, and he was surrounded by white-hot flame. The flame burned hot, his staff burst into splinters, and pieces of the staff scattered where he had been standing. When the flames were snuffed out, there was no trace of the wizard.

Duke Yarron put a steadying hand on Paedris' shoulder, as the court wizard swayed from momentary weakness. "Will you recover, Lord Salva? That fireball must have taken much of your strength."

Paedris leaned on his staff, catching his breath. "The fireball was not the problem, it was the spell I concealed the fireball inside, so the enemy did not see it until it was upon him. That sapped my strength." He straightened up, stretching his aching back. "I'm getting too old for this. Moving those rocks took far more effort than I expected."

"All my men, working together, could not have moved the smallest of those rocks. Rest, Lord Salva, my men and I can take the battle from here." Yarron turned to look down the valley, where his troops were advancing, now that the rockslide had ended. A jumble of rocks lay where the barricade had been, but his men were making their way around the boulders, using them as cover to send arrows into the massed enemy soldiers, who were disoriented and fearful at the sudden death of their wizard.

"Your men, yes. *You* stay here, Yarron. We did not come all this way so that LeVanne could be thrown into turmoil by the death of its Duke."

Duke Yarron bristled at the thought of not joining his men in battle, to wipe out the enemy who had invaded his land. The wizard had no actual authority over him. "My eldest son-"

"Is old enough, certainly, is he experienced? Acedor has been bold enough to attack the crown princess on your land, and to set up camp here. Here, in your backyard. Who best to lead LeVanne now, when the danger is so clear? You, or your son?"

Yarron's focus moved between his men, the wizard, and back to his men. He spat on the ground in disgust. "Your words ring true, Lord Salva, but it is not easy for an old warrior to stand aside, and let others do the fighting for me."

Paedris patted the Duke on the shoulder, and addressed him by his first name. "James, this is but a skirmish, the war is coming, and coming soon. There will be much fighting for all of us then. Save your strength, you will need it."

Yarron watched as his men charged down the rocky slope to the valley floor. "Will I? Does it matter, Lord Salva? In the long run, in my son's time, will it matter?" He looked at the wizard sharply. "You can no longer see the future as you once could, but your last vision showed the enemy's power is ascending-"

"Ascendant." The wizard interjected. Paedris grew irritated when amateurs tried to use knowledge that belonged only to wizards."

"-and that our power, your power, will inevitably fade."

"It is not written in stone, Yarron. The future can be altered. Even when we had the ability to glimpse the future, it was only that, a glimpse. A flickering, uncertain shadow, a mirage that is less distinct the closer you try to look at it. If I knew exactly what the future held, our King Adric would be alive-"

"Loathe I am to speak ill of my distant cousin, but Adric died because he was foolish and overconfident. You saw a future of death and destruction for the realm, and because Adric listened to your council, our army was there to stop the enemy. If Adric had listened to all of your advice, and the advice of his generals, he would have survived the day."

"Perhaps. That is my point, Yarron. The future is not written. Yes, the power of the enemy is ascendant now, and we do not as yet foresee a way to victory. I do not need fortune cards or magical spells to continue fighting in the face of the enemy's growing strength, I have *faith*. Faith gives me strength, and it should you as well."

"Mmm," Yarron grunted, pointing at the valley, where his men had routed the enemy and were skirmishing with small groups of survivors. "I have faith in my own men, Salva. That, and the power of our wizards."

"Fair enough," Paedris nodded. "Now, if you want to do something useful here, help me get down there. My powers will, I fear, soon be needed to help heal the wounded."

CHAPTER FOUR

"You see, see it, on the right there, the pointy tower?" Ariana gestured excitedly out the window of the royal coach. She was so eager to point out sights to Koren that she was blocking his view. He knelt on the cushion and stuck his head out the window, ignoring the disapproving frowns of the royal guards.

"The one made of dark grey stone? That is where Paedris lives?"

"Yes, and that's where you will live. My rooms are over toward the left, see the white building with the red roof?"

Koren didn't know whether Ariana was playing a trick on him. The castle was an immense building with battlements and towers, encircling the top of a hill, with a city spread out all around. Koren had never seen such a place. Still, he was somewhat disappointed. "I thought the royal palace would be more grand, like-" Koren stopped when he realized he was insulting Ariana's home.

"No, silly," the crown princess of Tarador punched him playfully on the arm, "you mean like in a fairy tale? It's a castle, a fortress; it was built a long time ago, when Tarador and Acedor were one land. Before the war." A frown passed briefly over the girl's face. "The palace was built inside the castle walls, when the first king came to live here. Don't you know anything about history?"

"We didn't need to know history to live on a farm." Koren grumbled.

"Well, you will simply have to learn. I can teach you. The first king of Tarador was Dagon the First, of course, he-"

"Ariana, stop hanging out the window like a monkey, and don't bore Koren to death with the royal lineage." Carlana ordered. "Koren doesn't need to have his head filled with useless facts to be Lord Salva's servant."

Koren took one last look at the forbidding tower where Ariana said the wizard lived, then sat back down on the plush cushion of the royal coach. He still could not believe he was riding in the royal coach, with the crown princess and the Regent. "Pardon me, ma'am, I mean, Lady, I mean, your Magnificence-"

Carlana couldn't help laughing. "Call me 'Your Highness', Koren. Dukes and Duchesses are 'Your Grace'. Ariana is also 'Your Highness' now. She will be 'Your Majesty', but not until she becomes Queen, and not while she has bits of straw stuck in her hair from hanging out the coach window like a wild monkey."

"Yes, your Maj-Highness. Am I really to live in the castle?"

"You are, Koren," Carlana confirmed, delighted to see the joy on the boy's face. Then, mindful of Paedris' warning not to let anyone know there was anything special about Koren, she added, "Not in the royal palace itself, of course. There are many servants living in the castle; cooks, gardeners, maids, why, even the stable hands could be said to live inside the castle walls, if they stretch the truth a little." Carlana had been reluctant to have Koren ride in the royal carriage with them, but Ariana had raised such a fuss about it, and Koren was still sore from the wounds he'd received while saving the crown princess, after all.

Koren relaxed back against the cushions of his seat, grinning. There had been no feast in his honor, and no knighthood, and no land granted to him, but whispered word of Koren's deeds had spread anyway. "Fancy me, Koren Bladewell, living in a palace. Why, my pare-" he had been about to say that his parents would be proud, but of course, his parents didn't care about him. He caught himself quickly, and continued "-pair, pair of shoes are the most expensive thing I've ever owned." He lifted his feet to admire the fine leather shoes Duke Yarron had given him, along with a complete set of clothes, including a warm winter coat.

Carlana had not been fooled by Koren's verbal trick, when he was about to say 'parents', she had looked way out the window, to avoid embarrassing the young man. When Ariana heard that his parents had abandoned Koren, she had demanded her mother send soldiers out to search for them. So far, there was no sign of Bodric and Amalie Bladewell, and Koren's uncle Ander said he didn't know where Amalie's cousin lived. Carlana had made a few discrete inquiries about the Baron who ruled Crickdon County, and learned the man cared little about the affairs of his commoner subjects, unless such matters filled his purse with gold, or his belly with food. And rumor had it that the Baron cared more about food than gold. Carlana's heart went out to the boy, now all alone in the world.

Worse, she couldn't tell him what Paedris had said, that Koren's reputation as a jinx was caused by his uncontrolled magical ability. The stories Koren had told, of exploding beer vats, and broken waterwheels, Paedris said were all manifestations of Koren exerting his will on the world, without knowing what he was doing, or having any ability to control the result. Truthfully, Carlana could not blame the people of Crebbs Ford for wanting the destructive boy out of their village before he caused any more damage. His parents, however, Carlana could not forgive. Whether they believed their son was a jinx or not, there was no excuse for abandoning an eleven year old boy in the wilderness. Koren still thought of himself as a jinx, in fact, the boy had been miserable when he warned Carlana about what a menace he was, and said that it was best if he went away, before he hurt someone. Paedris, bless the old scoundrel's heart, had laughed when Koren said he was a jinx, and announced such talk was utter nonsense, and he should know, he was the most powerful wizard in Tarador! Carlana wasn't sure Koren quite believed that he wasn't a jinx, but the boy had stopped talking about it. "I am sure you will enjoy living with Paedris." Carlana said quickly, to take the boy's mind away from his troubles. "Do you know, there are chambers in Lord Salva's tower that even I have never been into?"

"Really?" Koren asked in surprise.

"Really," Carlana laughed. "I hear that old rascal has spells blocking the doors inside the tower, and no one can enter unless he gives permission."

"Be careful in that tower, Koren," Ariana pleaded, "it is old and dusty, and sometimes there are strange lights and noises coming from there at night." The girl shuddered.

"I'm sure Lord Salva will keep you safe, Koren," Carlana added hastily, "as long as you follow his instructions, and don't go poking your nose into places you don't belong."

"Oh, no, your highness, I would never do that," Koren said, with a guilty little feeling in the back of his mind that, of course he would go poking his nose around the wizard's tower someday. Who could resist such temptation?

"You will come to the palace, to visit me?" Ariana asked. "We can have so much fun in the palace, and we have gardens, and stables for riding horses, and lots of games-"

"And much for you to learn, young lady, if you are ever going to rule this land." Carlana scolded. "There is a time for learning and a time for play. Koren may come to visit you, when you are finished with your lessons."

"What about Koren? Doesn't he need to learn, too?"

Carlana couldn't help the frown that flashed across her face. "Lord Salva will take care of Koren's education." She clasped her hands on her lap to stop a cold shudder from running up her spine. The wizard could not entirely be trusted. What plans he had for Koren, Carlana didn't know, and was quite sure she didn't want to know. Better the boy didn't know, either. "What Koren needs to learn as a wizard's servant is very different from what you need to learn as a crown princess and a lady."

"But, mother-"

"Don't you 'but mother' me, young lady. And I don't think Koren is really interested in learning heraldry, or court etiquette, or needlepoint, now, is he?"

All of that sounded deadly boring to Koren. "Uh, I don't think so, ma'am, I mean, your Highness." He sat back and looked out the window, the royal carriage was now passing through roads in the outskirts of the city of Linden that surrounded the royal castle. He had never imagined a city so big, never seen buildings bigger than the Golden Trout back in Crebbs Ford. The Golden Trout looked like a broken-down shack, maybe even a chicken coop, compared to most of the buildings here, and they were only yet in the poorer outlying section of the city. People were out in front of the buildings, enjoying the mid-day sunshine of a clear, late autumn day, waving and cheering as the royal carriage went by, everyone straining their necks to get a glimpse of the crown princess and the Regent. Koren was amused to see the excited, then perplexed looks on people's faces as they saw a boy staring back at them from the shadows of the coach, and realized they had no idea who this boy was. He waved back, at first gesturing enthusiastically, then mimicking Carlana's restrained, refined wave of holding up her arm, and gently rotating her wrist. The odd gesture was, he figured, some strange thing royal people did, like having more than one fork at the table. Koren had survived the multiple-fork test; the first night the royal party had stopped at an inn, by waiting to see what other people at the table were doing, and not doing anything unless the Regent or Ariana were doing it. For example, Koren noticed that royal people didn't eat soup in any way that made sense. The best way to eat soup was to hunch over the bowl, tilt it towards you, and scoop it into your mouth. But no! Royal people, Paedris had shown him, tilted the soup bowl *away* from them, and also tilted the spoon away from them, so that the side of the spoon closest to them didn't actually get any soup on it. While Paedris had explained that technique ensured there was no soup to drip off the near side of the spoon onto your fancy clothes, Koren thought it was only good for ensuring that so little soup got onto your spoon with each scoop, that the soup would be cold before you were done. Of course, since the soup was served, not in a proper bowl, but instead in a shallow dish that held barely two spoonfuls of soup, letting it get cold was not a problem.

Koren had only eaten dinner with the Regent and Ariana that first night on the road, after that, Koren ate his meals with the guards and other servants, and he traveled with them in their wagons. Carlana had explained to Ariana it was best to avoid drawing attention to Koren, and that explanation worked, for a while. It was on the last morning, as they approached the castle, that Ariana put her dainty little royal foot down and insisted that, since the royal carriage was 'royal' only because *she* was in it, Koren was going to be in the carriage, or the carriage wasn't going anywhere that day. Her mother the Regent discovered that no amount of arguing, ordering, scolding or pleading was going to change her daughter's mind. Carlana was torn between extreme annoyance at her stubborn young daughter, and being proud of the future ruler of Tarador asserting herself so forcefully. The royal guards obeyed the Regent by getting the carriage ready that morning, but when Carlana instructed them to bring the crown princess, the guards had stood around, shuffling their feet awkwardly, and looking off into the distance. They were generally making it clear there was no way those guards, who were trained and pledged to protect the crown princess with their very lives, were going to touch her against her will. No matter what the Regent wanted. The impasse between mother and daughter ended with Carlana allowing Koren to ride in the royal carriage, and Ariana realizing that she had pushed her mother about as far as she ever would.

Thus it was that Koren found himself dressed in fancy clothes that, he had to admit, fit him perfectly, and riding in the royal carriage with the crown princess and the Regent of Tarador, winding its way thru the city on its way to the royal palace. The royal carriage was near the front of a long trail of lesser carriages, wagons and men on horseback, all there to protect, provide for, and accompany the crown princess and Regent on their long tour throughout Tarador. Such a thing happening to poor farm boy Koren Bladewell, he had never imagined, not even in his wildest dreams back in tiny Crebbs Ford. He grinned ear to ear, continued to wave to the people, and gawked at the increasingly large, numerous and substantial buildings, as the royal carriage wound its way thru the city, up toward the gray castle on the hill.

While Koren was looking out the window, watching the city roll by, Ariana was watching Koren. Not openly staring at him, Ariana had been trained for far too long on how a proper princess had to behave, instead she looked out the window on his side of the carriage, with her attention on Koren, and not on the waving and cheering people who lined the road. When she saw that Koren was imitating her mother's restrained waving motion, she bit her lip to keep from laughing. That feeble gesture, which looked ridiculous even when her mother was doing it, was absurd when done with Koren's rough, strong hands. She had little memory of Koren holding onto her while they plunged down the raging river. He had touched her hand, briefly, when they met after Paedris declared the farm boy could get out of bed, but they had met in the duke's formal receiving hall, surrounded by people, wearing stiff, formal clothes. Ariana had been limited to holding out her hand, palm down, so Koren could kneel on one knee, take her hand in his, and kiss the back of her hand. Touching his future monarch was, according to her mother, supposed to be all the honor a common boy like Koren could ever want. Since her mother had never been a commoner, Ariana couldn't see how Carlana knew what common people wanted. Ariana herself didn't truly know what common people wanted, but certainly kneeling and brushing your lips on the back of a princess' hand could not compare to a real reward; like land, or money. Or a knighthood.

At the thought of Koren's hand touching hers, and his lips oh so briefly brushing against her skin, she unconsciously brushed the spot where his lips had lingered, tracing a circle around the spot with her fingertips.

While Ariana was watching Koren, Carlana was watching her daughter watch Koren, and the Regent knew exactly what the expression on her daughter's face meant. Knew what it meant that her daughter was brushing the fingertips of her left hand across the back of her right hand. Ariana was completely, hopelessly infatuated with her hero, this handsome, fresh-faced, young man who had risked his life to save a girl he didn't even know. He had saved her, not because she is a princess, but because she had needed rescuing, and because he was there, and because he could, or at least thought he had to try. He had saved her when the grown men who were there to protect her could not. Carlana was not surprised that her daughter's head was filled with romantic notions about her true hero, this handsome young man with the tangled curls of dark hair falling around his face, and the dreamy brown eyes-

Yes, Carlana could quite easily understand how her daughter could look at Koren the way she did. The mother of the crown princess needed to make sure the infatuation did not go too far, for Ariana could not be seen as becoming involved seriously with any young man now, especially not with a lowly commoner. Dangling the prospect of Ariana marrying a son of a duke was a way to keep the dukes supporting Ariana becoming queen on her sixteenth birthday. Without that prospect, it was far from guaranteed that an untested young girl could hang onto power, surrounded by powerful, ambitious and scheming dukes who lusted for the throne themselves.

Carlana would allow Ariana her girlish daydreams for now. Once they were in the palace, and Koren was busy with the wizard, there would be little time, Carlana thought, for Ariana and Koren to be together. Then Ariana's crush on Koren would fade over time, as she became distracted by everything going on around the royal palace.

The Regent had forgotten just how determined a young girl in love could be. And, in particular, she once again underestimated the determination of the young woman who would soon sit on the throne and rule Tarador.

After passing thru a busy section of the city that had many tall, stone buildings, the road was now in an area that did not appear to be as prosperous. Among the people lining the road, Koren saw a family of three; mother, father, and a boy around his age. The father had one hand on the boy's shoulder, and the boy was holding his mother's hand. The woman did not look much like Koren's mother, having blond hair and being quite tall, but this woman had her hair tied in a blue ribbon. Amalie Bladewell often had her hair tied with a blue ribbon, a ribbon that Bodric purchased new every year, without fail. Blue dye being rare and expensive, it was not a color most farm families in Crebbs Ford could afford; most people wore clothes of simple gray wool, or cotton in various shades of off-white or tan. Occasionally, clothes were red, if enough iron could be found to provide a color wash. But blue was unusual among poor people, unusual enough that it always reminded Koren of his mother.

Koren's hand froze in mid-wave, as he locked eyes with the boy standing with his parents on the side of the road, and felt a sharp pain of homesickness. He half rose out of his seat, enough so that his face was no longer in shadow, and the people could see him clearly. The family looked puzzled to see an unfamiliar face staring back at them from the royal carriage, and they waved uncertainly. Then the carriage swept past, and the family was gone. Koren slumped back in his seat, stricken. An unbidden tear welled up in his left eye, and trailed down his cheek.

Ariana had seen the family, having watched Koren, and guessed the significance, if not of the ribbon, then of the family, and the boy Koren's age. With a catch in her throat and a tear forming in her own eyes, she reached out to touch Koren's arm, but her mother nudged her foot. Shaking her head, Carlana silently mouthed 'give him privacy, Ariana', and the Regent put a hand over her own heart, to show she understood the pain Koren must be feeling.

Koren quickly discovered there were many children his age in the castle grounds, both royalty like Ariana, and commoners like himself. One of the first boys he saw, he met on his way to Paedris' tower. Koren was clutching his bundle of clothes and looking at the tower, trying to figure out how to get there from where he was. He was gawking up at the colorful flags flying from the battlements, when he collided with another boy. "Oof. Sorry." Koren said, as he dropped his bundle onto the ground.

The other boy had golden, shiny hair falling about his shoulders. He wore a magnificent red tunic, on the front of which was a hawk, embroidered in silver. And he looked down his nose at Koren, as if Koren were something foul he'd just stepped in. "Watch where you're going, you stupid oaf." The boy snapped, checking his tunic for damage, or dirt.

"Said I was sorry." Impulsively, Koren held a hand out. "I'm Koren Bladewell."

"Bladewell? Of?" The boy stared at Koren's hand, unsure what to do.

"Oh, of, um, of Crebbs Ford. It's in Crickdon County."

"Crickdon? Is that Winterthur province? So, the Bladewells of Crickdon. Never heard of you. You have the honor to be speaking to Kyre Falco, eldest son of Duke Regin Falco of Burwyck Province."

"Regin Falco?" It was Koren's turn to be confused. "Never heard of him, sorry."

"Never, never heard of Duke Falco?" Kyre sputtered, shocked.

"Um, never heard of Burwyck province, either."

"What? How could you have never- what kind of backwater farm boy are you?" Kyre took a step back. From the way Koren was dressed, Kyre assumed he was the son of a minor, unimportant noble, such as a baron or a viscount, perhaps a mere knight. But now Kyre considered that Koren might be a commoner servant. And Kyre had wasted his time talking to the lowborn boy? "What are you doing in the castle, boy?"

Koren shrugged and picked up his bundle, hoisting it onto his shoulder. "I'm Lord Salva's new servant."

Kyre looked at Koren in disgust. "Then, be along with you, boy! Hurry on about your business, and be more careful around your betters."

Koren remembered what Carlana said about how to address a Duke. He wondered if that applied to their sons as well. Koren bowed his head slightly. "Yes, Your Grace. Sorry to have disturbed you."

"Huh. You have proper manners, at least, boy." Kyre stepped around Koren and didn't give the servant boy another look.

When Kyre arrived at his quarters in the palace, he found Niles Forne lounging on a seat by the window. The Duke had sent Forne to the palace with Kyre, supposedly to help his son navigate the various intrigues in the royal court; Kyre knew the man was nothing more than a spy for his father. A spy, who in Kyre's opinion, paid far too much attention when Kyre did something bad, and barely noticed Kyre's many, many triumphs. "Forne." Kyre said dismissively as he removed his tunic and held it up to the light.

"Something wrong with your garment, young Sire?" Forne asked, looking down his long, narrow nose at the boy, without getting up from his seat.

"A stupid boy bumped into me in the courtyard, the wizard's servant?"

Forne sprung to his feet, with uncharacteristic excitement. "You met Lord Salva's servant? Pray tell, what is he like?"

"An ignorant farm boy, why?" Kyre draped the tunic over the back of a chair.

Forne sat back down. He could see he had work to do. "Ignorant farm boy he may be, but Koren Bladewell is the boy who rescued princess Ariana. In the course of one morning, he scared away a giant bear, saved her from plunging over a waterfall, and held off a troop of bandits by himself."

Kyre was not impressed. "And in the afternoon, did he slay a dragon and defeat Acedor's army?" He remarked flippantly. "This just a silly rumor."

"Sit down, Kyre." Forne said in a flat voice. There were times when Kyre was the heir of Burwyck province, and other times he was a spoiled, arrogant boy. And times when the spoiled boy part of him threatened his own inheritance. This was exactly the sort of situation Duke Falco expected Forne to handle, to guide his son. "It is not just a rumor, I have heard from good sources that what the *rumor* says is true. This boy Koren saved the life of our crown princess, even if the entire story isn't true. If you had been paying attention to me, or what is going on at court, you would know that Lord Salva was impressed with this ignorant farm boy, as you described him, and asked the Regent to appoint him as the wizard's personal servant. You would also know that princess Ariana considers Koren to be her hero." Forne paused. "Now that I think of it, I don't know why Carlana didn't grant the boy a knighthood, at least. That is curious, very curious. I shall have to make inquiries around the court. I have heard that, while Koren recovered from his wounds in Duke Yarron's castle, he and Ariana spent much time together, and now they are quite inseparable. He rode here from LeVanne in the royal coach."

Kyre sat down, chastened. Like all eldest sons and daughters of the Dukes who ruled Tarador's seven provinces, Kyre had on his eleventh birthday been sent to spend four years living at the royal palace. The custom was intended to ensure the future leaders were raised to be responsible, experienced, and loyal to the crown. There was also a darker purpose; while at the palace, they were hostages in case their parents had any ideas of overthrowing the ruling king or queen. Kyre's father had high hopes, as did the other six Dukes, that his son would marry Ariana someday, and toward that end, Kyre had been instructed to become close friends with the crown princess. So far, Ariana had been civil and polite to Kyre, but no more. "I should make an effort, a strong effort, to become friends with this Koren? If he thinks well of me, and speaks of me to Ariana-"

"Exactly, young Sire." Forne tactfully agreed with the obvious. "And something else, which can be worked to our advantage-"

"You mean *my* advantage, Forne."

Forne bowed ever so slightly; barely enough to show the respect due to Kyre as heir to the dukedom, not so much as to imply that Forne felt any more respect that he was obliged to. "The advantage of the Falcos, young Sire, I live to serve."

"Go on."

"Rumor has it, and my source on this is always accurate, that Koren was abandoned by his parents." Forne laid out the story of the Bladewell's banishment from Crebbs Ford, and how his parents drove away in their wagon, never to return. "My source tells me Koren blames himself for his parents abandoning him, that if he had not caused them so much trouble, they wouldn't have been forced to leave him alone in the wilderness. In the long term, Sire, it would be best if Koren were not here to be Ariana's friend, so that she would have to turn to someone else for friendship. If Koren could be convinced that his being a jinx is a danger to Ariana, or that Carlana will throw him out on the street once she grows tired of the boy-"

"I understand, Forne." Kyre said with a wicked smile. "My father was wise to send you here to serve me. Now there is only one problem you need to help me with."

"What is that, young Sire?"

Kyre didn't quite know how to say it, couldn't believe he would ever in his life have to say such a thing. "How does one apologize to a common-born servant?"

There was a pounding noise coming from the heavy wooden door at the base of the wizard's tower, three floors below where Koren had set down his satchel. "Hello?" Someone was shouting, although to Koren's ear, it sounded like 'Huhloo'?

Koren walked back to the stairway, and leaned out the narrow window to look down. There was a boy, a little older than Koren, dressed in faded, well-worn clothes, and a type of cloth cap that Koren had noticed many of the servants wore. Koren couldn't decide if the boy's hair was a dark blonde, or a light brown, it was mostly tucked under his cap. "Hey down there." Koren called out, since he didn't know what else to say.

"Hey yourself. Is that you up there, Koren?" The boy asked, although Koren at first didn't realize what he'd said, for the boy's accent was so strong that what Koren heard was something like 'Ay y'sell, izzat you uh thur, ko-en?'

"Uh, yes?" Koren guessed, still not sure what the boy had asked.

"You going to let me in? I ain't got all day, you know."

This time Koren figured, more from the fact that the boy was standing at the door than from his words, that he wanted to come into the tower. Koren hesitated. The tower didn't belong to Koren, he didn't know who else was allowed inside. "I'll be right down."

As he hurried down the stairs, Koren could hear through the windows that the boy outside was talking, either to Koren, or to himself. It sounded like "Be right down, he says, like him's royalty and me sitting here cooling my heels, sure, why not, I can just stand here until the sun goes down, nothing else to do with my time- hello!" The boy exclaimed as Koren pulled the heavy door open.

"It wasn't locked." Koren announced defensively.

"And I'll not be going in where I'm not invited." The boy said indignantly. "This here's your tower to take care of, got enough work, more than enough work, for myself. You can have this dusty old tower, with the weird goings-on in here, strange lights, and explosions, and smoke and mist coming out the windows all day and night, it's like to give any honest person the creeps, I say."

Koren gaped, he'd never heard anyone talk so much without pausing for breath. "Uh, hi? I'm Koren, Koren Bladewell of the Crickdon Bladewells, Winterthur province." Koren announced, assuming from his conversation with Kyre Falco that family name and origins were the usual form of greeting in the castle.

"And Cully's my name." The boy snatched off his cap and bowed mockingly. "Oh, the *Crickdon* Bladewells," Cully said, "everyone knows how high and mighty those Bladewells from Crickdon are, compared to the other no-account dirt farming Bladewells everywhere else. Pleased to meet you, your lordship. Cully Runnet, of the Runnets round here, least, round here the past few years. Before that, round anyplace my Ma and Pa could find work."

Koren's face was red. "I didn't mean- I'm just Koren. Lord Salva's new servant."

"I knows who you are, I got ears, I hear things. You can call me your official welcoming party of one." Cully jerked his thumb back over his shoulder, toward the palace. "I work in the hospital, mostly, sometimes in the kitchens, if they need help. My Ma's a physician in the hospital." He looked down at the bundle in his other hand, and gesture for Koren to move aside. "You gonna block the door all day?"

"Oh, I, uh, I don't know if I'm supposed to let people in."

"Oh, bah!" Cully elbowed his way past Koren, and headed up the stairs like he owned the place. "Been here enough times myself, bringing firewood and whatnot to the master wizard, you think he fetched his food and firewood and whatnot by hisself? The court wizard?" Cully shook his head at Koren's ignorance. "Like as not, he'd cast a spell and turn a toad into a servant to fetch his things. Or you into a toad, if you're not careful, and don't keep your nose clean and out of trouble, you hear me?"

Koren swallowed hard. "He can do that?"

"Seen it myself, I have." Cully declared, and Koren didn't know if he was joking or not. When he reached the landing on the third floor, Cully pushed open a door, went inside, and set down his bundle. "This be your room, I expect." The room was small, although bigger than the room where Koren had slept in his parent's home in Crebbs Ford, and there was a window, a wooden chest, and a bed frame with ropes for a mattress, and a small fireplace. "This here," Cully nudged the bundle with his foot, "is clothes for you, and bedding," he bent down to unwrap the bundle, "and lunch for both of us." The lunch was several loaves of good, crusty dark bread, and cheese, and a smoked sausage, and two ripe apples. "It's not much, but-"

"Not much?" Koren exclaimed. "It's a feast!"

Cully smiled, and winked as if Koren had passed some sort of test. "Aye, for the likes of you and me, a feast. For the Quality people round here, over in the palace, this is rough fare, why, they'd turn up their noses at such as we say is a feast. The Quality, they have roasted pheasant, and honey cakes, and tarts with strawberries and fresh cream." Cully spread the food out on top of the chest, and sliced the cheese and sausage with a knife from his pocket. He tore off a chunk of bread, layered it with sausage and cheese, and gestured for Koren to grab some food. "Come on, I'll show you around."

They climbed the tower, which was tall, but rather thin so that even at the bottom each level only had three or four rooms, with lots of closets and other cubbyholes. Koren reached out to tug open a door on the fourth level, when Cully slapped his hand away. "Don't you be touching that, you fool! You see the sign there, that's Lord Salva's sign." Cully pointed to a dark smudge on the door, like a smoke stain, that was vaguely in the shape of a lightning bolt. "Keep away from those, unless the wizard hisself tells you to go in there. Set off the banshees, otherwise, you will, shrieking demons that will wake up the whole castle, and bring a troop of guards pounding up the stairs."

"Banshees?" Koren looked closely at the door, thinking Cully was playing a trick on him. It looked like any other, old, worn wooden door.

Cully shook his head. "Ah, good thing for you I came along. Don't you know wizards set spells they call wards, to guard their things? You look for that sign on the door," he paused, biting one of his knuckles while he thought, "of course, there are also *invisible* wards, wind you."

"Invisible?" Koren swallowed hard, his throat suddenly dry, and not just from the bread he was eating. "How am I-"

"Don't worry yourself about it," Cully waved his hand assuringly, "I know which doors are warded. Or which doors are usually warded," he added under his breath, "you never can tell with wizards." He patted Koren on the shoulder. "I'll show you which doors not to open."

"What's behind the doors that are warded?" Koren asked innocently.

Cully snatched off his cap in exasperation. "There you go, already getting yourself in trouble, scheming to stick your nose where it don't belong! Can't leave well enough alone, can you? And of course, I'll get the blame, Cully, you should have warned the new boy, Cully, it's your fault, Cully, it's your fault, Cully this and Cully that, it's always me catches it hot when things go wrong around here."

Koren backed away, holding his hands up, although one hand was still filled with bread, cheese and smoked sausage. "I was just curious, that's all, I wouldn't get you into trouble. Had enough trouble myself." He said, trying to calm the other boy down.

"You best not." Cully mumbled, calming down as quickly as he had exploded. "What's behind those doors is none of our business, that's what's behind those doors. Especially not the business of a boy who just got to the castle, stepping right off the farm." His voice dropped to a conspiratorial whisper. "I seen behind a few o' those doors a time or two, strange stuff in there. Potions, and scrolls, and books likely filled with dark magic, powerful dark magic. You best stay away, if you can." He gestured for them to go up another floor in the tower. As they climbed, Cully patted Koren on the shoulder. "I hear you did get in trouble. Poaching in old Duke Yarron's woods, eh?"

"I didn't get in trouble for that!" Koren protested over a mouthful of sausage. "It was only a few fish, anyway."

"Only a few fish, you says. No deer, no rabbits, that must grow thick in the duke's private hunting reserve, and you wasn't tempted, even with a hungry belly?" Cully winked. "Don't you worry about it, the royalty taxes us, I say we tax them right back, by taking a couple deer once in a while, to fill our bellies." They stopped in front of a door that displayed the faint lightning bolt symbol, Cully pointed to it, and Koren nodded that he understood. "Only a few fish or not, you coulda got in big trouble, if you hadn't saved our princess. Say, is that story true?"

Koren hastened to repeat the story that Paedris had given to him. "I don't know which story you mean, there's a lot of wild tales going around, I hear. She fell in the river, and it was cold, and I was there to pull her out, before her guards could get there." The genius of Paedris' tale was that every word of it was true, so Koren didn't have to remember much of a lie.

Cully seemed disappointed. The stories he'd heard, of a giant bear, and a raging river, and bandits, were so much better than the truth, he wished he hadn't asked. "You saved her, whatever the story is. And isn't that like the Quality, huh? You save them, and the reward you get is to be stuck cleaning a dusty old tower for a wizard, who is likely as not to turn you into a frog someday, when he's brewing up potions and not paying attention."

Koren was about to protest that princess Ariana had treated him very well, and anyway, living in a castle was better than shivering and starving in the woods by himself over the coming winter. But just as he opened his mouth, Cully excitedly pointed out a large door, which Koren saw didn't have any lightning bolt symbol.

"This door! This one!"

Koren saw that it was a large door, heavier that the other doors in the tower, and the wood was reinforced by iron bands. It had a large but simple lock. "What about it?"

"Stay away! You stay away from this door. That lock may look simple to pick, if you know how, but this is one of those doors I told you about, that has invisible wards. Or it did. Anyways, you stay away, unless the master wizard tells you to go in there. And even then, you watch mind your business, and get out quick as you can."

"I will. Thanks, Cully." Being servant to a wizard was going to be a lot more complicated than Koren had thought.

"Now, here," Cully announced after they'd climbed another set of stairs, "is the wizard's bath room."

"A bath room?" Koren asked, peering over the other boy's shoulder to the partly open door. "What is a bath room for?"

"For bathing, you dimwit! What else would it be for?"

Koren's mouth dropped open. "There is an entire room just for taking baths?"

"Sure," Cully said matter of factly, enjoying the chance to play the role of a sophisticated castle resident, to Koren's country hick. "Where else would you bathe?"

Koren shrugged as he walked into the room. "We had a tub we'd put in the kitchen, that's where the stove is for heating the water."

"Oh." Cully was sorry for putting on airs in front of Koren. "That's what my family did, too. Before we got here, leastwise. The Quality, like the wizard, they use a room like this."

"Everyone has a room like this?" Koren's eyes fairly popped out of his head. Such luxury! He could scarcely imagine it!

"No, you dum-dum. Not me, and not you. But you think the princess bathes in a little metal tub? No, she has a bathing room that makes this," he gestured around the wizard's stone and tile bathing chamber, "look like a chicken coop."

Cully was going on about something, but Koren's brain was frozen on the image of the crown princess in her bathing room, her robe slipping down over her shoulders-

Koren coughed, shaking his head and thumping his chest. "Sorry." He needed to get his mind off the princess, get his mind away from what was probably a treasonous thought, certainly dangerous. Looking at the large bathing tub, he groaned. "Ahhh, I have to haul buckets of water all the way up here?" He tried to figure how many buckets of water he needed to haul up to the fourth floor of the tower. And how was he going to heat that much water? By the time he had a couple buckets of water heated and poured into the tub, the water already in the tub would be cold! Who ever saw a tub that big? The wizard was a tall man, and even he could stretch his legs all the way out. A person could duck their head completely under the water!

Startled, Koren realized Cully had been snapping his fingers in front of Koren's nose. "Hey, ho, you listening to me?"

"Huh, sorry."

"I *said*, you don't need to haul any water up here, it comes out of the tap." Cully pointed to a metal pipe which came out of the wall and extended over the lip of the tub. Koren had been wondering what it was used for.

"The tap?"

Cully blew out a long breath, flapping his lips in exasperation. "The tap, the pipe, the water pipe." He turned the valve on top of the pipe, and water flowed out, into the tub, splashing loudly in the stone-lined room.

Koren jumped back. "Are *you* a wizard?"

"What? Me, a wizard? What in the world makes you think I'm a wizard?"

Koren pointed to the splashing water with a shaky finger, water which came from nowhere he could see. "That's magic?"

"Magic? You think that's *magic*? It's plumbing, you numbskull."

"Plumbing." Koren repeated the word slowly. "What is plumbing?" Carefully, hesitatingly, he touched the pipe with a finger, then drew back. It hadn't hurt.

Cully himself had only a vague idea of what plumbing was and how it worked, but he wasn't going to let Koren know that. "There's water pipes like this running lots of places in the castle, and especially in the palace. It comes from, from the river, and there's wheels, and," he guessed, "pumps and stuff that push the water along. So, when you open the tap, water comes out."

"Even this high off the ground?" Koren held the pipe firmly, feeling it vibrate as water flowed out.

Cully scratched his head. "I heard this is about as high as it can go, which is why there isn't as much water coming out here as there would be if the tap was on the first floor. The water gets, I don't know, tired, from climbing up the pipe, or something like that." He shrugged.

Koren smiled. Water didn't get tired, Cully didn't know as much as he pretended. He turned the valve experimentally, and the water stopped flowing. Without the water splashing, he saw that the tub hadn't been filling, because the water was running down a drain hole in the bottom. The draining water swirled around, faster and faster, like a whirlpool in a fast-running stream. "Where does the water go?" He asked, relieved that he wouldn't need to haul buckets of soapy bath water back down the stairs, either.

This was a question Cully knew the answer to, because he had asked the same question when his family first came to the castle. "Down to a pipe in the ground, to another big pipe under the courtyard, then it goes down the hill to a marsh next to the river. The water coming out of the castle is, uh, dirty, which is not good to dump into the river, so it goes through the marsh first, and that, cleans it somehow? Before it gets to the river. It's all pretty smart, the royal engineers take care of the plumbing. They had the whole courtyard tore up a couple years ago, to replace pipes." He wrinkled his nose at the memory. "It kind of stunk bad for a few days, of course, the royals all went to the countryside that time. Can't have the Quality around while the castle's all tore up."

"But you had to stay here?" Koren asked sympathetically.

"Oh yeah, brother, don't you know it? When the royals and all the other high and mighties leave the castle, that's when the hard work gets done. Like to broke my back hauling stones this summer, when the princess went, well, you know, on her tour. The royals always get out of the palace in the summer, cause it gets too hot here. The princess has a couple summer palaces, up in the hills where it's cool. I never seen them places, they must be nice."

Koren thought Duke Yarron's castle was the most fabulous place he'd ever imagined, until he came to Linden and saw the royal castle. The palace inside the castle walls, where the royals lived, was grander still. And he didn't remember Duke Yarron's castle having 'plumbing', he had bathed there in a small metal tub, although servants had brought the hot water to him, along with scented soaps, and freshly cleaned towels. Now it was back to reality for Koren Bladewell. He glanced around the bath room. "Does the wizard always bathe in cold water?" He asked, shivering at the thought of being in that stone room, during winter, taking a cold bath. In warm weather, Koren's family had bathed in a swimming role in the creek that ran though the farm, the water came out of a spring up the the hills to the east, and was always chilly. Only in winter did the tub get hauled out of the attic and set up in the kitchen for bathing.

"What? No, you birdbrain," Cully said, rolling his eyes. Koren wondered if the other boy would eventually run out of different ways to say Koren was stupid. Cully nudged the metal box under the tub with his foot. "That's the heater for the tub, and see that stovepipe, going up the wall? It goes through that box up there," Cully pointed to the ceiling above the tub, "where the rinsing water is. You pull this chain here, and," he demonstrated, "warm water pours all over you, to rinse off the soap."

Koren shook his head in amazement. This 'plumbing' was truly incredible. How did people think of such things? The contrast between people who had luxuries like plumbing, and people like himself, could scarcely been greater.

"Nothing but the best for the Quality folk." Cully grumbled jealously. "Come on, I'll show you how the heater works."

The other side of the heater was a wood stove, in a room behind the bath room's wall. Cully explained that Koren would need to fire up the stove in the mornings, and run water into the tub, to prepare the wizard's bath in the mornings.

"He takes a bath *every* morning?"

"Sure," Cully nodded, "all the Quality folk do that. You'll need to wash up every day too."

Koren's eyebrows fairly met his hairline. "I have to take a bath every day?" His head was spinning. Perhaps being a wizard's servant was much harder than he had imagined.

"No. Well, if you're going to the palace, to carry messages for the wizard, then you'll need to be clean. They can't have the likes of you and me stinking up the place. And you'll need to wear clean clothes, with a freshly pressed shirt. Oh, don't worry about that," Cully hastened to add when he saw the other boy's distress, "there's a royal laundry you can use, that's where you'll do the wizard's laundry, too. Most days, unless you're going to the palace, you can just wash your face and hands," Cully winked, "and that's good enough. But make sure you wash the back of your hands, and scrub under your fingernails, they check that. The Quality don't miss anything, not if they could complain about it."

Koren looked skeptically at the wood stove. He would have to haul wood up the stairs. During the winter, it would be best to keep a small fire going all the time, with the coals banked to the side, so the heater didn't have to start cold. All that metal would take a long time to heat up. "Can't the wizard just," he waved vaguely toward the bath room, "heat the water by himself, with a spell or something?"

"Oh sure," Cully nodded knowingly, "I seen him do that once, when the heater box was being fixed. But he says it takes a lot of effort, even for a master wizard, and once he's in the tub and the water starts getting cold, he can't use the spell on the water with him in it, could he?" Cully winked.

"I guess not," Koren frowned. He knew absolutely nothing, maybe less than nothing, about magic.

Cully slapped Koren on the shoulder again. "You can count on me, bucko, we servants need to stick together, the Quality takes enough advantage of us by themselves." Cully glanced out the window. "Sun's getting low, I best be going. You know where the candles are, you'll be all right tonight, the wizard should be back in a few days. Take care of yourself, and don't touch anything!"

Kyre Falco just happened to be around the corner when Koren left the wizard's tower the next morning. Just happened to be there, just happened to be wearing his oldest, shabbiest set of clothing, and just happened to be carrying two delicious sticky buns. He just happened to have been waiting there for half an hour, growing impatient for the servant boy to come out of the tower. "Oh, hello. Koren, is it?" Kyre said with what he hoped would be seen as a cheery smile.

Koren bowed his head formally. "Good morning, your Grace."

"Call me Kyre, please, I am so tired of that 'Sire' and 'Your Grace' and "Your Highness' stuff, who can keep track of it?"

"It seemed to be important to you yesterday." Koren said warily. He still did not know how to deal with royalty; it was a new experience for him.

"Oh, that. Sorry about that. My father's advisor made me memorize the Ducal bloodlines yesterday. My head was so full of names that are supposed to be *so* important," Kyre rolled his eyes, "and I didn't recognize the Bladewells. Would you like a sticky bun? The kitchen gave me two of them."

"I- yes, thank you." Paedris was out somewhere with the army, Koren had slept in the tower by himself. The only thing he'd eaten the previous night was the remains of the loaf of bread Cully had brought. He didn't yet know where to go in the castle for food. "Where is the kitchen?"

Kyre couldn't help frowning. What a backwater oaf Koren was, didn't know his way around the castle at all? Then he covered his frown with a smile. "Come on, I'll show you, it's in the back of the dining hall. Do you ride? I was on my way to the stables, I feel like riding this morning." The stables were in the opposite direction from the wizard's tower, but Koren didn't know that. "What say I show you around the city?"

Koren hesitated. "I think I am supposed to be cleaning the tower-"

"Oh, you can do that later. Lord Salva isn't expected back for several days. I hear he helped the army win a smashing victory, should be a grand parade when the soldiers come back into the city."

Koren replied around a mouthful of sticky bun. "I'd love to ride a horse, your Grace." His first morning in the castle was shaping up very well indeed.

The royal stables were so large and grand that, when seeing them from the outside, Koren at first thought the building was part of the palace. Inside, Kyre introduced Koren to the stable master, loudly letting everyone know that Koren was his friend, and a guest of the Falcos that day, since Koren would normally only be allowed in the royal stables to care for the wizard's horse. They walked over to the stall where Kyre's horse was stabled, and Koren admired the animal while they put bridle and saddle on. The horse was a deep chestnut brown, with a white blaze on its forehead. "See this blaze, it has the shape of a falcon, see the wings here? These horses are bred in my family stables in Burwyck." Kyre announced with great pride. Koren thought the white blaze on the horse's forehead looked more like a blob of spilled milk than a falcon, but he didn't say so.

"Now, we need a horse for you." Kyre snapped his fingers. "Stable hand, you there, come here, good fellow. We need a horse for Koren, the wizard's personal and most trusted servant, you know." Koren almost blushed with pride as Kyre talked. "A gentle horse, hmm, to get you settled? These horses are bred and trained for war, they are not like the nags you are used to on the farm-"

They were interrupted by a commotion several stalls down the stable, a horse was snorting and kicking the walls, rearing up on its hind legs as three stable hands struggled to hold onto the reins. The horse was black, pure black, and a good two hands taller at the shoulder than even Kyre's horse. As Kyre led his horse out of the stall, the great black horse lashed out with a foreleg, knocking over two of the stable hands, and broke free, charging down the stable row toward Koren. In a panic, Kyre hurled himself into the stall, pulling his horse in with him. Koren flattened himself against the wall, but something made him reach out a hand to brush against the black horse's flank as it raced by. The horse skidded to a halt on the well-worn floor, and turned its head to look at Koren. It snorted; not threateningly, not friendly, merely curious.

"Good horse. Good horse." Koren said in a soothing voice, and he walked forward, despite the stable hands behind him shouting that the horse was dangerous, for him to get away, and run for his life. The horse stood still, its nostrils flaring, tilting its head side to side, unsure of the boy walking slowly closer. The horse lowered its head and allowed Koren to touch its muzzle; a shiver ran down the horse's spine as Koren laid his hand on it. "They have the bit too tight, don't they?" Koren said, as he undid the bridle, and let it fall to the straw on the floor. The horse tossed its head and whinnied like a pony, shivering from nose to tail. Impulsively, Koren climbed up the wall of the stable, got a firm handful of the horse's mane, and swung himself onto the horse's back. The stable hands gasped as Koren prodded the horse to gently walk down to the end of the stable, and back to its stall. He let himself drop to the ground in front of the stable master, who was staring, open-mouthed with shock. "Sir, the bit was cutting his lip." Koren explained, as if it were the most obvious thing under the sun.

"Wizard's servant, eh? I don't wonder if you have a spot o' wizard in you, too. No one has been able to ride that horse, lad, he's been nothing but trouble since the day he was born." The stable master held out his hand, but the horse shied away, until Koren patted his muzzle.

"You rode Thunderbolt." Kyre gaped at Koren with amazement.

"Aye, that he did, young Sire." The stable master agreed. "Son of king Adric's own horse, Thunderbolt is, or we'd not have kept him around, with the trouble he's been. Got the very devil in him, he does. Least, until this morning." One of the stable hands ran up to the stable master and whispered something in the man's ear, and the stable master turned and bowed deeply. "Princess Ariana! Welcome to the royal stables."

Kyre bowed to the princess, who was accompanied by her usual retinue of guards and maids. "Your Highness, good morning."

Ariana gave Kyre only a brief glance; she only had eyes for Koren. She thought he looked even better in his rough work clothes, than in the fine outfit he had been wearing in the royal carriage. "Your Grace," she said dismissively to Kyre, "hello, Koren."

Koren snickered, suppressing a laugh. "What's so funny?" Ariana demanded.

"Your Highness, Your Grace." Koren did his best to imitate the royal court's chief of protocol, an overly self-important man he'd met the day before.

Ariana laughed. "It is silly, isn't it? Especially when we're in the stables, with our royal feet stepping in horse manure." She turned to Kyre. "Good morning, *Kyre*."

Kyre was almost struck speechless, but he managed to say "good morning, um, Ariana," in a near-whisper. And he was smart enough to say only that, without gushing about how lovely she was, how pleased he was to see her. This was one of those moments when, his advisor Forne said, fewer words were better than more.

"What is going on here, Master of Horses?" Ariana resumed some of her royal princess authority when she addressed the stable master.

The stable master snatched off his cap, and bowed again to the princess. "Beg your pardon, Princess, but today I'm not the master of horses, young Koren here is. Tamed Thunderbolt, he did. I never thought I would live to see the day a man could ride that horse, but the boy here did, got that devil horse walking like a pony."

Ariana grew even more impressed with Koren. She walked over to Thunderbolt's stall, and reached out to pet the horse's nose. Thunderbolt gave a warning snort, and backed away, until Koren came to stand beside Ariana, and held out his hand to the horse. "Good Thunderbolt, good boy." The horse held out his head for Koren to scratch him under the chin, and allowed Ariana to pet him.

"Koren, I don't know what to say. Thunderbolt has been a trial for the stable hands since the day he was born." Ariana scratched Thunderbolt under the chin, and the horse closed his eyes in contentment. "Stable master, I grant this horse to Koren Bladewell."

"Ah, young Lady, that is, Your Highness, I don't know-" The stable master stammered in surprise.

"I am the crown princess of Tarador, am I not? And Thunderbolt is my royal property?"

"That he is, Your Highness." The stable master admitted.

Ariana turned to Koren and almost gave the surprised boy a hug, catching herself at the last moment. That would be most un-princess like behavior, so she wrapped her arms around the horse's neck instead. "Oh, Koren, I'm so happy for you. You'll have to feed him, and exercise him, and care for him, every day."

"I will." Koren said, his head bobbing up and down with delight. "Can I ride him now? Please, Ariana? Kyre was going to take me riding, to show me the city."

Ariana looked at Kyre warily. What game was the Falco heir playing with her friend? But Kyre disarmed her with a wry smile. "Koren wanted me to show him where the kitchens were first, of course, but I thought, since Lord Salva isn't here, Koren could have a bit of fun this morning."

Koren was looking at her so pleadingly, that Ariana smiled. She would have preferred to ride without Kyre Falco. "As I am in my riding clothes," the princess decided, "yes, let's all take a turn about the city, shall we?"

Kyre strode back into his quarters in the palace, where Niles Forne was as usual sitting by the window, reading a dusty old book. When he saw Kyre, Forne snapped the book shut and stood. "How was your morning, young Sire?"

"A triumph, Forne, a total and complete triumph!" Kyre said with a twinkle in his eye, and he pulled off his riding gloves, and tossed them on the floor for the servants to pick up later. "Koren now considers me his friend, Ariana called me by my first name, and the three of us went riding about the city this morning. *And* Ariana allowed me to help her get down off her horse several times. She even invited me to the opening of that maze she had built, out in the old gardens." Kyre paused, lost in thought. "What sort of attire is proper to wear in a royal maze?"

"I shall inquire in the court." Forne beamed with happiness. Duke Falco would be very pleased to receive this report! "Might I suggest, as a gesture of your new friendship, that you send your servants over to the wizard's tower, to help the boy clean the place, before Lord Salva returns?"

"Smashing idea, Forne, smashing! Yes, let's do that. In fact," Kyre paused, "I will go with them myself. Always wanted to see the inside of that tower, and I'll make sure my servants don't steal anything." Kyre was in such a joyous mood that even the idea of directing cleaning servants for the afternoon didn't seem so bad. "You know, Forne, it's too bad Koren is so low-born. He's not a bad sort at all, I actually enjoyed myself this morning. He's so grateful for anyone of consequence to pay the least attention to him, it is kind of pathetic. Did you know, Koren managed to ride Thunderbolt? Ariana granted the horse to him right on the spot. Amazing, it was."

"I'm sure it was, young Sire. Remember, please, he is lowborn, and not from any sort of good family. Koren Bladewell is a tool to be used, nothing more."

Kyre frowned. "You always have to remind me of my duties, don't you?" Kyre clapped his hands, loudly. "Servants! Bring me something to eat! The heir to the Falco line is hungry!"

The wizard's tower, except for the chambers Paedris had protected with a locking spell so no one could enter, had been scrubbed clean from top to bottom. Koren could not express how grateful he was that Kyre had brought his servants to the tower to help clean the place, and when the Regent heard what the Falco boy had done, Carlana sent the royal chambermaids to help also. Koren had mostly been instructed, politely but firmly by the other servants, that the tower would be cleaned faster if he stood out of the way and didn't 'help'. So Koren and Kyre had a grand time exploring the tall, narrow and forbidding tower, all the way to the platform on the roof, where there was a view over all the palace, the castle and the city of Linden, out to the countryside, and the hills to the east. On the way down the stairs, Koren paused to think a moment, but didn't say anything to Kyre. After everyone has left, he climbed back up to the roof, then counted steps all the way to the doorway on the bottom. Out in the courtyard, he looked at the tower. The windows were not evenly spaced, but something was wrong. He would have to ask the wizard about it, when Paedris returned.

The next morning, after going to the royal stables to feed and brush Thunderbolt, Koren stopped by the kitchens for breakfast. When he returned to the wizard's tower in mid-morning, he found a servant dressed in the uniform of the royal palace, waiting for him. The servant carried a hand-written note from Ariana, inviting him to join her for lunch in the palace.

Promptly at noon, having scrubbed himself clean, wearing clean and freshly pressed clothes, and his hair untangled as best he could get it, Koren presented himself at the servant's entrance to the palace. The guards were skeptical, even when Koren showed them Ariana's invitation. He waited ten minutes before Charl Fusting, the royal chief of protocol arrived, mumbling "Most irregular, most irregular indeed." With a look that suggested the man thought Koren was very likely to steal something valuable if he were allowed inside the palace gates, Fusting examined Koren's clothes, tugging the tunic sleeves, brushing bits of lint off, before giving up with an exasperated sigh. "There is nothing to be done here. Nothing! It's hopeless. I can't work miracles." Fusting turned and escorted Koren inside the palace. Up stairs, down stairs, through long, wide corridors where their footsteps echoed against the high ceilings, past grand public rooms, Koren hurried behind the chief of protocol, almost tripping over his own feet, because he was too busy gawking at the opulent building and not paying attention to where he was going. The palace was full of people; guards posted outside nearly every door, servants scurrying around on errands, and various nobles ranging from squires to knights and barons. Not knowing what else to do, Koren followed the example of the chief of protocol, and bowed to people when Fusting bowed.

While passing down a particularly grand hallway, lined with paintings of previous kings and queens of Tarador, Koren drifted to a stop. The men and women in the pictures, so regal, so grand, all appeared to be looking directly at him. Fusting stopped in front of a wide, double door, flanked by two guards. "The- dear me. What shall I call you?"

"Koren Bladewell, sir?"

"No, no. Your title, I mean. You're the wizard's servant, but of course, one doesn't announce servants. Servants aren't supposed to be invited to dine with royalty, either." The chief of protocol grumbled under his breath.

Koren had an idea. "I'm Koren Bladewell of Crickdon, if you please, sir."

Fusting snapped his fingers. "Of course you are!" He called out, in a clear voice "Koren Bladewell of Crickdon, here to see the crown princess."

Koren was expecting lunch with the crown princess to be stiff and formal, with a different fork to be used for each course. Instead, he found Ariana sitting in a sunlit room that overlooked the courtyard garden, attended by only a maid. When she saw Koren, she ran to him and hugged him, in a most undignified manner, while Charl Fusting looked away in everlasting horror. The chief of protocol backed away with a bow and scurried out the door, muttering to himself, his face white. When the door closed behind him, Ariana and Koren burst into laughter. "Most irregular, most irregular." Koren imitated the fussy Fusting.

"Oh, never mind him." Ariana laughed. "My mother says he's in charge of all the things that aren't important around the palace." She pointed to the table, covered by plates piled high with food. "Are you hungry? Let's eat first. I want to show you around the palace."

The palace was even bigger than Koren imagined, one room after another, until Koren was completely lost. "Does the palace ever end? Kyre told me it was big, but-"

"Kyre Falco?" Ariana looked unhappy. "Koren, you need to be careful about Kyre. The Falcos and the Trehaymes are not friends. You know the history of our families?"

Koren shook his head. "No." Apparently, he didn't know much of anything.

"The Falcos used to be rulers of Tarador, until seven hundred years ago."

Koren was completely surprised. "What happened?"

"The Falcos were the strongest of the seven Ducal families who broke away from Acedor, and Dagon Falco was chosen to be the first king of Tarador. At first, the Falcos were good rulers, I guess," Ariana shrugged to show she wasn't convinced, "but then they became lazy, and cared only about gold and jewels and building bigger palaces-" Ariana self-consciously touched her diamond necklace. "The Falcos built this big palace, we, we Trehaymes just live here. Anyway, Luis Falco was king seven hundred years ago, and he was terrible. Fat and lazy, and he didn't take care of the army. Acedor attacked, and they got all the way here, they surrounded the castle and destroyed the city. Luis Falco locked himself in the palace and hid under his bed. Well, maybe not really, but he didn't do anything useful. Some of the Dukes of Tarador fled, they thought the battle was lost. But Duke Aldus Trehayme, my ancestor, rallied what was left of the army, and they fell upon the enemy at night, during a terrible rainstorm. The enemy was surprised and defeated. When he got to the palace, Duke Trehayme found that Luis Falco had been killed by an assassin. And King Falco had no heir. Luis' brother claimed the throne, and in the confusion, several army commanders declared their support for him. Then it was discovered, of course, that the Cornerstone had been stolen during the battle. That ended any support for the Falcos. They had lost the Cornerstone! The Dukes then chose Aldus Trehayme to be their king. And Trehaymes have been the royal family ever since. And ever since, the Falcos have been scheming to reclaim the throne. That includes Kyre. Be careful around Kyre, I don't trust him."

Koren considered both that Kyre had been nice to him, and that Ariana had been nice and was the crown princess. "He's just a friend. And I'm just a servant. I couldn't help him even if I wanted to. And I don't." He hastened to add. "Um, Ariana, what is the Cornerstone?"

Ariana put her hands to her mouth and gasped. "You don't know about the Lost Cornerstone of Acedor?"

"No. Stories about ancient history aren't something that put food in your belly on a farm in Crickdon." Koren said defensively.

"But everyone knows the legend of the Lost Cornerstone! It's, wait, the chamber is right down this hallway. I'll show you." Ariana reached to grab hold of Koren's hand,

and she received a warm tingling feeling. A good feeling. Behind them, Nurelka discretely looked the other way. Ariana tugging a boy by the hand was not proper behavior for a princess!

The crown princess led the way down a corridor that was part of the original fortress; the walls were plain stone, the floor not covered in fancy rugs. They passed through several doorways, and at the end of the hallway came to a pair of heavy wooden doors. "There used to be guards here all the time, but my grandfather put an end to that. What's the sense in guarding something that has already been lost? The door is only locked at night. People don't come in here like they used to." She tugged on one of the large metal door handles. "Help me, Koren, it's heavy, and the hinges need to be oiled."

With the two of them pulling, the door swung ponderously open. Inside, Koren was surprised to see a large, empty stone chamber, with a high vaulted ceiling. In the ceiling were windows, which allowed sunlight to shine down upon a low, flat slab of stone that filled the center of the room. Their footsteps echoed in the emptiness. "I don't get it. There's nothing here." The floor was covered with a layer of dust, and cobwebs shown in the sunlight from the windows.

"Of course not, silly. This is where the Cornerstone used to be, before it was lost." Ariana hopped up onto the stone slab. "It was right here, before it was stolen. See, you can still tell where the Cornerstone rested."

Koren saw there were marks on the slab. He paced the corners. "Wow. It was huge."

"It would barely fit through those doors. See the scratches on the floor, leading toward the doors? That's where the enemy dragged the Cornerstone across the floor."

Koren looked around the chamber. There were no other doors. And the windows, far above, were too small. "But the other doors down the hallway are single doors, too narrow. How did the enemy get it out of the castle?"

Ariana raised her hands. "That's the mystery. No one knows. It couldn't have fit through the doors in the hallway, but it isn't here, so it must have been taken away. Most people think it is still here, in the castle somewhere. It's far too heavy to move without an army. This whole chamber was built around it, after the Cornerstone was brought here."

"What's so important about this cornerstone, anyway?"

"It's the original cornerstone, the first stone laid down when the castle was built for the first king of Acedor, when our people came across the sea. When the Dark One seized power in Acedor, much of the castle was knocked down, and during the battle, our army took the cornerstone and hauled it away to Tarador on a great wagon, pulled by dozen oxen. Legend says Acedor will not be restored to our people, until the Cornerstone is returned. So the enemy stole it, and hid it somewhere. My mother says without the Cornerstone, any talk of defeating Acedor is foolishness, and that is why she doesn't like it when Paedris tells her she has to send the army out to fight." All these heavy adult decision were going to be hers, in only a few years.

Koren got down on his knees and studied the scrape marks that were cut into the stone floor. Something about it wasn't right. He rose and stepped onto the pedestal where the Cornerstone used to rest. His skin tingled, and he stepped back. "Why do people think it's still here in the castle?"

"Because, um," Ariana bit her lips, trying to recall her history lessons. "I think the enemy was only in the castle for a few hours before Aldus Trehayme attacked. There wasn't enough time for the Cornerstone to have been hauled away." The crown princess held her hands out and shrugged. "Nobody knows. I have an idea," she said, with a mischievous grin. "We could look for it."

"Us? You and me?"

"Sure, why not? It will be fun!"

Koren looked around the empty chamber. "Where would we start?"

"Um," Ariana had no idea. "I don't know. Wait! We can search the scrolls in the royal library first. Mother is always saying I should read more."

Late that afternoon, Carlana found her daughter in her private chamber. Ariana was kneeling on a chair, elbows resting on a table, a table that was covered with scrolls. More scrolls were carefully stacked in baskets on the floor. Putting a finger to her lips to stop Ariana's maid from announcing her arrival, Carlana tiptoed along the wall to stand behind the heavy drapes.

"Look, see, this one is about Aldus Trehayme. Oh, it's just about his family line. Hmmph. What do you have?"

Carlana heard Koren's voice, speaking slowly, because his reading skills were not quite ready for deciphering ancient scrolls. "It says, it says, um, something about King Aldus sent a del, uh, a del-"

"Spell it out," Ariana suggested gently.

"D-e-l-e-g-"

"Delegation," Ariana guessed. "That means an official party, acting in the king's name. Go on."

"He sent a del-e-ga-tion to Ching-Do," Koren read carefully.

"That's an empire far to the east, a very powerful empire."

"The delegation was to seek wizards, to help defeat Acedor."

"Mother told me all our wizards were killed in that war, so there were none left to defend the kingdom."

"Then where did Paedris come from?" Koren asked, confused, and a little flustered, because Ariana was leaning close, and the warm scent of her perfumed hair was making him dizzy.

"Oh, he's from Stade, that's a land far away to the south, across the sea. All of the wizards from Tarador were killed. So, we brought wizards here from foreign lands. Besides, that war was a long time ago. Go on." Ariana encouraged.

Carlana stepped back from the drapes and whispered to the maid. "My daughter is reading scrolls? Historical scrolls?"

Nurelka nodded, and whispered back "Yes, ma'am. Been at it most of the day, she has, her and the boy. They carried the scrolls down from the library, and they've been very careful with them. Very proper, the two of them, don't you worry, ma'am. No funny stuff between them; your daughter knows better, and I think the boy is more than a little afraid still to be in the palace. Afraid of the princess, too."

Carlana peeked around the corner, to see Ariana and Koren hunched over a scroll, happily reading the ancient history of Tarador. The Regent didn't know how she felt about her daughter spending time with the wizard's servant, spending time so closely. But, if Koren was indeed to become the most powerful wizard in the land, as Paedris said, then it was important for Ariana to develop a good relationship now, before they each came into their powers.

But the two were not just queen-to-be and potential master wizard. They were also girl and boy. Girl and boy who had shared, and survived, a traumatic experience, which could naturally draw them closer. The girl, Carlana felt sure, was somewhat infatuated with her hero. The boy, and she knew Koren was a healthy young man, she was actually less worried about. While a boy Koren's age would have feelings about girls, Koren certainly knew that, in the end, he was a commoner, and Ariana was royalty, and that was the end of it. Just listening to Koren's awkward stammering when he spoke, Carlana had to smile. He looked like he was about to pass out, if Ariana got any closer. "Very well, let them be."

"Yes, ma'am. Should I get her dressed for dinner?"

Carlana shook her head. This was a good opportunity for the Regent to get a closer look at the boy wizard who would soon be a very important part of her daughter's life. "No, not tonight. I will inform the chief of protocol that I shall dine in my chambers tonight. Tell Ariana I would like her to join me, she can come dressed as she is. And she can bring her friend."

CHAPTER FIVE

When Paedris returned with the army two days later, Koren was ready. Standing on the wall above the main gate to the castle, Koren looked down at his new tunic, the same shade of purple that the wizard usually wore. With a yellow lightning bolt down the center, as an insignia. When they couldn't find a proper servant's outfit for Koren in the tower, Kyre had his maids cut up an old set of purple drapes to make several sets of tunics for Koren to wear, when Koren was going on about Lord Salva's official business in the castle. Since a lightning bolt was the court wizard's official insignia, Kyre decided on his own to add one to Koren's official outfits. Koren hoped Paedris would approve.

The army wound its way slowly up the streets of the city, through the gate in the thick walls of the castle. Koren thought he had never seen such a magnificent sight. Horses had been brushed until their coats shone, soldiers with polished armor gleaming, pennants of the nobles to which the various army units belonged, and at the head of the column, Paedris and the army unit's captain. The two men waved, and smiled and laughed. Paedris had a sack on his lap, from which he threw candies to the children in the crowd. It was a victorious army that marched in triumph through the gates of the castle.

Koren had not seen the wagon of wounded soldiers which had sped through the city's less-used northern gate ahead of the army, nor the horses that marched without riders because their masters were dead. It was a day for celebration, and all too rare occasion in the centuries-long war between Tarador and Acedor. When Paedris was through the gate, Koren raced down the stairs to greet the wizard.

Paedris heartily approved of Koren's new tunic, and never noticed the missing drapes. The wizard was also delighted to see how clean his tower was, although he did suspiciously check the wards on doors to rooms where he didn't want people intruding. Following the official ceremony to welcome the army, there was a feast, and Paedris brought Koren to the royal palace as his servant. Koren's job, according to Cully, was to stand against the wall behind the wizard's chair, and keep his master's glass full of wine. Mostly, Koren gawked at the assembled nobility, and had to be poked by the other servants to remind him of his duty. And, of course, he tried to eavesdrop on the conversation between Paedris and Carlana. Koren frowned when he learned the Regent and the court wizard did not seem to be on the best of terms. Apparently, Carlana had not wanted to send the army out, and even after the battle, she wasn't sure it had been wise to fight.

"That was a rather grand entrance, Lord Salva." Carlana said, holding a wine glass in front of her lips in an attempt to keep her words private. "Throwing candy to the children was a bit overdoing it, though, don't you think?"

Paedris gave the Regent an unfriendly smile; his lips curled appropriately, but his eyes glared at her. "The people need to celebrate a victory, Your Highness, it's good for morale. There have been too few victories recently; too many defeats. And far too much of Tarador doing nothing while Acedor's power grows to encircle us. The important thing is that I located the wizard who sent that bear to kill your daughter, and the force they intended to raid LeVanne with, in the confusion after Ariana's death. I also sensed a much larger force behind them, beyond the border. "

"And it was such an easy victory, Lord Salva." Carlana shot back. "Why, one wonders where was this enemy you warned us about, this terrible threat to the kingdom? Perhaps in the future, we can send you alone to fight our battles, and save the cost of raising an army."

"Do not underestimate our enemy, Carlana," Paedris deliberately used her first name, "we had the advantage of surprise this time, their raiding force was caught unawares. They thought they were safe, hidden in the Thrallren woods."

Carlana took a sip of wine, and spoke from behind the goblet, to prevent her voice from carrying. "The Thrallren woods, according my army captains, is impassable, and we didn't need to be concerned about an invasion from that direction."

Paedris shrugged. "So thought Duke Yarron, and those are his woods. His sheriffs patrol those woods, but I think it would be prudent to send, perhaps, two dozen Rangers to assist Yarron's sheriffs."

"Two dozen? Why not four dozen, or make it an even hundred Rangers? You are always quick to send my troops out to battle."

"I would think you'd like the idea of Rangers being in the field, where they can mostly live off the land. Here in their barracks, you have to pay for their keep." Paedris saw that remark caused a flash of anger from the Regent, so he hastened to continue "Yarron would no doubt be grateful for extra protection, and he is one of your strongest allies. Besides, a force of Rangers could also train some of Yarron's own troops, so they could eventually be entrusted with the task themselves."

"And a force of Rangers, operating on their own, could of course be trusted not to provoke the enemy? I think not." The Rangers, a small, elite force of the royal army, had a reputation for being aggressive, sometimes to the point of foolishness. "You defeated the enemy's raiding force. I think we will not face much of a threat for while."

Paedris could perhaps be forgiven his rudeness, for he was very tired. Healing Ariana and Koren, then riding out with the army patrol, destroying the enemy raiding force, battling the enemy wizard, and doing his best to heal the wounded on the long ride back, all had drained his strength. "Eight men died in this 'easy' victory you speak of, and many other men were wounded. The enemy has been bold enough to attack us because they sense Tarador is weak. Your late husband Adric knew the threat we face."

"Yes, and he died because he followed your advice, Paedris Don Salva." Carlana hissed under her breath. "My charge as Regent is to assure Ariana, and Tarador, survive to for her to assume the throne. This war has lasted for many years, I think it can wait until Ariana will becomes queen, and you can try persuading her to engage in military adventures. I will not go poking sticks into hornet's nests."

"Those hornets, dear lady, are going to be setting up their nests right here in this castle, if we do not fight them. It is the survival of all Tarador, and not just the Trehayme line, that should concern you."

Carlana was about to reply, when Baroness Sedgwick, alarmed by the argument that had grown loud enough for everyone at Carlana's end of the table to hear, stood up and proposed a toast to the wizard, for leading Tarador to victory. The distraction broke the tension, and the royal chamberlain clapped his hands for a troop of musicians and acrobats to perform for the crowd.

"Oh, I ate too much. Koren, this is one of the few times I appreciate wearing these silly formal robes, I can loosen the belt and get comfortable. Ahhhh." The wizard sighed contentedly as he sank back into his favorite chair, in his chamber near the top of the tower. "Koren, sit down, sit down, relax. Oh, put some more wood on the fire. And, do we have any more of that wine from Holdeness, the sweet red wine? Get the bottle, oh, and get two glasses, if you like sweet wine."

Koren smiled to himself at the wizard's idea of 'sit down and relax', it seemed to involve a lot of work for his servant. After he walked all the way down the stairs, out the door, and around the backside of the tower to fetch logs from the woodpile, walked back up to the pantry where the wine and glasses were kept, and returned to the wizard, he found the man asleep in the chair, his head lolled to the side, snoring softly. Koren had to set the wine down quickly and cover his mouth to stop from bursting out laughing. He poured a glass of wine, set it on the table next to the wizard, and put a log on the fire. When he closed the door to the stove, the creaking metal woke up the wizard with startled, interrupted snore.

"Snnnxxx- Uh! Oh, oh, it's you, Koren. I must have dozed off. Why, here's my wine." Paedris look a sip of the wine. "Ah, that's good. I'm more tired than I thought; it was a very long ride back, with few comforts. And less of a joyous welcome that I had hoped for, that didn't help matters." He grumbled into his wineglass. "Still, most things look better after a good night's sleep, eh? You had best get some rest, too, I hear you're going to a party tomorrow?"

Koren was suddenly embarrassed. "The princess is opening her maze in the garden, I hear many people are invited."

Many people, Paedris thought to himself, but only one commoner servant boy was likely invited. "I hear the princess has been inviting you to dine with her?"

Koren nodded, embarrassed. He knew tongues were wagging around the palace, about the servant boy who dined with the princess. Jealous, spiteful tongues.

Anyone who thought Koren might have romantic ideas about Ariana were idiots. Commoners, even if they were stupid, did not have romantic notions about royalty, certainly not when the royal person was the heir to the throne, and held the power of life and death over lowly born commoners. Koren's people were peasant farmers, who survived only on what they could grow on their land, or by illegal hunting in the forests that belonged to the local baron. At harvest time, the sheriff came to collect taxes based on the amount of land being farmed, whether it was a good year for crops or not. If there wasn't enough food left over for the family, they went hungry.

Koren wasn't just a commoner; he was a penniless servant, a farm boy who didn't even have a family. Did Koren sometimes get a funny feeling in his stomach, like butterflies, when he was around Ariana? Maybe so. When they were sitting around a table, looking at maps, and Ariana leaned close enough that Koren could smell her perfume, and the curls of her hair might brush against his hand, and she looked at him with that cute little smile-

Maybe Koren did daydream, just a little, about Ariana. When he wasn't thinking clearly. When he was thinking clearly, he remembered his place, and that place had no business even being around the crown princess.

So Koren grumbled uncomfortably when Paedris asked him about dining with the princess. "She's teaching me about history, and maps and stuff. There's a whole building full of scrolls and books, which she can borrow. She calls it a library."

"Good, good." Paedris was pleased that Koren was learning about Tarador, there was much the boy needed to know, even before he began his training in a few short years. Sensing that Koren didn't want to talk about Ariana, Paedris changed the subject. "Do you, uh, do you have something appropriate to wear to the party tomorrow?"

"Yes, sir, Ari- I mean, the princess, asked Master Fusting to help find clothing for me to wear."

"Ha, ha! Oh, so you have already had the displeasure of meeting Charl Fusting!" Paedris laughed. The wizard took a big gulp of wine and chuckled to himself.

Koren smiled while he recalled Fusting's immense distress at having to deal with finding the proper clothing for a mere grubby servant, a servant who needed clothing fit for an official occasion with the crown princess, which was clearly impossible, out of the question, except that she had insisted, and she was the crown princess, so Fusting had to do something, and so had scoured the palace for something Koren could wear. The chief of protocol had, after hours of grueling labor, selected several outfits that might, just might, possibly not be too outrageously horrible, if people didn't look too closely. And then Koren had ruined all Fusting's simply brilliant work by trying to put on a jacket backwards. The chief of protocol had fainted, and been taken away to rest, with cold towels on his forehead, and chilled wine to drink. Koren had shrugged, and gathered an armful of clothing for Ariana to choose from. The princess had so much fun making him try on outfits, that Koren wondered why she had asked Fusting to get involved in the first place. "I met him, yes sir. It was," Koren winked, "most irregular."

"Ha!" Paedris laughed. "I wish I had been there. A commoner, dining with the crown princess. Why, I bet there wasn't anything in his book of protocol to cover that, and Fusting loves referring to that stupid book. Be careful, Koren, you may be the death of that man someday. Oh!" Paedris' jaw stretched wide in a yawn. "I hope you have a good time at the party tomorrow."

"You wished to see me, your Highness?" Grand General Magrane, commander of the royal army, said as paused at the door, and bowed to the crown princess. After the tense dinner party, listening to the Regent and the court wizard arguing, all Magrane wanted to do was sleep, for soldiers needed to awaken early. He was still wearing his full dress uniform, which was heavy, and stiff and uncomfortable. Once long and black, Magrane's hair was now gray, and cut short, and his full beard partly covered a scar on the right side of his face.

"Yes, general." Ariana replied. "Please, come in, sit down. I wish to learn more about army strategy."

"Tonight?" Magrane asked, dreading a long night of looking over maps.

"No!" Ariana laughed. "And it doesn't have to be you, I don't want to take you away from your duties. I also don't want to wait until I have a crown on my head, to learn the tasks of being queen."

"That is wise, your Highness." Magrane thought for a moment. Who to assign the delicate task of teaching Ariana military strategy? A delicate, likely frustrating task, but one that could be rewarding, if the future queen thought well of the person. "I have a young man in mind, a Captain Raddick. He's a distant relative of the Magnicos. A promising young officer, in my opinion. He will be available, here in the castle, until the springtime. " And, Magrane thought sourly, perhaps all year, if the fickle Regent refused to send the royal army into the field once winter was over.

"Good, have this Captain Raddick speak with my secretary, soon. Now, general, my personal guards were with me all spring and summer, they must be tired, and in need of retraining, am I correct?"

"Yes, your Highness," Magrane answered warily, wondering why the princess had asked, "they will report for training in a fortnight, and be replaced by fresh men from the castle guard."

"The Thrallren woods are an excellent place for training, don't you think?" She asked with a slight smile.

"The Trall- your Highness, forgive me, but your mother-"

"Commands the royal army, she does *not* command my personal guard. Since mother won't send Rangers to help Yarron secure the Thrallren, I am sending my own guard there. For rest, and training, of course. I think thirty men from my personal guard should help Yarron sleep better at night, with his border more secure?" Ariana could not help smiling; she was well pleased with her self, for outmaneuvering her mother.

Magrane could not help smiling, behind his beard. Ariana Trehayme was going to be a formidable queen. The general only hoped he would survive the next few years, to see her safely on the throne.

The morning of Ariana's garden party started extra early for Koren. First, he grabbed a quick breakfast for himself; a small loaf of freshly baked bread, a sausage, and hot tea. Then, he fed and exercised Thunderbolt, and back to the wizard's tower. Paedris didn't drink tea in the mornings, he drank 'coffee'. Many of the army soldiers drank coffee in the mornings, they said it made them more alert. Koren had heard of coffee before, but never seen it. It was too expensive for most people, even tea was too dear for many poor farm families. Paedris had coffee beans brought in especially from his homeland twice a year; they were stored in metal pails in the root cellar to keep them cool. Koren needed to scoop out enough for a week to keep in the tower's pantry, and each morning, he carefully roasted a small handful of beans, ground them, and slowly poured boiling hot water over the grinds. The wizard liked his coffee strong, with a spoon of cream stirred in. Once the coffee was ready, Koren put the pot on the side of the stove, to keep it hot, but not too hot, and he ran over to the royal kitchens to fetch breakfast for the wizard. With the breakfast in a covered tray, which also went on the side of the stove, he put on an apron and crept up the stairs to listen whether the wizard was awake yet. That morning, the wizard was up, puttering around in his laboratory, so Koren dashed down the stairs and delivered breakfast, which was suitably appreciated. Paedris did not trust the royal kitchens to prepare his precious coffee, he had painstakingly shown Koren how to roast, grind and brew the bitter liquid, and exactly at what temperature it should be served. To the wizard's delight, Koren brewed perfect coffee! Knowing his servant had a busy day ahead, the wizard said Koren could clean up the dishes later. Gratefully, Koren ran back down the stairs to run the wizard's bath water and stoked the water heater stove. He had taken a bath the evening before, so now he got dressed in the party clothes that Ariana's maid had delivered the previous afternoon. The maid had even shown Koren how to wear the clothes, which was helpful, for he had no idea whether the shirt was supposed to be tucked into the pants or not, and whether the pants should be tucked into the boots (yes to both questions). He was dressed and ready an hour before the party was to start, plenty of time to duck back into the kitchens and scrounge up something more to eat. And borrow an apron, so he wouldn't drip strawberry jam onto his new jacket.

Ariana's party to open the new garden maze was, in Kyre's words, a smashing success. The weather was perfect, a brilliantly clear late autumn day, unseasonably warm. At Ariana's request, the royal gardener had been working on growing the maze for three years; the thick hedges occupied almost an acre of land in a garden outside the walls of the castle. Stone planters held some of the hedges, which could be moved to change the path of the maze, so Ariana and her guests would not get bored with it. There were three entrances, all leading eventually to the center, with many complicated dead-ends along the way. Ariana set up three teams of three, with her were Koren and a girl who was the daughter of some Baron, Kyre led one of the other teams. At the blare of a trumpet, the teams were off, running headlong down the maze. It took almost a quarter of an hour, but in the end, Ariana triumphantly led her team to the center, just ahead of Kyre. Koren could not remember the last time he had so much fun.

Afterward, there was a picnic on the great lawn of the garden, with kites to fly, games of kickball, and much general racing about and tomfoolery that the children's royal parents certainly would not have approved of, but that didn't matter, for Ariana hadn't invited any adults. And she said so.

On the advice of Niles Forne, Kyre did not act as though the princess were his new best friend, in fact, he rather left her alone. It was Koren who brought them together, choosing Kyre to play on Ariana's kickball team, without asking her first. The princess seemed cool to the idea, but Kyre was a good sport, even when he was knocked out of the game, and laughed and joked around so easily, Ariana had to wonder whether her opinion of Kyre Falco as devious and scheming was entirely correct.

After the fireworks that closed the party, Ariana went back to her royal apartments, Koren went to the wizard's tower, and Kyre reported to Niles Forne that the day had been another triumph for the Falcos.

While Koren enjoyed Ariana's party, and Kyre tried to impress the young princess, Paedris had invited Grand General Magrane to discuss recent information Magrane had received from his spy network, although that was really just an excuse to talk about future army strategy. Or, rather, what future army strategy should be, if the Regent had been willing to listen to either her army commander or her chief wizard. The general climbed the stairs with head held high, shoulder back, standing proud and tall. When he reached the study where Paedris was waiting, he dismissed his two guards to wait by the tower's front door, and slumped wearily into a chair by the fireplace. "Oh, Paedris, I am tired to the core of my bones. Perhaps I'm too old for this."

The wizard picked up the coffee pot from the side of the metal stove and poured a mug for his guest. "Nonsense, Leon," he said, returning the general's informality by using the man's first name, "you're in your prime, commanding the entire royal army. And you're younger than me."

"Ah," Magrane sighed as he sipped from the hot mug, "that is good coffee. You may be older in years than I am, but you are a wizard, after all."

"A wizard, yes, but having a longer life sometimes means having more than one lifetime of aches and pains. I dread the winters here, they make my joints ache. If it is going to rain, I can tell because my knees hurt, and that's no wizardry."

"We've earned our aches and pains, Paedris, from long service."

"And too many nights sleeping on the cold ground."

"Aye, that, too."

Paedris poured a mug of coffee for himself, and reached for a scroll the general had brought. "Where is that confounded glass? Oh," he realized he'd been sitting on it all morning, "here it is." He unrolled the scroll, which was written painstakingly in a cipher by the spy who had sent it to Magrane. The general had men who could decipher the document, one letter at a time, but Paedris had no patience for that. He held the glass, a thick, flat disc of clear glass, over the scroll, and looked through it. Because of the spell the wizard had cast on the glass, the words of the scroll appeared in plain writing to his eye. "Hmmm." He frowned. "This is not quite the good news we had hoped for, I am afraid."

Magrane snorted. "Who hoped for good news? I didn't. About the war, about our fortunes, there is no good news. Nor will there ever be."

"Come, Leon, surely you don't mean that."

"Paedris, we are men of action, and responsibility. You and I, here in private, need not tell each other happy fairy tales. We are losing this war; we have been losing for the last two hundred or so years. Our late king, and a few other kings and queens, may have halted our decline for a time, but year by year, our enemy grows stronger, and we do not. Our allies waver, those who have not already declared themselves neutral, or fallen under the sway of our enemy. I do not blame them, those smaller kingdoms, for if we cannot guarantee their protection, they must act to protect themselves. We know Lemonde allows pirates sponsored by Acedor to use two of their islands as a base, to raid our merchant ships." Lemonde was a small independent duchy at the eastern end of a large island off Tarador's southern shore. For centuries, part of Tarador's Royal Navy had been based in Lemonde's fine harbor, but thirty years ago, Tarador had found the expense of maintaining a large navy, stationing hundred of royal army troops in Lemonde, and paying an annual fee to the Duchess for use of the harbor, to be unsustainable. So, the troops had been withdrawn, the ships returned to Tarador, and the payments stopped. The Duchess had begged for at least two ships and a hundred soldiers, a token force at best, to remain. Harbor fees would stop, indeed, the Duchess offered to pay for the supplies the royal army troops needed. But the king who ruled Tarador at the time, struggling to deal with a drought, crop failures, and orcs raiding across the northern provinces, declared Tarador could no longer afford to support Lemonde. Three months after the Royal Navy ships departed for home, the Duchess of Lemonde received a notice that Acedor would be sending an envoy, and she would be wise to allow the envoy's ship into her harbor. Since then, two of Lemonde's strategically placed islands had essentially been ceded to Acedor. It had been a major defeat for Tarador, and the kingdom had been paying the price ever since. Allies learned from Lemonde that Tarador could not be relied on.

Magrane gulped the remains of his coffee, which was growing cold, made a sour face, and continued. "Without allies, without *committed* allies, we are alone. Alone, we cannot hope to stand against Acedor. Even powerful nations like Indus now refuse to extend us credit to buy supplies we need for our survival, they insist on being paid with gold, lest Acedor overwhelm us before we can pay our creditors. I fear that Ariana will be the last ruler of Tarador. And my fear, my lack of faith in our future, makes me unable to properly fulfill my duty to our future queen. A general who sees no hope of victory cannot lead an army. I intend to resign at the end of this year."

Paedris was greatly alarmed. Grand General Magrane was his best ally against the Regent, one of the few people of sufficient stature to make Carlana listen, who agreed with Paedris about the need to take action against the enemy. Mostly, the two men had argued fruitlessly with the Regent, but Paedris had hoped to change that soon. "General, I can understand your despair. Please remember," Paedris held his left hand open, and a searingly bright ball of fire briefly lit up the room, "that we have significant power on our side also."

Magrane blinked to clear his vision, seeing an after image of the fireball dancing in front of his eyes. "Paedris, I know you are a powerful wizard, perhaps the most powerful wizard in the land, but even you-"

"No, I-", Paedris caught himself before he revealed the truth. Not even Grand General Magrane could know about Koren. Carlana was safely within the castle, while Magrane went into the field with the army, where he might be captured. Captured, and given to an enemy wizard, who would strip the general's mind open, and reveal any secrets his mind held. "I do *not* despair. There are certain reasons, known only to wizards, why our fortunes will change dramatically, for the better, during Ariana's reign. Within a very few years."

Magrane looked up sharply at the wizard. "You speak truthfully? Not merely providing comfort to an old man?"

"Soon, other members of the Wizards Council will arrive here in Linden, to make plans for the future." Paedris leaned forward in his chair, elbows on his knees. "Believe me," he said as he added just a hint of reassuring magic behind his words, "this nation will survive. Leon, for the first time since I journeyed across the sea, to pledge my services to our long struggle against the enemy, I can see the end of this war. Within not just my lifetime, but yours." Paedris truly believed his words. The wizard held out his hand. "Keep your boots on, General, your nation needs you."

Magrane nodded. He had not wanted to resign, and whether he completely believed the wizard or not, he could see the wizard believed. He took the wizard's hand in a strong grip and shook it. "I know better than to ask for the secrets of wizards, but, agreed. We'll see this through to the end, you and I."

"Excellent! More coffee?"

"Koren! Koren? Now, where is that boy? Oh, there you are." The wizard announced, as Koren stepped breathlessly through the doorway, having run up two flights of stairs as quickly as he could. "I need to send this message to Duke Magnico, run this," he held out a rolled-up scroll of paper, "over to the telegraph."

Koren got a pained expression on his face, which the wizard failed to notice, as he had already turned his attention back to the bubbling glass containers on the laboratory workbench. Tell a griff? What is a 'griff', and what was Koren supposed to tell it? "Uh, sir, what is a griff?"

This got the astonished wizard's attention. "A griff?"

"Yes, sir, you wanted me to tell a griff something?" Koren assumed whatever he was to tell the griff was on the scroll.

Paedris chuckled softly. It had not occurred to him that Koren Bladewell, farm boy from tiny Crebbs Ford, had no idea what a telegraph was. "Not tell-a-griff. A *telegraph*. It is a series of towers across Tarador, with one visible from the next, to carry messages. You must have seen the one atop the hill to the east of the city? The office here is at army headquarters, across the courtyard."

Koren had indeed seen the tower, with a strange looking contraption on top; wooden arms somewhat like a windmill, only instead of sails, the arms had flags. "Is that what the tower is for, sir?"

"Yes, it is quite clever, I had never seen one before I came to Tarador," the wizard admitted, "the position of the arms, and the type of flags, spell out words. At night, colored lanterns are used, rather than flags. The first part of each message tells whom the message is from, the next part tells who the message is addressed to, then the actual message. Most royal, or army, messages, are put into a code, to keep them secret. There are such towers throughout Tarador, connecting Linden to each of the provincial capitals, and some of the Dukes have their own telegraph lines to connect them directly. With the telegraph system, a message can cross the nation from southeast to northwest in a single day! Depending on weather, of course; fog, rain or snow can block the view from one tower to the next."

"That is amazing, sir!" Koren was truly impressed, he had never imagined such a thing. Twice in his life, he had seen couriers riding fast horses through Crebbs Ford, headed toward the Baron's castle. He assumed all messages traveled by courier on horseback, how else could it be? "But, but I thought you sent messages by, uh, magic, or something. Like that hawk last week." A hawk had flown to the windowsill, and pecked at the window glass, until the wizard let it in, and retrieved a small message scroll that was tied to the bird's leg.

"Oh, yes, the army also uses pigeons, they are trained to fly to one place, like the royal palace, from wherever they are released. The problem you see, is that a pigeon can *only* fly to one place, which is not quite convenient. And pigeons, of course, can fall prey to falcons."

"But the hawk, sir?"

"Oh, the hawk. That was magic. I told the hawk to find a merchant I know, the man, well, he lives by the coast, and keeps an eye out for enemy agents around our ports. This merchant moves around quite a bit, so I couldn't send a message to a fixed address."

"How did the hawk find him, sir?"

"Huh? Oh," sometimes Paedris forgot how even simple magic wasn't obvious to ordinary people. "You see, I put a picture in the hawk's mind what the merchant looks like, hawks have exceptional eyes, of course. And I also told the hawk several places the merchant might be. That, uh, is rather odd, for birds don't see the world the way we do, they navigate by the position of the sun, and along invisible lines of energy. I don't know how to explain it. It is disturbing, that type of magic, so be in an animal's mind, however briefly. But, it might not work anyway, except that I have a piece of cloth with the merchant's scent on it. Those little metal boxes I keep in the cupboard? Each one has a cloth with a person's scent on it. The hawk delivers my message, then waits for a reply message to be tied to its leg, and returns to me."

"I was wondering what those little boxes were, sir." Invisible lines of energy? The world of wizards would truly be forever beyond Koren's comprehension. Ah, so what? It wasn't anything he needed to know as the wizard's servant. "I will carry your message to the telegraph office right away, sir."

While Kyre Falco was still glowing from the day, the party to open the maze was not quite a triumph for Koren. Servants in the castle had started whispering as soon as they saw Koren get out of the royal carriage on the return from LeVanne. Koren had gotten out of the carriage before it went through the castle gate; because Carlana was sure there would be a scandal if a young man were seen with the princess at the palace. Still, enough people saw Koren get out of the carriage, saw him wearing nice, clean clothes, and saw the princess lean out of the carriage, waving to him as the carriage drove through the gate. Then, the servant who brought to Koren the invitation to have lunch with the princess had told a few people, who told other people, who told other people. Word got around that this new boy, a poor, uneducated farm boy, a commoner, whose lot in life was to clean up after the wizard, this boy was putting on airs. Thinking he was better than the other servants.

It was bad enough that Koren was invited to the palace, to dine with the princess. When Koren was invited to the grand party that opened the royal maze, a party where a large number of servants were there working properly as servants, while Koren cavorted, and ran around, and laughed and ate fine food, with the royalty, right in front of the servants, well, clearly something had to be done to put the new boy back in his place.

Bart Loman didn't have the best of luck. What he had imagined, when he thought of showing this Koren Bladewell his proper place in the castle, was for Koren to be dressed in the fancy clothes he wore when he visited the palace to dine with the princess, where he no doubt drank tea from fine crystal cups, with his pinky finger in the air. Bart had imagined Koren smelling of flowery perfume, having his hair cleaned, combed and tied back in a fancy ribbon. The picture should have been of Koren striding across the courtyard, nose in the air, looking down on all the other servants.

What Bart Loman got instead was Koren, having exercised, fed and brushed Thunderbolt, and then worked for an hour in the stables hauling hay bales and mucking out stalls to pay for the horse's keep, walking back to the wizard's tower, bent low under a load of firewood slung over his shoulders. He was in old, patched and dirty second-hand clothing, his hair tangled with bits of hay stuck in it, and he smelled, well, he smelled like what his second-hand boots had stepped in at the stables.

Bart chewed on his lip while he thought. The gang of servants he had gathered looked at him, questioningly. Koren was supposed to be having lunch with the princess, in the palace, like he had done on the first day of the week for the past month! Why was he looking, and working, like a common servant? Working, in fact, harder than Bart Loman ever did, since Bart preferred shirking to working. Bart's personal motto was, in fact, why work when you can shirk? Bart didn't know that the Regent had declared her daughter needed to spend her time studying the history and customs of the Indus Empire, which was sending a new ambassador to Tarador soon, so Ariana had no time for lunches with Koren.

Seeing Koren working so hard didn't make Bart reconsider his plans, it only made him grit his teeth in anger. Not only was the new boy dining with royalty above his station, he was now also making other servants look bad! "Come on, boys, let's show him how things are done around here."

Bart glanced around; looking for guards, then strode out into the courtyard, leading his gang of a dozen servants. Bart stepped in front of Koren, blocking his path, while the others surrounded the tired young man.

Koren knew this was trouble. He had seen Bart around the castle; the other boy was fifteen, almost sixteen, tall and big for his age. Bart's straight black hair was pulled back like the way soldiers wore their hair, and the expression on his face was anything but friendly. He had a reputation as a bully, and Koren had avoided him, but that wouldn't work now. With a sigh, Koren set the firewood down behind him. "Hey, you're Bart, aren't you?"

"Aye, that's my name, your lordship." Bart said in a sneering voice, as he bowed mockingly. "Surprised you know the name of a lowly servant, your lordship being all high and mighty, and dining in the palace with the princess."

"I'm not a lord, I'm a servant." Koren protested. "The *wizard*'s servant," he added, knowing that most people feared Paedris.

"Aye, a servant when you have to be, when you're not putting on your fancy clothes, and dining with the princess, and having her show you around the palace like you're picking out which room you want for yourself. Being a servant like us isn't good enough for you, you're better than the likes of us here." Bart glanced at the other boys, seeing with satisfaction that his words had hit home; they were nodding, and muttering, and shaking fists at Koren. Bart kept going, before Koren could answer, "And you spreading fairy tales about how you're a *hero*, saving the princess from a bear, and a pack of wolves, and half the Acedor army, and then you sprouted wings, and flew her to safety." Bart got a good laugh from his boys from that joke. "What really happened that day, Sir Koren the Brave? Oh, I forgot, you didn't get a knighthood."

It was Koren's turn to grit his teeth. As much as he wanted to tell Bart that he had saved the princess, not once but three times, while the princess' personal guards had floundered uselessly in the water, he had promised Paedris that he would stick to the agreed story. "She fell into the water when the boat flipped over-"

"Ha!" Bart scoffed. "What I hear, is you fell into the water, tripped over your own feet and fell in, and she rescued you. Sounds a lot more likely a story, right, boys? Or you want us to believe fairy tales about you scaring away a bear, and a pack o' bandits?" All the servants laughed at that.

"You know what else I hear?" Bart continued. "I hear you're a jinx, you're cursed. Cursed, and there must be a reason for a curse like that, don't happen for no reason. What'd you do, to get a curse like that?"

"I'm not a jinx! Paedris says there is no such thing!"

Bart shook his head slowly. "Boys, he's as gullible as he is stupid. Course the wizard told you you're not a jinx! Told you what you want to hear, he did. Why you think he's got you living in his tower? So he can keep an eye on you, and stop your curse from hurting anyone else, that's why! It's plain as the nose on your face to anyone else, you're too dumb to see the truth."

Koren paused, mouth open. He had been thinking of a good insult to throw at Bart, but the other boy's words struck him. There was a ring of truth to what Bart said. The wizard had only offered to let Koren live with him, *after* Koren told him about being a terrible, dangerous jinx.

Bart laughed and pointed at Koren. "Look at that mouth open! A mouth like that needs a hook in it, doesn't it, fishy?"

"Shut up!" Was all Koren could think to say in return; any clever insults had temporarily left his brain.

Bart was encouraged by Koren's obvious anger. "And there's another thing; your parents abandoned you? I don't blame them. Any ungrateful son like you deserves to get dumped in the woods."

"I am not ungrateful!" Koren shot back hotly.

"Oh, no? Your family was forced out of their home, because of you. You caused all the trouble, you stinking, cursed *jinx*. The decent thing to do was for you to run away by yourself, and not make your parents leave their home, because of you."

"I, I didn't-" Koren didn't know what to say.

"Admit it! You didn't care about your par-" Bart's thought was cut off, when a hand grabbed the back of his shirt collar and yanked him back roughly.

"Bart!" Cully said as he released hold of the other boy's shirt collar. "You making trouble again, with your pack o' ruffians? Shirking, when you should be working?"

"Stay out of this, Cully!" Bart warned.

"Cully, I can fight my own battles." Koren said, but Bart's words about how he should have run away, and saved his parents from being exiled, that stung him badly. He didn't have much fight left in him.

Cully edged sideways to stand next to Koren. "Yeah, but you doesn't always have to fight your battles alone. Shoulda told you about old Bart here, the big lummox, he don't like to see anyone working round the castle, makes him look bad."

"I'm warning you, Cully!" Bart shouted as he raised his fists, looking around the courtyard to judge whether it was safe, for the moment, to get into a brawl.

"And I'm warning you, Bart Lummox, that I've thumped you before, and I'll thump you again." Cully stood his ground, not afraid of the bigger boy. "Now, you git! Git outa here, or I'll thump you bad enough, you'll be shirking in the hospital."

Bart took a step back. Cully had thumped him before, twice before. The smaller boy was surprisingly fast, and Cully fought *dirty*. Bart saw the stricken look on Koren's face, and knew he had hurt the wizard's brat badly enough with his words, fist weren't needed. And trouble would only get Bart assigned more working, and less shirking.

"Bah," Bart scoffed with a wave of his hand toward Koren, "his lordship's not worth our time, boys, let's leave him here with his servant Cully."

Cully helped Koren carry the firewood to the wizard's tower, then left, warning Koren to avoid Bart Loman. And also warning that, if Koren continued to dine at the palace like he was royalty, he shouldn't be surprised that some people, Cully included, got irritated at the special treatment.

Koren hauled the firewood up the stairs in several trips, and stacked it, and added some logs to the fire in the chamber where the wizard was working. When Koren brought lunch to the wizard, he paused on his way out the door, and asked "Paedris, sir, um, are you sure I'm not a jinx? That, you're not using your wizard power to stop me from hurting people, from making bad things happen?"

"What? Of course not, what a ridiculous idea. Who told you that?" Paedris was a powerful, master wizard. Unfortunately, he was also a terribly unskilled liar; while he spoke, he tried to smile, but the smile was not in his eyes. The frozen smile on his lips didn't convince Koren at all.

"Oh, no one. I, uh, was just wondering." Koren knew Paedris was lying.

"Well, you don't listen to such silly ideas, Koren."

"I won't, sir. Can I get more wood for the fire?"

"No, no, I'm fine. Are you all right?"

"Yes, sure. I'm, um, going to eat. Enjoy your lunch, sir." Koren went to his own room, where he sat on the bed, looking at his own plate of food, then pushed it away. He didn't feel like eating.

Bart's words had stung him, because Koren knew they were the truth. Why hadn't he left, on his own, without causing his parents to be exiled from the land they owned, the successful farm they had built themselves? He had been a bad son, an ungrateful son. It wasn't his parent's fault that their son was a jinx.

Tears rolled down Koren's cheeks, and he wiped them away angrily. His father had told him that moping around and feeling sorry for yourself didn't do anyone good. If you did something bad, hurt people you care about, then do something to make up for it. Or, at least, resolve not to do it again.

Koren stood up, went to the washbasin, and cleaned his hands and face. Then he got changed into his best clothes, scrounged up a few coins that Paedris had given him, and walked down the stairs.

Crebbs Ford had been too small, too poor to have a church; instead a priest had come through the town twice a year, in spring and during harvest season. The priest performed weddings, blessed people's crops and animals, and sometimes conducted a ceremony under the big oak tree in front of the Golden Trout, if the weather was nice. Koren's parents had only brought him into town twice to see priests; he remembered the first priest was an old man, who seemed tired, bored and anxious to get onto the next village. The second priest was a cheerful young woman, who had happily blessed the Bladewell's best cow. Koren had liked her. Within the walls of the castle, on the side opposite the wizard's tower, was a chapel for the royal family, although anyone could go there. Koren walked up the steps, pulled open one of the doors, and looked inside the cozy building. In the middle of the day, the chapel was empty. "Hello?" Koren called out, and stepped inside, carefully closing the door behind him. As it wasn't cold inside the chapel, someone must have a fire going in one of the side chambers.

Koren had never been inside a church, certainly nothing as grand as the royal chapel. The ceiling soared high above him, and the inside of the thick stone walls were painted a cheery blue. Tall windows along both sides were made of colored glass, depicting scenes of people doing good deeds; healing the sick, defending the weak, helping each other. Koren walked along one wall, gawking up at the beautiful windows, until he came to a window which showed a farm family; mother, father, son and daughter. The family looked happy, grateful for the help of their neighbors to harvest their crops. Koren reached up and traced the outline of the son with his fingertips. He remembered times like the one depicted in the window; families in Crebbs Ford always helped each other at planting and harvesting time.

Koren backed away from the window. The son's eyes in the painting were staring at him, following him as he moved. Staring at him, accusingly. It was creepy. He turned away from the window. "Hello? Mother Furliss?" He called out the name of the priest who called the chapel her home; Koren had met the kindly older woman once, when she had come to visit Paedris.

"Hah?" A man's voice answered. "What do you want?" Whoever the man was, he sounded irritated.

"I, uh, I'm looking for Mother Furliss? And, um, and I have a donation for the church, sir?"

"A donation, you say?" A rather unhappy-looking, almost bald man stepped out from a side chamber, still holding a chicken leg. He finished chewing, and wiped his mouth of the sleeve of his brown priest robes. "Oh." Seeing Koren, the man's face fell. A servant was unlikely to bring a substantial sum as a donation. Hardly worth the priest's time. "Give it here, boy."

Koren was uncertain, he thought donations went into a box, but the priest held out his hand, so Koren gave him the coins. The man frowned, bit into one of the coins to test it was real, and slipped them inside his robes. "Mother Furliss isn't here, she's out in the city this week, caring for the sick. I'm Father Gruch." Gruch's home church lay on the outskirts of the city, he only was assigned to the royal chapel a couple times a year, when Mother Furliss was called elsewhere. If it had been entirely up to Mother Furliss, Gruch would stay in his home chapel, but she needed to give all the priests under her care a chance to serve in the royal chapel.

Gruch wasn't unpopular only with Mother Furliss, he was unpopular with his flock in his home church. And any church he'd ever been in. Faith and a desire to serve are not what had called Emil Gruch to the church as a young man; poverty and laziness had motivated him. He was the fourth son of a merchant family that had fallen on hard times; his oldest brother would inherit the struggling business, which left Emil and his two other brothers to find their own ways in the world. Two brothers joined the army, which might have inspired Emil to follow them, except he saw how hard they worked, being outside in all kinds of weather. And then there was the danger, which did not appeal to Emil at all. When his brother Thomas was hit in the shoulder by an orc arrow, and came home to recover for three months, Emil decided army life was not for him. Fortunately for Emil, and unfortunately for the followers of the faith, the priest in Emil's hometown was elderly, and increasingly unable to manage by himself. Young Emil began helping the old priest, when he wasn't working in his parents' shop, and soon the old man had taught the young man the basic points of the scriptures, and the typical ceremonies of the faith. What he saw of priestly life did appeal to young Emil; a roof over your head, food provided not by your own sweat but by donations from the townspeople, respect from the people both common and royal. The work was not hard, either, if you didn't want to work hard at it, except for the part about caring for the sick. Emil didn't like that, didn't enjoy it to this day, and avoided those duties as much as possible.

Before the old priest died, he had, reluctantly, for he saw no great calling of faith in young Emil, written a letter of recommendation for the young man to be trained in the priesthood. Emil had seen studying at the monastery, where he had discovered to his dismay there were only two meals a day, and meager ones at that, as his ticket to an easy life. As he read all the proper scrolls, and said all the proper things, and did not cause trouble, the priests in charge of the monastery had not seen how they could deny him graduation, and ordination as a priest.

Unfortunately for Emil, he had not been as successful as a priest as he had imagined. He had to work harder than he wanted, and the ceremonies were so dull, and the ungrateful townspeople not so generous with their donations, and it seemed like there were always sick people he had to visit. Even when he was assigned to the royal chapel, two weeks a year, donations seemed to be significantly less than what Mother Furliss had told him was customary. So, Father Gruch was in even more of a bad mood than usual, when Koren interrupted his lunch. And then Gruch looked more closely at the young man, who had given such a pitiful donation. "Oh, you're the wizard's brat."

Wizards were a particular source of irritation and jealousy for Father Gruch. Just because wizards could touch, influence and command the spirit world to affect the world of the living, ordinary people thought wizards were sooooo powerful. Lies! Priests, Gruch told any and all who would listen, guided people's souls to their reward the spirit world, and wasn't that more powerful, and more useful, than the silly tricks wizards played with their skills? Especially since, Gruch hinted darkly, many, many wizards used their power for evil purposes, and even the best of them used foul, dark magics that were forbidden!

Koren bowed fearfully. This priest didn't seem very nice. "Yes, sir, Father Gruch, I am Lord Salva's servant."

The mention of the word 'Lord' made Gruch almost bite his tongue. How did a wizard merit the title 'Lord', when a dedicated servant of God like Emil Gruch only had the humble title of 'Father'? Gruch looked back at his lunch, which was growing cold already. "What did he send you here for, boy?"

"Oh, begging your pardon, sir, but the wizard didn't send me, he doesn't know I'm here. I came, you see, for, um, for spiritual guidance?" Koren wasn't sure those were the right words. "I want to know if a person can really be cursed, sir, Father."

"Hmmmm." Now, this might be interesting enough to interrupt lunch. "Spiritual guidance? You came to the right place, boy. I am a graduate of the Suyurdan monastery, and am an expert in the scriptures and the eternal mysteries." Gruch didn't know which mysteries were the eternal ones, but it sounded impressive. "Come with me." Gruch walked back into the side chamber where he had been eating lunch, and put the lunch plate on top of the stove to keep warm. He was about to wipe his hands on his robe, when he realized that was not quite the way to impress the boy, so he splashed some water on his hands, and dried them properly with a towel. Gruch draped the official scarf of his office around his shoulders, and waved Koren to sit opposite him. "What is troubling you, child? You can unburden yourself to me, you are safe in this house of the faith."

Koren, having never been in a chapel, was impressed, and intimidated. The priest was doing his best to appear kind and caring, but his expression was severe. "I, um, I want to know, can a person be cursed? Could a person be cursed, to be, to be a jinx, for example? To jinx other people, and cause bad things to happen, by accident?"

Even in his little church on the outskirts of the city, Emil Gruch had heard a vague rumor about something being strange with the wizard's new servant boy. A rumor whispered in confidence by another priest, who wasn't supposed to say anything. "This cursed person, this jinx, is this a friend of yours? Or it is you? Come, speak, and speak the truth, you cannot hide truth from God, boy."

Koren's mouth was dry. "Uh, sir, Father, it's me, sir. You see, strange things have been happening around me, since I was little. Sometimes, bad things. Paedris, I mean, Lord Salva, says there is no such thing as jinxes-"

"Of course there are! Why else would we have a word 'jinx' in our language?" Gruch interrupted. "Continue, boy."

"I don't mean for bad things to happen, and I don't *do* anything, bad things just seem to happen when I'm around."

"Um hmmm, um hmmm. And when did these bad things start? What is your earliest memory of these jinx things?" This was more interesting than Gruch had hoped, he had, for the moment, forgotten about his lunch.

Koren thought back. "I guess, when I was five or so." Koren listed some of the worst jinx incidents, ending with him destroying the grain mill.

"Yes, yes. And did you do something bad at that time, the first time you realized you're a jinx? Steal something, or disobey your parents, perhaps?"

"Oh, no, sir. Not, not anything like that."

Gruch leaned forward, his face very stern "Think, and answer truthfully. God does not curse people unless they have been wicked. What did you do?"

Koren felt tears welling up in his eyes. "I, I, I, um," he searched his memory, "that was about the time my parents wanted to have another baby. I remember my mother said she'd like a daughter, but I told her that I wanted a brother, to play with, and to help with my chores around the farm."

Father Gruch shook his head slowly. "You wicked, wicked boy. How could you be so selfish, to go against your dear mother's hopes for a daughter? And all because you were so lazy that you wanted someone else to milk the cows, and harvest the crops?"

Koren bowed his head in shame. "I didn't mean it."

"Come now, you meant it at the time didn't you?" One of the few things Father Gruch actually enjoyed about is job was reprimanding, and punishing, the wicked. And there were so many wicked, particularly among the people unfortunate enough to belong to his little church. The parts of the scriptures about God's righteous vengeance, although those were only the smallest part of the spiritual teachings, were Gruch's favorite parts to read.

"I guess so. Yes." Koren said in a whisper, unable to look the priest, the representative of God, in the eye. "God has cursed me?"

"What do you think, boy?" Gruch flashed a quick grin, before the boy could see. Clearly, the boy was cursed? How else could he be a jinx, and have all those bad things happen around him? There was no other explanation!

"What, what can I do? To lift the curse?"

"Oh, there's nothing you can *do*. God's will is not like a debt you can pay, boy! You don't bargain with the Almighty. You are going to be a jinx, and a curse and a danger to all around you, until, and if, God determines you have been punished enough. And that may not happen in your lifetime. What you can do is try to be good, from now on, and not give God reason to curse you more, and punish the people around you."

"Yes, sir, Father Gruch, sir. Sir? Could Paedris, Lord Salva, help me?"

Mention of the wizard's name angered Gruch. "No! You think wizards are more powerful than mere priests, because of their silly magic tricks?"

"No, no, sir." Koren stammered.

"You best not, boy!" The priest's voice thundered righteously. "Look to wizards for useless potions, and silly tricks, and smoke and lights. Look to a priest when you fear for your soul, boy. Your master wizard may be able to stop your jinx from hurting someone, if he is lucky, and is there in time, and sees what is happening," Gruch wasn't exactly clear on how jinx curses worked, but they had to be powerful, "but he cannot help you lift your curse." Gruch sniffed, and leapt to his feet. His lunch was burning on the stove. He raced over, scorched his fingers on the plate, shouted some very unspiritual words, and used the hem of his robe to lift the plate onto the table. The scent of the food reminded him of his hunger. His interest in the boy's curse was satisfied. "Begone, boy, think on your sins, repent and try to follow the path of righteousness. And remember! What is said in this chapel, in this holy house of God, between a priest and the faithful, is private and not to be repeated to anyone. Especially not to a wizard!"

CHAPTER SIX

"Oh!" Ariana exclaimed as she pulled the neck of her dress up to cover her mouth and nose. "What is that *smell*?"

The princess, with her guards and maids, had been crossing the palace courtyard, when there was a muffled explosion from the wizard's tower, and a burst of green light. Explosions and lights coming from that tower were not unusual, to the dismay of the residents of the castle. What was unusual was the thin, sickly greenish mist that poured down from the windows, and the mist smelled *terrible*. Like, as if some very large, stinky beast had died in the tower several days ago, and someone had unwisely just opened the door. Or, that same large beast had eaten something that didn't agree with it, and had the worst case of gas *ever*. Her maids began choking on the mist, and her guards, coughing and choking, grasped her arms to hustle her away to safety, when she saw the wizard and Koren stumble out the tower's doorway into the courtyard. "Wait!" She ordered her guards. "Help them."

The wizard, on his knees and choking, pulled a wand from inside his robes, and gasped out words in a language Ariana didn't understand. The mist stopped pouring from the windows, but it was too late. Tendrils of the mist had reached across the courtyard into the palace, and people were already running out into the courtyard, pinching their noses and looking around in disgust.

The guards helped Paedris and Koren to their feet, and the party staggered across the courtyard, gagging and coughing, to climb the stairs inside the wall that ringed the castle. Higher was better, as the heavy mist tended to cling to the ground. When they reached the top of the wall and could stick their faces into the wind that blew from the west, everyone hung over the wall, gasping for breath, trying to keep their stomachs from rebelling. "Lord Salva," Ariana managed to say, "what happened?" She glanced down into the courtyard, to see people frantically rushing around, trying to get away from the stench. She almost laughed when she saw Charl Fusting, the palace's chief of protocol, attempting to keep his dignity by striding stiffly, rather than running, and holding a handkerchief over his mouth. But then the breeze swirled a thick tendril of mist across the man, his eyes bulged and he ran in panic, tripped over his own feet, and fell into a puddle.

"I was-" Paedris paused to catch his breath, "brewing a healing potion. Or I thought I was." The wizard's eyes narrowed, and he turned angrily to his servant. "Koren, are you certain that was leaves of arrowroot that you brought?"

"Yes! And I ground it up real fine, like you said." Koren replied fearfully. Growing up on a farm, he was used to being around unpleasant smells sometimes, but he'd never even imagined anything smelling as bad as that mist. Had the foul mist been caused by his jinx, his curse?

"A single, narrow, silvery leaf, with serrated edges?"

Koren shook his head. "No, that's a spearleaf tree. Arrowroot leaves are dark green, and shaped like a triangle, with smooth edges."

Paedris rubbed his beard in frustration. "Ah! This is my fault, I should have considered that trees could be called different names in Crickdon than they are here."

"So, you mixed the wrong potion?" Ariana asked.

"It would seem so," the wizard admitted.

"What potion did you mix?"

"I don't know, it was a mistake," the wizard bit his lip in disgust, "but I'll be sure never to do that again!"

As the mist cleared, Ariana became aware of where the worst of the smell was now coming from. "Uh, Lord Salva, Koren, I think your clothes are," she wrinkled her nose, "rather fragrant."

Koren lifted his arm to his nose and sniffed his shirtsleeve. "Oh! Blast! That smell is in my clothes, and my hair now."

Ariana backed away, making sure to be upwind from the stinky pair. "Perhaps you two had better bathe, maybe in the stables?"

"Or a pigsty." One of her guards muttered under his breath.

Koren shivered as he scrubbed sand into his hair, then lathered his hair, for the fourth time, with a rough bar of soap. Taking a couple deep breaths, to steel his nerves, he plunged his head under the surface of the pond again and again, until he was gasping for breath. Sniffing, he still caught a whiff of that terrible smell. Or he imagined it. Or the smell now was in the pond water. Or in the tissues of his nose. Either way, he couldn't get himself any more clean without scraping his skin off, which he'd almost done. The stable master hadn't let him in, or even near the stables, when many of the horses panicked after getting a nose full of Koren. Paedris had been brought to the servant's bath in the castle, there to be attended by several servants who doubtless wished they'd volunteered to shovel out the stables that day, but Koren had been left to scoot out a rarely used castle gate, and bathe himself in a cold pond that lay half a mile from the imposing stone walls of the castle.

Fish had swum away in a hurry when Koren plunged into the pond, and not only because he'd disturbed them; he was polluting the water with a horrible stench. Standing up, wearing only short underpants, he looked in dismay at his clothes. There was no way he could ever get that smell out of the wool and cotton fabric of his clothes. Best to dig a hole, then, and bury them.

Would the cost of the clothes be taken from his pay? So far, all his clothes, and his meals, and everything he'd needed in the castle, had been free. When Paedris sent him out to get something from the city, the wizard gave him coins, and never bothered to count the coins that were returned to the brass money chest in the wizard's office. A chest full of coins, that was not even locked!

Koren scratched his now-itchy scalp, and put on the clean, rough work clothes he'd brought with him. The wizard was a good master to Koren, he could not ask for better. Around Crebbs Ford, there had been stories of sons or daughters who had been sent away to serve an apprenticeship, to learn a trade and secure their futures; stories of masters who abused their young charges, blamed them for everything that went wrong, demanded more money from their parents, and failed to provide any training. Koren knew of two boys who had run away from their abusive masters, run away and come home shamefully, for their parents had spent much hard-earned coins to get the apprenticed, and now the sons returned with no money and no trade learned. Or worse, for everyone had heard the tale of Annabelle Clintock, who had been excited to go away to be a house servant for the family of a knight. Everyone in the village had been excited for her, too, until she returned one day, clothes dirty, shoes missing, having walked most of the way home. The mistress of the house had beaten her for the slightest reason, the girls in the family were also cruel to her, and when the knight was at home, he had taken to sneaking up on Annabelle and kissing her roughly. Which the mistress of the house blamed on Annabelle. When the man tried to open the door to the tiny attic closet where she slept one dark night, she had escaped out the window, climbed down a rosebush, and made her way home to Crebbs Ford over the next week. Almost every family in the poor village had contributed something to the poor girl's family, Koren's family had donated a piglet, but her dreams of becoming a royal maid had been dashed.

Koren was willing to take abuse, up to a point; as a commoner it was simply part of life, that his betters would lord themselves over him. To a point, and no more. So, if Paedris insisted that Koren pay for the ruined clothes, he would do that. But he wasn't taking all the blame for stinking up half the castle.

"You wished to see me, Lady Trehayme?" Paedris said as he swept into Carlana's royal office chamber, cutting off the frustrated guard's attempt to announce the wizard. Technically, Carlana had *summoned* her court wizard, but Paedris had taken his time arriving at the palace. No one *summoned* Lord Paedris Don Salva de La Murta, and he certainly didn't respond to a summons from a timid Regent.

But if Carlana noticed the wizard's lateness, she didn't mention it. "Oh, yes, Paedris," she said, looking up from a pile of scrolls scattered across her desk, "come in, come in." She dismissed the guard with a gesture, and walked over by the window, where they could speak without being overheard. Also, where there was a breeze coming into the room. Paedris and Koren had been scrubbed until their skin was pink in the stables two days before, and declared that the smell was gone, but Carlana wasn't taking any chances. "I have news of Koren's parents."

Paedris' eyebrows shot up. "Indeed?"

"Yes," the Regent said with a frown, "his father only had one sibling, a brother, Koren's uncle," she checked the scroll for the name, "what is it, oh, 'Ander Bladewell', and he was no help. Koren's mother's family are traveling traders, one of my search parties located their caravan in Holdeness, where they're staying over the winter."

"Search parties?" Paedris asked in surprise. "I didn't know-"

"Ariana insisted. And we do owe the boy, after all. With the caravan are a couple of his mother's relatives; they knew where to find his mother's cousin, where his parents told Koren they were going. The cousin lives, or lived, in Surtagne."

"Lived?"

"The search party reports that he died four months before Koren left, um, Crab Ford, or something, his village. His mother wouldn't have known."

"I take it that the search party didn't find Koren's parents in Surtagne?"

Carlana shook her head. "No, and no one remembers his mother being there. I think his parents lied about where they were going, before they, they-" Carlana's hands gripped the rolled-up scroll, twisting it in anger, "dumped him on the side of the road. What kind of people would abandon their own children? If we ever do find them, I'd be tempted to hang the miserable wretches!"

Paedris took the scroll from the Regent, and laid it on the table. "Carlana, they believed their son was cursed, a jinx. Based on what Koren tells me happened around him in that village, I don't blame people for thinking he was a jinx, the fact is, he was dangerous. In the last incident, he destroyed the village's only grain mill, by accident, of course. The people of his village are poor farmers, they live year by year on their crops, and if they can't grind their grain, they have nothing much else to sell. His parents, well, they must have figured there was nothing they could do about a jinx."

"Koren! Koren!" Paedris called out from his laboratory. "Where is that boy?"

"Here, sir." Koren gasped, having dashed up two flights of stairs when he heard the wizard calling. "I was copying your book of healing potions, as you asked, sir."

"Oh, yes." Paedris said absentmindedly, having forgotten what he'd instructed Koren to do earlier. "Having any trouble with it?"

"No, sir. There are some foreign words, but I'm copying the letters on those."

"Not foreign, those are Old Lengish. The language you here in Tarador refer to as the 'Common Speech' is called Lengish everywhere else, and those words are from Lengish a long time ago, words that are not used anymore." Paedris thought the term 'Common Speech' showed how people in Tarador arrogantly considered their land to be the center of the world, which was not true. Although, in terms of the long struggle between light and darkness, between the underworld and the world of the real, Tarador truly was the center. And that was why Paedris had left his homeland.

"Oh. I didn't know, sir."

"No matter. I need you to go to the rooftop garden, and see if there is any basil left." Paedris had put the delicate plants inside glass boxes as the weather grew colder, to extend their growing season.

"Basil, sir?" Koren couldn't remember basil being used in any of the potions he'd read. But then, there were many, many potion books he hadn't touched yet, in the tower's library. "For a potion?"

"No," Paedris said with a wink, "for my dinner. The royal kitchens are preparing noodles with tomato sauce and meatballs, and the cooks here never use enough basil."

"Oh," Koren laughed, "yes, sir, I think the basil has not gone by yet." Koren never had tomato sauce, or noodles, before he came to Linden, now that dish was one of his favorites. Food in Winterthur province tended toward potatoes and gravy, which was filling, but rather bland after a while. Thinking about climbing the stairs all the way to the tower's roof reminded Koren of something that had been bothering him. "Uh, sir, I've been meaning to ask you a question, about the stairs to the rooftop."

"Mmm, I was wondering when you would ask me about that." Paedris said with a twinkle in his eye.

"I figured something was different about it, the second day I was here, sir." There was one set of stairs from the bottom of the tower to the fourth floor, then the stairs split, with one going only to the two top floors and the roof. "There aren't enough stairs, sir. I mean, I went outside and counted, and the windows aren't spaced evenly, but there aren't enough stairs to go from the fourth floor all the way up to the roof."

"Most people take a long time to notice, if they ever do. Come with me." Paedris led the way down one set of stairs to the fourth floor, where the other stairs were on the other side of the tower, behind a door. The wizard opened the heavy door, and walked ahead of Koren into the stairway, lit only by one narrow window that lay partway around the curve of the tower. Soon, too soon, they arrived at the landing on the eighth floor of the tower. Koren had been carefully counting steps.

"Tell me, what did you notice?" The wizard asked intently.

"The stairs are only enough to go up one floor, maybe a bit more. And the stairway curves too tightly into the tower, sir, we should be in the center of the fifth floor, but we're not, we're still up against the outside of the tower wall."

"Anything else?" Paedris said hopefully, with a raised eyebrow.

There weren't enough stairs, the passageway curved too tightly... what else could the wizard be hinting at? Koren mentally walked back through the lower doorway, up the stairs, past the window- "The window! Sir, the window should face west, with the afternoon light shining directly in, but it's not." The window was too high up the wall for Koren to see out and tell from the view which way the window was facing.

"Very good!" The wizard said delightedly as he clapped his hands. "Very good indeed! You are correct, there are not enough stairs to climb four floors, and the window faces north, even though it should face west. The answer, Koren, is *magic*, true magic." Paedris gestured Koren over to the upper doorway. "You see how the stone around this doorway is thicker than the tower walls?"

Koren peered at the dark stone. The doorway was thicker than his arm was long. He reached out gingerly and touched the stone, his fingertips tingled sharply, and he jerked his arm back.

"Ha!" Paedris chuckled. "Watch yourself there. This doorway, and the one below, are portals, between them the fabric of our world has been, the best way to explain it is *stretched*. That is how one flight of stairs can climb four floors in this tower. The truth is, there are no stairs, not in the real world. And there is no window. One thing you didn't notice is that footsteps don't echo in there, the sound is muffled, because there is no real stone in there."

Koren peered warily down the stairway, the stairway that didn't really exist, according to the wizard. "How did they build the tower that way?" He asked, completely astonished.

"The tower wasn't built like this, I added the staircase when I got here," the wizard said with obvious pride in his voice. "This tall tower may look impressive, but living here, with all these stairs, is painful for my old knees. I had the original stairway blocked up at the top and bottom; it's still there behind the stones. The workers installed these thick doorways, and I created the pathway between them. My original idea was to simply step directly from one doorway into another-"

"You can do that?" Koren's head was spinning.

"Yes. But then I thought that would be disturbing to any guests who are not wizards. Also, it takes more energy to go directly from one portal to another, and I was showing off already."

"What do you mean, sir?"

Paedris, the powerful wizard who could whisk people from one floor of the tower to another, looked sheepish. "I created the shortcut soon after I arrived here. All those stairs wore me out, I couldn't see myself using anything above the fifth floor, but with all the books, scrolls, and the equipment for my laboratory, there wasn't much room for me to have any living space. The portal was a way to make the upper floors practical, but in truth, I was showing off. I'd just arrived, I was a foreigner, and I was feeling rather full of myself. It was a way for me to impress the wizards of Tarador, because none of them could create such a portal." Paedris couldn't help mentioning the last part, with justifiable pride. "It was a lot more work than I intended, but once I started, I had to finish it."

Koren looked at his fingers, which were still tingling. "Sir, this is, it's *amazing*. Is, is it dangerous? What if you're in there, and the magic, uh, stops working?"

"Hmm." The wizard was uncomfortable with the question. It was a good question. He didn't know the answer. Not for certain. It had taken enormous energy to create the portals, over many months, and he had to renew the spell from time to time. Years ago, when he'd grown weary of renewing the spell, he had considered letting the portals decay, and using only the bottom four or five floors of the tower, but his pride wouldn't let that happen. Really, he thought the whole tall, narrow tower to be a silly place to live. It was intimidating to most people, and living there did add to his mystique as a wizard, and the tower was built for the first wizard of Tarador, so Paedris didn't have a choice in the matter. "Well, it doesn't simply stop working, it fades after a while, a long while, mind you, not overnight. You would notice the stairway getting dim, and," Paedris struggled to recall what a fading portal was like, as he'd been mostly very regular about renewing the spell, "it gets to be like walking through a thick fog, or walking through, sort of, water, I would say. And it takes longer to go from one end to another, you would notice that. But it wouldn't simply stop with someone inside, unless a person deliberately decided to live in there for a long time for some reason. No, what would happen is that, you would no longer be able walk through the doorways." While he was speaking, the wizard was wondering what would happen, if, say, an enemy wizard destroyed the portals, while someone was between them. Where would the person go? Likely, the person would pop back into the real world inside a wall, somewhere between the fourth and eighth floors. Releasing that much energy would destroy the tower.

But, no matter. Any wizard with the power to destroy the portals could use that energy much more effectively by doing something else, something even more destructive. Still, it was a good question, about what happened when a portal collapsed. Paedris didn't know anything in all the literature of wizardry to answer that question. He started constructing an experiment in his mind, he loved experiments. Perhaps he could create very small portals, and send in a bug, such as a beetle, and then collapse the portals. Of course, such a potentially destructive experiment could not be conducted in his tower, he would need to be somewhere out in the countryside-

"Huh? What?" Paedris suddenly realized Koren had been talking to him.

"The basil, sir, I'll go get it now?"

"Mmm, yes. I'll be in my study. I have an idea for an experiment that I want to write down, before I forget my thoughts."

Koren walked quickly up the stairs, the regular, normal, real, stone stairs up to the roof, and opened the glass case to collect basil. If Paedris was thinking up an experiment, Koren wanted to be far away. He wrapped a small handful of the fragrant herbs in a clean cloth, then sat for a moment, looking out to the west, over the rooftops of Linden. The top of the wizard's tower was the highest point for many miles, and the view was thrilling. That day, Koren wasn't thinking of the view. He was thinking about how he lived with an enormously powerful wizard, a man even more powerful that Koren had imagined. Paedris could stretch the fabric of the world! Koren didn't know what that meant, exactly, but one thing it meant was that he needed to remind himself, despite how nice, and jovial, and absent-minded Paedris was, that the man was the court wizard of Tarador, and Koren was a barely educated, homeless farm boy who had lucked into a place to live. Koren knew he had, since Paedris returned with the army, become overly familiar with the wizard, and not being properly respectful, or fearful, of the man's incredible power and station in life. If Koren hadn't saved the crown princess, it was likely he would never be able to look the wizard in the eye, in the extremely unlikely event they ever met.

Koren went back down the stairs to the upper doorway, which he now knew to be a portal to another world. He peered into the stairway that didn't exist, but as there didn't appear to be any fog, he took a deep breath, and ran though the nonexistent stairway as fast as he could, stopping only when he crashed into the reassuringly real stone hallway at the bottom. He looked fearfully back up through the lower portal, grateful that the wizard didn't send him up to the upper floors often.

Koren knew he was supposed to be quiet, and keep still, and not be noticed. He couldn't help craning his neck to gawk around the throne chamber. It was filled with nobles, and their servants. Of all the servants, he was the only one standing next to the crown princess, on the floor below the steps that led to the throne where Carlana sat, with Paedris standing by her side. Ariana leaned toward Koren, close enough that he could inhale her perfume. Seeing her in her formal gown reminded him that she was royalty, and he nothing but a common servant, and he felt a bit ashamed. "I wish I was wearing your robes, Koren, the collar of this dress is scratching my neck." She whispered.

"I don't think a crown princess is supposed to be wearing servant's robes." Koren whispered back. "Besides, that dress wouldn't fit me."

Ariana giggled at the thought of Koren wearing her frilly dress, and that brought a nasty look from her mother. Ariana bit her lip to stop laughing. "I hate this ceremony stuff, it's so boring."

The ceremony was to welcome a new ambassador from the Indus Empire, a powerful land far to the southeast. The tall door at the end of the chamber swung open, and chief of protocol Charl Fusting thumped his staff on the stone floor. In a loud and squeaky voice, he announced "Your Highness, Lord Salva, assembled guests, please welcome the representative from His Most Gracious Majesty, the Raj of Indus."

It was like a small parade. First, two tall warriors, wearing brightly polished armor, carrying poles with banners with the symbol of Indus; a golden tiger. Next, four girls, adorned with many layers of silk gowns that trailed on the floor behind them. The girls had small bells on the fingers, and danced and jingled the bells as they came into the chamber. The girls were followed by eight warriors, who carried large curved ceremonial swords, stomping their feet in rhythm on the stone floor. When the warriors stopped and backed away from each other, two tall women came through the doorway, put trumpets to their lips, and blew a loud salute.

Finally, the ambassador arrived, walking slowly, his head held high. He wore a costume covered in gold braid, and a tall hat with tassels. When he reached the bottom of the steps up to where Carlana sat, he bowed, and presented a sealed scroll to a guard, who carried it up the steps to the Regent. Carlana broke the seal, opened the scroll, read it carefully, and handed it to Paedris, who also read it, then nodded.

"I am Carlana Trehayme, Regent of Tarador, and this is Lord Paedris don Salva, master wizard. Your credentials from His Majesty the Raj appear to be in order. We recognize you as the official ambassador from the Indus Empire."

The ambassador bowed twice, to the Regent and to the wizard, it might have been Ariana's imagination but it seemed that he bowed more deeply to the wizard. "I am Usay Ulligrapat, the Bey of Begal, and I have the honor of being the representative of His Most Gracious Majesty the Raj."

Koren leaned over to whisper to Ariana. "What did he say his name is?"

"I think he said Oopsy Underpants." She whispered back with a wink.

Koren could not help snickering, and the maids who were standing behind Ariana burst into laughter.

"Oopsy Underpants!" One of the maids repeated, loud enough to be heard by the ambassador. Ariana tried to shush them into silence, but it was too late. The ambassador looked up at them, his face red. His warriors, angry at the insult to their ambassador, moved to surround him. Carlana was staring daggers at her daughter.

"Uh oh." Koren saw the wizard looking at him, and tried to put on his best innocent face. He knew Ariana was in big trouble. Before the ceremony, Carlana had told her daughter how important it was for Tarador to have friendly relations and support from the powerful Raj of Indus.

Carlana rose from her throne. "Ambassador, please excuse my daughter the crown princess, she is still a very silly young girl sometimes."

The ambassador was not satisfied by the Regent's apology. "What was the crown princess laughing at?"

Ariana knew she had to do something, or risk insulting the Raj. With Tarador at war, she could not afford to lose such an important ally. She stepped forward, and the crowd parted as she walked toward the ambassador. "Bey of Begal, I apologize to you, and to His Majesty the Raj. My servants were laughing because I could not pronounce your name correctly."

"My name?"

"Oo-say Ull-ig-ra-pat?" Ariana said very slowly. "Is that correct?"

"Yes. What is funny about my name? It is honored in my land!"

"And well it should be. It was Trypan Ulligrapat who led the army of Indus to victory against the Kuhlan Horde, are you related to him?"

The ambassador nodded. "Trypan was my ancestor."

Ariana bowed. "I am honored to speak to his descendant. If the Kuhlan Horde had not been stopped, they would have overrun Tarador, for we were at war with Acedor then, as we are now." Ariana put her arm through the ambassador's arm, and steered him toward the dining room, where a feast awaited. "Tell me, please, when the Horde came through the mountain passes, how did your ancestor get the idea to trap them by flooding the river valley?"

"You have read your history, young lady. Are you familiar with-"

The ambassador accepted Ariana's apology, and the dinner feast was very successful. Ariana smiled and laughed at the ambassador's jokes, and Carlana's army commanders talked about the great long-ago battle between Indus and the Kuhlan Horde. That was a subject about which the ambassador could speak for hour on end. After the dinner, a tired Ariana walked up to her chambers to collapse into bed. Carlana was waiting for her. Ariana hung her head. "I'm sorry, mommy. I was stupid and childish."

Carlana swept her daughter into her arms and kissed the top of her head. "No, you were wonderful. Yes, you shouldn't have laughed at him, what was so funny anyway?"

"Koren asked me the Bey's name, and I called him Oopsy Underpants."

"Oopsy-" Carlana burst into laughter. "That is funny. I would have laughed too."

"You're not mad at me?"

"I was. Don't do that again, we need our allies. Ariana, when you are the queen, you are going to make many mistakes. What you showed me tonight is that you can take responsibility, and fix your mistakes, by yourself." Carlana stepped back and looked at her daughter. "If you can stop being a silly girl, I think you might become a very good queen, someday."

"Yes, Mother."

On the day when the first significant snow of the season fell on the castle, the wizards arrived. When he discovered Koren's power, Paedris had sent word far and wide to other wizards, asking them for advice and help. One wizard Paedris had not invited was Dragotil, for that man had earned the displeasure of Lord Salva by failing to discover Koren's magical power, and thus Dragotil was on his way to a new assignment in a land far to the south of Tarador. The first wizard to enter the castle was a woman, slender, with dark hair and green eyes. She might have been young, or old, Koren couldn't tell, there was something very mysterious about her. Paedris whispered to Koren that her name was Chu Wing, and she was from Ching-Do, a very large empire far to the east. She had been visiting a wizard in the east of Tarador when the message from Paedris reached her, or she could not have arrived so soon. The wizard she rode in with was a man Koren would never have guessed was a wizard; he was of average height, with a round belly, curly red hair, and red freckles across his face. He looked like an innkeeper, not a wizard. Shomas Feany was his name, and he greeted Paedris with a ferocious hug that knocked Paedris' breath away.

Paedris instructed Koren to show the wizards to their rooms, which Koren had prepared a week before. Shomas quickly dropped his bundle on the bed, and set off for the royal kitchens. The woman let Koren carry her saddlebags for her, and he set them down carefully on the floor of her room.

"Madam Wing-" Koren began.

"Madam Chu." She corrected him. "In Ching-Do, our family name comes first."

"Oh." Koren blushed with embarrassment. "Madam Chu. Is there anything I can get for you?"

"No, I will dine later, with Lord Salva. Come here, boy, let me look at you."

Koren inched carefully forward, still wary of wizards. She held his chin in her hand, looking into his eyes and turning his head back and forth. Then she pressed a palm to Koren's forehead and closed her eyes. He felt suddenly very warm.

"Aay-ya!" Madam Chu exclaimed, and she released Koren, her eyes open wide, and she gasped to catch her breath, clutching her hands to her chest.

"Are you all right, Madam Chu?"

"I am- I am fine, Koren. Foolish, but fine. Leave me, please, we will speak later." She looked troubled, and her face was pale.

"Did I do something wrong?" Koren asked as he paused in the doorway.

"No. I was, you could say, I was testing Lord Salva."

The last of the three wizards arrived well after midnight, and raised a fuss because the castle gate was closed. Paedris roused Koren out of bed to fetch the man from the gate, stable his horse, carry up his bags, and bring whatever hot food was available from the royal kitchens. This man was tall, and thin, with very dark brown skin, and he was not friendly at all. Koren didn't blame the man for being grumpy; having travelled far and then kept waiting in the cold. Something about him reminded Koren of a bird, one of those tall, thin birds that stands at the water's edge, peering down into the water, waiting for fish. He too insisted on examining Koren, but only grunted, and remarked that Lord Salva had better know what he was talking about, to make a man ride many leagues in the cold weather. It was well after two in the morning before Koren collapsed into bed.

Over the next week, as the snow fell, and then melted, the four wizards met behind closed doors in the laboratory chamber on the fifth floor of the tower. Long into the night the wizards talked, and cast spells, and strange lights coming through the windows had people all over the castle talking. What was going on in there, people asked Koren, even Ariana asked him. But other than bringing food, and herbs and plants needed for potions, and cleaning up, Koren really didn't know what was going on. Of course, what Koren told people was that he *couldn't* say, but he hinted that of course he *knew*, he just wasn't *allowed* to say. It was all secret wizard things, dangerous for other people to know about. To Ariana, he told only the truth; he didn't know, but he was scared being around so many wizards, and not sleeping well.

On the ninth day after the wizards arrived, it was relatively warm, and sunny, and Paedris called for a break. Paedris, Madam Chu, and the late-arriving wizard who called himself Lord Mwazo rode out of the castle gate, to examine a ruined ancient city that lay across the river to the east. Shomas, who insisted Koren call him Shomas instead of Lord Feany, actually helped straighten up the tower a bit, then rode out with Koren to collect roots in the forest.

"That's a fine horse," Shomas said admiringly. His own horse looked like it should be pulling a heavy plow across a field, instead of carrying a wizard. "Is that the devil horse you tamed?"

"No sir," Koren replied, patting Thunderbolt on the neck, "he was never a devil, and I didn't tame him. He allows me to ride him."

"Ah. Yes, I understand, very good." Shomas said, with a wink. "How do you like living with a wizard, Koren?"

"Truly, sir, it's kind of frightening. I know you wizards mean well and all, but you're so powerful that I'm afraid Paedris will turn me into a frog by accident."

"Ha!" Shomas laughed. "Not all wizards are powerful, young Koren. Paedris is stronger than the three of us combined, by far. And Madam Chu is much stronger than either Mwazo or me. Of course, there are different kinds of strengths in magic. I am probably the best healer of us four, and I'm good with plants and animals, anything to do with nature, but I'm not so good at throwing fireballs." Shomas held his palm up, and only a feeble, flickering glow hovered above his hand. "Mwazo can't even do that. Uh, don't tell him I told you that."

"I won't, sir," Koren said, surprised. It had never occurred to him that there were different types of wizards, and that not all of them could throw fireballs.

"Mwazo has his own kind of strength, he is our expert on potions, and the arcane arts. There probably isn't a scroll about wizardry that old Mwazo hasn't read. And, he has looked deeper into the enemy's dark heart than anyone else dares." Shomas shivered at that thought, and waved his index finger in a circle, as if to ward off unseen evil. "That takes a special kind of strength that I do not have."

"And Madam Chu?

"Madam Chuuuu," Shomas drew the name out, "she is a mysterious one, isn't she? One of the court wizards of the emperor of Ching-Do, she is, and we're fortunate she was visiting my homeland when the message from Paedris arrived."

"There are more wizards that you four, sir?"

"Oh, yes, but there aren't many of us, that's for certain. No, the three of us are the only senior members of the Wizard's Council who could get here, before winter snows close the roads. There are other wizards, but not many, not many. Too few of us, compared to the ranks of the enemy." Shomas' voice trailed off, and he stared at the ground. Suddenly, he brightened, stopped his horse, and dropped to the ground. "Here, look, around this old tree, I think we'll find the roots Mwazo wants. Bring your shovel."

Koren brought a late supper to the four wizards, who were engrossed in reading. The supper was late, because the wizards had risen from bed late, eaten a late breakfast, then an early lunch, then a second lunch around the hour Shomas Feany called 'tea time'. There were books and scrolls covering every table, every shelf, and stacked four deep on the floor. Koren had to set the food tray in the hallway, and clean off a table, before he could set the plates and bowls out for the wizards.

Koren studied the four wizards, who were all lost in thought, their noses buried deep in books or scrolls, absent-mindedly sipping cups of tea. There was Paedris, with his dark hair and beard, from the land of Stade in the south. Madame Chu, from Ching-Do, so far to the east that Koren could scarcely imagine anything so far away. Shomas Feany, with the red hair and freckles of many people from his northern land. And Lord Mwazo, who had the dark skin and tightly curled black hair of his land far, far to the south even of Estada. Four wizards, from different lands, all together here in Linden, all for a common cause, whatever that was. Koren marveled that he, a boy from a simple farm in poor village of an unimportant county of Tarador, could be here, now, with four powerful and mysterious wizards. He was on his way out of the room, treading a narrow path through the scrolls, when Lord Mwazo cleared his throat. "Boy."

"Yes, sir." Koren bowed to the wizard. Lord Mwazo was a stickler for formality, and quick to take offense when he thought he was not being given proper respect as a powerful master wizard.

"Paedris," Mwazo said, without looking at Koren, "It is time. Nowhere do the scrolls tell us what we need to know."

"No," Paedris shook his head, "it is almost dark, and we dare not act while in the enemy's element. Tomorrow, in the sunshine, we shall find the answers you seek."

"That we all seek." Madam Chu added.

Paedris nodded. "That we all seek, yes."

Mwazo waved his hand dismissively at Koren. "Away with you, boy."

Koren bowed again and backed out the door, burning with curiosity. Lord Mwazo had wanted Koren to stay for something, something Paedris thought too dangerous to attempt in darkness. What wizardly act would need Koren to be involved? He shuddered. That night, Koren did not sleep well at all.

The next day dawned cloudy, with a chilly drizzle. The wizards had, for a change, gone to bed early, and so they were up early, and hungry. Koren fetched breakfast, then a mid-morning snack, then lunch. Still, the sun did not shine, and Paedris counseled patience, for he predicted sunshine in the afternoon. And to Koren's surprise, while he was clearing away dishes, the rain lifted, the clouds parted, and within an hour there was hardly a cloud in the sky. Paedris summoned Koren to follow, and the four wizards led the way to the platform on top of the wizard's tower, under the sunny sky. The top of the tower was one of Koren's favorite places to be, for it commanded a great view over the castle, the royal palace and the city, far out into the countryside.

The wizards sat on the benches that were built into the stone wall around the top of the tower, and Paedris told Koren to stand in the center. "Koren, don't be afraid, we only need to ask you some questions."

"Yes," Shomas added with a friendly smile, a few simple questions. "Sometimes, a wizard needs to work with, well, with-"

"With a person who doesn't have any magical power." Paedris suggested.

"Yes, someone without any magical powers, to compare, you understand?" Shomas finished with a questioning glance at the master wizard.

"I understand, Shomas, I mean, Lord Feany, sir."

"Tell us about your family." Madam Chu spoke up abruptly. Since the day she had touched Koren's forehead, she had hardly spoken to him.

Koren looked at the floor, his face burning red with shame. "I'm sorry, ma'am, but I don't have a family."

Chu's stern expression softened, as did her voice. "Koren, tell us about your parents, your mother and father, and their parents, and brothers and sisters. Everything you can remember; their names, where they came from. Everything you can remember. The good and the bad. There was good, wasn't there, Koren?"

Koren blinked away a tear. Yes, before he caused his family to be exiled from their village, there had been good times, much more than bad. "My mother's family I never met, they were from far away, I think. Her parents were traders, she met my father when the traders stopped in our village to repair their wagon. My mother has relatives, that's where my parents were going when they, they left, " Koren was about to say when they left *me*. "Le-left our village. They never told me where they were going." So I could never find them, Koren added to himself. Koren told them everything he could remember, about his uncle Ander, and his father's parents, who died when he was very young.

"Your family were farmers and traveling merchants, then." Shomas said. "No family stories of, oh, say, wizards, or knights, that sort of thing? Bladewell, hmm, there was a Sir Bladewell, a knight a long time ago, are you related to him?"

"No, sir. I don't think so. No knights, and no wizards. My father's uncle supposedly had a horse who could count to ten, but I think that was just a story." Why were four wizards interested in his family history?

"Hmmmf." Lord Mwazo looked down his long nose at Koren. "Common peasants, then."

"*You* were also born a common peasant, Cecil." Madam Chu admonished the proud wizard.

Cecil? Koren's eyes grew wide. He had never heard that Lord Mwazo had a first name. "Is it true, sir?"

"None of your business, boy." Mwazo snapped. "Lord Salva, we waste time, while the sun sinks in the sky."

Paedris nodded, and Shomas rose to speak with Koren. "Koren, we're going to do something, it's important, and you won't be hurt, I promise you."

"Am I to be tested, sir?" Koren asked anxiously.

"No," Paedris hastened to say, "it is us who will be tested. We need you to serve as a, as a, focus." Paedris avoided looking Koren in the eye, and his words did not ring true. The hair rose on the back of Koren's neck. Paedris was lying to him, again.

"Yes, the test will be for those who do not believe their own senses." Madam Chu looked pointedly at Mwazo, who snorted.

Koren swallowed hard, and nodded, and stood still. The four wizards stood around him, joined hands, and began chanting, strange foreign words. He began to feel warm, the way he had when Madam Chu touched his forehead. The feeling of warmth started at his toes, and swelled as it climbed his body, until the top of his head was uncomfortably warm. He felt faint, and his knees shook.

Suddenly, the wizards stopped chanting, and the warmth went away. All four of the wizards seemed slightly dazed, and Lord Mwazo fell to his knees, his face ashen. "Lord Salva, I apologize for doubting you." Mwazo gasped.

Madam Chu knelt at his side, concerned. "Cecil, do you need help?"

"No, no, Wing, I am fine, thank you." For the first time, Koren saw Mwazo smile.

"We have hope!" Shomas exclaimed, and threw his arms around Koren in another crushing hug that took the boy's breath away. "The legends say-"

"The legends are inconclusive, Shomas." Mwazo rose unsteadily to his feet, supported by Madam Chu. "I have made it my life's work to study the legends."

"Nevertheless, we do have hope." Paedris said. "Hope, and opportunity."

"And danger." Madam Chu added.

"Yes, danger. Koren, you may go now. It's a nice day, why don't you take Thunderbolt out for a ride?"

"Yes, sir." Koren bowed to the four wizards, and hurried down and out of the tower as fast as his shaky legs could carry him.

The joyous feeling of the wizards was short-lived. "What does this mean?" Shomas asked. "Out of nowhere, this immense power falls into our laps, and- and *we can't use it*! The boy is too young to control such power himself, and if we channeled such power through him, we may kill him."

Mwazo rapped his fist on the stone parapet in frustration. "It would certainly kill him. Yet, the enemy would not hesitate to channel power through the boy, use him up until he was a dry husk, and throw him away. Paedris, you were wise to hide the boy's power from him. Who else knows?" Mwazo asked.

"Us, and the Regent."

Chu bit her lip. "Perhaps it would be best if the Lady Carlana forgot what she has heard-"

"No." Paedris cut off Chu's treasonous thought. "She is the Regent. We may have disagreements, but we both serve Tarador. There will be no tampering with her memories, understood? Besides, Carlana has supported me completely about Koren."

"I sensed your blocking spell is wearing thin." Chu warned.

Paedris nodded agreement. "We need the four of us to cast a spell that will use Koren's own power to block his ability. It will wear off eventually, his power is too great to contain. He is already much stronger than all of us together."

"We will cast the spell tonight, after the boy is asleep." Chu declared. "The question still needs to be answered: what does it mean that we find this boy now, when the power of Acedor is growing beyond our ability to contain? Mwazo? You know the scrolls better than anyone."

Mwazo rubbed his chin. "There are many prophesies, of the final battle between Tarador and Acedor, or as I should say, between the forces of Light and the Darkness. This is not a battle for Tarador alone," Mwazo nodded to Paedris and Chu, who were from lands far away, "but for all free peoples. I cannot think of any mention of this boy in the scrolls. He is a complete mystery. But, you are correct, Madam Chu, it cannot be only a coincidence that Koren's power is rising now, when our need is becoming so dire. We must take hope from that."

"There is one thing I know for certain," Shomas said, pulling an apple from his pocket and biting into it, as his appetite returned. "As much wizardly power this boy has, so far in his life it has been balanced by bad luck. Think on that, Mwazo."

"Luck is not a-"

"And you are wrong about something, Lord Salva." Shomas continued, "There is such a thing as a jinx."

"What?" Chu exclaimed. Shomas Feany was not known as a philosopher.

"It seems to me that Koren's life has been jinxed. By now, he should be well on his way to becoming a powerful wizard, beyond the enemy's power to harm. His family should be wealthy beyond their dreams. Instead, he's sweeping floors and chopping wood, abandoned by his parents. You think it's a coincidence, that Koren happens to be in the wilderness, at the exact same time a magic-spelled beast attacks the crown princess of Acedor's greatest enemy?" Shomas asked with a raised eyebrow.

"It is not coincidence, and Koren is *not* a jinx." Lord Mwazo insisted, with surprising vehemence. "For us, for the forces of Light who struggle against the Darkness, he is the opposite of a jinx. For our young princess, he was a savior, unlooked for in the wilderness. When she needed him, he came without being called. For us now, facing what we all believe will be the final battle, he is Hope. No, Shomas, he may feel his own life has been jinxed, but he is the greatest stroke of luck we could wish for."

"If he remains on our side, if the enemy does not gain control of his power." Shomas warned.

Paedris let out a great sigh. "Yes. *If.*"

CHAPTER SEVEN

Koren stumbled out of bed late, unsure why he had slept so late and still felt so stupidly tired. It felt like he had hardly slept at all, and he had a vague memory of disturbing dreams involving wizards, wizards gathered around his bed in the dark of the night. He splashed cold water on his face, tried to drag a comb through his tangled hair, and hurried up the stairs. The wizards were not going to be happy about their breakfast being late!

To Koren's immense surprise, the four wizards were already sitting around the table, digging into a breakfast feast, and he could smell hot coffee. The wizard must have brewed the coffee himself that morning. Paedris waved to him. "Ah, there you are, young Koren! Had enough sleep, have you, Mister Woolyhead?" He said with a jovial wink. "Come, come, sit down. Shomas fetched enough food for an army."

Shomas patted his ample belly while stuffing a buttered muffin in his mouth. "I am hungry enough to eat like an army!"

Koren almost fainted when Lord Mwazo rose to pull out a chair for Koren, and then poured tea for him. "Jam?" Mwazo offered. "This strawberry jam goes particularly well on the muffins."

His head spinning, Koren managed to thank the wizards, and sat eating muffins, and bacon, and ham, and eggs, and bread that Paedris toasted over a fire in the corner of the room. The wizards talked about places they'd been, mutual friends they'd seen, or not seen in many years. Mwazo was in such a good mood that he poured out the rest of the teapot into his cup, and then performed what he called a 'trick'. With a mumbled incantation and waving his hands around, he made the teapot disappear, right before Koren's very eyes!

"Sir! How did you do that?" Koren asked, amazed. Paedris never did any 'tricks' with his wizardly skills; Koren had so far never seen him use any magic except for healing spells.

"It is now in the shadow realm, Koren." Mwazo said in a dramatic voice, with a wink at the other wizards.

"The shadow- what does that- where did it go?" Koren sputtered.

Mwazo waved his hand thru where the teapot had been. "The shadow realm is the land of spirits, it exists next to us, but we can't see it."

"We usually can't see it." Madame Chu corrected. "When the-"

"Yes, yes, don't fill the boy's head with details right now." Mwazo waved her away. "Now, watch this." The wizard closed his eyes in concentration, muttered some foreign words under his breath, and the teapot reappeared, right where it had been.

Koren clapped his hands with delight. "Oh, that is powerful magic, sir!"

Mwazo smiled, and took a short bow to acknowledge the applause. "No, it is truly very simple, that's why I call it a mere 'trick'. Casting an item into the shadow realm is one of the first tests of apprentice wizards' ability to control their power. You will-" Mwazo caught himself, as the other wizards eyebrows raised in alarm, "-er, that is, you will see truly powerful magic, during your time with Paedris."

Koren stood up to clear away the dishes, but Paedris waved for him to sit. "Relax! Relax, young man, you've been cleaning up after us tired old-"

"Who are you calling old?" Shomas interrupted.

"-gang of wizards for too long now. It is a fine day, let's all of us go out for a ride. I need to get out of this stuffy old tower, and it would be a shame to waste a sunny day, with winter approaching so quickly."

"Paedris," Lord Mwazo said slowly, while rummaging around in a great leather bag he'd brought, "I wonder. Ah, here it is." He pulled a small wood box from the bag, a battered old box made of ark, stained wood, with worn copper hinges.

"You wonder what, Cecil?" Paedris responded absent-mindedly, engaged simultaneously in reading a book, sipping tea, and toasting a crust of bread over the fire. It was late afternoon, not yet time for a hearty dinner, and the wizard was hungry again. True, he had a fine breakfast, a late, and very large breakfast, but they'd ridden far into the countryside, an endeavor that encouraged an appetite.

"I'd like to try something. With my cards." Mwazo opened the box, pulled out a stack of playing cards, and set them on the table. The cards were also well worn, but, unlike regular playing cards, these were blank on one side. The other side was inscribed with mysterious symbols well known by Mwazo, but some of the symbols were a bit of a mystery even to Paedris.

Paedris forced himself to pay attention. "Cards? Oh, your fortune cards." He frowned, then turned in surprise, which caused his almost perfectly done piece of toast to fall off the stick into the fire. "Oh, darn it! Have you found something new?" He asked excitedly, hopefully.

"No, not yet. I think thinking, about Koren, no, never mind, it's foolish."

"What is it?"

"A feeling. It's silly, forget about it."

Paedris set down his book and tea mug. "Cecil, you know better than I that sometimes a 'feeling' is the spirit world trying to talk to us. You are the most sensitive of us to the call of the spirits. What is your feeling telling you?"

"A vague feeling that, now, maybe something is different. That something has changed. I've had the feeling ever since I first met Koren. I would like to see if I can read the boy's future with these cards."

"We haven't been able to read fortunes in-"

"Yes, I know." Mwazo said quickly. "I know. I have a feeling, as you said."

"Let's see. Koren! Koren, come here!" Paedris walked over to a cabinet and got a thin needle.

"You called for me, sir?" Koren said, out of breath from racing up the stairs. From the state of the boy's clothing, the wizard surmised his servant had been scrubbing something, perhaps a floor, from the dirt on the knees of his pants.

"Yes, quite so." Paedris exchanged a glance with Lord Mwazo. He didn't wish to alarm Koren. "You seemed to enjoy Mwazo's magic tricks over the breakfast table, would you like to see some real magic?"

"Oh, yes, sir!"

"Good. Mwazo here would like to try reading your fortune. If we can. It requires a drop of your blood, a single tiny drop, you understand? I will prick your finger with this thin needle, and we'll put a drop of blood on this card."

Koren wasn't thrilled with the idea of a wizard needing his blood. That sounded vaguely like part of a spell wizards used to turn people into frogs, or something more horrible. He couldn't back out now, and he did want to see more magic, so he nodded.

Over the table, Paedris carefully pricked Koren's finger, and squeezed a drop of blood onto a blank card held by Lord Mwazo. The drop of blood was absorbed so quickly, it was as if it had fallen right through the card. "Hmmm. Still nothing." Paedris expressed disappointedly as the card remained blank. "Well, not every-"

"Shh!" Mwazo hissed. "The card is *not* blank!" He peered closely, intensely concentrating.

"Are you sure?" Paedris asked skeptically, leaning over to see the card closer. "The firelight can be-" The powerful wizard sucked in a breath. "Is it?"

"Do you see what I see?" Mwazo looked up hopefully. Looked up in hope, and confusion.

"I, don't understand. I can't truly *see* anything, it is as if the images-"

"Yes, yes!" Images flickered across the face of the card, impossibly fast. The wizards were unable to bring an image into focus, not a single one, not even when Paedris hurriedly cast a spell to slow their perception of time. Koren was greatly alarmed by that spell, for Paedris had been in such a frantic hurry that he hadn't explained what he was doing. Suddenly, the room had dimmed for a moment, the flames in the fireplace slowed so they appeared to be made of a sluggish liquid, which Koren found fascinating. The images on the card still flickered too fast for Koren to really see anything.

Then the spell dispersed, the room brightened, the fireplace went back to crackling flames, and the card was again blank, with no trace of blood on it.

"What did you see?" Paedris asked wearily, slumping into a chair. The time spell was draining, and casting it so hurriedly had exhausted the master wizard. His hand shook when he reached for a mug of tea.

"Nothing." Said Mwazo, master of his own type of wizardry. "I almost, no, nothing. But there was *something* there."

"What were all those pictures, sir? Lord Mwazo?" Koren asked innocently.

"Pictures?" Paedris looked up sharply.

Mwazo leaned forward eagerly. "Koren? You saw something? What was it?"

"It was," Koren fought for the proper words, "not something, sirs. It was more like *everything*. Everything, all at once. So fast, it all blurred together. Men on horses, and fighting, and skeletons, and fields of flowers, and sunshine and storms, and farmers bringing in crops, and people dancing, celebrating something, and, and, darkness, and something horrible. Horrible." He shuddered. "Also I think I saw the ocean, sirs, islands in the ocean. And mountains, tall mountains with their tops covered in ice, even at in summer time."

"Mwazo?" Paedris inquired with a raised eyebrow. "What does this mean?"

"It means," the lore master said with a deliberate look at Paedris, "that my fortune cards are still unable to see the future. What he saw sounds like a jumble of all the cards." He turned to Koren. "I'm sorry, Koren, sometimes this works and sometimes it doesn't. It is nearly time for dinner, why don't you run over to the kitchens and see what they're preparing for us?"

Koren knew when the wizards wanted to talk in private. "Yes, sirs." he bowed slightly, and left. If he was disappointed to not know more of his future, it didn't show, for he was still trying to recall more of the amazing images he'd seen.

"Lord Salva," Mwazo said after Koren had gone back down the stairs, "perhaps it is time to see your fortune."

"You think that will work?"

"I think it will help me understand what Koren's fortune means."

It didn't help Paedris, for the fortune card remained perfectly, frustratingly blank, as it had for everyone recently. Beginning, Mwazo recalled, twelve years ago, the ability of wizards to see the future, or to be more accurate, to see which possible futures were most likely to occur, had begun to fade. Within the last five years, the fortune cards had been blank, completely blank. Except today, except Koren's future.

"Hmmm. Blank again, as always." Paedris said in disappointment.

"Not quite." Mwazo announced, holding the card up to his eyes, and examining it from various angles. "There is something there. Two images, very faint, fading in and out, like they are trying to form, but the spirits yet lack the power."

"Which images?"

Mwazo carefully put the cards back in the box. "I would rather not tell you yet, for I very well could be wrong, and lead us all down the wrong path. I can say, with very little certainty, mind you, that I think, I get the impression that one image is a crown."

"A crown?" Paedris looked puzzled. For all his wizardly power, he lacked the lore master's insight into the arcane spirit world. "A crown is in my future?" The Don Salva family was sort of nobility in his home lands, but it had been many, many years since Paedris had been there, and many before that since he'd last exercised any of the legal powers of a Don. When he'd departed La Murta to fight the enemy in Tarador, he had left his lands to his children, except for leaving a large part of the olive groves to the townspeople.

"A crown *affects* your future, Lord Salva. A crown determines your future."

"Huh. I could have told you that, without using your cards. When the princess becomes queen-"

"No." Mwazo stood up, stretched his tall frame until his fingers nearly touched the ceiling, and strode over to stand closer to the fireplace, stirring the logs with a poker. "Not the jewel-encrusted crown of a queen, nor a princess. What I saw, what I think I saw, was a rather simple gold circle. And this future is soon, not far off, when your Ariana becomes queen."

"A simple gold circle? I've seen that many times, that's the Regent's crown." Paedris said sourly. "Her mother."

The next morning, the four wizards requested an audience with the Regent, to discuss 'matters of great importance to the future of Tarador', according to the note that Koren delivered to the palace chief of protocol. Carlana invited the wizards to dine in the palace that evening, which meant Koren was busy the whole day getting four sets of wizard robes cleaned and pressed. Even so, as they were about to leave the tower, Koren saw to his great distress that Shomas had a big stain down the front of his robe, from a blackberry pastry he had been eating.

"Shomas!" Madam Chu wagged a finger at her fellow wizard. "We are going to eat dinner in the palace. Couldn't you wait?"

"Oh, you know how these royal dinners go," Shomas grumbled, "lots of talk, and little bits of fancy food. A man needs something substantial to fill his belly." He tried to wipe away the stain, but only smeared it deeper into the fabric of his robe.

Koren brought a wet cloth to clean as best he could, but Madam Chu waved him aside. "Koren, dear, you have been so kind to us, let me take care of this for you." Touching her hand to the blob of jelly, she whispered words under her breath, and the robe was clean! "It's not really clean," she explained, "but the stain will be invisible for a while. Now, Shomas, try not to embarrass us tonight, please?"

Although Koren, in his official purple robes, escorted the wizards to Carlana's private dining chamber in the palace, he was not allowed to serve them at dinner. Even the palace servants, after they brought the food and drink, we told to wait outside, and the doors firmly shut. Koren stood in the hallway, wishing he had eaten something before coming to the palace. The door on the other side of the hallway opened, and Ariana waved him to join her. "I'm supposed to be working." Koren protested half-heartedly.

"Oh, don't worry about that, they'll be in there for hours. Mother and Paedris love to argue. Are you hungry?"

"I could eat." Koren admitted, when he saw the delicious dinner waiting in Ariana's private dining chamber. He still felt vaguely nervous around Ariana, although it wasn't as bad now. "Why aren't you in there with the wizards? You're the crown princess."

"Mother never lets me hear when she is talking about anything secret." Ariana stuck her lower lip out in a pout, and Koren thought that was the cutest thing he'd ever seen. "Do you know what they're talking about?"

Koren shook his head.

"Mother says it must be important, we haven't had this many wizards in the castle since I was a little girl."

"All they've been doing is talking, and reading a lot of dusty old books and scrolls. And they argue a lot. Except," Koren paused, with a buttered roll halfway to his mouth, "they stopped arguing a couple days ago." After they asked him questions about his family, and then held hands and chanted around him. And then he'd had a dream about the wizards standing over him, while he'd been asleep.

"What happened?"

"I, uh, I don't know." Koren lied. He didn't think Paedris wanted anyone to know what went on inside the wizard's tower. Whatever involved him couldn't be important, anyway. He shrugged. Who knew about wizards? "I guess they agreed, about whatever they were arguing about."

"That must be why they're with mother, to tell her what they decided. I hope Paedris doesn't try to get her to send the army out again in the spring; they have that argument every year. If Paedris thinks three more wizards are going to change my mother's mind, he is in for a surprise."

Koren frowned at Ariana's remark. The Regent was powerful, to be sure, but more powerful than the four wizards, or even Paedris alone? "Ari- Your Highness, do you know how powerful Lord Salva really is?"

"Your Highness?" Ariana asked with a tilt of her head. "Koren, please call me

Ariana, when we're alone. Or nearly alone," she added with a nod to her maid Nurelka, who sat discretely by the window. "I need someone who can talk to me as *me*, not by my official title. I have too many people who do that."

"Uh, oh, all right. Ariana." The name sounded strange in his mouth, saying it to her, in person. Being around the wizards, who were first formal, then friendly, and now dressed in their official robes and meeting in the royal palace with the Regent behind closed doors, had Koren confused again. "Do you know wizards can make things disappear, and then come back? I saw Lord Mwazo do that to a teapot, right in front of me. He sent it into the spirit world."

"I think I've heard of that. But I've never seen it. It must have been amazing!" Ariana hastened to add, when she saw Koren was disappointed his revelation was not something new to her. "Can Paedris do something like that? He hardly ever does any magic that I can see."

Koren knew that Paedris didn't show off his magical powers in public, because real magic was serious business, and he felt that the court wizard was not to be viewed as a circus performer. If people wanted to see silly magic 'tricks', they could give a couple coins to one of the charlatan street performers in Linden. "Anything Mwazo can do, Paedris can do. Uh, don't repeat that, please, Lord Mwazo is kind of touchy about his, I guess, status as a wizard."

"I would never tell anyone something you told me in confidence." Ariana said, while reaching out to hold Koren's right hand between her own hands. The gesture was so natural, offering reassurance between close friends, that she didn't realize what she was doing, until Nurelka discretely coughed in her corner by the window.

"Uh, thank you." Koren stammered out, flustered by the feel of the princess' warm, soft hand. Even after she released his hand, and looked a bit embarrassed herself, he could feel his hand tingle, and he self-consciously made his hand into a fist and tucked it behind his back. "I, uh, what was I, uh, saying?"

"You were, um, I, something about Lord Mwazo?" Ariana was thinking that Koren's hand had felt warm, and rough. Rough like the hand of a farmer, a worker, or a soldier. She liked that. So many of the royal boys, and men, that she knew, had soft hands, for they had never done any labor in their lives. Rough felt good.

"Oh, yeah." Now Koren felt warm all over, like when the wizards had been chanting around him on the rooftop, but for an entirely different, entirely natural and wonderful reason. To stall for time while his mind was overwhelmed, he took a goblet of water, but his hand shook, and he spilled a few droplets down his chin. Without thinking, he wiped his chin with the back of his shirtsleeve, an action that would have completely horrified Charl Fusting, with Koren wearing his best clothes, especially as those clothes were still barely, barely passable for an audience with the crown princess. "Ah, sorry." He said, and pulled a proper handkerchief out of his pocket. "So, uh, Lord Mwazo. He made a teapot disappear." Koren continued, while looking out the window to avoid looking at Ariana, because right then, he was having terribly improper thoughts about his future queen. Thoughts that could get a common-born boy like him hanged, or at least thrown in a dungeon. Ariana Trehayme was the highest-born person in Tarador, while he couldn't even claim the name Bladewell anymore, since his family had abandoned him. Thinking about his parents helped him focus, on something other than the warm, kind, beautiful, sweet-smelling girl standing close to him, with her soft skin and- "Do you know Paedris built a stairway that doesn't exist?" He blurted out.

"Doesn't exist? What do you mean?" Ariana asked, while watching her maid out of the corner of her eye. Ariana wished the kindly Nurelka would- just- go- *away*! But the woman had risen from her seat, and approached the table.

"Would you like hot tea, my lady?" Nurelka asked. "This pot has gone cold."

"No, it's fine, Nurry. We're fine." Ariana waved the woman away with irritation, but the maid, with a small, knowing smile, stood by the table.

"How could someone build a stairway that doesn't exist? You must be joking, young Koren." Nurelka prodded.

"No, it's true! He showed me." Koren explained about the magic portal in the tower, as best he could, and by the time he was halfway through the story, even Ariana was interested. Although she was still irritated at her maid. And irritated at the strict rules a crown princess had to follow. She would be the most powerful person in the realm soon, but right now, she couldn't even innocently hold hands with a boy. Or maybe not quite so innocently.

"You'll not catch me going into that tower, young Koren," Nurelka declared, "I don't know as how you do it, night after night, sleeping in there, with strange lights flashing, and the wizard casting spells." She shuddered, and put her hand to her forehead dramatically. "Didn't know wizards could make staircases out of thin air."

"I didn't either." Ariana said, troubled, but excited. What else could the wizard do? She'd seen him heal people, but when the wizard laid hands on a sick person, there wasn't anything to *see* when he did that. And she'd heard wizards could throw balls of glowing fire, but she'd never seen Paedris do that. "Can he fly?"

"No." Koren shook his head. "But he can walk on a rooftop, or along a ledge, like me strolling down a flat road. I saw him do that at Duke Yarron's castle. And he can talk to hawks, he can put pictures in a hawk's mind."

Ariana thought that she needed to have a talk with the Lord Salva, about what wizards could, and could not, do. She was learning about the army; strategy, tactics, and, Captain Raddick had been explaining to her, something called 'logistics'. Sending an army into the field, at the right place and the right time, was all good, but if that army didn't have proper weapons, and food, and hay or grain for their horses, and shelter if they were going to be out in the elements for long, then the most brilliant strategy in the world could not bring victory. Even simple things like spare parts to fix broken wagon wheels were important. And all the 'logistics' cost money, a lot of money. Ariana had been dismayed to see how much it was costing her own purse to keep her personal guard stationed in the Thrallren woods, her mother had insisted that money come from Ariana's own rather small sum of funds, and not from the royal treasury. The soldiers of her personal guard drew their monthly pay from the royal treasury, but when they were in the field, their supplies were paid by Ariana. And, although she was a princess, the crown princess, she didn't actually have much money of her own, not yet. That had been a lesson for the young girl to think ahead, and not act impulsively. "I wonder what they're talking about, in there." Ariana said as she looked into the hallway at the door to where her mother and the wizards were dining, and likely arguing.

"You are all in agreement, then?" Carlana asked.

The four wizards nodded, and Mwazo spoke. "The boy's power is truly frightening. Astonishing would be a better description. It was like looking into the noonday sun. And his power is still growing! Until he is ready to learn to control his power by himself, we need to keep his abilities hidden, even from the boy."

"Especially from the boy." Shomas added quietly.

"Are you certain that is necessary?" Carlana asked sharply. "You said that in a few short years, when his power becomes so great it is impossible to conceal, you will trust Koren with his immense power. Yet you do not trust the same boy now, when his power is so much less? It seems a contradiction."

The other wizards looked to Paedris, as he pondered how to respond. To give himself time to think, he drained the last drops from his wine glass, refilled it from the decanter in the middle of the table, swirled the wine in the glass, held the glass up to the light for inspection, and finally took a sip. "Ah, that is good wine. The issue is not whether Koren Bladewell, until recently a farm boy from a small, little noted village, can be trusted to use his power, the issue is whether he can be trusted *not* to use his power. To not use his power until he is ready to use it without injuring or killing himself, until he can actually control his power. If he tried to use his power now, it would certainly come to the notice of the enemy, and then Koren would be in grave danger, for he would be unable to control his power enough to defend himself. Can he be trusted to not use his power, if he saw someone in trouble, or he is attacked? No," Paedris shook his head, "the temptation is too great. Consider, Madam Regent, your own daughter. She, too, will be entrusted with immense power in a few short years. If she had the power, now, to defend you from your opponents on the Regency Council, could she be trusted to conceal such power, for years? No matter what the situation?"

The Regent took a sip of her own wine. "Perhaps not. No, she couldn't. Could anyone? Then, I don't see that we have other choice but to conceal the truth from Koren, but I fear you are playing with fire, and it will blow up in our faces someday."

"How so?" Paedris asked.

"Lord Salva, to you wizards, Koren is a mystery, a gift unlooked for, a reason to believe that we will win this war. You see his potential, as a weapon against Acedor. But he is also a young man, like any other young man. Consider this: Koren was exiled from his hometown, because he is a wizard. His parents abandoned him in the wilderness, because they were afraid of him. He lost his family because they didn't know the truth! He saved my daughter's life, and the only reward we gave him is a life of drudgery as a common servant. My daughter tells me that some of the other servants around the castle are mean to Koren, because they are jealous of him. Someday, not too far from now, Koren will learn that all his troubles are caused by his wizard power, and that we conspired to deceive him, and hide the truth from him. Lord Salva, you told me Koren's life has been jinxed, that he has been cheated, that his destiny has been stolen from him. We, here around this table, have conspired to continue that deception, to cheat him of the life that should rightfully be his, should have been his. These deceptions are well intended, I'm sure, but when he learns the truth, he is likely to be angry, an angry and very powerful young man. And the people who mistreated him might be very sorry about that."

The four wizards all looked down into their mugs of wine.

Paedris let out a long breath and slumped away from the table. "I fear the same, and have been afraid to say it. Whether Koren will ultimately resist the temptation to use his power for revenge, I cannot say. He is a decent boy, and very resilient. Most boys who went through everything that has happened to Koren would be bitter and angry. Koren is mostly happy, he is loyal to his friends, and the stable master tells me all the men there treat him with respect and affection. I have only known Koren for a short time, but I think the goodness of his character exceeds even his power."

Mwazo cleared his throat. "We too often use the word destiny lightly," he said in a tone that implied 'we' did not include himself. "Whatever the personal cost to him, I believe what has happened to Koren so far *is* his destiny, however unfortunate for the boy, and his family. If his power had been discovered early, he would not have been considered a jinx around his village, his family would not have been exiled from their home, his parents would not have abandoned him. He would not have been there, in the wilderness, when princess Ariana needed him. And Tarador would now be torn apart by the royal families fighting over succession to the throne, leaving us ripe for invasion by Acedor. If Koren has been jinxed, has been cheated, he has not been cheated by us, he has been cheated by his own destiny. I do not know where his destiny leads, but I cannot believe it a coincidence that he arrives here, now, unlooked for, just as our need for such power is greatest. Whether he accepts his destiny, or becomes bitter at it, will likely determine our own futures, and the future of this land."

Madame Chu nudged Paedris under the table. "Speaking of the future, Lady Trehayme-"

Carlana braced for the inevitable argument about sending the royal army out on adventures once the weather warmed, an argument for which she had a ready answer: no. No, not this year. Again.

"-Lord Mwazo wishes to read your fortune, if he can." Paedris continued.

Carlana was unprepared for this request. "Read my fortune? I thought you were no longer able to do that."

"Recent events have raised the possibility that may be changing." Mwazo said carefully. "We thought since, as Regent, you influence the fate of so many people, that the path of your fortune would be strong enough to overcome the difficulties we have communicating with the spirit world, in that area of magic."

"I see." Carlana saw right through Mwazo's clumsy attempt at flattery. "You wish a drop of my blood, I believe that is how your spell works?"

"Yes, Lady Carlana." Mwazo said with surprising hope. He hadn't expected this to be so easy.

It wasn't. "My answer is no." Carlana said, taking a sip of wine to conceal her sudden anger.

Chu spoke up. "We would not ask, if we were not confident the spell is beginning to work again-"

"I don't care." Carlana said with venom in her tone. "I don't want your so-called magic to work again. If it ever did. My husband died because he believed you knew the future. Yet you didn't foresee his death, did you?"

Paedris stare down at the table, a mixture of anger and guilt flooding through his mind. It was because of advice from Paedris that King Trehayme led his royal army out that fateful summer, led the royal army to stop what the enemy had intended as a surprise attack, to seize a vital river crossing, and therefore remove thousands of acres from the realm of Tarador. The magic of fortune-telling had already well faded by then, but

Paedris knew something bad, disastrous was about to happen, based on the fortune cards, and intelligence reports both magic and mundane.

Carlana saw an opening to shame her court wizard, who was far too arrogant for her. "My husband *died* because he-"

"Your husband died because he was a foolish ass." Shomas said quietly. As he rarely spoke in formal meetings, everyone turned to him in shock. "I must say, this is exceptional beer, my compliments to your brew master."

Carlana's face was beet red. "How *dare* you-"

"I dare, because I am not a citizen of Tarador, nor do I serve the royal court. I am a guest here, and guests, like children, may speak the simple truth. Your husband was wise to take Lord Salva's advice, and brave to lead his army into battle against our terrible enemy. He was foolish to think he should personally be at the head of the charge when they retook the bridge. The enemy was hoping to kill or capture the king of Tarador in battle, and he fell headlong into their trap. An army commander *commands*, he doesn't fight like a common soldier. A commander, a king, belongs in the rear, where can see, and direct the battle. That is his responsibility to the army that fights for him, while your husband put his royal guards in danger because he was reckless. Your husband saw a chance for personal glory, and he died because of that. Not because of any failure of magic, or wizardry."

Paedris agreed with everything Shomas said. Paedris had been there, at the battle, although he had been on the other side of the river, battling enemy wizards and a troop of orcs who had sworn to kill him. He had not seen the king personally at the head of the final charge until it was too late, for Paedris was too far away, and too hard-pressed by enemy wizards, to intervene. The final charge was successful, ensuring Tarador's victory in the battle, but it was a victory empty of joy. The king had taken a poisoned blade under the arm, a gap in his chainmail, and he succumbed hours later, despite the best efforts of Paedris and other wizards.

Agreeing with Shomas, believing he spoke the truth, was far different from agreeing with the other wizard's blunt talk. Paedris felt he needed to object to the harsh word of his fellow wizard. "Lord Feany, I insist you apologize to her Highness the Regent. Her husband was brave-"

But the Lady Carlana had heard enough, heard such talk before. That her husband had been impulsive, in battle, and in his choice of wife. Through eyes half blinded by tears, she stood up abruptly. "That will not be necessary. Lord Feany, I understand you plan to leave shortly, before the winter snows block the roads to your home? See that you do so. Good evening to you all." Without another word from anyone, she spun on her heels and left the room, slamming the heavy doors shut behind her.

After a minute of stunned silence, Chu spoke. "That could have gone better."

Shomas shook his head. "No it couldn't. She wasn't going to allow Cecil to read her fortune, no matter what we said. And she needed to hear the truth about King Adric."

"Shomas, she is a widow, still grieving-"

Shomas cut off Wing with an angry gesture. "She was a grieving widow, before she decided to become Regent. Once she put that Regent's crown on her head, she needed to put her grief away, and do her duty. Those in power most need to hear the truth, and not indulge in happy fantasies of what they wish to believe. If she believes that wizardry, not personal foolishness, led to her husband's death, we need to correct those notions.

Perhaps then she will not be so reluctant to send the royal army out to challenge the enemy, rather than sitting uselessly in garrison all season."

None of Lord Feany's companions could find fault with his reasoning. "Now, since there is nothing more to discuss, and I will be leaving Tarador sooner than expected, perhaps we should not let all this delicious food and drink go to waste, eh?"

Whatever the four wizards had discussed with the Regent, Koren saw that everyone left the dinner in a glum mood. Even Shomas, who ate his fill of the best the royal kitchens had to offer. The wizards talked late into the night, and awakened late, to be delighted that Koren had breakfast ready and their clothes cleaned. After Koren left to care for the horses, Madame Chu returned to the subject they'd discussed late the previous evening. "Cecil, you need the Regent's blood, because you think you saw a regency crown on your card?"

"Yes. It was more an impression, a feeling, than something I can say for certain that I saw. We must understand what the spirit world is trying to tell us. If we have a chance, any chance, to know any small part of the future, we must know it." Mwazo said vehemently. "The enemy is also blinded to the future, we can be sure the demon seeks any advantage he can seize. With the Regent of Tarador so adamantly against us, I do not see how we can do, what we must do."

"There is another way." Wing said hopefully. "Her daughter, the crown princess."

Mwazo shook his head. "No. Ariana will not become queen until her sixteenth birthday. Whatever the card tried to show me, that future is closer."

"I didn't mean Ariana's future. The Regent is her mother, so-" Her voice trailed off meaningfully.

"They are connected! Yes, yes, good thinking, Wing!" Shomas said with great enthusiasm. "Excellent."

"I don't quite understand." Paedris said, confused. In this area of magic, he was no master, to his embarrassment.

"Ariana's fate is connected to her mother through the Regency, and by blood." Wing explained. "We can use that close connection to divine her mother's future."

The four wizards agreed that approaching the crown princess with a request to use her blood for fortune telling, with her mother angry and watching the wizards closely, was not a good idea. Instead, Paedris casually mentioned to Koren that Mwazo wished to try telling the boy's fortune again that afternoon, and that he wanted to try casting the fortune of a girl also, as an experiment. And that Mwazo promised, if the fortune-telling spell didn't work, he was willing to perform other magical 'tricks' to make up for the disappointment. Paedris casually mentioned this to Koren, as Koren was going out the door, properly dressed, for lunch and reading old books with the crown princess. Naturally, Koren excitedly mentioned the fortune telling to Ariana, who exclaimed that, in case Koren hadn't noticed, she was a girl, and she very much wanted to see magic.

The spell didn't work, Mwazo said, and he expressed great disappointment, and had to entertain the princess by performing silly tricks. In truth, the spell had worked; he was much perplexed why Ariana's fortune was the same as Koren's; a blur of images. What could that mean? What were the spirits try to tell him through the cards? Or, worse, was the future as much a mystery to the spirit world as it was to Mwazo?

He finished his last trick, a simple spell which made Ariana's hair stand straight up, then he bowed deeply and announced that, regrettably, he must return to the wizard's tower, when a painting caught his eye as he walked out the door of her suite of rooms. "Your Highness, who is this in the picture?"

Ariana touched the gold-painted frame lovingly. "That is my grandmother, my father King Adric's mother, Queen Lilith."

"And this portrait was done while she was queen? Not before?"

"Yes, why?" Ariana titled her head. Wizards hardly ever took notice of the doings of the Taradoran royal court.

"The crown she wears, it is rather," he struggled for the right word, not wishing to cause insult, "understated, is it not?" Queen Lilith wore a simple gold band, wider on her forehead, where it was inscribed with the symbol of Tarador. No jewels, there was nothing fancy about it, that is, if you forgot that it was made of gold. "It is not unlike the regency crown your mother wears."

"Of course." Ariana said, as if it were the most obvious thing in the world. "That is a queen's everyday crown. The big ceremonial crown is much too heavy to wear every day, Lord Mwazo. You don't wear your formal robes every day, do you?"

Koren thought Lord Mwazo would indeed like to wear formal robes, and have everyone call him 'Lord Mwazo' every day, but he kept silent.

Mwazo stood rigid for a moment, his mouth open, as if he'd been struck by lightning. He put a hand to his mouth, breathed heavily, and recovered his senses. "You will wear such an every day crown, when you are queen, Your Highness?"

"Of course. I will wear *that* crown. It has been in the royal family for generations." She said with pride.

Mwazo fumbled for something to say, when all he wanted to do right then was get to the wizard's tower as quickly as he could. "I'm sure you will wear it well, Your Highness." He bowed awkwardly, one eye still on the painting, and fairly bolted out the door.

"What was that about?" Ariana asked with amusement.

Koren shrugged. "Wizards. If that's the strangest thing they do today, that will make me very happy."

Mwazo sprinted up the stairs of the tower, bursting in on his fellow wizards as Paedris was reading aloud from a scroll. "It's not a Regent's crown! It's the crown of a queen! A queen!" He shouted in excitement.

Shomas almost spilled his mug of beer when Mwazo surprised them. "Crown? What in the world are you going on about?"

Paedris took a guess. "The crown you think you saw, in my fortune card? It was not the Regent's crown? I thought the crown you saw was too simple, too plain to be the crown of a queen?"

Mwazo shook his head vigorously. "I was thinking of the fancy type of crown a queen wears on formal occasions. Paedris, but I've rarely met a queen when it was not a formal occasion. Ariana told me she would wear a very simple-looking gold band as a crown, for everyday use. She will only wear the big crown with all the jewels on formal occasions. You see what this means?"

"I have no idea, so please tell me." Shomas said.

"When I cast Paedris' fortune, I saw two symbols, and one symbol was a crown. We thought that meant the Regent, but I now know it is her daughter, the future queen."

"Wait," Madame Chu said, "you were sure the crown could not mean the princess, for she will not become queen until her sixteenth birthday?"

Mwazo's hands made two fists, and he knocked them together. "I cannot explain that. But the crown means Ariana, I am certain of it. I think something very exciting is about to happen! May I show you? May I cast your fortune now?"

Wing nodded. "Please."

Mwazo smiled broadly and clapped his hands in delight, the other three stood with mouths agape. On Wing's card, clearly visible, were two symbols: a lightning bolt; a white-hot streak of fire flashing across from top left to bottom right. And a crown, which, oddly, flickered from a simple gold circle to a shape more like a tiara, and back.

"What does this mean?" Wing asked in a near whisper. No wizard had seen a fortune card display an image in many years, all across the world.

"May I cast another card, before I answer?" Mwazo said with a raised eyebrow. "And not with one of us, I need someone who is not a wizard. We are too close to the spirit world, for me to be comfortable with interpreting what the spirits are trying to tell us. I need someone not affected by magical contact with the spirit world."

"Agreed." Paedris nodded. He walked to the window, opened it and leaned out. "How about, ah. Boy! You there, boy! Cully, is it? Yes, yes, you. Come up here, please. And bring your two companions with you. Yes, at once. Quickly, quickly, now!"

It was just Cully Runnet's luck to be crossing the courtyard while Paedris stuck his head out the window. He goaded his two companions, who had never been inside the forbidding tower, through the door, and up the stairs. It didn't help that Cully harshly told his friends not to touch anything, not a single thing, in the tower. The three boys warily edged into the chamber where the wizards were waiting, to find not one, not two, not three, but four wizards. Four wizards! And one of them was a pretty lady wizard.

It was all Cully could do to bow to the wizards without falling on his face, he was so nervous. The chamber, despite the winter sun peeking out between clouds, was dimly lit, the roaring fire tinted everything in the room with a light that Cully would have called golden, except with the place crowded with fearsome wizards, it was ominous. The room was crowded not only with wizards, it was cluttered, cabinets and tables were piled high with leather-bound books, ancient scrolls, glass jars and ceramic pots that Cully knew Paedris used for keeping roots, herbs, odd minerals and potions. That put Cully on edge, wondering what spells the wizards were planning to cast, spells that could not be good for three healthy boys. A burning log shifted in the fireplace and crashed onto the grate. That was enough, Cully was about to race back down the stairs, when a large wizard with red hair spoke from a chair in the corner "Well, come in, come on in, we don't bite, you know. I'm Shomas Feany, I assume you have names also?"

All three boys were tongue-tied, so much that they barely managed to stammer out their names. "Cully Runnet, Lord, um, Feany, sir."

"Stephen Bello."

"T-Toman Miller."

"Well, Cully, Stephen and Toman, we want to try telling your fortunes." Paedris smiled in a way he hoped would be reassuring. "All it will require is a moment of your time, and a single tiny drop of blood from each of you. When you're done, each of you will be paid a silver coin." Paedris pulled three shiny silver coins from a pouch, and laid them on the table by the window, in a shaft of winter sunlight. They glittered enticingly, and the boys almost forgot their fear.

Almost. A silver coin was not enough to overcome a lifetime of superstition about wizards. The idea of having blood taken had the three boys imagining horrible spells, where the blood would be used to turn them into undead creatures, or something even worse. Cully's two friends were shuffling their feet, considering running for the door, when Cully screwed up his courage. "I'm ready, Lord Salva."

"Come here, please." Mwazo said with a smile that was less reassuring than he intended. Madam Chu sought to calm the boys' fear by showing them the needles, and explaining "Lord Mwazo is going to lay three fortune cards on the table, and I am going to prick your finger with a needle. We will squeeze a tiny drop of blood onto the card, and then you can be on your way, with our thanks. And a silver coin."

Cully went first. He didn't flinch, and a truly tiny drop of blood dropped onto a card. He sucked on his finger, and nodded to his two friends. In a moment, it was done.

"A lightning bolt and a crown, sir? What does that mean?" Cully couldn't tear his eyes away from the mesmerizing images, the same images on all three cards. The crown spun, and flipped from one image to another, the lightning bolt fairly crackled with energy, so bright it almost caused spots in his eyes.

"That is wizard's business, Mister Runnet." Paedris said, not unkindly. "Thank you, gentlemen, you may run along now. Here are your coins. Oh, and you may take that tin of cookies with you."

"Yes, sir, Lord Salva sir, and Lords and Lady, ma'am." Cully said nervously, although not so nervous he didn't tuck the tin of cookies under his arm, before he bowed deeply, and the three fled down the stairs.

"So? Cecil? What does this mean?" Shomas said unhappily, having watched a tin of cookies disappear down the stairs, cookies he'd been planning to eat.

Mwazo frowned. "I don't know for certain. I will have to ponder this. Four people now have the same fortune, and I will wager my wizard's robes that if I cast the fortunes of every citizen in Linden, I would find the same two symbols. Except for two people; Koren, and the princess. Their fortunes are a blur of images, a blur of every image I've seen on a card. I am at a loss to tell you what that means."

Shomas pushed the cookies out of his mind. "It cannot be a coincidence that the two people whose fortunes are unreadable, are represented by the lightning bolt of a wizard, and the crown of a queen."

"Except Koren is not yet a wizard, and Ariana is not yet a queen. And you say this fortune will manifest soon?" Wing asked.

"Within the year, yes, unless I am very, very wrong." Mwazo answered. "The wizard can't be Koren, then, nor the queen Ariana, can it?"

"Again, we return to the question; what does this mean?" Paedris asked.

The four wizards stood, or sat, in silence, staring at the fireplace for inspiration. "I admit, this is not my area of expertise." Paedris said, after several minutes.

"Nor mine." Added Shomas.

"The mysteries of- oh!" Wing took in a sharp breath. She put a hand across her face, her knees wobbled, and she slumped into a chair.

Paedris was on his feet in a flash. "Wing, are you well?" Deep concern showed on his face, he knelt at her feet, and held her hands in his own.

"Yes, yes, thank you." She held his hands perhaps a moment too long, then pulled away gently. "Wild cards." She told Paedris.

It was his turn to gasp in surprise. "Could it be?"

"It makes sense, no?" Wing responded.

"Would the two of you mind explaining to the rest of us?" Shomas said, mildly irritated. A cookie would have improved his mood.

Wing smiled. "I was recalling something I have not thought about for many years, not since I was a little girl, learning the craft of magic, in a school high up in the mountains. There were cards there, cards used to tell fortunes, to foresee the future. These cards were not used, not even in training; they were in a sort of museum, a dusty old library of wizardry. I remember asking a very old wizard about this deck of cards, and he showed them to me, and told me such cards had not been used by wizards for many, many centuries, since the spell to create your picture cards was created." She pointed to Mwazo's deck of blank cards. "Before such picture-revealing cards were developed, wizards used a different type of cards?"

"Yes," Mwazo answered slowly, ransacking the depths of his memory. He was a student of wizardry, in addition to being a master of the arcane subject. "The art was very limited back then, a deck of cards had various hand-painted images. A wizard would shuffle the cards, and deal them one by one, the spirits were thought to have influence on which cards came to the top, to indicate the person's fortune."

"I've seen such cards, I don't remember where." Shomas said, half lost in thought. "There was a card with a skeleton, indicating death, a card with a sword, indicating battle, or fighting, or danger. It was very crude," he observed with a rather disparaging smile, wondering how wizards of that age managed to accomplish anything with their crude magics.

"Skeletons, yes," Wing agreed, "and swords, also lovers, and flowers, the sun and the moon. Among those in the deck was a special card, a card sometimes called the joker, or the trickster. A card that could represent any card, a card that presented any possibility, and all possibilities, at once. A wild card."

"A wild card." Mwazo pondered the idea. "I do seem to recall hearing such, in my studies of ancient magic. If a person drew a wild card, it was supposed to mean that person had no fate, that even the spirits did not know his or her future, that the person was entirely in control of their own destiny. That their future was not written. But, drawing such a card would be rare, exceedingly rare." He was silent a moment. "Do we now have two wild cards? Is it possible?"

"Is *what* possible?" Shomas almost shouted.

"Consider, Shomas," Paedris said, "four people, one a powerful wizard," he nodded to Madame Chu, "three are servant boys, who all have the same fortune, identical fortunes. A fortune which says their future will be largely determined by a lightning bolt and a crown; by a wizard and a queen. Now, consider two other people, one a future wizard, one a future queen. The cards for their futures are not fixed, their cards display images of every possible future. Their futures are not fixed in any way, for they control their own fates."

"And ours." Mwazo added in a near whisper. "Somehow, they control our fates."

"A boy and a girl?" Shomas scoffed. He rose from the chair to poke at the fire, pushing a log into a pile of glowing coals. "I mean no offense, Mwazo, but Koren is merely a boy, and Ariana a girl. They may very well become immensely powerful someday, but right now, Koren is mucking out stalls in the stables, and Ariana can't do anything without asking permission from her mother. A mother who says no to almost everything. Cecil, you are telling me these two children control my fate?"

"No, Shomas," Mwazo pointed to the cards, "that is what the spirits tell us. The spirits see this world as it truly is, not this illusion," he tapped the wooden table with a finger, "that we perceive as real. You do control your own fate, what the spirits are telling us is that, whatever you do, what we all do, ultimately does not matter. Koren and Ariana will decide the fate of this world. We only matter in how we affect them."

Shomas turned to Paedris in frustration. "You believe this nonsense?"

Paedris nodded gravely. "I do."

"I do, also." Wing added. She stood and began to pace in front of the fire. "More importantly, our enemy will. Our enemy has been as blind as we were to the future. Until a dozen years ago, when our ability to foresee the future began to fade, our enemy was content to bide its time, to chip away at our defenses, to be patient, for the enemy saw the same inevitable future we saw; we would be defeated, the barriers between this world and the underworld would be sundered, and demons would consume us. The demon is unspeakably ancient, it can wait, time is nothing to it."

She took a breath, and looked up into the faces of her fellow wizards. "When the future became unclear, the demon grew afraid for the first time, for its victory was no longer certain, and it didn't know why. It could no longer wait, so it has been on the attack for a decade. King Adric died not because the enemy is bold and confident, but because the enemy is fearful. Now, we see our fates are determined by a wizard and a queen. Our enemy will see the same, if it has not already."

Paedris nodded, his face grim. "Cecil, what has happened? Before, the fortune cards were blank. Now, they clearly show the images of lightning bolt and crown. What has changed?"

Paedris expected Lord Mwazo to ponder that question a while before answering, perhaps take a sip of wine while he considered the matter. Instead, he answered right away "Because the spirits have now seen the futures of Ariana and Koren."

"No one ever cast Ariana's fortune before today?" Wing asked, surprised.

Paedris shrugged. "Her mother has always forbidden it, that is why we needed to manipulate Ariana into requesting Cecil into casting her fortune. Without her mother knowing about it. Cecil, I didn't understand your answer," Paedris exchanged a puzzled look with Shomas. "This is not my area of expertise," he admitted.

"The spirits could not tell anyone's fortune before, because the spirits did not know anyone's future. We had not asked the right questions." Mwazo attempted to explain. "The spirits only look into the future when we ask them to; the future of this world is of no interest to them otherwise. Then, we asked the spirits to look into Koren, and then Ariana's futures, and the spirits now know that everyone's fate is tied to Ariana and Koren-"

"The enemy knows this also?" Shomas asked with great alarm.

"No, no, the enemy will only see what we have seen; a lightning bolt and a crown.

The enemy cannot cast the fortunes of Ariana and Koren without their blood. I expect the enemy will assume the wizard is you, Paedris, and that the crown belongs to Carlana. There is no reason for the enemy to think of a young servant boy, and a girl who has not yet come of age."

"Paedris, you and Carlana will be in great danger." Wing said, her voice half choked with concern.

"I see no change there," Paedris said, "the enemy has long sought my death, and the Regent is as securely protected as she can be. For Koren, and for Ariana, their apparent unimportance is their best defense for now. No, I don't see that anything has changed there. Except, that I expect our enemy to grow more desperate to strike at us, to end this war soon, by force, before the future escapes its grasp. Now, Lord Mwazo, there is one final card to cast. You know the card I speak of."

Mwazo's hands trembled when he reached for the deck of cards. "Yes," he spoke in a harsh whisper. "Do you think this is wise, Paedris? If I ask this question of the spirits, we will know, and the spirits will know. And the enemy will know also, for the enemy will ask the spirits the same question."

"Cecil, we must know. We have waited so long. We must know if this is the path forward, if this is our fate, our fortune, if the destiny of the world rests in the hands or two people so young, so unready."

Mwazo placed the two wild cards on the table, closed his eyes, muttered an incantation, and selected a card from the middle of the deck his fingers were so unsteady he almost dropped the card on the floor. In the tense silence, the sound of the card hitting the table made Shomas jump.

Mwazo took in a sharp breath.

Paedris bent over the table to look at the card and he, too, gasped. "Ascendant. Ascendant!" The card displayed a raging fire, reaching to the heavens. "Their power is ascendant."

"They are so young," Madame Chu said in a whisper. "We must protect them until they can protect themselves-"

There was a sound of feet pounding on the stairs, and the wizards became silent as Koren poked his head in the doorway. He had been walking back from visiting Ariana when he saw Cully, who told him about the fortune telling. And showed Koren the shiny silver coin he'd been paid. "Sirs? Madam? Can I do anything for you?" For some reason, Koren felt guilty to be wearing the fine clothes he used for visiting the palace, when he was supposed to be serving the wizards. He glanced around the room in dismay to see how cluttered it was. It had been clean that very morning, he had gotten out of bed early to scrub that very room until the floors shined, and now every flat surface was piled high with books, scrolls, empty cups and dishes, glasses, jars and crocks of roots, herbs and potions! He didn't need a magical card to foresee his immediate future; he would be up late, and getting up early, to clean again.

"Koren, hello." Paedris said, with a quick guilty look of his own, and averted his eyes to look at the fireplace.

Uh oh, Koren thought, what have they been up to while I was gone?

"Koren, come in, boy." Shomas called out, trying to suppress his grumpiness. He took a swig of beer from his mug, beer that had grown warm, and flat, and so Shomas made a sour face. In his fine clothes, clothes that were at odds with his current station in life as a servant boy, Koren looked to be play-acting. Shomas found it difficult to believe this good-natured, still fairly ignorant, innocent and clueless boy could somehow determine the fate of the entire world. "Did you, uh, have fun with the princess?" A sharp look from Paedris and the sudden redness of Koren's cheeks made Shomas hastily add "Mwazo says you two were looking at maps of the eastern border?"

"Oh, yes sir, her mother has been wishing the princess," he avoided calling her Ariana as that would seem far too familiar, "to learn about the Indus Empire. Because their new ambassador is here, I suppose." Koren noted that all four of the wizards appeared uncomfortable, he suspected they had been talking about him. Eager to get away, he began picking up dirty dishes. The large tankard that held beer was almost empty, and the beer at the bottom smelled stale. "Could I get you a fresh tankard of beer, sir," he asked Shomas, "and see if the kitchens have something to snack on, as it is hours before suppertime? Sometimes the kitchens have hot rolls, or salty pretzels."

"Ooh!" Shomas clapped his hands. "Yes, more beer, please."

To Koren's surprise, Mwazo rose from his chair and added dishes to the pile in Koren's arms. "I would dearly love a fresh hot pretzel, and I think, as Shomas seems so fond of it, I would try some of this beer."

Koren bowed as he backed out of the room, laden with dirty dishes. He could see that somehow, he needed to convince the royal kitchens to bake pretzels, whether they liked it or not.

Shomas left three days later, while Madam Chu and Lord Mwazo stayed in the castle for another week, then reluctantly had to leave, before the coming winter snows trapped them away from their homes. Koren was sorry to see them go, especially Lord Mwazo. The tall, thin wizard had become positively friendly, insisting that Koren put aside his chores to study books with him; learning about history, and, to Koren's surprise, wizardry. Mwazo did not, of course, show Koren how to cast spells, or create magical potions; instead they talked about the nature of light and dark magic, the history of wizards, and the rules that all good wizards had to live by. That seemed to be very important; Mwazo was very concerned that Koren learn about the heavy responsibilities of wizards, although Koren could not understand why a mere servant had to care about such things. Afternoons were spent in the cramped chamber Mwazo used as a study, reading books or scrolls in front of a warm fireplace, with hot tea and plenty of snacks to eat. Koren was sorry to see Mwazo leave, for it meant Koren went back to the drudgery of chores as the wizard's servant.

"Hey, Koren, ain't seen much of you the past fortnight." Cully said as he sidled up next to Koren in the royal kitchens, trying to squeeze in near the ovens, where it was warm. It was a raw, gray, nasty day outside, with rain, sleet, and freezing rain, thoroughly miserable weather to be out in. So Koren, and Cully, and many other servants, were taking any excuse not to be outside unless they had to. Koren had fed and brushed Thunderbolt, but the great horse had stuck his nose outside the stables, sniffed the damp, cold air, and walked back to his warm, dry stall. Having been warned about the coming weather by the wizard the previous day, Koren had plenty of firewood in the tower, so he didn't need to go outside to keep the stoves hot.

"I've been busy." Koren said with a yawn. He was sleepy, both from work and from the combination of being outside on the walk back from the stables, with wet clothes, and now being lulled toward sleep by the over-warm air in the kitchens. "All those wizards kept me hopping."

"What were they doing?" Cully asked curiously.

"Talking, and eating a lot, and making a mess. I don't know why the other three came here, so late in the year, Paed-, uh, Lord Salva didn't tell me." Koren yawned again, he couldn't help it. "He went back to bed after breakfast this morning, the wizard, I mean. Said this weather wasn't fit for man nor beast."

"Sounds like you need coffee, to keep you awake." Cully observed, trying to keep from yawning himself. Yawning was contagious, he thought.

"Never tried it." Koren admitted. "It smells good, when I grind the beans. What does it taste like?"

Cully shrugged. "It's bitter, if you drink it black. Put some cream in, and sugar, and it's good. You never tried it? But you brew it every morning for the wizard!"

"So?"

"So, you never took a sip yourself?"

Koren was surprised. "That's Lord Salva's coffee. He has the beans brought in from his homeland twice a year, it's expensive."

"Yeah, but, come on, you never took a little sip? The wizard wouldn't notice."

Koren wasn't sure about that. Wizards had ways of knowing things. And that didn't matter. Koren owed the roof over his head, and the food in his belly, to the wizard. He shook his head. "That would be stealing."

"Steal-" Cully stopped, when he realized Koren wasn't joking.

"You don't work for a wizard, Cully. He could turn me into a frog, if he thought I was stealing from him. This isn't a time of year to be without a roof over your head."

One especially dreary winter day, when the cold rain dripping down the gray stone walls of the tower had become such a commonplace sound that people only paid attention when it stopped for a blessed moment, Paedris put down his spoon, and pushed away the bowl with a sigh.

"Is the food bad, Lord Salva?" Koren asked. The cooks in the royal kitchens said they were beginning to run out of fresh fruits and vegetables as the winter dragged on, and the food had been less tasty recently.

"No, no, it's fine, I suppose. All this rain has me a bit out of sorts." Paedris looked out the window and shivered. The sky had been dropping a sloppy mix of snow and rain for the last two weeks, and everyone in the castle was heartily sick of it. "Somedays, I very much miss my homeland, it's warmer than here in the winter. Although, of course, that means it can be uncomfortably hot in the summer time." Paedris picked up a crust of bread and chewed it slowly. "And food there is better. All the cooks here know is this," Paedris made a sour face as he dipped a crust of bread into the gravy, then pushed his plate aside, "bland food of the north."

"Can I get you anything else, sir?"

"No, no, Koren, I'm just an old man thinking wistfully about the past. And waiting for this dreary winter to end. It seems like this winter will never end. Like the war, I'm afraid."

"Will the war end soon, sir?"

"What? This war has been going on for-" Paedris looked at Koren sharply. "Come here, sit down. We haven't talked about the war, now is a good time. What do you know of our enemy?"

"Uh." Koren thought about the stories he'd heard, likely mostly lies and exaggerations. People told children stories about Acedor to scare them.

"Let me guess," Paedris said with a dry humor, "you heard that if you were bad, Draylock would come on his terrible dragon, and take you away?"

"Yes, sir, something like that."

"Lord Draylock is a wizard named Mertis, he is a younger son of Duke Draylock of Savane province, in Acedor. Twin son, his brother was born a few minutes earlier, and so Mertis felt he had been cheated of his inheritance. Even though Mertis soon showed he had the power of a wizard, still he resented his brother, who would become Duke. Mertis grew jealous of other wizards in the court of Acedor, and went away for many years, it was later learned he had been studying dark magic. When he returned, he clouded the mind of the king, whispering of secret enemies, and under his spell, the king grew feeble and paranoid, he would not listen to the Wizards' Council. Mertis arranged to become the king's chancellor, then he became the real power in Acedor. He made plans to conquer other lands, but the Wizards' Council and several of the dukes had grown fearful of Mertis, and rebelled. The war was terrible, wizard against wizard, province against province. And brother against brother, for Mertis' own brother, by then the Duke of Draylock, had joined the rebellion."

"Why didn't all the Dukes rebel?"

"Because Mertis had cast spells on many of the dukes, so they were slaves to his will, but they didn't realize they were slaves. That is the cleverness of such an evil spell," Paedris spat out the words as if they made a sour taste in his mouth, "it makes the victims believe they are doing what they wanted in the first place. They actually believed Mertis was protecting the rightful king, and that Mertis' brother was conspiring against Acedor. In the battle, Mertis killed his elder brother, and declared himself Lord Draylock. After he captured Savane province and subdued his brother's remaining army, he turned and struck at his enemies, who had seized the royal castle, with the last of the Wizards' Council. They had hoped to restore the king to health and break the spell, but Mertis was too clever for them. When they tried to break the spell, the king died, and they lost all hope. Most of the wizards stayed behind to fight Mertis, while the rebel army retreated to the east beyond the border of Acedor, carrying the Cornerstone with them. Those rebels founded Tarador, and continued their fight to this day. Mertis let them go, for he had much to do to consolidate his control, and fighting the Wizards' Council drained his strength for many years."

"He defeated the Wizards' Council by himself? Dark magic is more powerful than good magic?"

"No!" Paedris almost shouted the answer. The power of dark magic was a subject that angered Paedris. "No, quite the opposite, Koren. Tell me, does it take more effort to plow a field, plant seeds and raise a field of corn, or to burn that field?"

Koren thought for a moment, sure this must be a trick question. "To burn a field takes no effort," he answered slowly, "once you get a fire started. Corn plants won't burn much if they're green, they need to be-"

"Yes, yes. My point is, it is so much easier to destroy, than to build. Dark magic is used only to destroy, it cannot *create* anything, it lack the strength to create, or to heal, or to build. Mertis didn't defeat the Wizards' Council by himself, he had an army behind him, and enough soldiers with swords, spears and arrows can overwhelm any wizard. And Mertis didn't care how many soldiers' lives he wasted to destroy the Wizards' Council, while the other wizards wanted as little blood shed as possible. Remember this, Koren, if you are ever faced with the enemy; know that many of their officers are under spells, and their will is not their own. They are slaves to Mertis, you should not hate them, you should pity them. The human soldiers of Acedor have their minds poisoned against us since the day they are born; they know only hatred, cruelty and fear. And the orcs, well, they needed no magical spells to join forces with Mertis."

"This Mertis is Draylock? And he's real?" Koren had always thought it was only a story, that there was no real Draylock. "Not the *same* Lord Draylock, he can't be, can he? Didn't this all happen a very long time ago?"

The wizard looked out the window for a long time, lost in thought. When he spoke, his voice was low and sounded as if he were far away. "The same. Mertis seized power in Acedor almost one thousand, seven hundred years ago now. And he is still alive, his body a mere husk by now, his life sustained through the power of dark magic, draining the life from young slaves, killing them to keep himself attached to this world by a thin cord. By now, there is nothing left of Mertis the man, for one of the great dangers of using dark magic is that the demons of the spirit world cannot be controlled for long. When Mertis chose to use dark magic, without knowing the risks, he himself became slave to a demon of the underworld. He cracked open a sliver of a gate, through which demons are trying to enter our world. That is what I fight against. If Tarador is defeated, the demons will grow so strong, they will tear asunder the borders between the spirit world and our world, and our world will descend into darkness, forever."

The next day, Koren went to the stables to feed, exercise and brush Thunderbolt. For much of the morning, he walked around in a daze, for he had slept hardly at all, his mind filled with thoughts of evil wizardry and demons. As he filled Thunderbolt's feed bucket from the oats bin, he asked the stable master "Sir? Do you think horses get tired of eating the same food, every day?"

"Huh?" The man asked, looking up from his account books. "They're horses. Why? Is Thunderbolt off his feed?" The stable master did not want to hear of any problems with Koren's horse; that devil beast had made his life difficult every day from its birth until Koren came into the stables.

"No, no, he eats fine, sir. It's, he likes it when I bring him carrots, and apples, but mostly he eats these oats, and hay. It's not very tasty."

"Tasty? What? Koren, what's this about?" The stable master put aside the account book and rose from the cubbyhole he used as an office.

"It's nothing, Paedris just said last night that he is tired of eating bland food. He meant, our food, here in Tarador."

"Oh, is that all?" The stable master cuffed Koren on the shoulder. "You should talk to Martel, you know Martel?"

"Yes, why Martel?" Martel was a friendly stable hand, a man with glossy dark hair and a full mustache he seemed to be proud of.

The stable master shrugged. "Martel is from Estada, like Paedris."

Koren blinked. "I thought he was from Stade." He pronounced the word 'shtade' in the Taradoran accent.

"Ha ha." The stable master chuckled. "Stade is what we in Tarador call Martel's homeland. *They* call it Estada."

Koren found Martel unloading bales of hay from a wagon, and pitched in to help. "Martel? You're from Estada, right? Paedris told me last night that he misses the food from your land."

Martel grunted. "The food here is what we feed to babies in Estada, it has no flavor. My wife, ah! She came here with me, she can cook real food! You should come to dinner at my house, I will show you what good food tastes like."

The dreary winter dragged on, and nothing much of importance happened around the castle. Koren was pleased to see that, compared to winters in Crebbs Ford; the season in Tarador's capital city was milder. Milder did not mean it was warm, in fact, having more rain than snow seemed to make the air more damp, and the cold seeped into Koren's clothes, some days worse than any cold he'd known in snowy Winterthur province. The cold dampness saturated the gray stones of the wizard's tower; Koren had to keep fires roaring in the stoves on both the floors of both the wizard's living and sleeping quarters, and the laboratory where he spent most of his time. The floor where Koren slept had no nice iron stove, just a small fireplace that seemed to let most of the heat go up the chimney. His little room was just warm enough in the evenings, but by the time he woke up in the mornings, he hated to crawl out from under the heavy pile of blankets of his bed. Fortunately, as a boy growing up in Winterthur, he had learned a few tricks to deal with cold mornings. When he went to bed, he rolled up clothes for morning and tucked them in next to him, so they would be warm when he put them on. And he had a small iron sort of basket that would hold hot coals overnight, usually there were one or two coals still glowing a dull orange in the morning, which he could use to get a fire started. His routine was to get dressed while still under the blankets, then wrap himself in a blanket and scurry across the floor to get a fire started. Once flames were flickering in the fireplace, he ducked back in bed for a quarter of an hour, while the fire raised the temperature of the room to a tolerable level. After that, he went up the stairs to stoke the fires in the stoves for the wizard, put water on for coffee, and went across the courtyard to fetch breakfast from the royal kitchens. The cooks there always had a covered tray ready for the wizard, while Koren could usually count on a bowl of porridge and maybe a buttered roll. Sometimes there was also an egg, or a piece of fruit for Koren, and he was always sure to thank the cooks for that. It still seemed like a bit of a miracle to Koren, how he got food at the castle. To get milk, he did not need to lead a cow into a barn, and get a pitcher, which he had first scrubbed clean and rinsed with boiling water, and sit next to the cow milking it. Instead, the royal kitchens had milk in cooled ceramic jugs. For butter, he did not have to skim the cream off the top of a pitcher, and spend what seemed like forever plunging a churn up and down to make butter; here it was ready in earthen crocks. Even his simple morning porridge was not oats he had gathered from a field during harvest season, the oats here were in big wooden bins. He didn't even have to start a fire, and cook the porridge by himself, the royal cooks did that for him, all he needed to do was bring a bowl for the cooks to ladle fresh steaming hot porridge into. And then they spooned fresh cream on top, and a couple cubes of maple sugar! Koren thought he was in heaven his first week living in the castle.

Winter evenings, when he lay in bed after putting out the candle, watching the fire slowly dying down to embers and feeling the cold creeping in, Koren considered how lucky he was to be inside, safe from the nasty weather, with a bed, and warm clothes and blankets, and a fireplace, and hot food waiting for him in the morning. He would not, he had realized after the second snowfall, have survived the winter on his own in the wilderness. The few supplies his parents had left him with were not enough for him to have made warm clothes, and construct a shelter, and assure enough food to last until springtime. As miserable as winter was in Linden, it was colder in the north, and without the royal carriage to whisk him from LeVanne, he would not have been able to walk much further south, not on his own, and with having to stop along the way to hunt, fish and forage for food. That thought had caused Koren to cry himself to sleep one particularly gray, cold and dreary night. When his parents had abandoned him, Koren had foolishly thought at first they had been careful to leave him with the means to survive on his own. He now knew they had not cared whether he lived or died, only that they were well rid of him, forever.

That was a hard thing for a boy to realize, alone on a cold and dark night.

As the winter wore on, Koren and Ariana continued to search the ancient scrolls for hints of where they might find the Cornerstone. Some days, Koren genuinely was eager to tackle the puzzle of what had happened to the Cornerstone. Most days, however, what he cared about was being in the royal palace, where he had a break from his duties, and where it was always warm, and well-lit by lamps and large windows, and there was always plenty of delicious food at Ariana's table. And there was also an opportunity to spend time with Ariana, with her smile, and her perfumed hair, and the way she tilted her head, and her voice that was music to Koren's ear, and the way she delicately bit her thumbnail when she was reading, and the way the curly locks of her hair kept falling forward around her face, and she would either toss her head, or brush the hair out of her face, tucking it behind her ear, and-

And Koren needed to concentrate on reading.

Reading the dusty old scrolls so far had done nothing but make Koren sneeze, until Ariana found a scroll about plans for expanding the castle, hundreds of years before the battle when the Cornerstone was lost. The plans showed there was a wide vault that ran almost underneath the Cornerstone's chamber. The vault had originally carried water, but the plans showed the vault had been blocked at both ends, and abandoned. Maybe, Ariana had said excitedly, the enemy had cut a hole in the floor, lowered the Cornerstone into the vault, and then replaced the floor!

When the princess and the servant boy found time to search for the Cornerstone, they looked for a way into the old vault. Mostly, Koren searched on his own, when he wasn't running errands for the wizard. When Ariana was able to join him, she had to bring along her personal guard, a gentle, older man named Duston who had retired from being a soldier. Duston's job was to keep Ariana, and her dignity as a princess, out of trouble. Including, avoiding scandals such as her sneaking around the castle with a handsome young boy. Duston had a daughter of his own, older than Ariana, and, although he took orders from Carlana, he felt the young princess needed freedom to be a girl. So, unless she was actually in danger, Duston pretty much let Ariana do what she wanted, under his supervision.

After two months of exploring the back walls of storerooms, and crawling in tight spaces between walls, Koren found what he thought must be a way into the old vault. At the end of a narrow crawlspace, there was an iron gate, with a lock corroded with centuries of rust. Koren met Ariana and Duston there one cold winter evening, after the princess had supposedly gone to sleep.

Koren pulled tools out of a leather bag. "The lock is rusted shut, but one of the hinges is broken. I brought a hammer and chisel to knock the other hinge open."

Ariana picked up the hammer, and looked at the gate. "Won't that make a lot of noise?" She gave the hammer to Koren.

"Yup, but the guard above us is wearing iron-soled shoes." Koren pointed at the low ceiling, and put a finger to his lips.

Ariana could hear, faintly through the rock, the clicking of a heavy man's shoes on a stone floor. They counted; the guard took eighteen steps in one direction, turned, and took eighteen steps back.

"You go back outside, and warn us if the guard stops."

"Us?" Duston asked skeptically.

"Uh," Koren said uncertainly, "I can't hold this gate by myself."

"Please, Duston." Ariana pleaded, in the little girl voice that she had been using to manipulate men since she was barely able to walk. "It won't hurt anything. Besides, I'm the crown princess, this gate belongs to me, doesn't it?"

Duston scratched his short gray beard while he thought. "Your mother, the Regent, may disagree with you there, young missy." He winked and smiled. "But she's never going to know, is she?"

"OK!" Ariana said with a grin, and walked back down to the entrance, which was behind stacked crates in a dusty storeroom. She counted "…sixteen, seventeen, eighteen, turn, and, one, two-"

Koren tapped the chisel with the hammer, knocking the hinge pin upward slightly. He tried to tap in rhythm with the faint sounds of the boots above.

"Seventeen, eighteen, Koren, stop!" Ariana whispered.

"Almost there."

The guard resumed his patrol, and Koren resumed tapping with the hammer, in time with the footfalls. "Almost there, Duston, hold the gate up a bit."

"Ugh, it's heavy for my old bones, hurry it up, if you can."

Just as the pin came out, and the gate sagged against the wall with a clanging sound, Ariana called out a warning. "The guard stopped walking!"

Koren sit still, his heart pounding. If they were caught, he could be in serious trouble. As the crown princess, all Ariana had to worry about was a scolding from her mother. Koren might be banished from the castle. He sighed with relief when he heard the guard above resume patrolling.

"Come, on." Koren called out, squeezing around the broken gate, and sliding down into the old vault. The crown princess was right behind him.

"Yuck!" Ariana said in disgust, lifting her shoe off the floor.

"Tsch." Duston exhaled in dismay. "I'll need to be cleaning those shoes before morning, lest your mother notice you weren't snug in your bed all night."

"The floor is wet. Must be water still seeping in from below. Be careful." Koren led the way, holding his torch out in front of him. The flickering flames cast eerie shadows on the curved walls of the old vault.

"How much further?" Ariana asked, trying to step around the slimiest of the puddles. She would ask Nurelka to clean the shoes.

Koren looked up. "We should be right under the hallway that leads to the Cornerstone chamber. But I don't see any signs that someone cut a hole in the roof. Look, the stones fit so close together there isn't any mortar between the blocks." He held the torch near the floor, and scraped slime away with his foot. "And there aren't any marks like there should be, if a heavy object was dragged down here." Now that they were in the vault, he could see it was barely wide enough to hold the Cornerstone. It had looked so much larger on the old scrolls.

"Let's keep going." Ariana suggested. "The other end can't be far."

The floor of the vault sloped downward, and the puddles grew deeper as they walked further into the vault. Koren had to brush spider webs away with his torch. Finally, they came to the end of the vault, a solid stone wall. If the Cornerstone had ever been there, it wasn't there now.

Ariana could sense Koren's disappointment. "Maybe it's behind this wall?"

"There's something carved into the stones here." Koren said. He wiped the grime away from the stone with a rag. "Oh!"

"What is it?"

Koren snorted in disgust. "It says 'Nestor was here, the Cornerstone is not. May you who read this inscription have better fortune'. And there's a date, but I can't read it."

"Nestor was the second Trehayme king of Tarador." Ariana exclaimed. She reached out and traced the carving with her fingers. "My ancestor wrote this with his own hand."

"We're not the first to search this vault for the Cornerstone."

"No," Ariana laughed. "Did you think we would really find the Cornerstone?"

Deep in his heart, Koren thought they would find the Cornerstone, that somehow it was his fate to find it. In fact, somehow he had been certain he would find it. "Yes, I guess so. You didn't? Then why search for it?"

Ariana shrugged. "It's more fun than doing needlepoint." She stuck out her tongue.

"Don't be discouraged, young man, you got a lot further than I did, back when I was your age, and searching for the Cornerstone myself." Duston held his torch close to the inscription, and traced Nestor's name with his finger in awe.

Koren shook his head. Finding Nestor's mocking inscription had taken all the fun out of searching for the Cornerstone. "Let's go, it's cold down here." He grumbled.

It was not until a week later that Ariana had another opportunity to invite Koren to lunch in her library. The table was laden with delicious treats, but Koren saw that Ariana had books and scrolls piled on top of a desk. "How about this one?" Ariana suggested. "It's a record of how the original castle was expanded-"

"This isn't about that stupid Cornerstone again, is it?"

"I thought you liked looking for the Cornerstone."

"I did, when I thought we had a real chance to find it. If King Nestor, with all his troops and advisors, couldn't find it, what chance do we have?"

Ariana bit her lower lip, and looked down to blink away a tear. She had so wanted to have a nice afternoon with Koren; the day was sunny and warm enough for the windows to be cracked open, the light breeze brought in scents that held the promise of springtime, Ariana had gone down to the royal kitchens herself to make sure her table was set with Koren's favorite honey cakes, but he had hardly touched the food. "Koren, what's wrong?"

"Nothing." Koren said, feeling a little guilty. He saw the honey cakes, and knew Ariana had gone to extra trouble to make him happy. "I'm tired, is all. This morning Thunderbolt was cranky and wanted to go for a long ride, and I didn't have time, because Paedris almost blew up his laboratory yesterday, and I had to straighten up."

Ariana had heard the explosion, and seen the yellow smoke rising from the highest chamber of the wizard's tower. "What was he doing?"

Koren managed a smile. "I never ask. It's better not to. Can I see that scroll?" The two sat quietly for a while, reading scrolls, or rather, Koren was engrossed in reading a scroll about the early days of the wizard's council, and Ariana was watching Koren. Whenever he looked up, she glanced away, pretending she was looking at a scroll, or a map, or nibbling on a honey cake. But she was looking at Koren, the way his thick curls of hair fell in front of his eyes, the curve of his jaw, the way his eyelids slowly blinked while he was reading. Her hero, the boy who had saved her from a bear, a raging river, and a pack of bandits. All by himself. And she couldn't even tell people how very brave he was, for that would draw the enemy's attention to him.

Ariana had heard about girls getting foolish crushes on boys; from listening to her maids, those silly girls fell in love with a different boy every week. Ariana was sure what she felt for Koren was different, of course it was. The boy she had a crush on was a true hero. But other girls probably thought their own crushes were true love, also. And true love was a romantic notion that a crown princess, and certainly not a queen, could not spend much time dreaming about. Queens married for political advantage, not for love. She sighed, loud enough for Koren to hear.

"Huh?" Koren asked. "Did you say something?"

"No. Um, Koren, do you ever think about getting married, someday?"

"Married?" A boy, who was not tired, and not intent on stuffing himself with honey cakes and reading about wizards, would have recognized the dreamy look on the crown princess's face, but Koren was very tired, and getting very stuffed with honey cakes. "No, I never thought about it, not really." Why did girls always want to talk about such things? "How about you?"

The dreamy look fell from Ariana's face. "Mother says I'll marry the son of a duke, whoever offers the best alliance within Tarador. Or maybe a prince from another kingdom. I'm sure mother will find someone suitable, someone horribly boring." She made a face.

"But, when you're queen, you could marry anyone you like!" Koren said with surprise. What good was being a queen if you couldn't do whatever you wanted?

"It's not like that. I have to think about what's best for Tarador, not only about what I want."

"I think that stinks! If I were king, I would marry any girl I liked."

"What kind of girl do you like?" Ariana asked, while twirling a stand of hair around her finger.

"Oh, I don't know, that's all too far away to think about now. It doesn't matter anyway. I'm living in a cubbyhole of the wizard's tower, that doesn't make me a good catch for girls."

"Some girls would think you're a good catch." Ariana said in a small voice. She hadn't thought about the subject of marriage from Koren's side. He was living in the royal castle, but in truth, he was only a penniless servant.

Koren shrugged. "Maybe someday, I can rent land for a farm somewhere. My father bought his own land, before he met my mother. My mother says he was the best catch in the whole village."

"You like farming?" Ariana asked, surprised. It didn't sound like fun to her.

"I know how to do it. You need a skill, if you're not going to be someone's servant your whole life. I mean, not you, you're a princess, and you'll be queen. You'll never have to worry about earning your keep."

The conversation was not going where Ariana wanted. "Would you like another honey cake?"

That evening, Koren was walking across the castle courtyard with Cully, after helping the other servant boy move furniture from a part of the castle that was going to be renovated. It was hard work, and the tired boys were headed to the kitchens to scrounge up whatever food was available. "Look, it's the princess," Cully whispered as he grabbed Koren's arm. Ariana was standing on a stone platform up against the castle wall, bundled up in fine, heavy clothes, her hair waving gently in the cold breeze. "She's reviewing the evening changing of the guard." Cully explained.

"I want to see," Koren said, standing on his toes to see above the crowd. "Let's go around the side." They squeezed their way along the wall, until they were in front, close to Ariana's personal guards. A guard held out a hand to prevent them getting closer, then recognized Koren and nodded. The boys stood quietly, waiting for the princess to signal the ceremony to begin. Ariana looked around the assembled crowd, from left to right, and when she saw Koren, she smiled, and winked at him, then gestured the guards to begin.

Cully at first thought the princess had smiled and winked at him, which froze him in place for a second. When he realized Koren had been the target of her affections, he looked at the other boy, and frowned. They stood silently until the guard had been changed, and the princess escorted back inside the castle. "Brother, you are in trouble," Cully said in a low voice, shaking his head.

"Huh? What do you mean?"

"I saw you making goo-goo eyes at the princess. What in the world are you thinking? Not thinking, you must be."

"I was not making... goo-goo eyes at Ari- at the princess."

"You should have seen your face, you were all 'Oh, I'm so in lu-uh-uv with her, the princess is my everything'." Cully said mockingly.

"Was not!" Koren said hotly, his face red from embarrassment.

"Was too! I know what I saw! Seriously, you must be crazy in the head, or something. She's the crown princess, she's going to be *Queen* soon. Her mother could have your head chopped off, if she saw you looking at the princess that way. Listen, brother, I know you're more used to being around goats than royalty, but they're up here,"

Cully stretched his hand up way high over his head, "and we're down there someplace," he pointed down at the muddy ground. "You can't even *think* about what you're thinking. You know that, right? She's going to marry some duke's son, or a prince from a foreign land. And you may not always be a servant, but you will always be common-born."

Koren looked down at the ground, miserably. "I know, I know all that. You don't need to tell me, I know who I am." A lowly servant, a boy without a family. "I'm grateful to be where I am, with a roof over my head, and food in my belly. I don't ask for more than that."

"Speaking of food in my belly, let's get to the kitchens, before all these guards going off duty eat everything."

Seeing Nestor's inscription had dampened Koren's enthusiasm for finding the Cornerstone, but reading the musty old scrolls in Ariana's library renewed his interest. If the weather had been warmer, he might have put it aside, but as it was still winter, and there wasn't much else to do, the itch to find the Cornerstone came back quickly. As the winter snows began to melt, and patches of stubbly grass appeared in the muddy fields around the castle, Koren returned to studying ancient scrolls for clues about where the Cornerstone could have gone. Ariana, he became convinced, was right. There was not enough time, during the battle, for the enemy to have carried the massive Cornerstone away. Yet, it was also clearly not hidden anywhere in the castle, which had been thoroughly searched by many generations of kings, queens, princes and princesses, as Nestor's note attested.

"Paedris," Koren asked one night, as he cleaned up the wizard's dinner plates, "do you know about the Cornerstone of Acedor?"

"Oh, ho! Is that where you have been sneaking off to, my curious little friend?" The wizard asked with a raised eyebrow.

"You don't know?" Koren asked, surprised. Didn't wizards know everything?

"Er, well, yes, of course I did," Paedris lied. "I was waiting for you to speak to me. I suppose every young person in the castle gets pulled into that fool's errand eventually. Don't worry, it's harmless fun, and you can learn a lot in the process."

"Did you ever search for the Cornerstone?"

"Me? Goodness, no. I haven't been that young in many years." The wizard was lost in thought for a moment. "Many, many years. No, I have never searched for it. Never even been to the old Cornerstone chamber, although I suppose I should someday."

"The scrolls say the enemy was not in the castle long enough, before Aldus Trehayme drove them away, for the Cornerstone to have been hauled away."

"That, young Koren, is why it is such a famous mystery!"

Melting of the winter snow couldn't come fast enough for Ariana, and the cold, gray weather wasn't the only issue weighing on her mind. She was running out of money, keeping her personal guard stationed in the Thrallren woods. The men, although they were helping themselves to game and fish in that dense forest, with Duke Yarron's permission, still needed an enormous amount of supplies for themselves and their horses; most of the money for those supplies came out of Ariana's personal account, which had almost run dry. Yarron had sent a private note offering to pay part of the cost out of his own pocket, so much he valued royal troops patrolling his borders, but Ariana had stubbornly insisted that supplies for royal troops be paid for with royal funds, so she had summoned the royal chancellor.

The chancellor was an old man, ancient to Ariana's young eyes; he became chancellor back when her grandfather was king of Tarador, and to Ariana's memory, always had white hair and a long white mustache. He had been Tarador's chancellor for twenty three years, serving two kings and now, one Regent. The years since Ariana's father died had aged him, perhaps more than all the other years combined, yet he had the energy of a younger man, and he was determined to remain in his job at least until Ariana sat on the throne. If that ever happened.

"Chancellor Kallron," Ariana bowed slightly in deference to the man's age, and he bowed lower in deference to her royalty. "Please come in, sit down. Would you like a glass of wine?"

"Wine? No, your Highness, I am afraid that at my age, it goes to my head far too easily." In truth, the chancellor rarely drank wine, or alcohol of any kind. He preferred to keep a clear head, while wine loosened other people's tongues, and he could listen to things that perhaps should not be said. He pointed to the teapot on the table. "If the tea is hot, I would appreciate a cup." Tea, for the chancellor, was far more than a beverage. The time spent placing a cup in front of him, carefully pouring tea from the pot, selecting a lump of sugar, adding a spoonful of cream, stirring the sweetened tea, setting the spoon down on a napkin, and finally raising the cup to his lips and sipping, all gave him time, time to observe. He needed time to observe the princess, for she had given no hint of what she wanted, when she sent the note inviting, or summoning, the chancellor. He preferred to know the purpose of a meeting before he walked into the room. To know the purpose, so he could plan, and assure that he walked out of the meeting with what he wanted, or at least to limit the damage.

What he observed gave him no clue as to what the princess wanted, although her clothes, casual by the standards expected of a crown princess, made it clear to him this was no formal matter of state. He also observed several open books on the table, pushed to the side, one book with a plate of cookies on top, and a half-nibbled cookie on a napkin in front of the princess. There was also a scroll on which the princess had been practicing her penmanship; indeed tiny smeared dots of ink stained her fingers, which she hadn't washed away before the chancellor arrived. So, she was relaxed, going about her day, and this particular meeting was not something she had prepared overmuch for. Unless, that is what she wanted the chancellor to think, to throw him off balance, although he did not think she had learned such guile yet. "You wished to speak with me, your Highness?" He said as he carefully set down the teacup in its saucer.

"Yes, I need to borrow money, to cover the expenses of stationing my personal guard in the Thrallren woods. You can arrange a loan from the royal treasury?"

The chancellor found the princess to be refreshingly direct, she did not waste time with pleasantries or talking around the issue; she just said what she wanted. Sometimes the chancellor forgot that the crown princess used to be the little girl he bounced on his knee when she was barely able to walk, and she likely still thought of him more as kindly Uncle Kallron, rather than as Chancellor Kallron. He had an answer ready, for Ariana's mother had already discussed the issue with him, and the princess was not going to like the answer. "Ah, yes, unfortunately, your Highness, your mother has directed me not to release any funds from the royal treasury to you. Her words to me were that if you wish to defy her by keeping your guard in the Thrallren, you can figure out how to pay for them yourself." Seeing the crestfallen look on the princess' face, he hastened to add "Perhaps your mother simply wishes you to ask her directly. I think that she was rather hurt by your actions." Having the Regent of the land also be the mother of the crown princess made Kallron's position between them terribly difficult, with affairs of state getting confused by personal feelings and family business.

The princess' face scrunched up with stubborn determination. "I am not going to go ask my mommy for money. I don't want the money to buy something silly like a new dress, I *need* the money to protect our borders, since my mother hasn't see fit to do it properly herself."

Kallron couldn't completely suppress a wry smile. "Yes, your mother told me you would say that. Perhaps this is an opportunity for you to develop your diplomatic skills? When you are queen, there will be many times when you will need to persuade others to do as you wish, rather than merely issuing others."

"I know, I know, you keep telling me that." She shook her head, and brushed aside the curls of hair that cascaded over her face. "And I will, but not now. I just can't think straight when it's my mother I'm talking to."

Nor can she, when she is talking to you, the chancellor thought, but kept silent.

"Then, I shall have to borrow money from one of the merchant banking houses. You can arrange that?"

The chancellor nodded. This too, he had anticipated, when Carlana told him her daughter could not borrow from the royal treasury. "I can, however, I must warn you, it will be expensive, particularly as you will be borrowing the money for several years."

"Expensive? Why? They know I'll pay them back once I become queen." Who would hesitate to loan money to the monarch of the realm?

"Forgive an old man for rambling on a bit, your Highness, but I think this is a good opportunity to instruct you about banking and finance. Just a bit, I promise." He added, but instead of the frown he expected when he mentioned 'instruction', the princess leaned forward attentively. The prospect of becoming queen in just a few years had made her interested in subjects that had tended to bore her when she was younger. "The banking houses in Tarador get most of their money from foreign lands-"

"Why? We don't have enough money here in Tarador?"

"Certainly there are enough coins going around, your Highness, but the war with Acedor, particularly recently, our needs for grain, war materials and, well, almost everything, exceeds the amounts available within our borders. To make up the difference, we have needed to buy from foreigners. Even the royal treasury borrows temporarily from the merchant banking houses, to tide us over during the year, until harvest time when taxes are collected. The amount we have had to pay to borrow money has been increasing every year since your father died. And those are short-term loans, backed by the full credit of the state."

"The cost to borrow is going up, because foreigners are afraid my mother will lose the war?"

"The fear that *Tarador* will lose the war does drive up the cost of borrowing." The chancellor was uncomfortable with Ariana criticizing the Regent he owed his loyalty to.

"But mostly the fear is that the costs of the war, of defending our borders," he looked the princess in the eye at that remark, "will stretch our resources so much, that we will not be able to repay the loans. Or at least not repay them on time, which is almost as bad, as far as the banking houses are concerned. It is uncertainty, you see, that drives fear, and fear drives the cost of borrowing."

"You're saying it would be expensive me to borrow money, because people fear the royal treasury will be empty by the time I become queen, and I won't be able to pay them?" She had seen the gold and silver in the royal treasury vault beneath the palace, and couldn't imagine it ever going empty. And that was only one vault, which she had been told was rather small, as vaults go.

"Yes, and there are other fears, when the borrower is yourself. This would be a personal loan to you, but paid back with future state funds. That is an unusual arrangement, and the banking houses won't like it."

Ariana's cheeks flushed red. "They think I may decide not to pay them once I am on the throne? They question my honor?"

"Your honor, no. May I speak frankly, your Highness?"

"Always, chancellor." Now she was being formal.

"In addition to the risk that Tarador may lose the war, or that the war may deplete our finances, with loaning money to you, there are two other risks. First, there is the risk that if the war begins to go badly against us, your mother may be replaced as Regent, and that would present the risk of the Trehayme family losing the throne. In which case, you will not become queen."

Hearing this, Ariana's face became pale, as if she'd just fallen ill. "And the second reason?" She asked, fearing she knew the answer.

"Forgive me for saying this, your Highness, but the second reason is-"

"If I am killed before my sixteenth birthday."

"Unpleasant though it is to think about, yes, your Highness. That is a risk that must be considered, by any banking house. If you do not become queen, whoever sits on the throne would be under no obligation to repay your personal debts."

Ariana looked out the window and bit her fingernails for a moment while she thought. "Wait here please, chancellor." She rose from the chair and walked across the room, through the doorway to her bedchamber, where her maid Nurelka was discretely waiting. It only took her a minute to come back, with a thick red folded cloth in her hands. She sat back down, and unfolded the cloth to reveal a gold ring with a large rectangular emerald, surrounded by six diamonds. "Would a banking house be happy if they could hold onto this, until I repay them?"

The chancellor's eyebrows flew up in surprise. "Your Highness, royal jewels can't be used for-"

"Oh, hush, chancellor, my father's mother gave this to me on my fourth birthday, so it's my personal property. It belonged to her mother. I rarely wear it, because it's rather an old style, with that chunky emerald and the scrollwork on the gold."

The chancellor reflected that the 'chunkiness' of the emerald came from its substantial size, which made the gem very valuable. "Your Highness, at the risk of sounding like Charl Fusting, this is indeed most irregular." The thought of royal jewels ending up in a pawnshop horrified him. Sometimes he needed to remind himself that he worked for people who owned palaces and had their own armies. Fabulous jewels were nothing but baubles to such people.

"Like I said, I rarely wear it, I don't think it would be recognized by anyone outside the palace. It's not doing me any good by sitting at the bottom of a drawer. How much do you think I could borrow against this ring?"

Kallron's mind was racing to think of how he could discretely, with the *utmost discretion*, have someone approach a merchant banker with the large and distinctive ring. "Your Highness, you could easily borrow enough funds to keep your guard in the Thrallren for years. This ring is, in fact, far too valuable to-"

"No, use this one. I may need additional money in the future, and I don't want to keep going back to the banking houses. You can arrange it?"

"If you insist, your Highness, certainly I can handle this discretely."

"Thank you. As part of your discretion, you will not mention this to my mother."

"I will have to tell your mother the truth if she asks, your Highness."

Ariana laughed. "Oh, she will, she will. Don't mention it until then, I rather like the idea of my mother waiting a while, thinking I'll come crawling to her for money."

Walking slowly so as not to spill anything, Koren climbed the steps of the tower, up to Paedris' study. It had taken him most of the day to prepare a special dinner for Paedris. The cooks in the royal kitchens had looked skeptically at the strange foreign spices Martel had given to Koren, and had turned up their noses at the scents as Koren was cooking, but he thought it smelled and tasted delicious. The wizard looked away from the scroll he was studying, and sniffed the air, his eyebrows lifted in surprise. "It can't be! Is that tordalla soup?"

Koren set the tray down, and lifted the covers to show the food. "Tordalla soup, and chicken in-fi-er-no, I think that's how you say the word, with corn cakes and rice."

The wizard almost trembled with delight as he lifted a spoon to his lips and tasted the soup. "Oh, that is splendid. The pepper is perfectly roasted, just a hint of sweetness. There is a new cook from Estada in the royal kitchens?"

"Oh, uh, no." Koren shifted from one foot to the other, embarrassed. "I made it."

"You?" Paedris looked at the food, then cut off a piece of chicken and closed his eyes as he tasted it. "Perfection. Perfection! Where, when, how did you learn to cook, to cook food from my homeland?"

"Do you know Martel Vazan, he works in the stables? He and his wife Izella are from Estada, from Tas Herridos?"

Paedris shook his head. "I don't know this Martel, Tas Herridos is in the far south of Estada, a long way from my home in La Murta. I didn't know one of my countrymen was here in the castle! He showed you how to cook?"

"No, his wife Izella showed me. I hope you like it."

"Like it?" The wizard rose from the chair and embraced Koren in a bear hug. When he sat back down, Paedris had to brush away a tear. "Thank you, Koren. People don't, they don't think of wizards as being human. We are. We have parents, and homes, and some of us have families, too. I had a family, one time. I have a grand daughter named Izella, although I haven't seen her in a long time. She is probably a grandmother by now." Paedris ate another bite of the chicken. "Ah, this reminds me of home. Sit down, eat!"

Koren wasn't much hungry, he'd been snacking on the food while he was cooking it, but he got a bowl of soup and a corn cake. "You had a family, sir?" The words were hardly out of his mouth, before he feared whether he should have asked such a personal question. Lord Salva was so often friendly that Koren sometimes for forgot about being merely a servant.

"Yes, I was married once." Paedris' right eyebrow raised in question. "You're surprised? Don't worry, most people are. When I was a young, and foolish wizard, feeling full of myself, and not yet aware of the great responsibility that comes with great power," the wizard paused to give Koren a sharp look, although Koren couldn't imagine why, "I was in the court of King Manello of Estada. I fell in love with a girl there, one of the king's nieces. My master, Cydall the wizard, warned me against it, but she was so, so, kind, and gentle. We met when she saw a butterfly knocked to the ground by a passing carriage, she held it carefully in her hand, and brought it to me, asking if I could heal its broken wing."

Koren waited while the wizard was lost in thought. After a minute had gone by, Koren loudly dropped his spoon on the table. "Sorry, sir. You were saying?"

"Eh? Oh, yes. The butterfly. I healed it, the wing was only bent, not broken, and she brought it to the window, and it flew away. Arposa, that's the Estadan word for butterfly, that's what I called her, after that. Arposa. We had four children, they grew up to be good people, all of them. My grandchildren, too, all good people, I had seventeen grandchildren."

"Had, sir?"

Paedris took a deep breath, composed himself, and ate another spoonful of soup. "Yes, had. They're dead now, most of them. Koren, how old do you think I am?"

"Uh, well, sir," Koren considered what to say, adults seemed to be offended if people though they looked old, "your hair has gray streaks, so maybe you are, fifty? But I've heard wizards live a long time, so, maybe, seventy?"

Paedris shook his head. "Koren, I am one hundred and eighty two years old. Wizards age slowly, we can use the power of the spirits to renew our bodies. So, I remained young, while my Arposa grew old. I was able to slow her aging, at a great strain to my powers, but in the end, she passed, as we all will, some day. So, you see, Koren, my master Cydall was right, it is not wise for a wizard to marry a regular person; it can only lead to heartache. And it can be cruel, for your love to see you remain young and healthy, while they become old and frail. My children have all passed, and most of my grandchildren also. When my last child died, I left Estada, to come here, and dedicate my power to defeating Acedor. That is my life now."

That sounded terribly sad to Koren. "Yes, sir."

"That's enough speaking of the past. We have this delicious food, let's enjoy."

Kyre Falco was in a foul mood. Rumors of Ariana roaming around the castle with Koren had reached his ears, and he was jealous. How could the crown princess choose to spend time with a commoner boy like Koren, instead of royalty like Kyre? Koren was nothing but a servant. He didn't even have a family!

Kyre was not the only person in the castle who didn't like to hear of Ariana spending time with a common servant. Duke Falco had ordered Kyre to become friends with Ariana, and Koren was in the way; Niles Forne decided something had to be done, to get rid of Koren. The man's scheming little mind had considered having Koren kidnapped, but since the boy was under the wizard's protection, such a plan was far too risky. No, this needed a careful plan, not something to be rushed into. He would start by making the castle an unpleasant place for Koren to live.

"He's coming. You know what to do?" Kyre whispered, as he stepped back into the shadows.

"We'll take care of it, your Grace." The boy Niles Forne had chosen for the task was a nephew of Baron Pendran, a vassal of Kyre's father. Utri was only a year older than Koren, but big for his age, with a round face and curly brownish hair. He had been trying to grow a mustache, but the hair on his upper lip was sparse, like a brown cat had rubbed up against him, and left some fur behind. "That stupid farm boy won't know you're involved."

Utri Pendran and three of his servants swaggered out into the courtyard, talking loudly and tossing a ball between them. Koren immediately sensed the group was trouble, and moved aside, but one of the boys ran next to him, to catch the ball. The boy pretended to trip, and fell into Koren, knocking them both to the ground. "Watch where you're going!" Utri shouted as he sprang to his feet.

Koren stood up warily and brushed the dirt off his clean shirt. He had been on his back from the palace, after having lunch with Ariana and looking at old maps, which Ariana loved to do. "Me watch out? You're the clumsy one!"

"Watch your mouth when you're speaking to your betters, boy." Utri snarled, and his servants laughed as they surrounded Koren.

Koren didn't recognize Utri, who had arrived at the castle only a week earlier. "Better? How? Better at tripping over your own feet?"

Utri's eyes narrowed. Now he was genuinely angry, not play-acting for Kyre. "You're the wizard's brat, aren't you? Koren?"

"Koren Bladewell."

"What I hear is, you're just Koren." Utri snarled. "You don't have a family name, because you don't have a family. Your family dumped you on the side of a road. Ha! What kind of scum were your parents?"

Before he could think, Koren jumped at Utri, knocking him to the ground and pounding the bigger boy with his fists. The three Pendran servants joined in, punching and kicking Koren, until they were pulled apart by a guard.

"What's this?" The guard asked, as he held Utri by his collar.

"Release me!" Utri demanded. "I'm the eldest nephew of Baron Pendran!"

To Koren's surprise, the guard stepped away from Utri. "Sorry, young sir, I didn't recognize you." The man scowled at Koren. "Koren, I expected better of you. Brawling in the courtyard? You be on your way."

"He attacked me!" Utri protested. "I demand satisfaction! It is my right, I am a Pendran, and he is a common servant."

The guard, who was also a common servant, was used to dealing with fights between the boys in the castle. "Yes, the law is on your side. So, if you want to fight, you can fight in the sparring ring."

Koren had never been in the sparring ring, where soldiers and guards trained. Kyre had invited Koren to watch him spar, but Koren had never been inside the ring. The guard opened the gate, and said gruffly "in you go. Just you, Utri, you'll not bring your friends along this time."

"I get to choose the weapons." Utri pointed out. "He hit me first."

The guard was surprised; he assumed the two boys would fight with their fists. "What's your weapon?"

"Swords." Utri said with a smile. He was good with a sword.

The guard frowned, then snapped his fingers. "Fine. Swords you want, swords you'll get." He opened the weapons locker, and pulled out two wooden, padded practice swords. Utri took one, tested it for balance, and cut the air with a series of strokes. "It'll do." He announced with a wink toward his servants.

The guard handed Koren the other sword. "Have you ever used a sword?" he asked in a low voice.

Koren shook his head. Other than play-fighting with sticks, the only weapons he'd ever held was a knife or a bow. Swords weren't any use on a farm.

"I can't tell you much in a short time, but even with the padding, these swords can hurt." The guard warned. "Normally you'd be wearing a padded jacket, but, as this is a duel, well, you'll have to do your best. I'll stop the fight if you are hurt bad."

Then the guard stepped outside the ring, and closed the gate behind him.

Utri held up his sword. Niles Forne's plan had not involved Utri whacking Koren with a sword, but Utri was enjoying the change in plan. He would teach the servant boy a lesson, and then the Falco family would owe the Pendrans a favor. "Do you yield?" Utri had never known anyone to yield before the fight had begun, but it was part of the rules that the question had to be asked.

Koren gritted his teeth. Why was he fighting? Utri had only told the truth about him; he had no family. But the smug Pendran boy had insulted Koren's parents, who were good people. It wasn't their fault they had to rid themselves of such a trouble-making son. "It's cold out here, but Hell will freeze over before I yield to you."

Utri grinned. This was going to be fun.

Koren held up his sword the way he had seen Kyre get ready to fight. Utri suddenly lashed out, sweeping his sword at Koren's face. Without Koren realizing what he was doing, his right hand raised his sword and blocked Utri's sword, knocking the other boy back.

Utri stepped away, warily. Koren had blocked him, blocked him so hard that Utri's arm hurt. The servant boy must have had combat training! Utri had intended to toy with Koren, smack him around until his whole body was bruised. It was not going to be that easy. Utri swept the sword up again, but at the last moment switched the sword to his left hand, aiming at Koren's exposed ribs.

And again, Koren's sword moved so fast it was a blur, this time hitting the flat of the blade against Utri's left hand, and Utri dropped the sword. "Ow!" Utri shouted, cradling his injured hand. "That hurt!"

"Oh, and you weren't trying to hurt me?" Koren asked. Was sword fighting this easy? It didn't look easy when other people were fighting. "Do you yield?" He asked with a smirk. "Or do you want me to smack you again? I can do this all day, if you want some bruises."

Utri's ears burned. A Pendran yield to a servant boy? He lunged for his sword, picked it up with his right hand, and stabbed at Koren's legs.

Koren knocked the sword aside, and Utri grabbed for his legs, tackling Koren and the two boys fell to the dirt, rolling around and punching each other.

"Enough!" A man's voice roared.

It was the royal weapons master, a tall, gruff man, who was never seen without his well-worn stiff leather combat vest. "You!" He pointed at Utri. "You're done. Step outside the ring." Utri started to sputter a protest, but the weapons master grabbed him by the front of his shirt, and tossed him toward the open gate. "You lost, boy. Be grateful I stopped the fight before you got hurt, or made an even bigger fool of yourself." The weapons master served the Regent, the Pendran family meant nothing to him. "And you!" He pointed at Koren, and he picked up the sword Utri had dropped. "Who trained you to fight like that?"

"N-no one, sir." Koren replied, surprised.

"You're either a liar, or the best natural sword fighter I ever saw. On guard!" Without another word, the weapons master stabbed the point of the padded sword directly at Koren's throat. The blow never landed, for Koren's sword flicked up and knocked it aside. But fighting the weapons master was not like fighting spoiled Utri Pendran, for the man was not discouraged. The force of Koren's sword caused the man to turn to the left, and he spun with the movement, his sword sweeping around to catch Koren off guard.

It didn't happen. Koren sword was waiting for him when the man turned, and the weapons master staggered backward, trying to catch his breath. Koren's sword had caught him under the ribs.

The fight went on, weapons master against servant boy, sword clashing against sword, until both had sweat dripping down their brows, despite the mid-winter cold. A crowd had gathered to watch the spectacle. Word of the weapons master fighting the wizard's boy swept through the castle like a wildfire! The excitement finally reached the ear of Carlana, who, by chance, was walking through the castle with Paedris. Both hurried to the windows that overlooked the sparring ring. The man and the boy circled each other, swords drooping toward the dirt, their arms too tired to hold them up.

"How can Koren have a chance against my master of weapons?" Carlana asked the wizard in a harsh whisper. "You said he couldn't use his powers!"

Paedris frowned. He should have anticipated this event. "He can't *project* his powers outside himself. Using a sword like that is within him, I can't block that."

"Someone needs to stop this, before people figure out that Koren is no ordinary boy." Carlana leaned out the window. "Hold! Drop your weapons!"

Hearing his Regent's voice, the weapons master dropped his sword to the dirt. Koren was so tired that he was slow to respond, until the sword fell out of his hand.

"The boy fights like a demon, your Highness." The weapons master gasped between breaths. "His technique his terrible, but I've never seen anyone so fast. Except you, of course, Lord Salva. Does the boy have a bit of wizard in him?"

Carlana exchanged a warning glance with Paedris. This is exactly what she was worried about. "Ho!" Paedris exclaimed. "A wizard? Koren? No, he is a farm boy, and a slow-witted one at that. But, since he is my servant, he wouldn't be much use guarding my tower while I sleep unless he could fight, now would he? I cast a spell on the boy, so he won't trip over his own sword."

The crowd, mostly soldiers and guards, murmured at that remark. Could the royal wizard cast a spell on them, also, to give them such lightning speed?

"I know what you're all thinking, and the answer is no. You think casting such a spell is easy? I don't have the energy to cover all of you. You lazy slugs must learn to fight the hard way!"

The weapons master bowed to the royal wizard. "Lord Salva, since the boy is your servant, would you mind if I trained him? He is fast, but unskilled."

Paedris stroked his beard, then nodded. "When he has time, yes, it would be good for him to get some exercise."

When Koren left the sparring ring, Utri was waiting. "You didn't beat me." The boy glared at him. "It wasn't a fair fight."

"I never said it was. The next time you want a good spanking, you know where to find me, Lord Putrid. Bring your friends, there's plenty more where that," Koren pointed to the angry bruise on Utri's left cheek, "came from." He brushed past Utri and his gang of servants, who instinctively stepped back warily. He was famished, and sore all over, even though the weapons master had barely touched him with his sword. When he walked out into the courtyard, Kyre ran up to him. "Koren, I'm sorry about Utri, he's a bully. Baron Pendran is a vassal of my father, I can ask for Utri to be sent home."

"No, I need to fight my own battles." Koren knew there were many Utris in the world; somehow he had to deal with them. "Besides, I don't think Utri will want to fight me again, after today." He grinned at that thought. Koren was still in a daze, over how fast he was with a sword.

Kyre held onto Koren's arm. "You need to be careful. Paedris is using you, and he doesn't care if you get hurt."

"What do you mean?"

"He put a spell on you, without telling you. Who knows what else he's done?"

"Paedris wouldn't hurt me." Koren protested.

Kyre shook his head. "Koren, you think Paedris is your friend. He's not. He's the royal wizard, and you are his servant, that's all you are. You're not the first servant Paedris had in that tower."

Koren blinked. Of course Paedris must have had other servants before him, but Koren had not thought much about it. "What are you saying? What happened to the others?"

"I hear most of them ran away. Some, nobody knows what happened to them." Kyre hinted darkly. "You be careful. Paedris is so powerful, he may hurt you without meaning to. But don't think he cares about you, you're just a servant. And Ariana may like looking at old maps with you, but never forget that she is the crown princess, and you're a commoner. Carlana will make sure Ariana never forgets that."

"I just want to be her friend."

"Koren, I may be your only real friend in this castle," Kyre lied, "because I don't need anything from you."

Koren shrugged. A minute ago, he had been happy that he beat Utri, and held his own against the weapons master. "I guess. If Paedris wants to hurt me, what can I do about it? Like you said, I'm just a servant. I don't even have a family to run home to."

"I think you need to be ready to run away, if something bad happens. Ariana can't help you; she's not yet the queen. And Carlana doesn't like you."

Carlana had never really been friendly to Koren. Having been thrown out of one home, he didn't like the idea of running away from another. Koren sighed.

"Here," Kyre reached into his pocket and pulled out a leather pouch, "take this."

Koren looked in the pouch. It held four gold coins. He was shocked. "I can't take this!" He had never seen so much money in his life.

Kyre waved his hand, as if gold coins were nothing special to him. "Take it, take it. If you need to run, you'll need to run far, and never come back. I'd like to offer you sanctuary, but if the Falcos defy the Regent, that would be treason."

"OK, I'll hold it someplace safe, and hope I never need it."

Kyre frowned. "I think you will, and sooner than you think." If Niles Forne's plan worked, Kyre said to himself, Koren would need it soon.

"You gave him *what*?" Niles Forne asked, shocked.

"It's only four gold coins, Forne, the Falcos can afford it." Kyre added defensively. "Besides, we want Koren to go far way, right? How far do you think he would get without money? Four gold coins is a good investment."

"Hmmf. Your *reasoning* is sound, young sire, but I think your *reason* is not. You feel sorry for this boy."

"Koren didn't do anything. It's not his fault." Kyre protested.

Forne snorted. "Koren is not your friend. His own parents didn't want him. I think you forget sometimes that Duke Falco is not only your father, he is your liege lord, and he gave you an order to get rid of Koren, so Ariana will need to find someone else as a companion."

"I know my father's orders, Forne."

"Knowing, and obeying, are two different things. You need to do both."

That evening, Niles Forne scribbled a letter to Duke Falco, informing him of the day's events. That Koren had been wizard-spelled to be blindingly fast with a sword was dismaying, but no great problem. The castle had been made a less pleasant place for Koren, Kyre had warned him he was in danger from Paedris, and Koren was now thinking maybe he needed to run away in the future. Now all Forne needed to do is give Koren a reason to think the time to run was *now*. But, Forne added to the letter, "I fear your son, although following my instructions, is sympathetic to the Bladewell boy. Kyre must take care, lest he become soft." Softness, Forne knew, was not allowed in the Falco family.

CHAPTER EIGHT

Koren had thought he could train with the weapons master when he wanted to, when he had time and felt like sparring. No such luck. Paedris had worked out a schedule with the weapons master, and Koren now had to report to the sparring ring three times a week, in addition to his own work for Paedris. And caring for Thunderbolt, and working in the stables to pay for the horse's keep. And the three times a week tutoring in writing, history and mathematics that Paedris had insisted for Koren. With the weapons master, there was training with the sword, of course, but also Koren learned to use a shield, a pike, a spear and a bow. The bow he liked best, he had always been deadly accurate with arrows when hunting, and now he never missed a target, even when Koren was on horseback and the target was also moving. The sword training was the worst. Instead of a chance to show off, and whack the weapons master with a practice sword, the training involved what the weapons master called Forms; endless repetitions of swinging the sword around, and placing his feet in exactly the correct position, and bending his elbow just so, until Koren's whole body ached, and his arms felt like they would fall off from weariness. Koren thought that, after training with the weapons master and the man's stupid Forms, that he was going to curl up in the Form of a ball, and be stuck in that Form forever, because he was so stiff and sore.

Between his two jobs, caring for his horse, and combat training, Koren decided he needed to forget about silly things like looking for a lost Cornerstone.

Koren was cleaning up after the wizard's dinner, when he lifted a knife, and balanced it on his finger, like the weapons master showed him to do with swords. "Sir," he asked, "I'm training to use weapons."

"Hmm? Yes, the weapons master tells me you are learning quickly." The weapons master had sounded overjoyed to have such a talented and obedient student, rather than the clumsy, arrogant royal children he was used to.

"Yes, sir. I am doing my best, sir." And Koren had the bruises and aching muscles to prove his efforts. "Am I going to get a real sword, sir? To protect you?"

"Eh? Why would I need you to protect-" Paedris sucked in a breath. Having to remember all the lies he'd told was getting to be all too much. "Oh, certainly, yes, of course, now that you are gaining skill, it is time for you to get a sword of your own. Yes, yes, that is a capital idea." Paedris hoped to venture out with the army in the summer, and would take Koren with him. For that, the boy needed weapons of his own, weapons he was familiar with, rather than whatever second-hand gear the army had available. Perhaps the weapons master had, no, Paedris had a better idea. Koren was working very hard, the boy deserved a reward. Something nice, but something that didn't seem like an indulgence. "A sword is a very personal thing, it needs to feel right in your hand. You should start with a short sword." The wizard saw Koren's face fall, so he hastened to add "The short sword is carried by most archers, as a secondary weapon. With your remarkable skill with a bow, it is unlikely you will be called upon to fight at short range." And, if Paedris could help it, Koren would not be called upon to fight at all, until he mastered his immense magical power. "Tomorrow, go to Hedurmur's in Linden, you know where the flower fountain is, near the clock tower? Hedurmur's shop is down the street to the north a block or two; I haven't been there in some time. Ask people when you get near, tell them you want to buy a sword from the dwarf."

"A dwarf? Hedurmur is a dwarf, sir?" Koren had seen dwarves around the castle; the dwarves had an ambassador who visited the castle at least once a week from his home just outside the main gate. And he'd seen dwarves in Crebbs Ford, a wagon came through the village to use the bridge once a year or so, and would stop outside the Golden Trout to sell their fine metalworking. But Koren had never spoken to a dwarf. Twice he had gone with his father to buy items from the dwarves, their metal plow blades lasted almost forever, his father had said, and needed sharpening only once each season. The first time, Koren had stayed under a tree with the family wagon while his father bargained for a good price, the second time Koren had shyly stood beside his father, watching the dwarves with fascination. Dwarves were, to his surprise, not as short as he expected, most were a good four or more feet tall! It was amusing to see some of the less-tall humans stretching themselves to full height when around the dwarves, when that height was not much more than half a foot taller than the visitors. The few dwarf women Koren had seen were lovely; petite with bright eyes, looking no different from miniature human women. It was the dwarf men who were somewhat exotic, being much more broad than a human man of the same height, and stronger. The stories Koren had heard of dwarves being inordinately proud of their beards appeared to be true, all the dwarf men Koren had seen had thick, luxurious beards, some adorned with beads or even gold ringlets.

"Yes, he is the chief of his clan here, he operates a metal shop. Take this," the wizard pulled a gold and silver token out of this pocket and gave it to Koren, it felt heavier than it should have, and was rather warm, "and go to Hedurmur, tell him I want you to have a proper sword, he can put it on my account."

"Oh, yes sir, thank you sir!"

Koren awoke early the next morning, eager to get his chores done and go into the city to see the dwarf. By two glasses before noon, his horse had been exercised, groomed and fed, the stoves in the tower were well stocked with wood and burning nicely, the wizard's dining area had been cleaned up after breakfast, and the wizard himself was happily puttering away in his laboratory, sipping from a fresh pot of coffee. Koren walked out through the main gate, greeting the guards, feeling the token Paedris had given him laying heavy in his pocket. Even in winter, the city of Linden was busy; wagons rolling about the streets, the markets open although the people selling wares were bundled up against the cold, huddling over small stoves while they waited for customers. Many of the merchants knew Koren, and called out to him, offering roots, spices and other such things he often bought for the wizard, but this day he only smiled and waved back. When he arrived at the fountain in front of the clock tower, he wandered north up several streets until he found the building that must belong to the dwarf. The front of the building looked like the entrance to a cave, Koren wondered how the dwarves had brought such large, heavy pieces of stone through the city streets, until he realized the stones were fake, being made of plaster. He ran his hand over the fake rock, which needed to be repainted in spots, where the bare plaster showed through. Suddenly, the heavy wood door was yanked open, and Koren was face to face with a dwarf. Or face to chest, since the top of the dwarf's head came up not quite to Koren's chin. The dwarf shrugged. "You humans think all dwarves live in caves, so we added this ridiculous facade on the building. You have business here?" He asked gruffly, looking skeptically at Koren's rough workman clothing.

"Yes, uh, sir?" Koren said, unsure how to address the dwarf. Or man, since the dwarf was a man, with a grey beard that draped halfway to his belt. "Lord Salva sent me?" He pulled the token out of his pocket and held it up.

"The wizard!" The dwarf exclaimed in surprise. "Come in, come in, kind sir. My name's Leggard, at your service. Why, we haven't heard from Lord Salva in many seasons. Too long!" He held the door open just wide enough for Koren to pass through, then closed it firmly. "My old bones can't stand this cold anymore." They entered a dark, low-ceilinged chamber that Leggard said apologetically was also just for show, through a larger door, and into a large, cheery room, with a cozy fire in the stone fireplace, and windows in the ceiling. Koren thought that having windows in a roof was strange, but they did let in a lot of light. The dwarf bowed to a figure sitting in a large leather chair in front of the fireplace. "Hedurmur, Lord Salva's servant to see you."

Hedurmur stood up, he was younger than Koren expected. Perhaps very young, for Hedurmur's beard was a mere dark shadow on his face. Although, he had lines on his face, so was he old, or was that just the way dwarves were? Koren must have been staring, for Hedurmur self-consciously ran a hand over his chin. "Odd looking isn't it?" The dwarf chuckled. "My face feels naked without it, and cold, too, bad time of year to be without a beard, I tell you. Magnificent beard I had, until an accident at the forge three days ago, and singed half of it off. Figured it best to shave it all off, and start over."

"Um, um, yes, Master Hedurmur, sir. I'm Koren, sir, Lord Salva's servant." Koren's own hand touched the wispy fuzz on his own face, before he realized what he was doing. He checked hopefully for beard growth in a polished metal mirror every morning, but so far he had been disappointed.

"Leggard, get our friend Koren here a drink, we have some mead, uh, hmm," Hedurmur considered Koren for a moment, "you are rather young, aren't you, eh? Hard for us to tell with you humans sometimes. Leggard, put some tea on to brew, I could use a cup myself, on this cold day. Koren, come sit by the fire while we discuss what brings you here today."

Koren explained about his need for a sword, and Hedurmur nodded when he heard the wizard had suggested a short sword.

"Mmm, a short sword, just the thing, just the thing, indeed. I've heard about you, Koren, your sparring with the weapons master. Heard you have incredible skill with a bow. If you'll be fighting, it will either be with a bow, at long range, or sword for short quarters. In close combat, a short sword is both faster and less clumsy that a broad sword. Leave the big showy metal to knight cavalry, and to the idiot sons of royalty so they can play at being soldiers. When your life is at stake, you want to move quickly, slash and stab, slash and stab. No room for a long sword in close combat, you get unlucky and the tip gets caught on something, and next eyeblink you're looking at your guts spilled out onto the ground." Hedurmur saw Koren's face go white at that thought; he'd forgotten how young the boy was. The dwarf coughed, and sipped tea while Koren stared into the fire for a moment, nervously slurping tea from his own cup. "Ah, if you're ever in trouble, you'll have the master wizard by your side, eh? Let's go find you a sword."

Hedurmur led the way into a room that was filled with weapons, both finished and in rough form. The dwarf selected a half dozen finished blades, thought as minute, and unlocked a cabinet to get out another blade, then carried them into yet another door, which opened into a long, narrow corridor, at the end of which was a door to a well-equipped blacksmith shop. Hedurmur walked through, shouting greetings and orders to several dwarf blacksmiths over the din of forges, bellows, pounding hammers, the hissing of hot metal being quenched in barrels of oil. Coming from the hot, closed air of the shop into an open courtyard was a shock; the cold winter air actually felt good. "Try these swords. Feel the balance, swing them around. If you find one that's close to what you want, I'll send for more of that type. And we can always modify a sword, or make a new one for you."

Koren didn't need Hedurmur's shop to change anything for him; the fourth sword he picked up was the one. As soon as he picked it up, he knew, it simply felt right in his hand, like it was a part of him. He was pretty sure this was the blade Hedurmur had taken from the locked cabinet, whatever that meant.

"You're sure, then?" Hedurmur asked, almost disappointed that he wouldn't be creating a custom sword for the wizard's servant.

"I'm sure, sir. Like it was made for me, it's perfect."

"Huh. Let's see how you use it." Hedurmur strapped a blunt brass covering over Koren's sword, and picked up a practice axe. They began sparring, slowly at first.

Koren had never sparred against a battle-axe, nor against an opponent shorter than he was. Shorter, but also stronger. Instead of using the proper forms and techniques, because Koren didn't know the proper technique for defending against an axe, he had to fall back on his speed and instinct, or he'd be falling on his behind in the dirt. The weapons master, Koren decided, need to teach axe fighting, and fighting against shorter enemies. Orcs were short in stature like dwarves, weren't they? And fought with axes.

On his third time being knocked to the ground, Hedurmur held up a hand in surrender. "Ah, if I still had a beard, I'd have to shave it off in shame, young Koren. With your speed, I'd wager you could beat me, or most anyone, with that sword. Or with a feather." The dwarf grumbled under his breath.

Koren was sore, and his arms felt ready to fall off. "I was lucky, sir, I've never fought an axe, or a dwarf." He swung his right shoulder around slowly, to loosen it. "You're very strong, sir."

"Bless you for taking it easy on an old dwarf's ego, I'll be sore in the morning, I wager. That's the sword for you, no question about it. I'll have it sharpened, and we'll deliver it to the wizard's tower tomorrow. What about the grip?" It was plain, rough brown leather. "I can make it nice, inscribe your name on it?"

Koren shook his head. He wasn't buying the sword; the money would come from the wizard's pockets. The sword would be Koren's to use while he served the wizard, but it would not be his property, any more than the brooms, mops or other tools around the tower. "No, sir, it is fine the way it is. Thank you, sir, this is a fine blade."

"None finer." Hedurmur beamed with pride, as he held the sword up and sighted down its length. "People think the strength of our metal comes from the way we work the metal in our forges, or the mixture of oil we use in the quench, or the quality of the ores we mine up in the mountains. The truth is, it's all that combined, plus more." He winked. "And that's all I'll say about it now. Give my regards to the wizard, please."

The Lady Carlana Trehayme, Regent of Tarador and mother of the crown princess, closed the heavy accounts book with a loud thump and rubbed her tired eyes. "Enough of these accounts for tonight, I am weary of keeping track of grain storage-"

"Forgive me, your Highness," Chancellor Kallron interrupted gently, "we must-"

"Enough!" Carlana fairly shouted, and emphatically slapped the leather cover of the accounts book. She picked up her half-empty wine glass and drained it in one long drink, then waved away the servant who was coming to refill the glass. "Yes, we need to look at this, but not tonight. Not tonight. Tomorrow morning, then we can look at this again, after I have breakfast, and perhaps a ride into the countryside. The wizard promised the weather would be better tomorrow; these cloudy, chilly days have me down. I do so need a ride."

Kallron rose from his chair, gathered up his books and scrolls, and bowed slightly to the Regent. "Certainly, your Highness." He would be up late, again, reviewing the royal accounts by himself, only royalty could decide when they wanted to work, or not. The rest of the world worked when they had to, which was all the time. "I shall wait upon you in the morning."

"Wait, Chancellor, before you go, how is my daughter able to maintain her personal guard in the Thrallren? I received a report from my captain there," she absent-mindedly searched for the particular scroll amongst the disorderly pile on her table before giving up, "and her troops are still there, with no sign they are preparing to leave anytime soon. In fact, the commander of her guard ordered new pack mules. Surely she has run out of money by now." Carlana had expected her daughter to raise the subject, and apologize, but the princess had not mentioned it once.

"Oh, that." Kallron had been dreading this question from the Regent. "Your daughter has been able to obtain a loan, from a merchant banker, a substantial loan. She will be able to fund her personal guard until she becomes queen."

"My daughter dealt with a banker? When? How did she-" Her eyes narrowed. "She didn't, *you* did, didn't you?"

"Not personally, I had it handled with extreme discretion. The banking house does not know the loan was to your daughter."

"Those tight-fisted merchants don't loan money to strangers. What did you do?" She asked suspiciously.

The chancellor felt like a fish on the end of a hook, dangling in front of the Regent. "The princess gave me an emerald ring, to use as surety for the loan. The merchant was led to believe the loan is to an unnamed baroness. Your daughter said she rarely wore this ring, so it is unlikely to be recognized?"

Carlana didn't know whether to be angry, proud or amused. "I know that ring. It's ugly, it's been in the family for years, but I don't think anyone has ever liked it." She smiled, with only one side of her mouth. "My daughter has out maneuvered me, I suppose I should be proud."

"She is a very determined young woman, your Highness. And clever."

"Determined and clever may also be viewed as stubborn and sneaky, chancellor. It does not help that my chancellor went behind my back."

"Please understand, I am in a very difficult position, your Highness. Legally, I am your daughter's chancellor, and I am responsible to her for personal matters. This did not affect state funds or property, and your daughter ordered me not to tell you."

"Don't make this a habit, chancellor."

Koren stored his tools in a closet on the second level of the wizard's tower, it was a cramped, dark room with no window. He was putting his tools back, one day after cleaning up after one of the wizard's explosive potion experiments, when he knocked a chisel off the shelf. It struck the floor, cutting a chip out of the stone. Koren wasn't concerned about damage to the floor, it was already scarred from centuries of hard use. He picked up the chisel, the same chisel he had used to break the iron gate in his failed search for the Cornerstone. The chisel was unharmed by its fall. He was about to place it back on the shelf, when the deep scratch in the floor caught his eye.

Getting down on his knees, Koren inspected the mark the chisel had made in the stone floor. It looked familiar. Without thinking what he was doing, he picked up a hammer, and used the chisel to make the gouge in the stone longer.

"Son of a-" He exclaimed.

The marks made by the chisel looked exactly like the scrape marks in the floor of the Cornerstone chamber! Everyone assumed the marks had been caused by the enemy dragging the Cornerstone across the floor. But, if those marks had been made by a chisel, the enemy must have carved the marks to make the people of Tarador *think* the Cornerstone had been hauled away. The scrolls Koren had read all said those scrape marks proved the Cornerstone had been dragged off its platform, and across the floor. Could he be the first person to see the truth?

But if the Cornerstone had not been dragged away, what had happened to it?

"Ho, young master Bladewell, are you ready?" The weapons master asked, as he wiped down the sword he had been using to spar against one of the royal brats he had to train. Or, had to waste his time with, since most of them were not serious about learning weapons craft. His time with Koren was, by contrast, pure delight, for the wizard's servant was diligent and never complained. And, having never used weapons other than a bow before, Koren had no bad habits the weapons master needed to correct.

"Yes, sir. I have a new sword, sir, Paedris bought it for me to use."

"The wizard bought it for you?" The man said with a frown. "A soldier should choose his own weapons."

"Oh, I did, sir, I chose this blade, I should say that Paedris paid for it. Hedurmur-"

"Hedurmur? You have a dwarvish blade? Give it here, let me see it." The man demanded eagerly. "Hmm, yes, a fine blade," he cut the air with it, and tested its balance, "a fine blade indeed! *I* don't have such a blade. This is true dwarfish make, not one of the human-made blades the dwarves only finish, this comes from the forges of Kzod itself." He sighted down the blade suspiciously, and tested the sharpness of the edge by lightly running it along one of the thick, heavy leather armor vests that hung on the wall of the weapons storeroom. Even with very light pressure, the blade sliced right through the leather, as if it were passing through water. The weapons master whistled admiringly. "Koren, try something for me," he asked as he handed the sword back to the boy, "test the edge by running your thumb along it. Carefully, go lightly!"

Koren did as he was asked, and was disappointed to feel the edge was dull. "Sir, I'm sorry, I only got this blade two days ago, I don't know why it isn't sharp." He said with shame. A soldier cares for his weapons; he should have honed it that morning.

"Ha! It is sharp," the weapons master held up the sliced-open vest to demonstrate, "that you have there is a magic-spelled blade. Dwarvish magic. It can't cut you. And it will almost never go dull, so don't you bother trying to sharpen it. Paedris himself has such a blade, yes, him and the old king, Ariana's father. Our wizard paid a handsome sum for a blade like that, I reckon. Don't you let anyone monkey with that blade; they'd slice themselves open to the bone before they knew it. Now, let's put a brass guard on your new blade, and see how you use it."

"Yes, sir," Koren said while gazing in awe at his sword. Neither Hedurmur nor Paedris had mentioned anything special about the blade. "Uh, sir, could you teach me to fight against an axe?"

"Hedurmur thumped you good, then?" The weapons master smiled. "All right, it's time you learned to fight against our foul orc enemy."

"Hello, Kyre!" Koren shouted across the courtyard, waving at his friend.

Kyre was still sore from his own sparring session with the weapons master the day before, and in a foul mood. It was late, and the early spring night was cold, he wanted to hurry across the courtyard and relax in front of a warm fire, not waste time chatting with the wizard's servant. And Niles Forne had again scolded Kyre for going out riding with Koren, rather than attending to his duties. Riding horses with the wizard's servant was one of the few times in a week that Kyre could relax and forget about rank and protocol for a while, for Koren knew nothing about either. "Koren, when we're in public, it is proper for you to call me 'your Grace'. I'm not a kitchen servant you can shout at." Forne's suggestion that Kyre was not loyal to his father had stung him, and Kyre had been avoiding Koren for a week.

"I am sorry, your Grace." Koren bowed slightly, the smile falling away from his face. "Good evening to you."

Kyre grunted and was about to walk away, when Koren spoke again. He had spent most of the day cooped up in the tower by himself, and was eager to talk to someone, anyone. And, being a teenage boy, he couldn't resist teasing his friend. "Full moon tonight, your Grace."

Kyre spun around, angry to be delayed in the cold by stupid small talk, when he had an idea. "Yes," he agreed with a wicked smile, "it is a full moon. Koren, you've been here in the castle a while now, have you ever climbed the old bell tower on the night of a full moon?"

Koren looked up at the bell tower, part of the original fortress. It was no longer part of the outer wall, so no guards patrolled on top of it. "No, why? I've been up there in daylight."

"It's a tradition. Young royal men do it to prove they are brave. But don't worry about it, you're just a servant." Kyre turned as if to leave.

Koren was hooked. "I can do it! What's so scary about an old tower?" Koren looked up at the stone spire. It wasn't even very tall, as towers go.

"The tower isn't scary, it's the full moon. When the enemy captured the castle, they were let inside by traitors, and one of the traitors killed the guards on top of that tower, before they could warn of the attack. The ghosts of those guards still patrol that tower, and you can only see them in the light of a full moon."

"Really?" Paedris had never mentioned that there was anything special about the light of a full moon.

"Really." Kyre said, as if he were a wizard himself. "I've been up there, you can hear them and see them." Kyre's felt butterflies in his stomach when he remembered being paralyzed by fear on the stairs of the tower. He had never actually gone all the way to the top of the tower in darkness, although he'd never admit that to anyone. "Of course," he said haughtily, "I wasn't scared. Koren, you don't have to do this."

And so, of course, Koren had to do it.

The steps that wound their way upward in the old bell tower were worn down in the center; so smooth they were almost slippery. This tower was even older than the tower where Paedris lived, the windows there were mere narrow slits, spaced wide apart. Koren had to feel his way, hugging the outside wall. When he reached what he thought was halfway up to the roof, he stopped. Was that voices he heard? He couldn't tell if it were voices, or his imagination. He peered out the window slit. The moon had gone behind a cloud during his climb, it was now so dark he could barely see his hand in front of his face.

Koren kept climbing, occasionally stumbling on an uneven step, until he saw an opening above him, dimly lit against the patchy clouds. The stone steps ended on a flat wooden floor. What Koren remembered from the one time he had been atop the tower, in full sunlight, was that the railing along the edge was rather low, so he inched forward until his foot touched the railing. He glanced down, where he could barely see Kyre in the shadows of the courtyard, looking up at the tower. "Ha!" Koren said to himself, this was not such a big deal. Kyre had been playing a trick on him, there were no ghosts. He waved down at Kyre, but the ducal heir couldn't see, it was too dark. Koren looked up at the clouds, if he waited a moment, the moon would be visible again, and he could prove to Kyre that he, Koren Bladewell, had climbed to the top of the tower by himself, and was not afraid at all.

Then the moon came out, illuminating the courtyard with a cold silvery light, Koren was sure Kyre could see him. He stood at the railing, waving his arms, calling out in a loud whisper. "Kyre! I'm up here! Kyre! Hey, I'm up at the-"

Koren suddenly became aware of voices behind him. Someone else had climbed up the tower behind him? He turned and-

Saw ghosts.

They wore uniforms with the symbol of Tarador, and armor in an old style, and carried swords that glinted brightly in the moonlight. "Whooo goooes theeere?" the voices called, as the ghosts moved to surround him, reaching out to grab him. He felt icy fingers on his arm, and he panicked. He later didn't remember bursting between the ghosts, evading their bony, outstretched fingers, leaping through the opening in the floor, tumbling down the first couple stairs, taking the rest three at a time, bouncing off the hard

stone walls all the way down, until he stumbled through the doorway to sprawl at Kyre's feet in the courtyard.

Kyre's eyes were as wide as Koren's. He had not expected Koren to actually reach the top of the tower!

"Did you-" Koren gasped between breaths, "did you see them?"

Kyre nodded vigorously. "They were all around you! You shouldn't have been standing near the railing like that!"

"When I," Koren caught his breath, "got to the top, there was nothing, it was dark. I didn't see them until the clouds went away. Where did they come from?"

Kyre shuddered, as if he could feel the icy hands of the ghosts on his skin. "They are always there! In the light of a full moon, the shadow realm becomes visible to us, here in the real world." Kyre spoke as if he were a wizard himself. "Did they hurt you?"

Koren held up his arm, which still felt cold. He rolled up the sleeve, and saw faint red marks, where the ghosts had touched him. "N-no. It f-feels cold, but it doesn't hurt."

Kyre felt ill, as if he were going to faint. "Come on, let's get you in front of a fire, and something hot to drink."

"That sounds good," Koren said, rubbing the marks on his arm to take away the chill. Suddenly, he looked up at the full moon. *The ghosts are always there.* Koren's mouth dropped open. *The shadow realm becomes visible in the light of a full moon!* "I- I have to go." He turned and ran as fast as he could toward the castle.

"Wait! Where are you going?" Kyre asked, startled, but Koren had already disappeared around a corner.

Koren knew there was no way the royal guards were going to let him inside the palace, at such a late hour, without an appointment. But the Cornerstone chamber was not truly part of the palace itself, only attached to it, and so Koren ran all the way around, to the door of the corridor that led to the Cornerstone chamber. The guard there nodded to Koren and opened the door for him; servants often used that corridor as a short cut between parts of the palace and the kitchens. But when Koren got to the chamber, the heavy doors were locked shut. He tried to look through the crack between the doors, and was frustrated to see only darkness.

There were windows, set high up in the chamber wall, near the roof! He could look through those windows. If he could get up there. He turned around and raced back down the corridor, up two flights of stairs and opened a window, careful not to let it squeak. Below the window was a roof, which led to the outside wall of the Cornerstone chamber. If he could manage to crawl along the wall to a window, he could see inside the chamber.

After his last experience climbing out a window and onto a roof, when he very nearly fell to his death, Koren was not eager to repeat the experience. He looked up at the moon, it was halfway down toward the horizon already, and clouds were building. He took a deep breath, and put his trembling right foot out the window onto the roof.

Koren was about to yank open the door to the wizard's bedchamber, when he realized that was a foolish idea. Paedris set ward spells every night, if Koren had yanked opened the door, he might have set off howling banshees and been blasted back across the hallway. Ever since Kyre warned Koren that the wizard saw him as nothing but a servant, Koren had been very careful around the powerful sorcerer. Perhaps he should forget about the Cornerstone, and let Paedris sleep? No, this was too important. He used his fist to pound on the door. "Paedris! Lord Salva, please, you must come quickly."

The face that appeared when Paedris opened the door was that of an old man, befuddled by sleep, no more a wizard than Koren was. "What time is- Koren, what are you doing?" Paedris asked with a jaw-stretching yawn.

"Please, sir, put on your robe, you must come quickly. The moon is setting sir, please hurry!"

It was a sleepy and grumpy Paedris who ordered the guard to unlock the door to the Cornerstone chamber. The wizard half suspected his servant was playing a prank on him, perhaps something Carlana had ordered. "Koren, if this is a joke, it is most certainly not-" The wizard halted in mid-speech, gaping with his mouth wide open.

"You see it? Oh, sir, you see it?" Koren gasped in relief that the light of the full moon still shone through one window, down upon the Cornerstone's resting place.

"See what?" The guard asked, stepping into the chamber. "Nothing here but dust, Lord Salva. I think your servant is playing a trick on you."

"No," Paedris said in a harsh whisper, "it is the enemy that has been playing a trick on us, on *me*. For centuries. And I have been a fool not to see the truth! Koren, how did you know?"

Koren knelt down and ran a finger along the scrape marks on the floor. "When I realized these marks had been cut with a chisel, sir, I knew the enemy only wanted us to *think* they had dragged the Cornerstone away. They must have sent the Cornerstone into the shadow realm, like the way Lord Mwazo made that teapot disappear."

"Cut by a chisel, hmmm? Cut by a chisel?" Paedris roared with laughter. "Kings and queens have searched for the Cornerstone, but only this boy thought about a common stone-cutting tool! And a teapot!"

The guard edged back toward the door. The wizard had clearly gone mad. "Begging your pardon, Lord Salva, but are you well?"

"Yes, yes, man, we are all well tonight! Koren, hold my hand, and concentrate on the Cornerstone. Quickly, before the moonlight is gone!" Holding Koren's hand in a painfully tight grip, Paedris muttered words in a language Koren didn't understand, then shouted at the stone and gestured with his staff. There was a blinding flash of light, and there, in front of them, was the Cornerstone, where it had been all along.

"May I, may I touch it, sir?" Koren asked in awe, after Paedris released his hand. His body felt odd, and tingled all over.

"Yes, but I think you should attend to our guard first. I'm afraid the poor fellow has fainted."

"You do understand, Koren?" Paedris asked, the next morning, when the wizard surprised his loyal servant by waking him up, and bringing him a fresh pot of tea. Koren should have known this did not mean good news.

"I guess so." Koren mumbled, staring at his shoes. He had gone to bed glowing with excitement from his triumph in the Cornerstone chamber, dreaming of glory. But, after Koren had gone to sleep, Carlana and Paedris had decided that credit for finding the

Cornerstone must go to Ariana, not to Koren. Everyone must believe that the crown princess had unraveled the legendary mystery; it would strengthen her hand in the future when dealing with the Dukes. For credit to go to a common servant, when generations of royalty had failed to discover the truth, would make the royal family a laughingstock. And Koren, after all, was nothing but a common-born servant. He didn't matter. He had saved a princess not once but three times, *and* found the legendary Cornerstone. What more did he have to do, to be more than a servant boy? Or would nothing he ever did be good enough?

"You know who really found the Cornerstone, and I do. And Carlana and Ariana both know, Koren. But no one else can know." The guard who fainted had been sworn to secrecy, and he was anyway not eager to talk about the events of that night. Paedris had agonized over, once again, denying Koren credit for a remarkable accomplishment. For saving Ariana's life, Koren should have, at the very least, been rewarded with a grant of land. And for finding the Cornerstone, when wizards and kings had failed for countless years? Why, a knighthood would be the barest minimum reward!

Unfortunately, word that the Cornerstone had been found would soon reach the enemy's ears. If the enemy heard a story that the crown princess had found the Cornerstone, their assumption would be that the truth was her royal wizard had really been responsible, and the enemy would not inquire further. But if the enemy heard that the royal wizard's servant had found the Cornerstone, then the enemy would look closely at this unknown servant boy, the same boy, who, according to rumors, had saved the princess from the magic-spelled bear the enemy had sent to kill the girl. It would not take long for the enemy to discover there was something odd, very odd, and interesting, about the wizard's remarkable servant boy.

Paedris could not allow the enemy's eye to be turned on Koren.

"It's not fair." Koren grumbled. "I know, life isn't fair. Loyalty runs uphill," he said with a wink, "and the smelly stuff gets dumped on my head. Oh, what the hell, now I can stop looking for the stupid thing. Paedris, why could I see the Cornerstone, and the guard could not?"

"Er, oh, I, um, well," the wizard stumbled over his own tongue, "you see, Koren, I think that living here, being around powerful magic all the time, you have become, well, rather sensitive to it. Nothing to worry about. Say, I hear the kitchen is baking cream cakes this morning," Paedris hurried to change the subject, "why don't you bring us a plate of them, and we'll have our own celebration?"

Koren was not the only person in the castle unhappy that he was not given credit for finding the Cornerstone. Every time well-meaning people praised her for finding the Cornerstone, Ariana felt like a complete fraud. Her mother had declared a feast to celebrate the discovery of the fabled Cornerstone, fortunately for Ariana the feast was not to be for another six weeks, to allow time for the Dukes and Duchesses to travel to the castle. Perhaps by then her face would not burn with shame when people gushed over how clever she was.

Ariana wanted to tell Koren that she didn't like stealing the credit for finding the Cornerstone, but the very next morning after the unveiling of the Cornerstone, having stuffed themselves with cream cakes, Paedris and Koren had ridden their horses out of the castle, and they weren't supposed to return for five whole days! Ariana was miserable, expecting that Koren might think it was her idea to steal the credit from him.

Being out of the castle, riding about the countryside with Paedris and two of the royal guards, almost made Koren forget his disappointment over not being able to tell people that he had found the Cornerstone. Almost. The purpose of riding out of the castle had been to give Koren's anger time to cool off; gathering rare roots for potions had only been an excuse. It was difficult to find roots in the winter, even if a week of warmer weather had caused much of the snow to melt; Koren knew Paedris didn't need roots badly enough to roam around the countryside in winter, so he enjoyed simply being out of the castle, seeing something different than the gray stone walls. During the day, they rode along country lanes, Paedris mostly letting Koren decide where he wanted to go. In the late afternoons, they stopped at inns, where Paedris was given the finest room available, and the kitchen staff scurried around frantically to make a dinner good enough for the court wizard. What surprised and amused Koren was how the innkeepers and workers bowed and scraped to *Koren*, asking what his favorite foods were, helping him care for the horses, putting away the baggage, making sure he saw them taking special care setting up his own room. It was the first time in his life that people, especially adults, deferred to him. In the castle, Koren was just another servant. Out in the countryside, Koren was the person closest to the powerful master wizard Lord Paedris Don Salva de la Murta, and because people were afraid to speak to the wizard, they spoke to Koren. A few people even offered him money, if Koren would ask the wizard for a favor. Koren always refused the money, of course, and also refused to ask favors from the wizard, whether paid or not. He didn't have to; when people heard a wizard was in the village, they flocked around the inn. Most people wanted merely to see the wizard, and the soldiers had to shoo people away to keep them from following the wizard all day, or he would get no peace at all. Some people wanted the wizard to bless them, or their fields, or their animals; Paedris gently explained that blessings were the province of priests, not wizards. And there was always a family in each village who wanted the wizard to heal a sick person. Sometimes Paedris could help, and sadly sometimes he could not, and sometimes he declared the sick person only had a bad cold, and needed to rest, to be kept warm, and to drink a hearty chicken broth with vegetables.

One morning, in a very small village up in the hills east of Linden, where the tiny inn had only two rooms and Koren had to share a room with the two snoring soldiers; a man was waiting when they stepped outside after a surprisingly good breakfast. The man was wearing what must have been his best clothes, but he was clearly a poor farmer, with his clothes much patched, collar and cuffs frayed. When he saw the wizard, the man snatched his cap off and knelt on one knee. "Please, my lord Salva, my wife, she's with child, and she's sick, very sick. Could you please look at her, kind sir?"

Paedris, who had slept well, having suffered no snoring companions in his room, and feeling good after a delicious breakfast served in front of a fire in the inn's cozy common room, took pity on the man, asking him questions about his wife. The man led the way, riding an old plow horse, several miles deeper into the hills, to a small but well-kept farmhouse at the end of the road. As they came around the bend in the road, Koren admired the man's property; a barn well banked against winter winds with stacks of hay on the north side, healthy-looking animals grazing in the fenced paddock, rolling fields separated by lines of trees as windbreaks. The neat stacks of firewood, even now that winter was waning, were impressive, enough surely for another year. Right then, Koren knew his fondest dream was to have a farm just like this one.

As they approached the house, the man called out, and two children ran out, a blonde-haired girl a few years younger than Koren, and a boy Koren guessed to be six years old. "Papa! Papa! Come quickly, mama is burning up with fever!" The girl cried out, tears streaming down her face.

"Melissa! This here's the master wizard of all Tarador, show your respect." Her father admonished his children. The girl curtsied and the boy bowed, avoiding looking the great and powerful wizard in the eye.

Paedris feared he was too late, or could not help, when he entered the farmhouse and saw the woman. She was laying on top of the bedcovers, and sweating although the fire in the stove was low, and inside the house was cold enough the wizard could almost see his breath. She was also shivering, and when he felt her forehead, she was indeed burning up. First, Paedris told her husband to stoke the fire, to warm up the house. While her skin was hot, her insides were cold, Paedris explained, hence the shivering.

The wizard covered the woman with a blanket, knelt beside the bed, and made her drink water. He laid his hands on her, closed his eyes, and summoned his senses.

"Sir?" Koren asked quietly. "What do you see, or, or feel?"

"A wizard can sense-" Paedris had been about to explain how a wizard could sense sickness inside a person, or animal, sense something wrong, and isolate it, and act upon it, and then strengthen the surrounding tissues. He had been about to explain, as a wizard to an apprentice, when he caught himself and remembered Koren was not yet an apprentice. That if he explained how to sense corruption inside a person's body, and how to send healing force flowing from wizard to patient, Koren may realize he, too, could sense that. And that might get Koren to thinking he, too, had wizardly power. That might make Koren realize his ability to calm frantic animals, like Thunderbolt, was in fact part of his power as a wizard. And for Koren to realize the truth, now, too soon, would be a disaster. So instead of explaining, Paedris snapped "Koren, stop bothering me when I'm working. Go boil some water, and get me clean cloths."

"Yes, sir, sorry, sir." Koren mumbled, and hastened away to help the father bringing in firewood. When the fire was roaring in the stove, and a pot of water was on to boil, Koren brought a bag of clean cloths, and the wizard's satchel of potions, then went out to help the two children with farm chores. Chores around a farm waited for no one, they did not care whether someone in the house was sick, or even dying. He helped the girl get the family's two cows into the barn, and milked one cow while she milked the other, and her little brother fed the goats and pigs. Then Koren tended the plow horse, bringing the animal into the barn, brushing its old coat, and bringing in a bale of hay.

"Sir? Is momma going to be all right?" The girl asked, and Koren momentarily turned around to look for the wizard, for no one had ever called him 'sir' before. He was not much older than the girl, which certainly didn't merit him being called 'sir'. But he was a companion of the great and powerful wizard, and he now wore fine clothes, and he lived in a castle. To the girl, he must seem like a grand figure.

"You don't have to call me sir, miss. I lived on a farm like this, before I came to serve the wizard."

"Really?" The girl asked, wide-eyed.

"Really. I'm no one special, just a servant. I chop wood, and fetch food, and clean up after my master. As far as your mother, I don't know whether she will be well, but I do know that Lord Salva is the most powerful wizard in all the land, more powerful than you can know, more powerful than I could have imagined," Koren said with a shudder as he thought of the staircase that didn't exist, and disappearing teapots, "so if anyone can help your mother, he can. And if he can, he will. Lord Salva is a good man, which is why our enemy fears him so. Now, let's bring this milk to your father, and see if the wizard needs anything."

When they got back into the house, Koren at first feared the worst, for the mother was laying in bed, with the blanket pulled up to her chin, and she appeared not to be moving. The wizard's face was drained of color, he and the father were huddled by the stove, heads nearly touching, talking quietly. The girl, seeing this, flung her arms around Koren and sobbed on his shoulder, while her little brother clung to his waist. "No, don't cry, little ones," the father called out softly, "your mother is going to be fine, and the baby too. Lord Salva has worked a miracle on her-"

"No miracle," the wizard protested, "merely a good dose of the right potion, and some help from a touch of magic." From the wizard's tired eyes, the woman had needed more than just 'some' help from magic, healing her had been a strain on even his great powers. In his hand was a thick slice of bread, slathered with butter and jam, for the use of magic had made him hungry again, as it always did. Koren noted the wizard's hand shook slightly. "Her fever has broken. Keep your wife warm, and let her rest, she needs rest, and quiet, and fruit juice if you have it, and a broth, chicken broth is best, I find."

"Yes, my lord," the man replied, looking at the wizard worshipfully, which would have annoyed Paedris. "Apple cider I have, and we've a pot of chicken soup frozen in the shed, I'll heat it and give her spoonfuls, as you instructed."

A bit later, outside, the man tearfully offered to give Paedris sacks of grain, or a goat, or even his prize cow, but the wizard refused. "I don't know how else to thank you, Lord Salva." The man said, choking back tears.

"You don't owe me anything," the wizard insisted. "You pay your taxes? Your taxes help pay for my keep. And for the royal army that keeps the enemy from all of our doors. My servant says you have an admirable farm, that you work hard and are a good steward of the land. Live a good life, and take care of your family, that is all I ask." In the end, Paedris accepted a small jar of maple syrup, mostly because he thought the man would feel better about having given something back to the wizard. "Now, Koren, we need to get on our way. I believe I saw a ruined castle on our way up this road, and I've never been in these hills before. I feel like exploring this morning."

"Oh, yes, sir, please, sir. I'd love to do that." Koren said with genuine enthusiasm. He loved poking around old tumbled down castles, cities and even just the foundations of long-ago farmsteads. It was now mid-morning, a sunny day warming up nicely, although the wizard warned cold and snow were on the way. Best to enjoy the good weather while it lasted, and be thankful that he would rest his head that night under the roof of an inn, with a full belly. After they had ridden out onto the road, Koren asked "Do you feel up to a ride today, sir? We could go back to that inn, for a meal."

"Yes, yes, I'm fine now, Koren. That was a good thing we did this morning, Koren." Paedris declared, and he did indeed look much better, with color returning to his face, and his eyelids no longer drooping. Wizards did recover faster than ordinary people, perhaps that was magic also. "Although lunch does sound good, I think the innkeeper mentioned he would have chops on the grill and potatoes later today. And I believe his wife was cutting up apples to bake a pie, so certainly we can't let that good woman's efforts go to waste, eh?" The wizard said with a chuckle. "We must go back down this road anyway, so we'll stop by that ruined keep." The wizard looked up at the cloudless sky. "This nice stretch of weather won't last past midday tomorrow, I fear. Best we start making our way back to Linden."

The wizard was right, the weather did turn foul, with clouds and cold, and a drizzle, with sleet falling at night. The day they returned to the castle, a wet snow fell, covering the roads and making the horses slip in the mud.

Paedris hurried from the stable up to his tower, telling Koren his old bones needed to get out of the cold. It took Koren two hours to get the horses groomed and fed and settled in their stalls, and the saddles cleaned and stored away. With the work done, Koren headed up to the royal kitchens with a gang of boys to see what they could find to eat. The boys were in a playful mood because of the unexpected early spring snowfall, laughing and joking, running around the weary Koren. When they came through the gate in the castle wall, a boy in front saw some of his friends on the other side of the courtyard, and with a shout, threw a snowball. The packed ball of wet snow arced high through the air toward the surprised boy, but it was Koren's friends who were most surprised, for while the snowball was in the air, Ariana came around the corner, and the intended target ducked out of the way. The snowball hit Ariana squarely in the chest, splattering her all over, and soaking her dress. The crown princess sputtered, melting chunks of snow dripping down her face.

There was a tense moment as the pair of royal guards in Ariana's party reached for their weapons, and Koren and his friends froze in horror. Assaulting royalty could get a person, even a young boy, thrown into the dungeon.

Ariana held up one hand to stay her guards, while her other hand wiped the melting snow off her face. Without a word, she bent down to scoop snow from the courtyard and packed it into a ball. "Charge!" She shouted, and the fight was on.

Snowballs flew back and forth, and the fight raged, with the royal guards stepping aside and letting the children have fun. Soon everyone had been thoroughly smacked with snow. The ruckus attracted the attention of Carlana, who was walking down a corridor where windows overlooked the courtyard. "Oh, dear, what a shame," one of the Regent's maids exclaimed. "That is no way for a young lady to-"

"Oh, hush, Matilda." Carlana said with a wistful smile. "She is young, and growing up too fast. Let her be a girl for a while longer."

Down in the courtyard, the two sides had moved closer, each side barely having time to pack the snow into balls before throwing. Koren took shelter behind a wagon, as he stood up to throw, he caught two well-aimed snowballs right in his face. He fell backwards onto the cobblestones.

Ariana put her hands to her mouth in fear for Koren. Forgetting about the fight, she raced around the back of the wagon to see if Koren was injured, slipped in the snow, and fell right on top of him.

"Ooof!" Koren tried to catch his breath, with Ariana's knee digging into his stomach. "You're heavy!"

"Oh no, did I hurt you?!" Ariana cried in distress. When she had seen Koren across the courtyard, her only thought had been to run over to him, and tell him it was terribly unfair that he was not getting proper credit for finding the Cornerstone, and that it hadn't been her idea, and that someday she would be queen, and then she could see that he was recognized as a hero for saving her, and she was so sorry-

And Koren's face was only inches from hers, and he looked so cute, with his mop of dark curly hair falling across his eyes, and his face wet with melting snow, and his eyes sparkling-

In the corridor above, Carlana's saw that her daughter, the future queen, was laying on top of a commoner boy, and going to kiss him, right in the courtyard of the castle! Her maids also saw what was going to happen, and gasped in shock. Carlana's hands flew to the window, fingers fumbling with the handle to fling the window open.

Ariana had never kissed a boy before, but it seemed so natural. She closed her eyes, and-

And shrieked in shock as Koren stuffed a handful of snow down the back of her dress. They both jumped to their feet, Koren laughing and grinning, Ariana hopping around, tugging on her dress as the cold slush dripped down her back. "Oh, you are the most rotten-"

"Ha! I got you!" Koren laughed, dancing away as Ariana tried to tackle him.

Up in the window, Carlana pressed a hand to her heart in relief. Matilda the maid observed knowingly "Girls at her age are interested in boys, before the boys are ready."

"Yes. Still, I think you were right the first time, it is time that I treat my daughter as a young lady, instead of a girl." The Regent sighed. "I wish she never had to grow up."

"Every mother wishes so, your Highness."

Ariana gave up trying to catch Koren, and rubbed her back up against the wagon to soothe her wet, frozen skin. Around them the snowball fight had died down, with the combatants trying to wipe the snow off their own sodden clothes. "Sorry about the snow." Koren said, regretting that he'd stuffed snow in her clothes. It had been an impulsive act, that now seemed immature and stupid. "Can I help?"

"No, I got it." Ariana laughed. "Koren, I'm sorry, about-" She looked around her, people were too close for her to speak freely. "About, you know."

Koren frowned, then shrugged, his mouth dry with nervousness at being so close to her, his stomach dancing with butterflies. "Paedris explained it to me. You're the crown princess, I'm a servant. Besides, it was your idea for us to look for, you know."

"Still, it's not fair."

"Life isn't fair." Koren said with a wink.

"People tell me that all the time."

"So."

"So. Uh," Ariana didn't know what to say. A moment before, she had been about to kiss Koren. "How was your, um, where did you go?"

Koren scuffed his boots on cobblestones. Talking to Ariana was suddenly awkward, and he didn't know why. "Oh, nowhere special, digging roots for potions, and

Paedris was healing people along the way. It was fun, to be out of the castle for a while."

"Good. That's good. Really, uh, really good."

"Your Highness?" A guard asked, coming around the wagon. "You should change out of those wet clothes before you catch a sickness."

"Yes, I suppose. Koren, will I see you sometime?"

Koren made an exaggerated bow. "Most certainly, Your Highness."

"I agree, this is not good." Paedris muttered. He took a sip of wine, taking time to gather his thoughts. "Still, I am not surprised. He is a young boy, and, princess or not, she is a young girl. And you told me she has admired Koren as a hero since the day he saved her." And their fates are tied, although he said nothing of that to the Regent.

"Has Koren said anything to you?" Carlana asked. She had not mentioned to her daughter that she saw her almost kissing Koren, but she would have to talk to Ariana about it someday.

"No, nothing special. Of course, he does talk about Ariana often, but I expected that was because he was excited to be invited to the palace. Not many servant boys get invited to lunch with the crown princess." Paedris swirled the wine in his glass, then gulped it and set the glass down. The discussion had him too upset to enjoy a fine wine. "We shall have to keep them apart, I suppose."

"I do think that is best."

"In the summer, I would likely be out with the army anyway," Paedris glanced at the Regent to see her reaction to the idea of the army fighting again. Carlana's frown deepened, so he dropped the subject. "Until then, I can take Koren with me to visit Rellanon." As he said it, the idea sounded better and better to Paedris. Rellanon province lay to the southeast of Linden, where springtime came sooner. Duke Magnico, a steady friend of the Trehaymes, had a cozy guesthouse where Paedris could stay, away in the hills, surrounded, as Paedris remembered, by well-tended gardens, and a lake stocked with fat trout. Yes, that sounded like a very good idea. And not just because it would keep Koren and Ariana apart, for young passions to cool. "Such a journey would keep me away for several weeks, probably until the Cornerstone festival."

"You could leave soon, then?"

"Ariana, we need to talk." Carlana said, as she waved her maids away for privacy. Mother and daughter, Regent and crown princess, had been discussing plans for the Cornerstone festival, and while Carlana had been concerned about seating arrangements for the guests, Ariana had been talking Koren this, and Koren that, half her words were Koren, Koren, Koren.

After the maids had closed the door behind them, Carlana took her daughter's hand gently in her own. "Ariana, I understand that Koren has done wonderful things, amazing things. I understand why you admire him, but, you do know there can never be anything between you two?"

"What?" Ariana protested, a bit too forcefully. "I don't," tears in her eyes told that she had been about to lie. "It's not fair! Koren should be a knight already, for saving me. Now he finds the Cornerstone, and he gets nothing for it?"

"You know why we can't-"

"I know why, and I hate it. It's not fair to Koren. It's not fair to anyone!" She angrily wiped away her tears with a napkin. "Sometimes I hate being princess. Everyone thinks it's so great to be a princess, and it's not. I can't even be friends with a boy, because all the Dukes and Duchesses want me to marry one of their horrible sons!"

"We can't all marry for love, Ariana. Not many women do, I'm afraid."

"Did you?" Ariana asked through a sniffle. "Did you love Daddy?"

Carlana pursed her lips, paused for a moment, then shook her head. "Not when I married him, I didn't love him. I was afraid of him. But later, yes, when I saw how kind he was, how much he cared for me, and his people, and then how much he loved you. Yes, I did grow to love him, very dearly."

"You were afraid of Daddy?" Ariana asked, surprised. Afraid of the man who crawled around the palace on his knees, pretending to be a horse, with his little daughter on his back? Afraid of the man who tucked her into bed at night, with a kiss, and a bedtime story, not leaving that task to maids?

"You have to understand, I was merely the daughter of a minor baron, and my parents weren't especially rich or powerful. My parents' greatest dream was that I would marry the younger son of a duke someday, or perhaps a wealthy merchant. Their true hope was my sister, and she was supposed to go attend the duchess when your father visited. But my sister fell ill, and I went in her stead, and my mother told to stay out of the way and not call attention to myself." Carlana said the last with a touch of still-fresh bitterness, a wound that had not fully healed. "Your father noticed me when I was practicing archery, which ladies were allowed to do, and later he noticed me again when I was singing in the choir during dinner one evening. I was in the back row of the choir, mind you, and I don't know how he heard my voice among all the others. He called me forth to sing for him, and I was so nervous I almost fainted, and then I forgot the words to the song. He knew the words, and he sang along with me-"

Ariana laughed. "Daddy couldn't sing!"

"Oh, his voice was atrocious." Carlana laughed also. "But he sang anyway, in front of all the guests, until I remembered the words. That was, the first kind thing he ever did for me." Carlana remembered with a wistful smile.

"Then why were you afraid of him?"

"Why? Because he was the king, silly girl! He had the power of life and death over us all. He was young, and strong, and so handsome, and all the girls fawned over him. I feared he only wanted to toy with me, like some men do to poor servant girls. And when his emissary came to my parents, to ask for my hand in marriage, I didn't know what to think. I'd never lived in a palace! Many of the noble ladies here were terribly jealous of me, and they were mean to me."

"Mean to you? But you were marrying the king!"

"Much of the court thought your father made a terrible mistake choosing me, for I brought nothing to the match; no money, no influence, no political advantage. I arrived at the palace a month before the wedding, and stayed in the royal apartments. The ladies were sure a dumb country girl like me would soon make a fool of myself in the royal court, and your father would change his mind. I think that just made him more determined to marry me."

Ariana had never before heard the story of how her parents had met. "Do you think I'll marry a man who loves me?"

Carlana pulled her daughter close and hugged her. "Oh, honey, I think you'll be a good queen someday, and *all* your people will love you."

Seeing Ariana almost kiss Koren, and talking with her daughter about silly dreams of marriage, made up Carlana's mind about something she had been considering for almost two years. Considering for years, and secretly negotiating for years, and never reaching the point when she felt comfortable committing herself. It was time to put comfort aside, she decided, and take the type of action her critics said she was not capable of.

She sent for the ambassador from the Indus Empire, to meet in her private chambers. The Bey of Begal arrived with an aide and a pair of guards, and was mildly surprised to see that the Regent of Tarador was alone in her ornate sitting room, except for an elderly woman he did not recognize. "Ambassador Ulligrapat, please have your guards wait outside the door. I wish to discuss something with you, in private." The Regent said.

Usay Ulligrapat bowed, and gestured for his guards to leave. "May my aide remain, Your Highness?" He was hopeful about the absence of the royal chancellor, who almost always accompanied Carlana when discussing matters of state. Hopeful, for there were certain matters of state he had been discussing with the Regent, which her chancellor was not aware of.

"Yes, please, I wish your aide to join us, as we require witnesses. For this purpose, I have invited the royal scribe; she is the official keeper of records for the realm. Including records which need to remain secret for a time."

The Ambassador's heart leapt in his chest, soaring with hope that he would soon achieve the result for which the Emperor had sent him so far from Indus. He bowed to the woman he now knew as the royal scribe, for her odd robes now made sense. Her sleeves were short, the bottoms of the sleeves were rolled up and pinned near her elbows, Usay supposed that was to keep her sleeves away from fresh ink on documents.

"Please, Ambassador, sit." Carlana said, gesturing to the chair across the low table from where she was seated. It was a rather intimate setting, a setting Carlana had chosen to emphasize the intimate, and sensitive, nature of their discussions. "Would you like tea? We recently acquired a supply of Masala Sahm tea leaves."

The royal scribe had heard gossip around the castle of how shockingly expensive a single bag of this special tea had been, a bag no larger than a loaf of bread. The Regent must have been very eager to court favor with the ambassador, to pay so much for a bag of dried leaves. While the Regent and the Ambassador exchanged endless and meaningless pleasantries, the scribe considered how much the price of the ordinary tea she drank at breakfast had soared in price over the past few years. The steep increase in price was a sign, she had been told by the people who dealt with the realm's finances, of how foreigners feared that Tarador was slowly losing the war, for foreigners no longer gave credit to Taradoran merchants, and those merchants were forced to pay in silver or gold. The scribe kept a neutral expression on her face, and glanced out the window, bored of the Regent's verbal sparring with the foreigner. She was thinking of her son, who had recently become apprenticed to a merchant, and would be leaving home in the springtime to travel far and wide, perhaps even across the sea. Would her son ever travel as far as Indus? The scribe shuddered at the thought of such a long and dangerous journey to a strange foreign land, where people-

"I have decided to sign the treaty." Carlana interrupted her scribe's thoughts.

The Ambassador's perpetual expression of a pleasant half smile broke into a genuine smile. The scribe thought the man was pleased that his mission to Tarador had been successful, and he could now look forward to returning home, leaving behind the cold winter rains of Linden. The Ambassador's reserve broke so much that he clapped his hands in delight. "Thank you, Your Highness, we are most grateful. The prince will be so pleased, I know that he is eager to finally meet you, having heard so much about you."

"And I look forward to meeting him."

"The prince is very handsome, Your Highness, he is considered-"

"Yes, I have seen the portrait. Ambassador, I will sign the treaty, with conditions, there are several issues we have not addressed."

The Ambassador's broad smile did not waiver. Conditions were to be expected, and would not stand in the way of Usay Ulligrapat returning to Indus in triumph, to be rewarded by the Raj himself, a grateful Raj. The Bey of Begal was a king in his own right, king of a land almost half the size of all Tarador, which is why the Emperor of Indus had sent the Bey to Tarador as his personal representative, to complete negotiation of the treaty.

"The treaty specifies loan guarantees to Tarador of eight hundred thousand rajtees, which is acceptable," Carlana said while trying to keep all expression from her face, "however, the treaty does not specify the exchange rate between Indus rajtees and Taradoran florins. We require the treaty to be enforced at the rate of exchange that is in effect at the time, for both initiation of the loan guarantees, and for repayment."

The Bey's smile slipped ever so slightly, then returned. With the value of Tarador's currency slipping, such a floating exchange rate would make the treaty more expensive for Indus, which would not please the Raj. The Raj would be pleased, however, that the loan price the Bey had negotiated was less than half of what the Raj had allowed. "Of course, Your Highness. We did not specify an exchange rate, for we expected the rate to vary over the years," he lied smoothly.

The scribe glanced out the window again, as the two leaders discussed the dull minutiae of finance. She had been interested to hear that a prince of Indus would be apparently arriving in Linden, to meet Carlana. Why had the Ambassador said 'finally'? Had the Regent been corresponding with a prince, and why? And why would it matter whether the prince was handsome or not?

"Agreed." Carlana said with a nod. "The same conditions will apply, at the time, to the dowry."

Dowry! The scribe almost gasped aloud in surprise. A dowry was an exchange of gifts or money in consideration of marriage. Marriage! The Regent was negotiating to marry a foreign prince! Oh, what a clever woman the Regent is, to make such a bold move in Tarador's time of need!

"Of course, Your Highness," the Bey said with his smile not wavering, "it is entirely reasonable for such conditions to apply to the dowry. Of course. We are in agreement."

"With the financial details settled, then, we can discuss the wedding ceremony." Carlana was not smiling, her lips drawn tightly. "The marriage will be here, in Linden, in the royal chapel, and will be officiated by a Taradoran priest." Hopefully, thought Carlana, Mother Furliss would perform the marriage ceremony.

"Of course, Your Highness, we would be honored for the ceremony uniting our two peoples to be held here, in Linden."

The scribe fairly quivered with excitement at the prospect of a royal wedding in the palace. Even if the people of Indus were foreigners, those of Indus she had seen in Linden were elegant and exotic. The wedding would be a spectacle, an event to lift the spirits of the people of Tarador.

"Our traditions require-" The Bey began to say.

"Yes, I understand the imperial priests must perform their own ceremony, at the heart of the empire in Indus." Carlana said. "So be it, we have no objection."

The scribe wondered at the strange customs of foreigners. The Regent was wise to let them perform their pagan ceremonies far from the borders of Tarador. What manner of dress would the Regent wear for the wedding, the scribe wondered? In addition to her authority as Regent, the Lady Carlana was a former queen of the realm, and mother of the crown princess. Would Carlana be getting married to this foreign prince as the Regent, or as the crown mother, or both? The scribe could not recall an instance in the long history of Tarador when a Regent had married while in office. An office Carlana Trehayme would hold only until Ariana came of age on her sixteenth birthday. The powerful empire of Indus would not marry a prince of the empire to a mere Regent, no, the empire sought marriage because Carlana was the crown mother, and through her, Indus could cement ties to her daughter, the future queen.

The scribe thought fondly, and a bit sadly, of the crown princess. The princess had been only two years old when the woman who was now the royal scribe came to the palace to serve in the royal library, and became the official head scribe six years later. The princess had grown into a young woman in that time, and had seen much tragedy and sadness. The invasion of Tarador's western border by Acedor's army, the untimely death of her father in battle, and the long, grinding, wearying war that had been raging hot and cold as long as the princess could remember. The prospect of becoming queen, something most girls could only dream of excitedly, only meant crushing responsibility falling onto Ariana's shoulders. And she, too, would someday have to seek a husband who could bring an advantage to her realm. Marrying for love was not something a crown princess or a queen could even dream about. It was so sad that such a kind and lovely girl-

"However," Carlana continued, "my daughter will not be traveling to Indus. You will perform your ceremony without Ariana."

The scribe gasped out loud, shocked. The Regent was not marrying a foreign prince; she was marrying off her own daughter!

Carlana and the Ambassador turned sharply to look at the scribe, whose face was red. "Will this be a problem, Your Highness?" The Ambassador asked.

"No," Carlana answered with a withering stare at her royal scribe.

The scribe looked at the floor and curtsied. "No, Your Highness, Your Grace Ambassador Ulligrapat. I was startled is all. The office of the royal scribe has ever been discrete concerning official documents."

Carlana turned back to the Ambassador. "This agreement will remain secret until the day before my daughter comes of age."

The smile was gone from Usay's face, replaced by a neutral expression. "His Majesty the Emperor is, as I have stated, uncomfortable with this treaty remaining secret for so long."

"And we have explained that such secrecy protects the crown princess." Carlana's smile was also gone. "As long as the dukes and duchesses believe there is a possibility that Ariana will marry one of their sons, they will remain content with supporting the Regency. If they learned she has been promised to a foreign prince, even a favored prince of powerful empire, some of the provinces could be tempted into, shall we say, adventures or intrigue."

Usay openly frowned, then regained his neutral expression. The Emperor was not concerned about the secrecy of the treaty document, for many agreements between nations were secret, he was concerned for the Regent of Tarador's reason for insisting on secrecy. Carlana needed secrecy simply because her hold on power was weak. A weak Regent was not able to provide a strong guarantee that the Empire would receive in the future, the agreed benefit from the loan guarantees that took effect immediately.

Ultimately, it did not matter, Usay knew. The negotiations for the secret betrothal of Carlana's daughter to the Emperor's second son had started with the Emperor offering loans, loan guarantees and even part of his army and navy to Tarador, for the Emperor feared that Tarador would be conquered by the Enemy. Against the common demon Enemy, Tarador's fight was the fight of all peoples, and if Tarador were to fall, Indus would not last long. Usay nodded. "Tarador's internal political matters are your concern, Your Highness. We are agreed, then? The terms we discussed here can be added to the treaty document now, and my aide and your scribe can act as witnesses?"

Carlana tried to keep her eagerness from showing. Tarador needed this treaty, she needed this treaty. Tarador needed the money from loans, to keep fighting the war, until and after Ariana became queen. Ariana would not be happy when she learned, shortly before her sixteenth birthday, that she was betrothed to a foreign prince. The people of Indus felt it was the responsibility of parents to find a good match for their children; this match would be good for Ariana, good for her station as queen and good to ensure the future of the realm. Ariana needed to put aside silly girlish dreams of marrying a servant boy, or a wizard, and think about her responsibilities. Prince Noredon would be a good companion, and his presence in the royal household would bring strength and stability to Ariana's reign, for she could rely on a powerful empire as an ally. With a signed treaty in hand, Carlana could simply smile to herself when people accused her of inaction while Acedor pressed in on Tarador's borders. Merchants would notice their trading partners were allowing credit again. The royal army would see new supplies and reinforcements, including foreign mercenaries. Ariana would see less pressure on her mother from the Regency Council. All of which would ensure Tarador's future and ease Ariana's path to the throne.

Her daughter would be unhappy, her daughter would be furious. Her daughter would live to become queen. "Yes," Carlana stood up and offered her hand for the Ambassador to shake. "We shall sign the treaty today."

Koren trudged down a hallway inside the castle, bent over by a bundle of laundry that weighed almost as much as he did. He was dead tired, having just arrived back at the castle that morning. Staying at Duke Magnico's guest house, a hunting lodge, had been an idyllically peacefully couple of weeks, almost a holiday for Koren. The Duke had been fairly bursting with pride to have the court wizard staying at his hunting lodge, knowing the other Dukes would be burning with jealousy, particularly as Paedris had agreed to ride back with Magnico, when the Duke journeyed to Linden for the Cornerstone Festival. When the royal courier reached the Duke, announcing that Paedris desired to stay at the Duke's hunting lodge, the Duke had sent his servants into frantic action; scrubbing the already clean lodge top to bottom, stocking the kitchen with food, filling the wine cellar with the wizard's favorite vintages, and clearing winter leaves and brush from the gardens. When they arrived, Paedris and Koren found fresh early blooming flowers planted up against the lodge, where the thick timbers provided warmth to the soil, and a retinue of Magnico's servants ready to take care of the court wizard, and do most of Koren's work also. Koren did not have to chop wood, or clean anything except the room Paedris used as a study. Staying at the lodge was a grand time for Koren, the Duke's library was well stocked with books and maps, the lake was full of fish, and there was an entire countryside for Koren to explore while riding Thunderbolt. He had ranged far and wide, sometimes staying away overnight, with the wizard's permission, although the wizard had insisted that at least two guards accompany Koren on his rides. At first, the guards had resented being assigned to a lowly servant, which was unheard of. Why did a mere servant boy need to be guarded, especially deep inside Tarador? Koren didn't understand it either, thinking the wizard didn't trust him not to get lost, but he obeyed his master. And the guards, after getting to know Koren, treated the rides as a holiday also, and a chance to hunt game on their Duke's private lands. During their weeks at the lodge, the first true signs of spring had arrived, with daffodils popping their bright yellow flowers out of the ground, and fruit trees beginning to bloom, and bees buzzing slowly around, as if they, too, needed to shake off their winter doldrums. Koren had been sad when Paedris announced it was time to ride back to Linden, and although it was fun traveling with the Duke's caravan, now that he was back at the royal castle, there was much work to be done. Such as a large pile of laundry, wet and muddy from long days on the road.

He stopped at the bottom of a staircase, set the bundle of dirty clothes down on the floor, and sat on a step to rest. Two young maids came along the hallway and paused at a window, just around a corner. Koren could faintly hear them talking.

"Oh, look, that's Kyre Falco over there. He is soooo handsome." One girl said with a sigh.

"You keep dreaming, Mariska." The other girl laughed. "He is cute."

"Did you hear about Kyre? Susan, you know Susan, she's a maid for the Falcos, she told me the truth is, it was Kyre's idea to look for the Cornerstone in the moonlight."

"No!"

"It's true, Tasha! Kyre heard Ariana was searching for the Cornerstone, and he reminded her about the guards in the old tower, the ghosts who only come out in a full moon? Kyre figured out the Cornerstone had never been moved, he could tell by the marks in the floor there."

"He is clever, that one. And more clever to let the princess take the credit."

"You know, the princess is sweet on him?"

"Ariana? No!" Tasha laughed. "She's a Trehayme, he's a Falco. Like oil and water, they are, never will mix."

"Say what you will, but I've seen the way she looks at him."

"You, Mariska? When are you ever around princess Ariana?"

The girl named Mariska sniffed. "Well, I am, sometimes, and I know what I've seen. Sweet on him, she is."

"Ha! Time to get moving, the dining hall won't clean itself. Oh, hello, um," Tasha was startled to notice Karen around the corner, "You're, uh, Koren, is it?"

Koren's ears were burning. Kyre was getting credit for his accomplishment? Angrily, Koren jumped to his feet and slung the bag of laundry over his shoulder, but it was too heavy, and he fell against the wall, spilling dirty laundry on the floor.

The two girls laughed. "Maybe you should take two trips, next time." Mariska laughed, while Tasha bent down to help him scoop sheets back into the bag.

Koren mumbled thanks, picked up the bag, and staggered up the stairs as fast as he could. Kyre Falco had girls in the castle dreaming about him, while Koren was hauling firewood and laundry, and the maids couldn't even remember his name! "Ariana, sweet on Kyre Falco? Ha!" Koren muttered to himself, then froze on the stairs. He remembered Ariana talking about marriage, she'd said she would probably marry the son of a duke.

Kyre was the son of a duke.

Perhaps much had happened while Koren was away.

Oh no.

Had Ariana been trying to tell him something, that day weeks ago, while he was stuffing his face with honey cakes and not really listening to her? Ariana was his friend, and Kyre was his friend, so he should be happy for them. He wasn't. He wasn't happy to think about Ariana with another boy, even though he knew it was useless for a peasant boy to dream about the princess. He was a peasant, a lowly farm boy, a common servant. The class structure in Tarador was rigid, if you were born a commoner, that's where you stayed, and you should know your place.

Koren knew his place, but he didn't have to like it.

Around the corner, the two maids paused to look out the window. "He's cute too." Tasha said softly.

"Who?" Mariska asked. The only men she saw in the courtyard below were a pair of guards, their faces hidden under shadow by their helmets.

"Koren, the wizard's boy. He's cute. And everyone knows *he* spends a lot of time with the princess."

"He's cute," Mariska admitted. "I don't know why the princess invites him to dine with her, he's just a servant like us. I don't take tea with Ariana."

"Koren does. If the princess if sweet on anyone, it's Koren."

"What? Oh, such talk! Where do you get these ideas, Tasha?"

"If she's not sweet on him, and he's a commoner, then why does she spend so much time with him, huh?"

Ariana forced a smile to freeze on her face, and she waved appropriately. But she was bored, terribly bored. With all the Dukes and Duchesses gathered in Linden and such Barons, Baronesses and lower-ranked royalty as had been able to make the journey for the Cornerstone festival, Ariana had to endure endless dinners, parties, receptions and, worst of all, watch spoiled royal boys show off for her. At least when they were racing horses across the field, she could get interested in watching the horses, regardless of the riders. Sitting in the royal box above the sparring ring, watching the sons of Dukes and

Barons play fight and hoping to catch her favorable eye, she was completely uninterested. She did her duty; smiling, waving, congratulating the winners, engaging in small talk with the parents who were so hopeful the future queen would find their eligible sons appealing. She found none of them appealing. Not appealing in *that* way. Oh, to be sure, some of them were handsome, and charming, and well spoken, and quick with a blade or skilled with a bow, and she appreciated any person who could handle a horse with grace and not brute force.

But none of them were as quick with a blade, nor skilled with a bow, as Koren. Not one of them could have ridden Thunderbolt, nor even gotten close to that horse without catching a hoof in the belly, or a bite on the arm. For all their well-polished and well-practiced charm, none of them had the simple, honest grace of Koren. For all their play-acting in the sparring ring, none of them had ever faced true danger, had ever stood up to an enormous bear, nor plunged into a raging, icy river, nor faced a gang of bandits with only a small knife. None of these royal brats had risked death to save the life of a girl they didn't know, risked death when no one was watching, for no gain but because it was the right thing to do. None of them had saved her life, not even once, while Koren had done it thrice in a single morning. And for all their cleverness, their witty words, none of them had solved an ancient mystery, found a Cornerstone that had been hidden for centuries in the spirit world, and given hope to a weary nation that they might someday see victory in a war that had lasted over a thousand years.

And not one of them, nor all of them together, were as handsome as Koren Bladewell, in the eyes of the crown princess. When a match was ended, and the victor held up his sword triumphantly, chest swelled with pride, face flushed from exertion, eyes twinkling, smiling up at the crown princess, Ariana could not help comparing that son of the Duke or Baron to a common farm boy, and find the royal boys lacking. Their fine clothes and polished armor, their shining combed hair, their soft hands that had never done an honest day of work in their lives, could not compare to Koren's disheveled servant's clothes, and his tangled curly hair, and his rough hands, hands rough from a life of honest labor.

If her mother thought that sending Koren away would make Ariana's feelings cool, her mother was wrong. Mother and daughter had argued after Koren left, mother insisting the journey away from the castle had been the wizard's idea, Ariana not believing a word of it. The wizard suddenly had decided, while spring rains were soaking the ground, to ride many leagues on muddy roads, to an isolated hunting lodge? And it was merely a coincidence that the wizard decided to go on this 'sabbatical' just after Ariana almost kissed Koren? Ariana wasn't fooled. Nor was she discouraged. Perhaps there was much of her father in her, for people trying to keep something away from her only made her want it all the more. Her father had wanted to marry the daughter of a minor Baron, a land-rich but money-poor family that could bring nothing to the marriage but the girl who the king admired and loved. Adric Trehayme's advisors and his court had all been against the match, to no avail, for Adric was king and he would do as he wished. Most people, to this very day, considered Adric to have been impulsive and rash in that decision. Ariana, facing the suffocating constraints of her role, found much to admire in her father's action, and thought she understood why he had done that. Tarador was embodied in the king or queen, and the king or queen needed to think of Tarador first and above all, but sometimes, the person who held the office of king or queen needed to be themselves, or there would be nothing left of them.

Being away from Koren, and seeing all the eligible royal boys vying for her attention, brought Ariana to a decision, a decision she kept to herself. Once she became queen, she would grant Koren Bladewell a knighthood, and a grant of land. Land near Linden, so he would not be far away. She would brush aside the protests of her mother, and her advisors, and her court wizard if needed, and grant Koren the honors he should have had already. Until she became queen, she would bide her time, and tell no one of her decision. No one, except for one person, the future Sir Koren Bladewell. If she could not make Koren a knight now, she could at least tell him of her intentions, and trust him to keep quiet. Now that she had made her decision, she could hardly wait to tell Koren, so much so that she almost wrote a letter to be delivered to him in Relannon. No, a letter simply would not do, letters could be read by prying eyes. And she wanted to see Koren's face when she told him, see the surprise and joy on his face. She imagined seeing his face like that, over and over, and although she was burning up inside to tell him, she *would* wait for the right moment. She would wait until after the Cornerstone festival, after the Dukes had all departed, and the castle was back to normal. The weather should be delightfully warm by then, she would invite Koren out to a picnic lunch in the gazebo by the lake of the royal gardens. Perhaps for his fourteenth birthday, which would be soon. Yes, that would be the perfect setting, so she would wait for the perfect day, and everything would be perfect.

Until then, she kept the smile frozen on her face, and waved, and politely talked about nothing, and waited.

Now that all the Dukes and Duchesses had arrived for the Cornerstone festival, Koren was doubly busy, as were all the servants in the castle. Only two Dukes, close friends and allies of the Trehaymes, stayed in the royal palace, the other families maintained homes in the city. Koren was exhausted from running into the city and back, carrying gifts and messages to and from the wizard. Then there were the dinners Paedris was invited to, the lunches Paedris hosted in return, the daily rides out into the countryside, and the quiet meetings Paedris had with the army generals and captains. The only break Koren got was that the weapons master was too busy for Koren's training; the sparring ring was constantly busy with young royals eager to prove their prowess.

After he found the Cornerstone, and Carlana announced a festival to celebrate *Ariana's* great accomplishment, he had been angry. Then, like everyone in the castle and the surrounding city, he had become swept up in the excitement of the festival; every day, wagons streamed through the city gate bearing food, entertainers, even a circus with strange, giant animals that Paedris said were 'elephants'. Now, with two days remaining before the festival, Koren only wanted the event to be over, so he could rest. Let Ariana be given credit for finding the Cornerstone, she would have to sit through endless speeches and wear hot, scratchy clothes. Koren mostly wanted simply to sleep.

Koren feeling worn out was not good enough for Niles Forne, who now had his Duke living in the city, and Regin Falco was questioning why his son's advisor had been unable to get rid of a simple servant boy. The commoner boy was getting far too much attention from the princess. Excuses would not do, Duke Falco insisted Koren be gone by the end of the summer. One way, or another.

As long as Koren thought he had friendship and support from the crown princess, Forne reasoned, there would be little reason for the boy to leave. How then, to show Koren that he was nothing but a lowly servant to Ariana and her mother? Forne's latest plan was why Kyre sought out Koren in the stables.

"Hey, Koren, I haven't seen you around lately." Kyre said, trying to lean casually against the worn stall door.

"I've been busy." Koren barely looked up from his work.

"I have an idea," Kyre said, as if it had just occurred to him. "The Regency Council, that is the royal family and all the Dukes and Duchesses, are meeting tomorrow, to talk about the war, and strategy and all that stuff. You want to come as my guest? Paedris can't make you work while you're with me, right?" He winked.

"Oh, I don't know, uh, I don't think I'm supposed to wear my fancy servant's clothes if I'm not with Paedris, and he said he's skipping the Council meetings, they're all just posturing and speeches."

"I've got clothes you can wear. Come on, it will be fun. You can learn a lot, watching the dukes and duchesses arguing." Which is why Kyre's father was making him go. "You may hear something Lord Salva needs to hear. And, Ariana will be there."

"Oh, then, sure." Koren was eager to see the princess again. "Ok, I'll go."

"Hold!" Duke Bargann grumbled, pointing one of his pudgy fingers across to table at Koren, who was sitting in the row of chairs behind Kyre and his father. "Who is this boy? I don't recognize him."

Regin Falco drew himself upright in his chair, and fixed Bargann with an icy stare. "He is a close friend of my son, and a guest of the Falcos. Kyre can attest to his good character."

Bargann snorted, and waved his hand. "I don't care if he's your knight champion, Falco. Meetings of the Regency Council are for royalty only. That's the law. Regent Carlana, you allow this?"

Carlana winced. A petty dispute to start the meeting was the last thing she needed, and she silently cursed Koren for causing the trouble. Defending the Falcos in formal session of the Council almost made her choke on her words. "If Duke Falco wants-"

Bargann cut her off. "I don't care what Falco wants, the law is clear. I remind you, it is the law that put you on that throne now, instead of your daughter."

"Mother!" Ariana leaned to whisper harshly in her mother's ear.

"Not now, Ariana." Carlana whispered back. She could not understand why Bargann was arguing with Falco, those two were strong allies. What was really going on, she wondered? "The law is the law, and we must follow the law more than anyone else. You are the crown princess, you need to speak."

Ariana swallowed her anger, the taste bitter in her mouth. She stared straight ahead to avoid looking at Koren while she spoke, her voice barely above a whisper. "The law is clear. Koren must leave."

Koren's face burned with shame, he looked down, avoiding everyone's eyes. He had been hoping, expecting, even, that Ariana would speak up for him. Instead, he had been dismissed. Koren pushed his chair back and stood up. Remembering his manners, he bowed to Duke Falco, then to the throne, although he couldn't look at any of them.

Taking extra care not to stumble over his own feet, he walked out of the hall with what little dignity he had left.

Apparently, much indeed had happened while he had been away.

Hours later, Kyre found Koren chopping wood, out behind the stables. Koren had changed into his grubby work clothes, and must have been chopping wood for a while, because he had a large pile of wood already cut, split and stacked. "Koren, I'm sorry. It's my fault, I knew the law, but no one has enforced it for years. Bargann was being a jerk. Ariana should have told Bargann to be silent."

"She could do that?" Koren asked, so surprised that he almost sank the axe into his foot, instead of a log.

Kyre shrugged. "She's the crown princess, and Carlana is the Regent. The law is the law, but sometimes the law is whatever the royal family says it is. Allowing only royalty into the Regency Council is more of a tradition than a law."

Koren acted like he didn't care, while his teeth clenched in anger. Ariana could have saved him from being humiliated in front of the assembled royals, instead she had dismissed him? "It doesn't matter, it was probably boring anyway."

"I think Carlana is mad at you for causing a scene." Kyre placed a new log on the chopping block. "I'd stay out of her sight for a while, if I were you."

Koren took aim with the axe, and split the wood with one angry blow. "I haven't been to the palace in a long time, and I've never seen the Regent while I'm doing laundry, or splitting wood."

Koren slowly climbed the stairs of the tower, carrying dinner for Paedris. The scent of the roast beef and potatoes were making his mouth water, but he was so tired from chopping wood, that all he really wanted was to skip eating, and crawl into bed. The door was open; the wizard was looking at a pile of scrolls on the table, shifting them from one pile to another. "Ah, Koren, there you are. Set the food down over there, please. We have much to do tonight, and time is short."

"Tonight, sir?" Koren groaned. The sun was already setting when Koren had crossed the courtyard from the royal kitchens.

"Yes." Paedris said as he dug through a chest and pulled out a well-worn pair of traveling boots. "We are leaving tonight."

Koren's shoulders slumped. "Leaving again, sir? So soon?"

Paedris paused to stare at his servant. "Oh, I forgot to tell you. Yes, the Regent has refused to send the army out this summer, despite my advice, and the advice of, well, we can discuss that later." The wizard moved his lips like he had something sour in his mouth. "The point is, she has agreed I should visit one of our allies, to strengthen our alliance in advance of the summer. We are bringing an army troop with us, a full century of soldiers. Captain Raddick and I decided we would leave as soon as possible, before the Regent changes her mind. It is unfortunate that we'll miss the festival, but it cannot be helped. How soon can you be packed?"

Now Koren regretted not getting dinner for himself. "Uh, how long will we be gone, sir?"

"The journey to Hoffsta will be three weeks, better plan on four if we run into bad weather. Don't worry about food, the army quartermaster will take care of that. I'll need my best robes for when we are in Hoffsta, let's see, um-"

Koren bowed and started to back out of the room, before the wizard decided to pack the entire contents of the tower. "I will take care of it, sir. We should be ready in a turn of the glass?"

"Very well, good, good. Send word to Captain Raddick to expect us then."

It was two turns of the glass before the army troop rode out the gates of the castle, amidst much cursing, shouting, and general complaining about the lateness of the hour. And at the prospect of missing the festival, where there was sure to be food and drink and much merriment. As they wound their way down through the streets of the city, Koren took a look back at the gray stone walls of the castle, and the white palace lit by torches. Despite being tired and hungry, Koren was glad to be getting away from the castle, away from the maids who barely knew his name, away from the royals and their stupid rules, away from being embarrassed in front of a hall full of people, away from fickle princesses who liked him one day and ignored him the next. As far as Koren was concerned that night, he didn't care if he ever came back.

CHAPTER NINE

Ariana woke late, hiding her eyes from the bright sunshine as her maid pulled the curtains from her window. She had stayed up very late, with her mother and the Dukes, discussing boring affairs of state until she was barely able to keep her eyes open. What she had wanted to do last night, instead of listening to Dukes give speeches, was to find Koren and tell him how sorry she was that he had been cast out of the Regency Council meeting. Any rule that said a true hero like Koren could not attend such a meeting was a stupid rule, and she intended to change those rules when she wore the queen's crown on her heard. And make Koren royalty anyway, by granting him the knighthood he should have already! This morning, she would start by inviting her hero to lunch, to apologize in person. And maybe tell him about his future knighthood that very day, if the moment seemed to be right. After all, there was no reason she had to wait for his birthday to give him a present. "Good morning, Suzanna, it looks like a fine day." Ariana said as she sat up, stretched her arms and yawned.

The maid curtsied. "Good morning, your Highness. It is indeed a fine day, will you be taking a ride before your lessons?"

"I will have breakfast first. Bring me a pen and paper, I wish to send a note to invite Koren Bladewell to lunch with me today."

"But, my lady-"

Ariana waved away her maid's protest. "I know what my mother says about me having boys here in my chambers, so we will dine in the royal hall. And I don't care what my mother thinks." She added almost under her breath. Her mother should be the one to apologize to Koren, but since that would never happen, Ariana would do it herself.

"But, my lady, the wizard and his servant rode out with Captain Raddick last night. Going to Hoffsta, they are."

"Hoffsta?" Ariana exclaimed. She remembered her mother discussing Hoffsta with some of the dukes, she couldn't remember what was said. "But that is so far away! Koren won't be back for months?"

"Yes, my lady. You won't be needing the pen and paper, then?"

"No!" Ariana shouted, and pulled the covers over her head, to hide her tears. Koren had left the castle before she could tell him she was sorry. "He must think I'm a horrible," she sobbed to herself. Sending Koren away again must have been her mother's idea! She threw the covers off, and slid her feet onto the floor. "Get my dress, I will speak with my mother right away."

"No, I didn't send Lord Salva away to get Koren out of the castle, whatever gave you that silly idea?" Carlana asked as she bit into a piece of buttered toast. "If you had been paying attention the past week, Paedris wants me to send the army out again this summer, and he persuaded more than half the Dukes to agree with him. I told them that I am not risking the army on another adventure, but what I did agree to was sending a troop of soldiers, and Lord Salva, to Hoffsta. King Perannin of Hoffsta is nervous about Acedor raiding his coast, and he was been wavering in his alliance with Tarador. Paedris and Captain Raddick are going there, to show our support for Hoffsta."

"But they left in the middle of the night! I didn't get a chance to tell Koren I was sorry for throwing him out of the council meeting!"

Carlana shrugged. "Departing in the night was Captain Raddick's decision. And crown princesses do not apologize to servant boys. You did nothing wrong, Ariana, Koren should not have been there. If anyone is to blame, it is the Falcos."

Ariana still had her arms across her chest, defiant. "You can't blame-"

"Why *was* Koren with the Falcos?" Carlana interrupted. "He had no business being there. The wizard's boy sitting with our political rivals?"

"Kyre is Koren's friend." Ariana said with a frown.

Carlana's laugh was bitter. "Falcos do not make friends with servant boys. What game is Regin playing? It disturbs me that a boy my daughter is so infatuated with is-"

"I don't have a crush on Koren." Ariana protested weakly.

Carlana appraised her daughter with a cool eye, then held out her hand. "Ariana, dear, sit down, please. You forget, I was your age one time, and I know what it is like to have a crush on a boy." The Regent sighed. "Koren saved your life, and he discovered the Cornerstone, of course he's a hero to you-"

"He's a hero to everyone! If everyone knew."

"If everyone knew, the enemy would know, and it would not be healthy for Koren to have the enemy's eye fixed upon him."

"The enemy's eye is fixed on us."

"Yes, and that is why we live in a castle, surrounded by soldiers, and you take a dozen guards with you whenever you ride outside these walls. Koren is under Lord Salva's protection, that is why he was brought to live with Paedris. Ariana," Carlana took her daughter's hands in her own, "I also think Koren is an extraordinary boy, and I see why you admire him. But you do understand that you are a princess, and he is a commoner, and there can never be anything between you?"

Ariana nodded reluctantly, defiant. "Yes, mother."

"Good. Someday, there will be the proper time to recognize Koren for his achievements, I promise you that. Until then, would you like to do something that might help Koren?"

"Yes?" Ariana's mood brightened.

"Find out why Kyre brought Koren to sit with the Falcos. Kyre must have known Koren would be humiliated, what we need to know is why. Why are the Falcos interested in the wizard's servant?"

Koren found he greatly enjoyed riding with the army. The soldiers, except for those few who resented his wizard-spelled skill with the sword, liked him and treated him as one of their own. Koren ate his meals while sitting around a campfire with the soldiers. The soldiers were happy to have someone who had not already heard all their stories, lies and jokes; and Koren was happy to hear the stories, lies and jokes, even when he couldn't tell the difference between them. When Captain Raddick decided it was time, at the end of a long day of riding, for drill with weapons, formations both on foot and horseback, and other training, Koren took his place with the soldiers, griping and complaining just as they did. Although he did not take a turn standing guard at night, he rose early to bring coffee and hot food to the soldiers who were up guarding the camp, in the wee hours of the morning.

Carrying the pail of hot coffee, Koren carefully stepped around the sleeping forms of soldiers until he came to the edge of the campsite. Koren knew his vision at night was far better than most people, it had been that way ever since he could remember, so he didn't think it was the result of another spell Paedris had cast on him. He had no trouble following the faint trail of flattened grass up to where the sentries were posted. He also could move very quietly, so he took care to make noise as he approached the guards, lest he startle a guard, and be the target of an arrow in the darkness.

"Halt! Who goes there?" A woman's voice called out.

"Koren Bladewell. The password is 'cornstalk'."

"Yes it is." The woman chuckled. "Advance and be recognized. Did you bring something to eat?"

"Just coffee, the cooks don't have breakfast ready yet." Seeing the disappointment on the soldiers' faces, Koren reached into his pocket with a smile. "But I do have this sweetcake that Paedris didn't eat last night."

"Ah, give it here, my good man."

Koren split the sweetcake into three pieces, and sat eating quietly with the two soldiers, looking off into the darkness. As they were still inside Tarador, no one expected an enemy attack, and the sentries were bored.

"Let me see your face." The woman named Blogel said, and studied Koren's cheek in the dim moonlight. "Huh. You'll have a bruise, nothing more. If they do that again, you call for me, we'll teach them a lesson. They hit you hard." Yesterday, Koren had been sparring with two soldiers who resented his wizard-spelled combat skills; Koren found he could usually hold off three soldiers, if they were only using practice swords. After getting whacked with Koren's sword too many times, the men called three of their friends, and in the melee, Koren had taken a hard blow to the face, before an officer stepped in and broke up the fight. The five men were now on punishment duty, and Koren would try to avoid them when he could.

"I hit them harder." Koren said with a grin. And that was the truth, he had hit them hard, even with the padding wrapped around Koren's dwarf-made short sword, it still hurt to get whacked on the arm or in the belly.

"And you did, you did!" Blogel agreed, patting Koren on the back. She liked the young servant boy, he reminded her of her brother, back on the family farm. With women making up only fourteen of the hundred soldiers in Raddick's century, the women tended to stick together, and they had sort of adopted Koren, looking after the boy. "Tell me, that story I heard, about you rescuing the princess from a bear, or bandits, or something, was that true?"

"Bah!" The other soldier, a man named Kreger, snorted. "Next you'll be believing the boy pulled the Cornerstone out of his pocket, and gave it to the princess."

"Let the boy speak, Kreger. True or not, it's a good story."

Koren took a deep breath, and repeated the story Paedris told him to use, if the subject ever came up. "There was a bear, a really big one, and the guards say they found bandits in the woods, later. The bear came out of the woods, it was being chased by a swarm of bees, and it knocked over the boat. I pulled the princess out of the river."

"Huh," Blogel sounded disappointed, "she could have drowned, I guess, if you hadn't been there."

Koren grinned and nodded vigorously. "Princesses can't swim, with all those fancy clothes they wear."

Blogel laughed. "Wait 'til she gets the crown on her head, she really won't be able to swim then."

"I hear what you were doing in those woods was poaching Duke Yarron's deer?" Kreger asked.

"I didn't see any signs against poaching." Koren grumbled. "And mostly, it was fish, anyway."

"Lucky you saved the princess, then, before Yarron's sheriff caught you." Kreger looked at Koren sharply. "Dukes don't take kindly to poachers."

Blogel slapped her fellow guard on the head. "Give the boy his due, Kreger! Besides, can you tell me you've never taken a deer or two, when you were hungry and the sheriff wasn't looking?"

"Well," Kreger grunted, then smiled, "maybe. Got to keep them darned lazy sheriffs on their toes, right?"

"Quite right, quite right." Blogel took a sip of coffee. "So, Koren, you ever thought of being a soldier?"

Koren looked down at the ground. Soldiers came from common folk, but the officers only took men from good families, who could vouch for their character. Without a family, Koren didn't think being a soldier was an option for him. "I, uh, I work for Paedris, that's what I do."

"Yes, of course, but what about your future?" Kreger asked. "You're not going to live in a cubbyhole in the wizard's tower forever, are you? A young man like yourself needs to think of the future. Do you have a girl? Women like men who have a future ahead of them. If you're not going to be a soldier, are you going to learn a trade, or rent some land to farm? You come from farmers, don't you?"

Koren glumly admitted he had not thought much beyond being the wizard's servant. He had saved almost every coin Paedris had paid to him, little as that was. "I do know farming, I suppose it would be nice to have land of my own, someday."

"There you go!" Kreger said encouragingly. "I have a little plot of land myself, a couple acres set aside, plan to live there someday when I'm done soldiering, and be lord o' my own land."

"Ha! You, a lord?" Blogel laughed. "Your soldiering will be done when a orc splits you with an axe."

"Don't listen to her, Koren. Be on your way, now, there's more of us needing coffee this morn. You think on what we said about your future, hear?"

"Paedris, how long do you, uh, think you want me to work for you?"

The wizard's eyebrows flew up, and set down the mug of coffee he had been drinking. "You don't like being here?" It had never occurred to Paedris that a lowly peasant boy would not enjoy being the court wizard's servant.

"Um, yes, sir, I am very grateful, it's great living in the castle, I mean, in your tower, sir. It's just that, most boys my age would be learning a trade, for the future. If I'm ever to, to get married, someday, I would need a place of my own."

"Married?" Paedris exclaimed, astonished. Koren had been spending time with Ariana-

No! It couldn't be! Koren had rescued the princess, but surely he was not such a fool that he considered her a sweetheart? This could be a disaster! Paedris was so shocked by the unexpected conversation that his face took on a scowl that Koren mistook for anger. "You have a girl in mind?"

"No! Sir. Not now. I don't have a trade, or own any land, my mother would say I'm not a good catch? But, someday-" Koren looked at the floor, embarrassed. Then he blurted out "I can't live in a cubbyhole forever, sir."

Paedris felt a shiver of relief. There was no romance with the princess; Koren was nothing but a normal boy, wanting to know of his future. But what could Paedris say? That Koren would, in a short few years, replace Paedris as the most powerful wizard in Tarador, and have a castle of his own to live in? The wizard cleared his throat. "Koren, in your young life, you have already rescued a princess and found the lost Cornerstone. You may stay here as long as you like, personally I don't know what I would do without you. But I can certainly understand that a young man like you needs to think of the future. Have you considered a trade you would like to be trained in?"

"I know how to farm, sir, raise crops, and I'm good with animals. Someday, I suppose, I would like land of my own."

"Hmmm." Paedris rubbed his beard while he thought. "Koren, when I agreed to take the position here as court wizard, I didn't only get fancy robes and an awkward old tower to live in. There is a grant of land that comes with it, the land was supposed to be a country escape for me. I've only been to see my land once or twice, it's about two days' ride to the north, but it's nice enough. The family down the road farms my land, and we split the money from sale of the crops. If you like, in a few years, you could live there, and raise crops for me. I think I remember there is a small house, and a barn." Paedris had a flash of inspiration. "In fact, I will make a bargain with you. If you remain here as my servant, until your sixteenth birthday, then I will give a quarter of my land to you."

"Give me, sir?" Koren gaped at the wizard.

"I certainly have no need for it, I don't know the first thing about farming."

"My own land." Koren said in a whisper.

"It's not much, mind you, a quarter of the land is only about fifty acres."

"Fifty acres?!"

Paedris was taken aback. "Is that too small for a farm?"

"No!" Fifty acres was more land than his family had owned! Now Koren had to sit down, his shaky legs could not support him. "No, it's very generous, sir. Fifty acres."

"Here, drink this, you look pale." While Koren gratefully drank the coffee, Paedris pondered how to get out of the sticky mess he'd talked himself into. Technically, he didn't *own* the land he had just promised to give to Koren. The Trehaymes owned it, the land was for Paedris to use while he served as the court wizard, but he didn't *own* it. Perhaps Paedris could persuade Carlana to give the land to Koren, as a well-deserved reward for his service to Tarador? A quiet grant of land would not likely attract the enemy's attention to Koren. And if Carlana did not agree, Paedris himself would buy land for Koren; the wizard had enough money of his own. Raising the money would require selling some of his own land in Estada, perhaps he should write to his nephew there? Yes, the more Paedris thought, the more he liked the idea of Koren being away from the castle, away from prying eyes, while Paedris trained him in wizardry. The way the boy's power was growing, by the time Koren was sixteen, there would be no way Paedris could hide the truth from him any longer. "Huh?" Paedris realized Koren has been saying something.

"Sir, how can I ever thank you?"

"Bah!" The wizard waved his hand. "It is the least I could do, considering all you have done for Tarador. Now, finish your breakfast, Captain Raddick wants us packed and ready to ride in half a glass."

By the time Ariana was able to ask Kyre about why Koren had been with the Falcos in the Regency Council meeting, her anger had only grown. She'd been forced to wait for the end of the Council meetings, then the three days of the Cornerstone Festival, then Kyre had joined other royal boys in a hunting expedition that had lasted six whole days! She had been miserable during the Cornerstone Festival, feeling nauseous when people praised her for finding that fabled lost object. She had practiced what she would say to the Falco boy, clever words to trap him in the lies he would inevitably tell. She was determined to get the truth out of Kyre Falco.

Kyre was feeling particularly good that day, the hunting expedition had been fun, with far more racing about across the countryside on horseback and general tomfoolery than hunting, a chance for young royals to get away from the formality of the royal castle, showing off, pretending they were 'roughing it' when all their meals were cooked for them, and they slept every night in comfortable lodges or in large, fancy tents that were set up by servants. One night, Kyre had insisted that one of his older servants, who was not feeling well and suffered especially from the still-cold nights, sleep in Kyre's tent, while Kyre put his bedroll under the simple tarp his guards shared. Other royal boys laughed at him when he helped cook breakfast and brought food to his ill servant, then helped take down and pack away the tents, but Kyre didn't mind their jeers. His servants worked hard for him, and he trusted his guards with his life. Such loyalty deserved to be rewarded, rather than the disdain and abuse many royals gave to the common-born people who served them. Kyre wished his father understood that; it took so little effort to make common people happy, they were grateful for even simple gestures from royalty. Treating people fairly, and with dignity, not only ensured their loyalty, it felt good. Kyre's father felt that any familiarity with servants would lead only to shirking of duty and, eventually, questioning of orders, and disobedience. It is far more proper, Regin Falco advised, for servants to fear their masters, lest they assume undeserved equality with their royal betters. Kyre Falco wondered if his father considered whether, in case of a dire threat, who would be more reliable; people who served only out of fear, or those served from a sense of loyalty? Loyalty had to work both ways.

So, Kyre was feeling good, after having earned his father's grudging pleasure for Kyre successfully getting Koren to leave the castle for several months at least, after enjoying a smashingly good time at the Cornerstone festival, and coming back tired but happy from the hunting expedition. And now being called to an audience with the crown princess, in her private chambers! Kyre had asked Niles Forne what the princess wanted, but his advisor had no idea, having returned to the castle only a few hours before the invitation from the princess arrived. Forne had been frantic, calling in all his informants, but no one had anything useful to report. The princess had been tired after the festival, and kept mostly to herself, receiving few visitors other than for her official duties, which didn't give Forne any clue as to why Kyre had been invited to the palace. All Forne was able to do was to get Kyre properly dressed, and send him on his way.

Thus it was that Kyre had no idea what Ariana wanted to talk about, when he was announced at the door to her private chambers in the palace. He had no idea, but he was hopeful. He had done well in the games before the Cornerstone festival, winning several sparring contests, and a long horse race. Perhaps he had caught the eye of the princess? Ariana was in her study, a small but pleasant room with a large window that gave a view out over the gardens. "Your Highness," he said as he bowed deeply to the princess, then he turned and gave a short bow to her maid. "Mistress Hodgins," he addressed Nurelka, "I have heard that you like pine honey, please accept this jar I bought in the Wendurn hills."

"I," Nurelka didn't know what to do, being taken aback by Kyre's gesture. Honey from the pine forest in the Wendurn hills was the best in the land, and her favorite. She looked to Ariana for guidance; the princess seemed to be as surprised as Nurelka was. Ariana flicked her wrist in a gesture intended to be unseen by Kyre Falco, Nurelka accepted the jar of honey, curtsied and responded properly. "Thank you, your Grace," she said, and retreated to the far corner of the room.

Kyre's gesture had thrown Ariana off, and that irritated her. Instead of beginning with the usual meaningless niceties, she went right to the question she wanted to ask. "Why was Koren Bladewell sitting with the Falcos?"

It was Kyre's turn to be taken aback. Koren Bladewell had been the last thing on his mind, the boy was gone, and would be away for months, perhaps the entire summer. He lamely slipped into a lie. "I thought he would enjoy it, seeing everyone sitting around arguing. I wanted to get him away from his chores for an afternoon."

"You invited Koren to be nice, because you are such close friends?" Ariana asked, her voice dripping with sarcasm.

"We are friends." Although Koren deserved a better friend than Kyre.

"You, Kyre Falco, friends with a common servant, a boy who doesn't even have a family? I think anyone would find that hard to believe."

"His is my friend." Or he thinks he is, Kyre thought guiltily. "He's the only person I know who doesn't want something from me. When Koren goes out riding with me, it's because he enjoys being outside the castle walls on his horse, and not because he wants a favor from me or my family." Kyre spoke quickly because it was the truth, he didn't need to wait while he thought up a good lie. "Everything else around here is politics," he looked the princess directly in the eye as he spoke, "and I grow sick of it sometimes."

"A Falco who doesn't enjoy the game of scheming for power? Are you quite certain you are Kyre Falco?"

Kyre was genuinely hurt. "You don't know me at all." He responded hotly, forgetting he was speaking to the crown princess. "You know what your family thinks of my family, the history of people long dead. How would you like it if people judged you only by what they think of your mother?"

Ariana knew she would not like that at all. "I am to believe that you invited Koren to sit with you, out of your well-known kindness to the common people? Why did your father's lap dog Duke Bargann object?"

Kyre shrugged. He'd repeated the lie enough times now that he almost half believed it. "Bargann sometimes gets a burr under his saddle, and needs to show he's not beholden to my father. They've had a dispute going since the beginning of the winter, I don't know what it's about," he said truthfully, even though he was certain the dispute had nothing to do with Koren Bladewell. Niles Forne had arranged for Duke Bargann to object to Koren being in the Regency Council meeting, and Bargann had played his part, likely hoping this small favor would help gain leverage in his dispute with the Falcos. Except apparently now that favor, the whole plan, had backfired on the Falcos, earned the ire of the crown princess. Kyre's father was not going to be pleased about this. Impulsively, Kyre asked "Is that why Koren left before the Cornerstone festival?" Kyre couldn't remember now whether Koren had left the same day he'd been ejected from the Regency Council, or shortly after. It hadn't seemed important at the time, and Kyre had been very busy.

"No," Ariana said with a haughty toss of her head, to cover her own frustration at mishandling the conversation. Kyre's gift to Nurelka had thrown Ariana completely off her plan; all her carefully crafted questions, to steer the Falco heir into revealing the truth, had vanished when she amateurishly blurted out the question on her mind. Ariana's mother was not going to be pleased about this. "Lord Salva has business in Hoffsta, which you would know if you'd been paying attention during the discussions, he left as soon as Captain Raddick had his troops ready."

Kyre appeared to take a moment to consider Ariana's announcement. He spoke slowly and formally, while his mind raced to think. "My mistake, your Highness, I did not remember. I spoke to Koren after the Regency Council meeting, to apologize for any embarrassment caused to him, and Koren didn't mention that he was planning to leave the castle." Kyre was telling the truth, Koren had been upset, but why hadn't he said anything about going to Hoffsta? Had Koren suspected that Kyre set him up? "Will that be all, your Highness?" Kyre needed to talk to Fore about this terrible development, figure out a way to make certain none of the blame came back to Kyre.

Ariana, more disgusted with herself than with Kyre Falco, simply nodded, her cheeks red with a mixture of anger and embarrassment. She was not going to let the matter drop, but she needed to be more subtle in the future.

CHAPTER TEN

Koren's head was still spinning while they rode that morning. He had plenty of time to think, because Captain Raddick was not pressing his men to ride fast that morning, they only had five leagues to go, before stopping in a village for the middle of the day. Paedris noticed that his servant was distracted. "Ah, I see you have rejoined us, Koren."

Koren's face grew red with embarrassment. "Yes, sir. I was thinking on something. Nothing important."

"Now that you've thunk," Paedris said with a twinkle in his eye, "I want you to do a favor for me. When we get to the village of Longshire, ride ahead with Raddick, and see if they have a room at the inn. After sleeping on a cot these last three weeks, my back could use a real bed for the night."

"I thought we were only stopping here for the afternoon, sir?"

Paedris chuckled. "That is Captain Raddick's plan. But, as I'm sure there will be a child, or a prize cow, or a chicken, that needs to be healed, why, it wouldn't be right for the court wizard to ignore the needy. Could keep us here until well after dark."

"Oh, yes, sir." Koren winked. "Certainly, sir."

It was a fine day, the sky clear, the air fresh and warming, and the late morning sun drying the last of the dew that was still clinging to the underside of fence rails alongside the road. The air smelled like fresh, clean earth, the homey scent of plowed fields where seeds had only just begun to sprout. There were only a few wispy clouds on the horizon to the south, where Paedris said was the sea that formed Tarador's southern border. The Sea! Koren very much wanted to see that great body of water; everyone who had seen it said he would be amazed. The biggest body of water Koren had ever seen was a lake, and that not a large one, barely more than a pond. He had seen paintings of the sea, and of the great ships with their towering white sails. It was hard to imagine a ship, as big as a barn, moving across the water. Up ahead of him, across the fields and around a bend in the road, he could see a barn, and beyond that, the roofs of a village.

It was pleasant to be riding with the army, alongside the wizard, under a clear blue sky. He had a fine horse, a full belly, and not a care in the world at the moment. Here, it didn't matter whether Dukes thought he belonged, or whether maids remembered his name, or whether a fickle princess liked for him to be around that day, or not. Here, he only had to ride, and provide for the wizard's needs and comforts, and keep out of trouble. Koren was thoroughly enjoying himself, out in the countryside where he belonged, instead of behind the grim stone walls of a castle. The country they rode through reminded him of Crickdon; low, gently rolling hills, open farm fields where the crops were beginning to come out of the ground and rise toward the sky, neatly fenced pastures with sheep-

Pastures with sheep.

Just sheep.

No people.

Koren rose from the saddle, looking all around, front and back. He sat back down, opened his mouth to speak, closed it, opened it, and closed it again. He stared at the sheep, then at the buildings of the village ahead, unsure of himself.

His servant's odd behavior had not escaped the attention of the wizard. Had not escaped the attention, nor annoyance, of the wizard, who was trying to concentrate. "Koren, if you have something to say, please say it, and stop fidgeting."

"Sir, it's the sheep."

"Eh? What about them?" They looked like ordinary sheep to Paedris.

"They're alone. No shepherd, not even a dog. No farmer would leave his sheep alone like that, sir, they're too valuable. And too stupid."

"Uh," Paedris knew very little, zero actually, about the care and raising of sheep, "maybe the shepherd is-"

Koren continued excitedly, keeping his voice low. "And the village ahead, Longshire. Look, sir, see? There's no smoke coming from any of the chimneys. That big white building must be an inn, or a tavern. The kitchen there should have a cooking fire, for the noonday meal." Koren closed his eyes. "And, and, sir, I have a feeling like we're being watched."

Paedris shaded his eyes with a hand, and peered ahead at the cluster of buildings that made up the small village of Longshire. Koren was correct, none of the chimneys had smoke coming from them. The wizard bit his lip while he thought. "I don't see *anyone* in these fields. That is odd, isn't it?"

"Sir, now that I think about it, I don't remember seeing anyone for the past several leagues we've ridden. Not since we passed by that farm where the man was repairing the roof of his barn." Koren had waved to the man, who had paused in his work to wave back. "Sorry I've been so wooly headed this morning."

Paedris closed his eyes tightly in concentration. "I don't sense anything."

"Then that's good, right, sir?"

"You don't understand. I can't sense *anything*. I fear some other wizard is in the area, and has cast a spell to dampen my senses. Damn it!" Paedris cursed under his breath, the first time Koren had ever heard him curse. "We've all been wooly headed this morning. Koren, I want you to make your way up to Captain Raddick, and tell him I think we are being watched. I know this area well; just beyond the village there is a crossroads that leads to a bridge, the only bridge across the river for several leagues. Tell Raddick that I advise him to make straight through the village, and get across that bridge, if trouble strikes. Go now, but don't ride too quickly, if there are eyes watching us, I don't want to alert them yet."

"Yes, my lord." Koren tugged back on the reins, let Thunderbolt fall behind the wizard's horse, crossed to the other side of the army column, then he nudged Thunderbolt into a slow trot, and crouched down in the saddle. As he passed by troops, he greeted them laughing and joking, trying to act casually. He itched at the delay, for he and Paedris had been riding at the rear of the column, just ahead of the supply wagons. He slowed Thunderbolt to a walk as he finally approached the front of the column, where Captain Raddick rode.

Koren saluted, his right hand to his temple, although he was not sure a servant, and not a proper soldier, was supposed to use that greeting. During the entire journey, Koren had never spoken to Raddick; he had dealt with Raddick's lieutenants instead. "Sir? Captain Raddick?"

Raddick had been discussing something with one of his lieutenants, and was annoyed by the interruption. "Yes? Boy, I'm busy. I'll talk to you later."

"Begging your pardon, Captain sir, this is wizard business, and it can't wait," Koren insisted. Raddick was intimidating, but nowhere near as intimidating as Paedris.

Raddick turned his attention from the lieutenant. The wizard wouldn't interrupt army business unless it was important. "Speak, boy."

Nervously, Koren blurted out "Sir, those sheep are alone, no shepherd or dog around. We haven't seen anyone in the fields since we passed that barn a few leagues back. None of the buildings in the village have smoke from their chimneys. And Paedris says there must be a wizard around, because he can't sense anything, nothing at all, which I guess is unusual, for a wizard. He says he feels like we're being watched." Koren wasn't sure how wizard senses worked.

"Whoa, whoa, slow down, boy. Sheep?" Raddick twisted in the saddle to peer at the sheep contentedly grazing in the pasture the army column was passing by.

"Yes, sir, I think-" Koren stopped as Raddick waved his hand for silence.

"You're right. There's no one in the fields. And the village ahead appears deserted." Raddick was alarmed now, he exchanged a glance with his lieutenant, who nodded grimly and said a very bad word under his breath. They were deep inside Tarador, so Raddick had not bothered to have scouts ride on the army column's flanks. Deep inside Tarador, but less than fifteen leagues from the seacoast. Could the enemy have landed a raiding party, which had traveled so far inland? It was difficult to believe, but the enemy had been shockingly bold recently, even including an invasion of the Thrallren woods. Raddick didn't know the full story of how Ariana had been attacked, but Raddick did know Ariana's visit to LeVanne province had been cut short, and her guard doubled. "I am a damned fool! What else did the wizard say?" Raddick resisted the urge to gallop back to confer with the wizard himself.

"He advises that, if we're attacked, you go straight through the village, and across the bridge, he says it's the only bridge across the river for several leagues." They had passed another bridge that morning, but it was so old that part of the center span had fallen into the river; it was useless as a bridge.

Raddick nodded agreement. He had ridden the road before. He was not in a good position, if the enemy had planned an ambush, they had planned it well. Just across the field to the east, the river had steep banks on both sides, and was rushing deep and rapidly with the spring rains. The only way across the river was the bridge beyond the village ahead. Behind, the road went through a gap between two hills, which would be easy for the enemy to block. Ahead, the road squeezed between buildings in the village. His supply wagons could not travel across the fields and pastures, they were separated by stone walls, wood fences and tree lines which acted as windbreaks between the fields. It was a good place for a prepared battle, not good for an escape attempt.

Raddick made a quick decision. "Pentric," he turned back to his lieutenant, "when the wizard gives his signal, we ride through the town, enemy there or not. Leave the wagons; we get the men and horses across that bridge yonder. Boy, drop back slowly and tell Lord Salva that we await-"

While Koren was talking to Captain Raddick, Paedris called two soldiers, a man and a woman, and gave them orders. Here, in the royal army, he did have command authority. "Don't reach for your weapons," he began in a low voice, "the enemy is near. I said, *don't* reach for your weapons!" He added in annoyance as the younger soldier automatically gripped her sword and rose half out of the saddle. "What are your names?"

The older man, a veteran of many battles, with a white scar across his forehead to prove it, answered "Arteman, Lord Salva. I was with you at the battle of the Thrallren Woods, sir. This undisciplined young one is Dartenon." Dartenon tried to relax, but the inexperienced young soldier could not help glancing at the tree line atop a low ridge to the west. Arteman cuffed his companion on the side of her helmet. "Look straight ahead, you fool. What are your orders, my lord?"

"Though it seems unlikely here, and on this fine spring morn, the enemy will attack, soon. I have advised Captain Raddick to make straight through the village, and across the bridge, if he can. You two find my servant, and get him to safety."

"My lord?" Arteman asked in surprise. A servant's place was by his master's side, especially a wizard-spelled expert fighter like Koren Bladewell.

Angrily, for he was running out of time, Paedris grabbed the front of Arteman's leather vest. "You get Koren to safety, even if it costs your lives, do you hear me?" The wizard added a compulsion spell under his words, and the two soldiers stiffened.

"Yes, my lord." They said in unison.

"I only hope we have time-" Paedris began, before there was a terrible roar from the west, and the enemy stepped forward from the tree line. "Go, you fools!"

Koren caused the enemy to spring their trap too early, for the enemy had seen Raddick giving orders to his lieutenants, and seen Dartenon grasp her sword. The enemy's plan had been to let the Taradoran royal army's column pass by to the south, then emerge from the tree line and cut the road behind them, while enemy soldiers in the village ahead set up a barricade across the road. Instead, at the instant the enemy was sighted, two of Raddick's lieutenants spurred their horses, and led ten soldiers toward the village as fast as they could ride. Another soldier spun his horse around and raced back along the column to tell the supply men to cut their horses loose, and abandon the wagons. Raddick's horse reared up as its master pulled back on the reins, and Raddick stood in the stirrups and raised his sword high, crying out to the men behind him "To me, to me!" More and more of the enemy were emerging from the tree line, Raddick realized he was facing a substantial force, not a mere raiding party landed from a single ship. There were easily three hundred of the enemy mounted on horseback, and he could see a few enemy soldiers in the village ahead, belatedly scrambling to set up a barricade. His two lieutenants were almost at the village; the enemy dropped the tree they intended to use as a barricade and fumbled for their bows. The main body of the enemy charged from the tree line with another roar, racing down the pasture, scattering the panicked sheep. Raddick waved his men forward with his sword, letting them pass him by, so he could attend to the rear of the column. As Raddick wheeled his horse around to face the enemy, there was a shout of dismay from his men. Fireballs from three enemy wizards lashed out, and even Raddick winced in terror, before Paedris deflected the fireballs to splash into the pasture, well short of their target! A cheer went up from the royal army soldiers, and Raddick saw Paedris spur his horse to leap the fence, and race away across the pasture with the three enemy wizards following him.

Koren had momentarily frozen at first sight of the enemy, while Thunderbolt strained at the reins. Seeing Raddick's horse rear up, Koren figured he no longer needed to worry about alerting the enemy, so he urged his horse on, and soon wind roared in his ears as he raced back alongside the road, passing the soldiers who were all moving forward as fast as their own horses could move. When the enemy threw fireballs at Paedris, Koren flinched like everyone else, and Thunderbolt veered off the road in fear. It was not the horse's fault, Thunderbolt had never been trained as a warhorse, and few horses could stand the sight and smell of fire, especially magical fire. As he struggled to control his horse, Koren saw Paedris deflect the fireballs, which fell short to scorch the pasture grass. When the wizard's horse jumped the fence and raced away across the pasture, Koren was stunned. Why would the wizard leave him? He managed to get Thunderbolt pointed in the right direction, and was about to urge the horse onward, when his way was blocked by two soldiers. "Out of my way!" Koren waved frantically, anxious to find a way through the chaos of soldiers who were struggling to control their own horses, and help Paedris.

"Come with us!" One of the soldiers shouted at him, and tried to grab the reins.

"No! I must-"

"Lord Salva told us to get you to safety! Those are our orders!" The man stared into Koren's eyes with such intensity that Koren hesitated.

"Paedris ordered me away?" Koren couldn't believe it. "But I'm his servant."

"Fat lot of good your sword will do against wizard fire, boy, you'd just get in the way. I've seen Lord Salva in battle; he's an army all to himself. I'm Arteman, she is Dartenon. You have a helmet? Put it on. Now, come with us, or we're lost."

Koren fumbled to get his helmet untied, and jammed the uncomfortable armor on his head, it was a bit too big and he had to tilt it back to keep it out of his eyes. The three tried to gallop up the road, but it was now jammed between the fences by other soldiers on horseback, and riderless horses that had been cut loose from the wagons. The enemy was now halfway across the pasture, having split in two groups to cut off the royal army front and back. Koren stood up from the saddle to watch Paedris; his master was riding away across the pasture at an angle, heading for a gap in the trees that separated the sheep pasture from the next field. The three enemy wizards were chasing Paedris, as Koren watched, fireballs flew back and forth, neither side getting a hit, and then Paedris' horse plunged through the tree line gap to the next field, and he was gone from sight. Koren turned to look ahead, where Raddick's lead troops had forced their way into the village, sweeping aside the barricade. The Captain himself was behind Koren, leading the men from the wagons. "We're not going to make it!" Koren shouted, seeing that the enemy would cut the road before he reached the village.

"The boy's right!" Arteman hauled in the reins, causing his horse to skid to a halt on the muddy dirt road, and the old soldier slid off onto the ground. "Help me!" The soldier called out as he began pulling apart the tall split-rail fence that lined the east side of the road. Koren and Dartenon joined him, along with a half-dozen other soldiers, they swiftly opened a twenty-foot gap in the fence, and soldiers began to guide their horses into the field without waiting for orders; they could see the enemy almost upon them.

Captain Raddick rode up, about to rebuke his men for stopping, when he saw the gap in the fence, judged how close the enemy was, and recognized Arteman. "Arteman, good thinking. On with you, then, around the village, get across the bridge and don't let anything delay you. Archers! Give these men cover!" Raddick spurred his horse onward, to hold off the enemy.

Back on their horses, Koren, Arteman and Dartenon rode across the field at a fast trot, looking backwards to see whether all the soldiers were following them. A dozen soldiers had gone past the gap in the fence and were riding hard after Captain Raddick, swords drawn, charging into the lead group of enemy soldiers, who had reached the road, and jumped their horses over the low stone fence there. Only a few of the royal army soldiers who had gone through the fence had bows and arrows, they all jumped off their horses and knelt behind the fence. While Koren's magical skill could hit a moving target from horseback, the other archers needed to steady their aim. Arrows thudded into the enemy soldiers, breaking up their formation just as Raddick and his soldiers slammed into the enemy with a ringing of steel on steel.

Koren stood up in his stirrups, transfixed by the sight of his first battle. He had never seen the enemy, now he saw them up close, not more than fifty yards away. They were terrifying, Koren felt his legs turning to jelly as he stared, transfixed. The enemy's helmets were covered with black feathers, the faceplate of their helmets were fashioned and painted to look like skulls, and they wore bones and teeth on a string around their necks, or woven into their beards. To Koren, they looked like demons from a nightmare, come to life. He knew, from talking to Paedris and some of Raddick's men, those scary faceplates interfered with the enemy soldier's vision, but even knowing that, Koren found his hands shaking. Unlike the swords of the royal army, which gleamed bright from being kept constantly cleaned and oiled, the enemy's swords were never cleaned, left covered with blood and gore from previous battles. Only the sharp edges were bare steel, a cut from such a dirty blade made for certain sickness, and some of the enemy's blades were dipped in poison.

Despite his fear, Koren reined Thunderbolt to a halt. The handful of royal archers were losing their battle, there simply weren't enough of them, though they were shooting as fast as they could, and now from close range, for the enemy was now in the road, and making for the gap in the fence. In a few moments, the archers would need to leap back on their horses, or be overrun. "The archers! I can help!" Koren called out.

Arteman cursed Koren's foolishness. "Move! That's an order! You don't even have a bow, you young idiot!" He whacked Thunderbolt on the horse's left flank with the flat of his sword, and the horse shot forward in fright, beyond Koren's control. To keep Koren moving, Arteman kept his horse pressing sideways into Thunderbolt's flank, urging him forward. Koren reluctantly followed Arteman's orders, while looking backward at the archers. Only three of the archers made it back to their horses, the others had waited too long, and were now tangled with the enemy, fighting with swords. Their bows were discarded on the ground, useless in close combat. Koren let Thunderbolt run on by himself, the fight both horrified and fascinated him so he couldn't tear his eyes away. For all the exhausting hours Koren had spent sparring with the weapons master, he had never seen real combat, with men falling, with blood, and screams and terror and confusion. Now, only now, could he see the value in the weapons master's endless, tedious 'Forms'. In combat, real combat, no one had time to think, a soldier needed to *act*, without hesitation. The endless repetitions of Forms had taught a soldier's *muscles* how to move a sword, a shield, a pike or whatever weapon he had, without waiting for his slow brain to decide what to do.

"Make for the bridge!" Arteman called out, holding his sword in the air to rally the men to him. Those who could followed Arteman, urging their horses on in what was now a race. To get to the bridge beyond the village, the royal army men needed to go through a field between the river bluff on the left and the buildings of the small village on the right. Koren tried to judge, the field they must ride through was maybe two hundred yards wide? Royal army soldiers were still fighting with enemy troops in the village, those few royal army men who had forced their way through the village were guarding the entrance to the bridge, but there were only three of them, and the enemy was now alert to the need to seize that bridge, having failed to spring their trap in the village.

Koren tore his eyes away from watching the fate of the archers behind, and concentrated on where he was going. He knew Thunderbolt could easily outpace any of the royal army's horses, but it would be foolish to be out front by himself, and if he got to the bridge first by himself, what would he do then? He held Thunderbolt back, despite the horse chomping at the bit and fighting the reins, keeping pace with Arteman and Dartenon. Their three horses reached the edge of the field, and jumped a low stone wall. The next field had been planted with corn, which was not yet even knee-high; the horses had no problem finding solid ground for their hooves. They were just passing the barn that was the last building of the village, and Koren was looking ahead to the three royal army soldiers guarding the bridge, when Dartenon gave an agonized cry, leaned to the right, and fell off her horse.

Koren and Arteman wheeled their horses around as one, to see Dartenon on her knees, an arrow protruding from her upper right leg. A group of enemy archers were crouched in the shadow of the barn. Koren opened his mouth to shout for the woman to get back on her horse, when another arrow hit the young soldier square in the chest. Dartenon's head snapped back, and she fell to the ground without a sound.

Koren was halfway out of his saddle when he felt Arteman's hand on the collar of his vest. "No! You can't help her!" The man shouted.

"But, I, we have to-"

Arteman pulled Koren close so they were face to face. "This is not a game, it's war! If you don't want to die like Dartenon, ride for the bridge."

Koren had never seen anyone die in battle before; his mind was awhirl of confusion while he let Arteman lead the way toward the bridge. Tears blurred Koren's vision as Thunderbolt carried him toward safety. Enemy troops were now riding out of the village in an attempt to cut off their escape; it was going to be close. Some instinct caused Koren to duck, just before an arrow whizzed past where his head had been. He was turning to see where the arrow had come from, when there was a sound like a sharp axe hitting soft wood, and Arteman gasped. An arrow was sticking out of the old soldier's back! Koren leaned over to stop Arteman was falling off his horse, but the horses moved apart, and he was too late. Arteman fell forward, rolling out of the saddle face first, and fell to the ground. One of his horse's hooves kicked him in the head by accident as the soldier fell, throwing his helmet off. The horse stumbled and fell, rolling over then scrambling up and running off in fright.

Koren hopped down to the ground; horrified the old soldier may already be dead. Arteman lay on his side, and groaned when Koren reached him, his eyes fluttering, unfocused. The arrow was not in deep, it had hit a thick strap on the leather vest, Koren was able to quickly wiggle it out, as the man grunted in pain. Pulling the ripped vest open, Koren could see white bone in the wound; the tip must have hit a rib. Painful, but lucky for Arteman, and the arrowhead looked clean, Koren licked it and spit out, it didn't taste like poison. The old soldier was not so lucky about the wound on his head. The horse's hoof had caught him in the right temple; there was a deep gash in the shape of a horseshoe, and a lot of blood. When Koren tried to help him up, Arteman only groaned, could not keep his legs under him. The man's eyes were closed, his head lolled from side to side. There was no way Koren could get the man onto Thunderbolt's back by himself. Something, a sound, a movement of air, caused Koren to spin around. Before he realized what he was doing, his short sword was in his hand, and the blade flicked out to knock aside an arrow that had been aimed at Arteman.

"How the hell did you-" Exclaimed a passing soldier, astonished as Koren stood up, and this time, his sword blade neatly sliced the next arrow's shaft in two, with the tip diving into the ground.

"Help me!" Koren pleaded. "I can't get Arteman onto my horse."

"Damned fool you are, and damned fool I am too, but-" The man waved to another soldier, and together the two men quickly picked up Arteman and flopped him face down on Thunderbolt's back, then they were off.

Jamming his sword back into its sheath, Koren climbed up into the saddle, and this time, dug his heels into the horse's side and loosed the reins. Thunderbolt *moved*, surging forward so fast that Koren almost fell off backwards, the horse's hooves digging clods of dirt out of the ground and flinging them backwards in his headlong flight. In less than twenty strides, the great horse had passed the horses of the two soldiers who stopped to help Koren, their mouths gaping open as Thunderbolt, nostrils flaring, passed them as if they were standing still. Passed them while carrying two people on his back. If Koren had time, he would have fairly burst with pride about his horse, but all he could think of then was to get Arteman to the bridge.

And with a clatter of hooves on wood, they were on the bridge. Some instinct caused Koren to hop off, and hand Thunderbolt's reins to a passing rider. "Take Arteman across the bridge, he's hurt badly!" He shouted, and the man took hold of the reins and guided Thunderbolt across the bridge at a trot.

Koren ran over to the royal army men guarding the bridge entrance, who were now seven soldiers, including three archers. Leaving his sword in its sheath, Koren asked breathlessly "What can I do? Can I give you arrows while you shoot?"

One of the archers nodded, and indicated his quiver of arrows on the ground. But another archer held up his right wrist, which lay at an unnatural angle to his arm, it was sprained badly. "Not much use I am with this bow." The man said with disgust, and spat on the ground. "Can you use a bow?"

Before Koren could answer, another soldier snapped "don't waste your bow on a boy! I'll take the bow myself before-"

"Shut your mouth, Teegan." Answered another of the archers. "Koren here is the wizard's boy, and if you haven't seen his archery lessons with the weapons master, I have. Wizard skill he has with a bow, never misses, and he can shoot an arrow further than any of us. Hedris, give him your bow."

Koren felt much better with a bow in his hand. Calmer. With purpose. The injured soldier called Hedris handed him an arrow, and Koren sighted along it, then realized he was insulting a royal archer, who of course would have checked his own arrows. "Sorry."

Hedris shook his head side to side. "Don't be, I'd do the same. Always check weapons you're not familiar with. If you have the time. I think our time is about up." He pointed toward the village. The surviving royal army soldiers, with Captain Raddick and two of his lieutenants at the rear, were past the village and riding at full speed toward the bridge, pursued by the enemy. To the west, more of the enemy were riding to cut them off, and the enemy was ahead. "Hit the lead riders. Koren, you take the right." The head archer ordered, and the two royal army archers, and Koren, nocked arrows to strings, and drew back. The enemy rider Koren sighted on would be colliding with the royal army men in a few seconds, and the shot was at extreme range. Koren steadied his aim, stilled his breathing, and-

-hesitated.

The enemy soldier's face was scrunched up in an angry grimace, and his spear was held forward, reaching out toward the royal army.

Koren had never killed anyone, never fired an arrow, or swung a sword, in anger. Seeing the enemy's face, the face of a real person, he hesitated. The two other archers let their arrows fly, and either missed, or their arrows fell short.

"Koren." Hedris hissed in a loud whisper. "You've probably never killed a man, I know it's not an easy thing to do. Shoot. Shoot now, or more of our soldiers die."

Koren blinked, feeling his eyelids sting from the salt of dried tears, tears that had welled up in his eyes when Dartenon died. Thinking of that brave woman, Koren aimed slightly in front of the enemy rider, pulled the bowstring back as far as it would go, and waited a couple heartbeats. Paedris may have given him magical fighting powers with the sword, but Koren had always been deadly accurate with a bow, as far back as he could remember, hunting rabbits and deer around his parent's farm. He always *knew* just when to let an arrow fly. When he sensed the moment was right, he released the bowstring. "Another." He said to Hedris, while selecting another target, not needing to watch the arrow. The arrow would hit its target.

Koren never missed.

The enemy rider leveled his spear at a royal army soldier, and opened his mouth to let out a battle cry. Koren's first arrow impacted right in the roof of his mouth, cutting off his scream.

After that first shot, the battle was a blur for Koren. Take an arrow from Hedris, fit it to the bowstring, select a target, draw back the bowstring, wait for the right moment, and release. Again, and again, and again and again. Koren was having an effect on the battle, after five of their fellows died from arrows fired at such distance, other enemy riders veered off, trying to keep at longer range. The royal army took the opportunity to break through, and then Koren and the two other archers had to be careful, for their own men were blocking their shots. They switched their focus to the enemy soldiers riding in from the west, charging the bridge directly. Koren had time only to fire two more arrows, then Raddick's horse pounded onto the bridge, and the Captain shouted for his men to retreat. Koren followed the soldiers, running fast as he could, turning to fire another arrow. One royal army soldier was hit by an enemy arrow, and fell over the side of the bridge into the rushing water below. When Koren reached the far side, completely out of breath, he ducked aside to clear a path for the archers who had taken up position across the end of the bridge, blocking the enemy's path. Two archers were using flints to set fire to the oil-soaked rags they had wrapped around their arrows, as Koren and the last of the royal army raced safely past, they let the flaming arrows fly, aiming at the middle of the bridge. The arrows hit, and started small fires in the dry old timbers of the bridge deck. But enemy soldiers were charging fast across the bridge, led by a very large man on a massive warhorse. The man was entirely clad in black armor, as was the front of his horse. As Koren watched, two royal army archers shot at the enemy, but their arrows glanced off his armor. The warhorse did not shy away from the flames, but leaped over, and suddenly loomed before them. The enemy soldier raised a bloodstained battle-axe, and even the most battle-hardened royal army soldier felt fear.

Without asking, or much thought, Koren pulled an arrow from another archer's quiver, nocked it, aimed and fired in one smooth motion. The arrow took the enemy soldier right in the one gap in his armor: his throat. A cheer went up from the men around Koren as the huge man crashed to the bridge deck, and his panicked horse wheeled around, riderless, to leap back through the flames.

Two, three, five more flaming arrows hit the bridge, and it was ablaze, effectively blocking the enemy's path. The enemy sent arrows through the flames, and shouted insults, but Raddick had gotten most of his force safely out of the ambush. The battle was over, for the moment. He left a guard at the end of the now flaming bridge, and gathered his remaining lieutenants to discuss what to do next. Koren ran over and removed his helmet. "Captain, sir, what about Paedris? Lord Salva is in danger!"

"What the-?" Captain Raddick was startled to see Koren, startled and then angry. "What are you doing here, boy?" Raddick had lost track of Koren after the enemy emerged from the tree line, the last he had seen of the wizard's servant was of the boy riding back along the army column. When the wizard jumped the fence and rode away across the fields, Raddick had assumed Koren would have followed. "You didn't follow the wizard?"

"No, sir, I-"

"Your place is with your master, boy!" Raddick angrily waved his hand for silence when Koren tried to explain. Part of the anger was because Raddick had considered Koren to be an honorable person; he knew that the wizard and most of Raddick's soldiers liked Koren. Now Koren had disappointed him severely. "Lord Salva used his magical powers to give you lightning speed with that sword, so you could protect him, and you run away at the first sign of trouble? No, I don't want to hear excuses! Go see if you can help with the wounded, and stay out of my sight, you coward." The Captain dismissed Koren with a disgusted look, and turned to bark orders at his lieutenants.

"But, but I-" Koren stammered, totally surprised by the Captain's reaction. "Sir-" The words died in his mouth, as he realized only three people in the world knew he wasn't a coward, that Paedris had ordered Koren away. Dartenon lay dead, on a field across the river. Arteman was with the wounded, unconscious and uncertain to survive the day. And Paedris himself? Paedris was on his own, pursued by three enemy wizards. On the other side of the river, where there were hundreds of enemy soldiers.

"Come with me." Said an older soldier Koren didn't know, who had overheard Raddick's disgusted outburst. The man's clothes were spattered with blood, some of it was his own, from a ragged cut on his forearm, and one side of his beard was crusted with blood. He looked no worse than most of the royal army men. "Name's Porten, and you're Koren, right?"

"I'm not, I'm not a-" Koren self-consciously wiped at the drops of blood on this own face, blood that belonged to Arteman. Koren himself had not gotten even a scratch during the battle.

"Best you stay away from the Captain for a while, and do what he says. Can you help with the wounded?" The man asked gently. He knew this was the young man's first battle, and the old soldier remembered his own first battle, how shocked, scared and disoriented he had been, all those years ago.

Koren nodded. He was in shock, but not so much from the battle, which was still only a blur, as if it hadn't really happened. His shock was from Captain Raddick calling him a coward. "I'm *not* a coward!" Coward? In his first battle, he had fought hard, and killed enemy soldiers, without any real combat training! If Raddick hadn't been so busy, he would have seen Koren shooting arrows, seen that it was Koren who stopped that last, huge enemy soldier. "I've helped Paedris when he's healed people, but I don't know about potions or spells or anything like that."

"Healer's got his own potions, whatever he could carry with him since his wagon's on the other side of the river. Do what you can, and don't you worry about the Captain. He just lost a battle, and a lot of our men, on our own territory. He's not in a good mood about anything, so best stay out of his way for while."

"We can't just leave Paedris."

Porten gestured toward the enemy troops across the river, troops who were still firing arrows, when they thought they had a good shot. "Long as the enemy holds that side of the river, and we're over here, there's not much we can do to help the wizard, but you can help our men here. Come on now, time's wasting."

Koren knew what it was like to be truly tired before, from long days on his parent's farm, or surviving on his own in the wilderness, or working as the wizard's servant; he found a new meaning for *tired* that day. Already worn out from the unexpected battle, he spent the rest of the day doing whatever the royal army's healer needed done, and the man had Koren running ragged. Finding and chopping wood for a fire, hauling water from the river, dodging enemy arrows that still flew from the west riverbank, tending to the suffering wounded as best he knew how, which wasn't much. After Koren collected wood and got a fire roaring, and set kettles of water boiling to clean bandages, the healer asked Koren if he knew where to find bloodroot, which Koren knew could often be found growing along old stone fences and the cellars of abandoned homes. Riding frantically far around the countryside, Koren managed to gather two solid fistfuls of bloodroot leaves, and when he got back, even Thunderbolt was foaming with sweat, and unsteady on his great legs. The healer, without the magical skills of a wizard, and with most of his supplies in his wagon across the river, was doing the best he could to help the wounded.

"You found bloodroot? Give it here, give it here!" The man shouted excitedly. He wiped his hands off on a rag, then took a small pinch of bloodroot and crushed it between his fingers, inhaling deeply. "Ahhh, fresh! Good, very good, and more than a handful!" The healer had not expected Koren to find much, if any, of the rare plant, especially since Koren had no idea where to look, having never been in that part of Tarador before. "How did you find it?"

Koren gave a weary shrug. "South on the road, a quarter mile, I saw an overgrown lane, figured it used to lead up to an old farm. There's an abandoned farm house, the bloodroot was growing around the foundation stones." The bloodroot had been tangled with an old, thick rosebush; Koren's hands and arms were scratched and bleeding from being ripped up by the thorns.

The healer looked up sharply at Koren, with new respect. He knew little of the wizard's young servant, having never met the boy before Koren joined the army expedition. "Hmm. That was good thinking. Now, hurry, you know how to prepare a potion of bloodroot?"

"Sir, I've done it many times for Paed-, for Lord Salva. Wrap them in clean cloth, plunge into boiling water for a couple seconds, then gently squeeze the cloth to bruise the leaves, to bring out the juice, or sap, or whatever it is."

"Yes, yes, quickly, quickly! Only three leaves per cloth, we have too many wounded, and too few leaves. I only hope we are not too late." The healer glanced at the row of wounded men laying on blankets in the shade under a grove of trees. Koren saw that, while he had been searching for bloodroot, two men must have died; there were two empty blood-stained blankets in the row.

Bloodroot was very effective at stopping wounds from bleeding. It also stung the skin, by the time Koren had prepared all the bandages his thorn-scratched hands felt like they were on fire. He ran back and forth from the kettle to the healer, giving the man fresh bandages as needed. When all the bloodroot had been used up, Koren hurriedly tended to Thunderbolt, giving the horse water, and removing the saddle before brushing his glossy coat. The horse had eaten his fill of hay in the fields around the abandoned farm while Koren had collected the bloodroot, which was fortunate, considering that all the feed grain for the army's horses was in wagons across the river. The east side of the river was mostly woods and overgrown meadows, which provided little for the horses to eat. The soldiers all had field rations, of dried meat and fruit, in their packs, but their horses mostly went hungry.

The healer next instructed Koren to make a vegetable broth, from a dried mix the man had, and give it to the wounded men, to up keep their strength. As the day wore on into evening, Koren sat with the men who had recovered enough to speak, trying and failing to reassure them that everything would be all right.

"Sir?" Koren approached the healer, who had his meager supply of potion bottles laid out on a blanket. The man was holding bottles toward the setting sun, trying to see how much was left in each bottle. "I gave everyone the broth like you said, everyone who would take it. Arteman hasn't awakened."

The healer didn't know that Koren was almost desperate for Arteman to awaken, as the old soldier was the only person around who could tell Captain Raddick that Koren was not a coward, that Paedris had ordered Koren away. If the wizard didn't survive his own battle across the river, Koren could never prove he wasn't a coward.

"Arteman is an old soldier, veteran of many a campaign." The healer answered with great weariness. "This may be his last battle, and I fear he must fight this one alone. If he cannot recover on his own now, he'll need a wizard to heal him."

CHAPTER ELEVEN

Captain Raddick sent riders out north, east and south, to see whether the enemy was on the east side of the river also. Even the wounded soldiers struggled to sit up when the first of the riders returned as the sun was setting, everyone in camp was anxious for news. The news was good, as far as it went. There was no sign of the enemy on the east side of the river. Raddick, fearful the enemy would use small boats to sneak troops across the river in the darkness, but unable to move the wounded without wagons, ordered his men to cut down trees to create a makeshift barricade, and posted sentries along the riverbank. As darkness fell, Koren found himself with two soldiers on a bluff above the river, cutting down trees. Portis had seen Captain Raddick start making his rounds among the wounded men, and had pulled Koren away, to keep the boy out of Raddick's sight a while longer.

"You think the enemy will really try to cross the river tonight, Portis?" The other soldier asked, as he wiped sweat away from his eyes.

"Don't matter what I think, nor you; the Captain says we build barricades, then that's what we do."

"If I wanted to be a lumberjack, I wouldn't have joined the army." The other man grumbled. He looked down at the swiftly flowing, dark water. "Enemy'd have to be a fool to try getting across that, at night."

"You think so? And what would you have said the odds were we'd be ambushed this morning, huh?" Portis swung the ax, and it bit a shallow cut into the tree with a dull thudding sound, instead of a solid 'Thunk'. There was only one ax for the three men, and not even a proper wood-chopping axe. Raddick's men had to build barricades with the axe blade of the half dozen halberds that some men had carried as secondary weapons. The long pole handle of the halberds had been cut down to make it able to be swung as an axe, but the halberd blade was longer and thinner than a useful wood-chopping axe. Still, the soldiers needed to make do with what tools they had. The rest of their tools, food, supplies, medicines and weapons were in wagons left behind, across the river. "Koren, bring that stone, we need to sharpen the blade again."

"Sharpen it much more, and there won't be any blade left." The grumpy man grumbled, as he sat down on the ground.

"What're you sittin' for, Loxa, you lazy good for nothing? You sharpen it this time, maybe that'll learn you against complain' so much. Koren, you give Loxa the stone, I'm setting down for a rest."

Koren handed the sharpening stone to the grumpy Loxa, who sat down and began to run the stone over the axe blade. Koren's job in the three-man team was to drive two horses to drag the felled trees down to where they would be set into the barricade. Portis had put him in charge of two horses which usually pulled the cook's wagon; beasts that were strong and sturdy, not fast. If they had been cutting the trees for lumber, the branches would have been trimmed off before Koren hitched the logs to the horses. For a barricade, what Raddick wanted were trees with tangled, thick branches, which made them very difficult for the horses to drag through the woods. The trees were constantly getting snagged on other trees, rocks and pretty much everything, and Koren had to haul on the branches with all his might to get them unsnagged. By the time he had delivered four trees to the barricade, he had used up all the swear words he learned from the royal army, and started inventing new curses of his own.

"Looks like we could get some rain." Loxa observed.

"Huh? Why you say that?" Portis grunted, laying backing against a tree, with his eyes closed.

Loxa pointed to the northwest with the sharpening stone. "Lightning in the clouds, over yonder there. Storm's coming."

"That's funny looking lightning." Koren said, and hopped on a tree stump to get a better view. "I've never seen lightning like that."

Portis roused himself to see what was so interesting about lightning. "What the hell is wrong with you two, can't you let an honest, hard-working man rest?"

Loxa snorted with laughter. "If you were honest, or hard-work-"

"Quiet!" Portis exclaimed. "That's not lightning, you fool, you ever see lightning red and blue like that? That's wizard fire! The light from wizard fire, reflected on the clouds above."

"Paedris! He's alive!" Koren shouted excitedly. Now that he knew what he was seeing, he could tell Portis was right. It was wizard fire, glowing off the bottom of the thin, low-lying clouds to the northwest. Glowing blue, and red. That morning, the enemy wizards had thrown red fire, and Paedris blue.

"Course he's alive all right, the old rascal, alive and giving the enemy hell, by the look of it." Portis said with pride in his voice. "That's our wizard, he is."

"I never seen wizard fire until this morning," Loxa said defensively. "You seen old Paedris fight before?"

"Well, sure," Portis said, "wasn't I with him when we-"

"We need to help him!" Koren interrupted.

"Help him?! I told you before-"

"Before we didn't know where he was, or that he was still alive, and fighting. If there's a battle, that means he didn't get away. He could be trapped somewhere. He needs our help."

"You know where he is, do you, you who never been in these parts before?"

"He's, he's," Koren waited for another flash of light, "he's over there, somewhere." He waved his hand in the general direction of the light. To the northwest, beyond the village, up the river. "We can follow the light to find him!"

"Koren, lad, your heart is in the right place, but you need to use your head too." Portis tapped his temple with a finger. "That's on the other side of the river, we can't even get over there." Portis pointed down toward the black, rushing water that was now barely visible in the vanishing twilight.

"We burned the bridge behind us, for real this time." Loxa added. "No way to get across, that I know. Nearest bridge is leagues north of here?"

"Aye, listen to Loxa, lad, he's right. Nothing we can do tonight to help Paedris." Portis said. "Best we stay here, and build a barricade, so we can stay behind it until dawn, and some of us can catch a few winks of sleep."

"No." Koren dropped the horses' reins on the ground. "I'm *not* in the army, I'm not a soldier, I'm a servant. And I belong with Paedris." And he turned and hurried down the hill without another word.

"What?" Loxa exclaimed, "You can't just-"

Portis grasped the younger soldier's arm. "Let him be, Loxa, let him be. This is his first battle, and he's right, he's not a soldier. We'll get these last two trees cut and drag them down to the road. Koren will be back, I think, he can't go far."

Koren held Thunderbolt to a fast trot, although he could feel the great horse straining to run. The road was dark and unfamiliar, Koren could not risk the horse stepping into a hole and injuring a leg. The moon was half-lit, high in the sky, but ducked behind clouds too often for Koren to see the road ahead with confidence. This road, on the east side of the river, seemed to be less used than the west side road the army had traveled. The road here was more narrow, deeply rutted, with overhanging trees, and in places old stone walls had partly tumbled into the road. Several times Thunderbolt had stumbled and nearly thrown Koren off when the horse stepped on a stone. Even with his excellent night vision, Koren was afraid to let his horse run in the darkness.

An hour after seeing the wizard fire in the sky, Koren was doubting whether he had been right to run off to rescue Paedris. What was he going to do, by himself? After he had run down the hill and found Thunderbolt, he had ridden away as fast as he could, pausing only to lean down from the saddle to snatch a bow and quiver of arrows from the ground next to a sleeping soldier. Koren had let loose the reins; Thunderbolt had surged off into the night, chased by a chorus of shouts from the alarmed soldiers. Koren had urged Thunderbolt onward, to bolt through the last gap in the almost-finished barricade, then they were gone, Koren barely hearing the shouting behind him over the wind whistling in his ears. Soon as they were around the first bend in the road, where the light from the campfires and torches of the royal army was blocked by trees, they were plunged into sudden darkness, and Koren had pulled back on the reins, and held Thunderbolt to a brisk trot since then. At first, Koren had been afraid of Captain Raddick sending men to pursue him, but in the confusion of setting up barricades and preparing for a night defense, no one thought much of the wizard's servant riding out of camp on his horse; the few soldiers who noticed him going assumed Koren had been sent on another errand by the healer.

He had gotten away; he had a strong horse, a bow, a quiver of arrows, his short sword, and no idea how he was going to rescue the court wizard. No idea how he was going to get to Paedris, to even get across the river. When the road ran through farm fields, where Koren could see the sky to the west, he would sometimes see wizard fire reflected off the clouds, so he had a very rough idea of the direction he needed to go. The river, however, was still an impossible barrier. Once, when the road ran close to the top of the bluff above the river, Koren had gotten off Thunderbolt and walked to the edge. When the half moon peeked out from behind the clouds, he saw there was a steep drop to dark, rushing water. White foam boiled around the rocks, the river was still in spring flood, there was no way Thunderbolt could get across, and Koren would be gambling his life to swim across, even without weapons.

He stared down at the river, at the swiftly flowing black water, and doubted himself. What was he doing, in the dark, all alone? What did he hope to accomplish, one person, with a single quiver of arrows and a short sword, against enemy wizards and scores of battle-hardened soldiers? Maybe he should ride back to camp, tell Portis he was right, and do whatever he was ordered to do.

Give up? Give up, and ride back to the safety of the camp, where he could chop wood, and boil water, safely surrounded by the royal army? Give up like a coward?

Koren had not been angry during the battle, he hadn't had time. After, he was in shock, and scrambling to follow the healer's orders. It was only now, alone with his thoughts in the darkness, which he was free to consider what had happened since the morning, a perfectly pleasant spring morning. And he was angry. The battle was still a blur in his mind, the fighting so unexpected, so brief and intense, that he only remembered bits and pieces, such as when Dartenon fell, and the look on the face of that enemy soldier on the bridge, when Koren's arrow caught him in the throat. He wasn't angry about the battle, he was angry that Captain Raddick had called him a coward.

Koren may be a jinx, may have been cursed by God, may have been a terrible son, may have been abandoned by his parents. But he was *not* a coward. And he was going to prove that, or die trying.

He sprung to his feet, ran back to Thunderbolt, and continued north on the road, anger fueling his determination.

They were nearly past the crossroads before Koren realized another road led off to the left. He dropped to the ground, and walked carefully along what he thought was the center of the road, feeling grass and weeds brushing against his legs. This road, wherever it led, had not seen much traffic in a long time. He waited for the moonlight, the clouds were thinning and ragged, he should soon have some light to guide him for a few hours, until the moon set over the hills to the west. When the clouds slid aside, Koren got a decent look at the road in front of him. It was overgrown, with brush crowding the sides, a downed tree blocking the way. It looked like someone had made an attempt to chop the tree in half, to move it, but then had given up. The road didn't appear to be a promising way for Koren to get across the river.

Unless-

That morning, he had ridden past another little-used crossroads on the west side of the river, and one of the soldiers who had been in the area before said the road to the east led to an old bridge, which was not used because the center span had fallen in the river. That road had also been overgrown. Maybe the weed-choked road ahead went to the old bridge. Even if the bridge could no longer carry wagons, or horses, it might be possible for Koren to somehow use the bridge supports to cross the river.

The moonlight helped Koren see at least the outlines of the road, and any trees that had fallen across it, but after Thunderbolt stumbled twice on objects unseen under the weeds, Koren dropped down and walked, leading the way. By the time they reached the bridge, the moonlight was steady, and Koren could just barely see wizard fire, not reflected on the scattered clouds, but as a flickering glow on the western skyline, through the trees atop a hill. He must be getting closer to the wizard!

Leaving Thunderbolt behind, Koren cautiously walked out onto the bridge. It was narrow, only wide enough for one wagon, but substantial, being built of stone. Leaning over the railing, he could see the bridge was a series of stone arches, soaring high above the river below. Each arch ended in a sort of tower, rising from the river, white rapids glinted in the moonlight around the base of the towers. The gray stone surface of the bridge ended after four arches, replaced by a wooden bridge in the center, which at one time reached across to the stone tower on the other side. Some time ago, the wood structure had sagged and tilted to one side; it still reached almost all the way across, but many deck boards were missing, and the other end of the wood bridge deck was below the stone road surface on the other side. Someone had tied a sturdy rope all the way across, Koren tugged hard on the rope, it felt safe. Safe enough for him, carrying his small pack, short sword, bow and arrows? He edged out onto the sagging bridge, feeling for steady footing, holding tightly to the rope. Halfway to the other side, he felt the bridge shift and sway under his weight. With his legs shaking, he inched his way back toward the security of the stone arch. He could gather up his pack, sword, bow and arrows, and make it across. Even if the floor of the bridge gave way, he could hang onto the rope. There was no way for Thunderbolt to get across; the wood bridge sagged so much there was a gap half as high as Koren was tall at the far end. Surely not even Thunderbolt's legs could jump that high.

"Good horse, good boy, Thunderbolt." Koren hugged the horse's neck and stroked his shoulder. He left the saddle on, but took off the bridle and reins, tucking them into a saddlebag. "You know your way back to the army, right? You'll be fine, you'll be fine." He said, more to convince himself than to calm the horse. Koren hated to leave his horse alone, but didn't know what else to do. "Now go, go, good boy." Koren gave the horse a swat on the rump, and Thunderbolt trotted off the bridge, then turned and stood, watching and waiting. "Go! Go away!" Koren shouted, but Thunderbolt simply snorted, stomped his feet a few times and flicked his tail nervously.

Shrugging his shoulders, Koren turned and ran to the edge of the stone arch, taking a firm grip on the rope. Knowing what to expect, he was not alarmed when the wood bridge swayed and sagged. Trying to keep tension in the rope, so it could take his full weight if the wood structure of the bridge fell, he walked carefully across, feeling for a solid surface before he placed his foot down on the wood deck. There was little wind that night; he could hear the roar of the water rushing under the bridge, and the creaking of the timbers, and the blood pounding in his ears. When he reached the end of the wood structure, he had to climb up to the stone road surface, hauling himself up on the rope. The stones at the edge were loose, the first time he tried to pull himself over the edge, the stone crumbled and he fell back onto the wood deck, which lurched to the side with a cracking sound. Koren held tightly onto the rope, taking his weight off his feet, but he could feel a strong vibration, and then the entire wood bridge was swaying wildly. With a loud clatter of hooves, Koren swung around on the rope to see the now-panicked horse racing across the bridge toward him, lurching from one side to the other as the wood surface gave way beneath Thunderbolt's weight!

Koren was about to shout for Thunderbolt to go back, then he saw in a flash that the horse's only chance to survive was to keep going, as fast as he could. Desperation gave him strength, and Koren heaved himself up the rope to roll onto the stone surface of the arch. He barely spun around in time to see Thunderbolt, eyes wide open in terror, launch himself into the air on his great legs, with the wood bridge span rocking and sagging beneath his hooves. Koren rolled aside just before the horse crashed down belly first on the stone bridge surface, legs splayed out front and back. Thunderbolt's back legs were hanging in the air, hooves scrambling as the stones on the edge of the bridge broke loose underneath him. Koren flung his arms around the horse's neck, and felt himself being dragged over the edge, when Thunderbolt rolled on his side, almost crushing Koren, but managing to get his back legs onto the bridge. Still terrified, Thunderbolt scrambled up and raced off toward the other end of the bridge, one hoof glancing Koren's leg and slamming him back into the stone bridge railing, and almost over the edge. He had his own split second of terror as he hung out over the river, before pulling himself back from the edge, because even the stone bridge began shaking as the wood span splintered and began dropping into the river. On hands and knees, and then running so fast his feet barely touched the bridge, he followed his horse until they were both safely on solid ground.

Perhaps it was the shock of nearly dying and losing his beloved horse, but Koren found himself falling to his knees, hugging Thunderbolt's left foreleg, and laughing out loud, laughing uncontrollably. The image frozen in his mind was of Thunderbolt, the mighty terror of the royal stables, flying through the air to flop down awkwardly, sprawled on the bridge. Koren had never seen a horse land on its belly, and he didn't think Thunderbolt had either. When he could stop laughing, he walked around the horse, checking for injuries. With Koren's hands touching him, Thunderbolt quickly stopped shaking and panting, and playfully nipped Koren's hair. "You *stupid*, crazy horse." Koren muttered. "What were you thinking? You're smarter than that!" The ground shook as the wood span broke loose from the stone bridge on the far side, and crashed into the river with a tremendous splash.

"I guess we'll not be going back that way, huh, boy?" Koren said nervously. Now he was committed, effectively stranded on the enemy's side of the river. He took the bridle out of the saddlebag and put it back on, then swung himself atop Thunderbolt. "Let's get out of here. If the enemy is within a league, they surely heard that bridge fall into the river."

Koren urged Thunderbolt into an easy trot, feeling whether the horse was limping, but everything seemed to be normal. He urged the horse into a slow gallop, trusting Thunderbolt to find his way through the weeds on the road in the half moonlight. He shook his head in amazement at his horse. That the horse could jump off a collapsing bridge, jump higher than Koren was tall, was amazing. That any horse could land so awkwardly, and not be seriously injured, but be able to carry a rider at a gallop; Koren didn't know what to think.

It was no more than a mile to the crossroads Koren had ridden by that very morning, which now seemed a lifetime ago. He recognized the pair of tall, old oak trees that stood on the northwest side of the main road. Behind them stretched a hay field, the patchy hay barely tall enough to reach Koren's knees, the field ended in a line of trees atop a hill to the west. Through those trees came flashes of light; wizard fire, much brighter than he had seen before! He must be close now. Excited and scared at the same time, he guided Thunderbolt along a slight depression in the field that led up the hill. The depression must have been an old road, a very old road. The crossroads at one time had gone four ways. Wherever the abandoned road went, it was in the same direction as the wizard fire, and that was where Koren was going.

The ancient road used to go through the trees, but trees had long ago grown tall and filled in the gap. What he saw from the top of the hill made him unbuckle the guard around his sword, and take the bow off his shoulder to hold in his left hand. The line of trees was thin, maybe fifty yards deep. On the other side of the trees was a field that sloped down to a shallow valley, with a stream shining in the moonlight. And the tumbled-down stone ruins of a small castle, where the wizard firelight was coming from. A dozen or more riderless horses stood outside the castle walls on the far side, the wall closest to Koren had mostly fallen down, with brush and trees grown up between the stones. There was a section where only a few stones lay on the ground, half buried, that was probably where the castle gate used to be. Thunderbolt could jump over one of the large stones, and then they'd be in the courtyard of the ruined castle. With the enemy.

And then what?

Then he'd find Paedris, and help however he could. Captain Raddick was right, the wizard had given Koren magical fighting skills to serve as a personal guard; where he belonged was with Paedris, not taking shelter with the royal army.

Koren realized with sudden clarity that he wasn't afraid of dying. His life for the past year was a gift. He could have died alone in the woods, from illness, cold, starvation, snakebite, a thousand things could have gone wrong for a boy alone in the wilderness. Or he could have drowned in the raging river, when he was trying to hang onto a girl he didn't even know. He could have been killed by the bandits, or by Duke Yarron's men, or he could have fallen off the roof of Yarron's palace. He could have died that very morning, in battle, despite Paedris' effort to send him away to safety. He could even have died that very night by falling into the river, when his inexplicably foolish horse had insisted on following him, even at the risk of his own life. Thunderbolt. He was not afraid for his own life, but he regretted risking the horse's life. "I'm sorry to bring you into this," he said as he patted the horse's neck, "this isn't your fight. But if Paedris is hurt, I can't carry him out of there all by myself."

The horse whinnied like a pony, and craned its neck to look up at him. "You and me, boy, you and me, right to the end." Koren said softly, and when he looked in the horse's eye, he had the odd feeling that the animal *understood* him. Surely that was not possible? Thunderbolt winked slowly, tossed his head, and reared up on his back legs, as if eager to get going.

He was surprised that he was able to ride all the way down, through the field, splashing across the stream and up to the castle, without any alarm being raised by the enemy. What he had expected was to see soldiers running out, or to hear an arrow whistling past his ear. Everyone inside the castle must be focused on the battle between the wizards; this close to the castle walls, the burnt, rotten-egg sulphur smell of wizard fire was overpowering, and the flashes of light were intense enough to leave spots swimming before his eyes. As Thunderbolt galloped up the gentle slope toward the ruined gate, Koren could feel the horse's muscles quiver with excitement, or fear, or both. With a sharp snort, the horse gathered himself and sprung into the air, to leap over a large stone block, and into what used to be the courtyard of what Koren now realized used to be a fortress, not any rich nobleman's castle. Scattered around the courtyard were large stone blocks, and piles of smaller stones.

There was a flash of wizard fire, illuminating the courtyard with harsh red light, exposing all to Koren's eyes. And exposing him. He reined Thunderbolt to a halt behind a large pile of stones, and for a moment, everyone froze.

Across the courtyard, taking shelter behind stones, were enemy soldiers. Bodies of a half dozen other soldiers were laying on the ground, bodies scorched by wizard fire. Some looked as if they had tried to climb the walls to shoot arrows down at Paedris, but from the broken and scorched bodies of the dead, the others must have realized that was a foolish idea. Behind other stones in the middle of the courtyard were two enemy wizards, only two. A blackened and cracked pile of stones nearby must have been where the third enemy wizard met his end. With shock, Koren realized Paedris must have sent a blast of wizard fire *through* a block of stone, to kill that wizard. He had no idea Paedris was so powerful, the court wizard so rarely showed his true abilities.

And there was Paedris himself, huddled behind two large stones. No, not huddled, he was slumped over, looking tired and lost. His purple robes were blackened, his face shown with sweat in the moonlight, and his hands shook. But what Koren saw in the court wizard's face when their eyes met was not fear, but shock. Complete shock, not at a rescuer appearing, but that his rescuer was *Koren*. They had only a split second to exchange a glance, horror showing in Paedris' face, when everything happened at once.

The enemy wizards quickly recovered from their surprise at the unexpected arrival of Koren, the one to the left reached back with one hand and began gathering a fireball to throw. But Koren was faster, so fast he was barely aware of what he was doing. In one motion, he slid off Thunderbolt, had an arrow nocked on the bowstring before he realized his arm had even reached back into the quiver. Then the arrow was flying on its way toward the wizard; before Koren's feet touched the ground, two other arrows followed it, all flying straight and true. It was like living in a dream where the world moved so slowly as to be almost frozen. Koren could clearly see the three arrows tracking in on the wizard, the arrows seeming to be suspended on invisible strings in the air, see that wizard's ugly, scarred face change from anger to shock to fear. The hand that had been gathering a fireball flexed open, letting the fireball dissipate to nothingness, while the other hand swept the wizard's staff up, up into the path of the first arrow. The first arrow was barely knocked aside, its sharp tip slicing the wizard's shoulder as it flew by. The second arrow was well and truly blocked, the staff by now up in the front of the wizard, his lips moving rapidly, chanting a spell; the second arrow sprang aside directly to the left of the direction it had been flying.

But the third arrow-

The third arrow bored in, relentless, unstoppable. Koren's vision was so clear, in the slowed time, that he could see the feathers of the fletching at the rear of the arrow waving slightly, as they guided the shaft through the air. The sharp tip shone brightly in the moonlight. The wizard's lips froze in mid-chant as he realized to his terror that he would not have time to deflect this arrow, that he, mighty mage of Acedor, was about to be struck by an *arrow*, a weapon used by lowly soldiers. An arrow, of all things!

And then the third arrow struck, struck with a solid thunking sound, piercing the wizard's robes, slicing into and through the wizard until even the feathers were half buried in the man's chest. The man half rose up in utter shock, turning toward the other enemy wizard, who was equally shocked, shock so deeply as to be beyond belief. The stricken man's hand released his staff to fall toward the ground, and touched the back end of the now blood-soaked arrow that protruded from his chest. His fingertips had no more than brushed the arrow, when he was incinerated by a searingly bright blue fireball.

Paedris had not been sitting idly by as Koren fought. Taking advantage of the enemy wizard's surprise and weakness, and exposure from rising up from behind the stone, the court wizard of Tarador had flung a fireball at the enemy who had besieged him for countless hours.

"Koren!" Paedris shouted, his voice hoarse from weakness and thirst. "You idiot! Get out of here!"

"No! I came to rescue you!" Koren shouted, as he slapped Thunderbolt on the rump, and the horse bolted away, startled.

Paedris' heart sank, and he felt icy cold with fear. The enemy had set a trap for him, a trap to kill or capture Tarador's court wizard. Now, because a young man was far more brave than sensible, the enemy might unknowingly destroy Tarador's true greatest weapon, or worse, capture Koren! The remaining enemy wizard could not have missed the astonishing fact that the boy who suddenly appeared in their midst must be a wizard; no one else could possibly have killed a mage of Acedor with a mere arrow. No one but a wizard could have set three arrows in flight before the first was halfway to its target. How could Koren have been so stupid? Why could he not follow orders, or had the two soldiers Paedris instructed to keep Koren safe failed in their duty? All these thoughts raced through Paedris' mind in a flash, and then there was no time for thought, because the enemy struck back, and time slowed again.

As Koren reached back for another arrow, it was his turn to be stricken with fear. The last enemy wizard had seen an opportunity in the brief second while Koren and Paedris had shouted to each other. An opportunity for a desperate attack; an angry red fireball was already streaking through the air toward Koren.

Koren's right hand, which had been reaching back for an arrow, turned to flash in front of his face, palm outward in an instinctive, and futile, last gesture of the doomed. Out of the corner of his eye, Koren could see Paedris' mouth open in terror as the old wizard shouted "Noooooooooooo!" and then Koren cringed, closed his eyes and prepared to die. The fireball struck, enveloping Koren in searing heat-

-and washed over and around him. The fireball *flowed* around Koren like he was a rock and the ball of fire was a fast-flowing stream. It parted around him, rejoining into a single ball of flame behind him, and slammed into the stone wall. Stone chips exploded outward in a violent explosion and Koren ducked, flinging himself to the ground. Sharp shards of stone pelted him, inflicting numerous small cuts through his clothing.

If the enemy wizard has been shocked by the death of his fellow mage, that did not compare to his utter incomprehension that Koren had survived the most powerful fireball the wizard was capable of throwing. Survived, it appeared, without even scorching the boy's tangled mess of hair. Unable to speak, or really even to think, the enemy wizard stood halfway up, to gape at the boy, who was now pushing himself to his knees, shaking his head. From behind a pair of stones rose up the man who had been the Acedor raiding force's prey; the powerful court wizard of Tarador.

The two adversaries locked eyes for an instant, as the mage of Acedor gestured toward Koren, his mouth forming a silent question. No wizard could survive being struck by a fireball; a powerful wizard like Paedris could knock a fireball aside, or block it to splash in front of him, but no one could survive being struck by searing magical fire. Not even, thought the mage, his own dark Master. That boy-

could the boy

possibly

be-

Paedris nodded, in answer to the question. "Yes." He said simply, then reached down deep inside himself, gathered his last remaining strength, and the last enemy wizard disappeared in a blaze of blue fire.

"Paedris!" Koren shouted, as he watched the wizard sink to his knees, and fall facedown in the dirt and weeds that covered the ground of the old courtyard.

The enemy soldiers, cowering in fear and dismay after their three mages were burnt to a crisp, had regained a bit of their courage. True courage was not needed, for many soldiers of Acedor were under a compulsion, and that magical urge now reasserted itself. While Koren was straining to lift the wizard onto the kneeling horse, one soldier worked up the nerve to quickly glance above the pile of rocks he was hiding behind. What he saw emboldened him, and he motioned to his fellows. He saw the wizard of Tarador, unconscious or nearly so, and the boy. By themselves. The boy had survived a fireball, but surely that was the work of the Taradoran wizard, and not the boy? He looked like merely an ordinary boy. One boy, and there were eight veteran soldiers of Acedor arrayed against him.

Koren's first notion that the enemy was back was an arrow that just missed his head, barely missed because he had reflexively ducked his head aside at the last second. He had heard the whistle of the arrow in flight, or the twanging sound of a bowstring, or had it been something else? With a last desperate heave, he managed to get Paedris on the back of Thunderbolt, and he spun to face the enemy. He had only a split second to batter aside another arrow with his bow, and dodge a third, before he could nock an arrow of his own, and let it fly. A second arrow was on its way to another target before the first arrow had reached halfway across the courtyard, and the first arrow was traveling at blazing speed.

The enemy soldier who had been boldest paid the price for his actions, for he had been reaching for another arrow, when Koren's first missile caught him square in the chest, flinging him backwards. He sprawled, instantly dead, across a pile of stones. Koren's second target had the good fortune, or sense, to drop down as soon as he had loosed his own poorly aimed arrow. But Koren's second arrow still hit the top of the enemy's helmet with enough force to slam his face into a stone and make stars appear in his eyes.

"Koren, no! You must, *you* must get away. Everything depends on it. We are lost if-" Paedris muttered feverishly, almost in a whisper. Seeing Koren survive being struck by a fireball had not only shocked Paedris to his core, it terrified him. If Koren was that unimaginably strong now, what would he be when he gain his full powers? And could anyone control such power?

"Shhhh, quiet, sir, you mustn't strain yourself, you're weak with fever." Koren was afraid for the wizard's life, the man's pulse was weak and alternately racing and slow. He could not imagine the effort it had taken for Paedris to fight off, then kill, three enemy wizards. If the enemy had invaded Tarador to set a trap for the court wizard, they must have sent three of their most powerful wizards. That Paedris survived was a miracle, and now his life hung by a thread. Koren tied a strap across the wizard, to hold him onto the horse, and then grasped the bridle to look Thunderbolt in the eyes. "I don't know if Paedris had cast a spell on you, too, or if it is something else, but I think you can understand me somewhat. You need to carry Paedris out of here, fast as you can, get back to the road and go north, toward home. I'll follow you as I can," Koren added as he heard a clatter of stones announcing the enemy soldiers were again looking for an opportunity to attack. "Now, go!" Koren shouted, and swatted Thunderbolt on the rump. The horse took two steps forward, stopped, turned to look back at Koren, tossed his head, and was gone, leaping over the half-buried stone of the ruined gate.

CHAPTER TWELVE

Koren wrinkled his nose before stepping into the water, breaking the solid green scum of algae on top. The water was disgusting, and smelled worse, but he could not see any choice. He was trapped, with only two ways out. Forward was the channel of water, the surface of the water a good two feet below the roof of the ancient drainage channel where Koren stood, but the roof stones of the vault sloped down and disappeared under the water ahead. Behind him were enemy troops, with plenty of arrows, swords, spears, and most important, a cask of oil, and torches to light it. When Paedris escaped, Koren discovered he had only two arrows left in his quiver, and although those two arrows claimed two enemy soldiers, there were many of the enemy left, far more than Koren expected. Right after Thunderbolt carried the wizard away, several soldiers had blocked the gap in the wall where the gate used to be, cutting off Koren's escape route. And although Koren's fighting skills were more than a match for two, or even three, enemy soldiers, they had arrows, and he didn't. He quickly found himself taking hasty shelter behind a stone, with no way out. After an arrow got through his guard and made a shallow cut in his leg, he decided he needed to dash for the wall, or he would be trapped there, and worn down eventually. As he got up onto the balls of his feet to run for freedom, he planted the tip of his sword into the soil for balance, and was surprised to see the sword sink into the soft ground. Digging with the sword, he discovered that he wasn't crouched on the ground at all, he was on the rotted remnants of a wood hatch that covered an old drainage channel, like the old, blocked-off vault under the Cornerstone chamber in Linden. He had tugged the crumbling hatch aside enough to squeeze through, hoping to follow the channel out to where it surely must run into the stream outside the walls.

And now he was certainly well and truly trapped. The enemy had taken a long time to learn that Koren wasn't still crouched behind the stone, then they had quickly discovered the hole leading down to the drainage channel, when the first soldier stepped on the rotted wood, and fell through. Since then, pairs of soldiers had taken turns going down into the channel, but because Koren was able to take shelter behind rocks that had fallen from the ceiling, the enemy was not able to use arrows with any effect. And the channel wasn't tall enough to stand up in, which made sword fighting impractical. After Koren's sword chopped the points off a couple spears, the enemy had retreated above ground, to shout insults down at Koren, some of them in the harsh, guttural language of Acedor, but enough in the common tongue that Koren could understand. Even if he didn't know the language, Koren could have figured that the enemy soldiers were not shouting words of encouragement to him, or offering food and fresh water. When they grew tired of shouting insults, the enemy had stopped to think, and that is when the trouble really started for Koren. Two of the soldiers had small casks of oil with them, why Koren didn't know, although it was likely for some evil rites the mages of Acedor used to practice their foul magics. One soldier had come down into the channel, rolling a cask before him, and then had pulled out the stopper, letting the oil out. Because the channel sloped downward toward Koren, the oil was now flowing in his direction, forming a thick sheen on top of the water. He could barely see there, underground, only the light of the enemy's torches above and moonlight came weakly down through the hole Koren had 'escaped' through. It was clear that the enemy would soon toss a flaming torch down into the channel, and set the oil on fire.

So, Koren inched forward, until his head scraped the top of the chamber, and the water was up to his nose. He tilted his head up, breathed in as deeply as he could. His only hope was to swim, or crawl, down the channel to where it emptied into the stream. If the old channel wasn't blocked along the way.

What Koren didn't know, as he took one last breath and slipped beneath the water, was that the enemy had found the other end of the channel where it emptied into the stream, and had three soldiers positioned there, ready to strike if he ever made it that far.

Koren hadn't heard any sounds from enemy soldiers for what he judged was several hours now; by the color of the light, he guessed the sun was setting. He had never made it to the end of the channel at the stream; the way was blocked by the collapsed roof of the channel, and by thick roots. After a few seconds of trying to squeeze by the roots, with his air running out and blood pounding in his ears, he had turned around to see flickering orange light behind him. The enemy had set the oil on fire, he could not return. He lay on his back in the water, about to accept his fate, when his eyes caught the faintest glimmer of light above him. Clawing his way upward with his bare hands, he found a narrow tunnel that led to the surface; barely enough room for his face so that he could breathe. Air! He had air. And cover, for while enemy soldiers had walked the length of the channel above the ground, stabbing downward with the spears and shouting insults, they had not discovered Koren's hiding place. Toward morning, when sunlight filtered down through the hole, Koren realized that a long time ago, a tree had grown over the channel, and grown large, its roots seeking the water below. Eventually, the roots had collapsed the roof of the channel, then later, the tree must have blow over in a storm. The hole Koren was in was where a root had rotted away. Working slowly and quietly, he had managed to gouge out a space big enough for his head, neck and one arm, the rest of his body was submerged in the water, and he was chilled to the bone. Also hungry, and thirsty. He knew better than to drink stagnant water, he could still smell the stink of the green scum of algae that lay on top of the water. A brief rain shower before dawn, with water streaming down the roots into his parched mouth, was the only water he'd drunk since he left the royal army, the night before.

It was time to get out of the hole, while he still could. Moving with stiff muscles, he carefully reached above, and scooped one handful of dirt at a time to rain down on his head and shoulders. When he couldn't see anymore, he plunged down into the water, washing away the dirt. The sun had set before Koren was able to squeeze himself up out of the hole to look around. All appeared quiet, he couldn't see any enemy soldiers. A pair of deer grazed in the field, near the tree line; Koren knew it was unlikely deer would expose themselves if people were around, especially people on horses. The enemy must have left the area. His sword was tossed out first, then he wriggled to break free of the roots and rocks. With legs too stiff and cold to walk, he had to crawl to the stream, where he disciplined himself to scrub his face and hands clean with sand, before moving upstream to drink the clear water. Sipping, rather than gulping as he wanted to, he drank his fill slowly. When he was almost able to stand, he stumbled painfully downstream to a pool, where he scrubbed the muck off the rest of himself, and his clothes, as best he could.

Sitting by the stream in the silvery moonlight, trying to stretch his leg muscles so he could walk upright, he realized with a start that very day was his fourteenth birthday. It was not his best birthday. Perhaps it was the worst. His thirteenth birthday had been interrupted by the people of Crebbs Ford announcing that he, Koren, had been banished from Crickdon County. That had been a bad birthday, certainly. But this was his first birthday without his parents, without his mother baking a special treat for him, without his father helping with Koren's morning chores, so they could go fishing most of the day. Fishing, sitting by a stream like this one, talking, or sitting together in comfortable silence. Bring home fresh fish, which Koren and his father cleaned and cooked, served with butter and toasted bread crumbs, carrots and potatoes. Koren's mouth watered just thinking of such good food. Or, at that moment, any food at all, he was so hungry. Still, he was alive, and being alive meant a chance for a better day ahead.

On achingly stiff legs, he walked slowly back to the road, where he looked both ways in the fading light. He was alone. Ready to duck out of the road if he heard anyone coming, he trudged north, hopefully following Thunderbolt and the wizard.

After walking north along the road through the night and half the next morning, he heard the sound of hooves, and ducked behind a tree, his short sword ready. To his surprise and delight, it was Thunderbolt, trotting along, looking lost, and as tired as Koren was! The horse had no saddle, and his coat appeared to have been brushed, so Koren assumed the smart beast had carried the wizard to a village, or farm, somewhere people tended to lost horses and injured wizards. After a joyous greeting, Koren had ridden the horse for only a quarter of an hour, when the horse's wobbly legs told Koren it was time to stop. Finding a field with grass for Thunderbolt to graze, and fresh water to drink, the two settled down to catch much-needed sleep, and had awakened later than Koren intended. The sun was low in the western sky, it was almost nighttime. With the two refreshed, watered, and at least Thunderbolt's belly full, they returned to the road and proceeded north at a steady trot, until they found the way blocked by a royal army patrol. The patrol was commanded by a sergeant, a man sent hurriedly south to block the road after the royal army was alerted by riders sent north from Captain Raddick, and the sergeant was following the vague orders he'd been given, without any imagination. Block the road, keep lookout for enemy forces, keep any civilians out of harm's way. Koren was a civilian, so Koren had been kept with seven farm families, who had been hastily gathered up from their homes, and ordered to stay with the supposed safety of the royal army. Keeping civilians safe, with enemy troops possibly roaming around the countryside, was easier with the civilians in one place, rather than wandering around by themselves and getting into trouble. And so, Koren had been forced to stay with the sergeant's two dozen troops, most of whom were untrained reserves called up from the local militia in the emergency. Three days had gone by, with Koren fuming at the delay, before a regular royal army unit arrived in the late afternoon, three hundred soldiers galloping down the road, spears in the air and banners flying.

As soon he was able, he sought out the Captain of the army unit, a red-haired woman he didn't know called Glennis MacKurt. "Captain, ma'am, I'm Lord Paedris Don Salva's servant, we got separated at the battle of Longshire."

"Huh, who?" MacKurt was irritated to be interrupted; she had too much to worry about already. "Who are you?"

"Lord Salva, ma'am, the court wizard? I'm his servant, Koren Bladewell. I sent him away on my horse three nights ago, he was badly injured. I need to find him!"

MacKurt frowned. If this boy truly was the master wizard's servant, MacKurt needed to pay attention. She didn't need people at the royal court hearing bad things about Captain MacKurt. "Sent him away?"

"Yes, ma'am, he killed three enemy wizards, but the enemy still surrounded us, and he was injured, so I sent him away on my horse," Koren pointed toward Thunderbolt. "My horse came back the next morning, but I don't know where Lord Salva is! I've been stuck here wasting time for three days!"

MacKurt thought for a minute. "The wizard is gravely ill, he is on his way to the royal palace hospital, we passed his wagon as we rode south yesterday. I didn't hear anything about his servant, though. Can you prove you are his servant?"

"Begging your pardon, Captain," one of MacKurt's lieutenants spoke, "if that devil horse is the boy's, then he must be the wizard's servant. I've never met the boy, but I remember that horse from when I stabled General Magrane's horse last year. The stable hands hated that horse, and I hear the wizard's servant is the only one who can ride him."

MacKurt considered the horse, then Koren. "That could be true, could be. I've also heard the wizard has given his servant magical fighting skills. If you are his servant, surely you could best one of my soldiers with a sword?"

Koren gritted his teeth and fumed with anger. Paedris was gravely ill, and she wanted him to waste time performing tricks? "If Lord Salva is sick, I need to go to him now! I know where he keeps his potions and things, in his tower."

MacKurt's eyes narrowed. "And yet you refuse to prove who you are?"

Koren had enough of delaying. "Behind me is an oak tree, with a target the sergeant's men have been using for archery practice?" He knew the tree was a good twenty yards behind him. Without warning, he pulled out his short sword, which caused alarm among MacKurt's men, but Koren threw the sword backwards over his shoulder, without looking. There was a gasp from the soldiers as the sword embedded itself in the center of the target.

MacKurt's eyebrows rose in surprise, but there was a twinkle in her eyes, and she made a short bow from the saddle. "Very well done, master servant. I envy you your skills. You may be on your way, with an escort. Lieutenant Meers, we need to send back a courier anyway, to report our progress. Select a courier to ride north with Lord Salva's servant. And, Koren, your name is? Give the wizard my best wishes for a speedy recovery." MacKurt's smile faded. "We need his great power in this war, and sooner than later, I fear."

Any thoughts Koren had of racing north on a well-rested Thunderbolt were dashed when the courier set off at a fast pace, then settled into an easy trot. The courier was named Lenner Smith, and at barely seventeen, he wasn't all that much older than Koren. Perhaps self-conscious of his youth in the royal army, Lenner had worked hard to grow a respectable beard.

"Mister Smith, I thought couriers rode fast?"

"Call me Lenner, Koren, we'll be riding together for a while. It's a long way to the royal palace, can't be wearing out the horses. We'll change horses tomorrow evening, at Hereford."

Koren shook his head. "I won't leave Thunderbolt, and he doesn't need to be spared a fast run. Can't we go faster?"

The courier shook his head. "You won't get far on this road without me, the army has checkpoints every few leagues, now. I have a pass," Lenner patted his vest, where he carried a scroll written by Captain MacKurt, "but you'll be held there, without me." Lenner also wore a vest with the royal army crest on it, and his horse's saddle was army-issue. Koren wasn't wearing any sort of uniform. "The whole countryside is up in arms, after we heard about the battle. You were there?" Lenner asked excitedly. "What happened? I was in Dunladdon when we got the call to move south, haven't heard much more than that we got raided?"

Koren sighed, and scratched his head in frustration at the slow pace. If he was going to be stuck with the courier for days, he might as well tell the tale. "It wasn't just a raid, Lenner, we were ambushed by three wizards and-"

"Are you sure Lord Salva said it was his summer retreat? The land that used to be one of the king's hunting grounds?" Lenner asked, a couple days later. Having exhausted the battle of Longshire as a subject for conversation while they rode, Koren and Lenner had been talking about farming that morning. Lenner had grown up in Linden City outside the royal palace, where his father was a scribe in the royal archives. Other than growing some vegetables and herbs in the yard behind their home, Lenner and his family knew nothing about farming. They were riding by a farm Koren admired, with nicely rolling fields of corn and a well-kept barn, when Koren excitedly mentioned Paedris' promise to give him land to farm, on his sixteenth birthday. Lenner had tilted his head skeptically, and asked the question.

"Yes," Koren answered, "Paedris, I mean Lord Salva said a couple there farms it for him. I wonder what type-"

"Wait, Koren. Hmmm."

"What?" Koren asked.

"Uh, I don't, uh, hmmm." Lenner struggled to find words. "Uh, if it's the same land, and I don't know of any other, the wizard can't give it to you. He doesn't own it."

"What? Are you sure?"

Lenner nodded seriously. "Uh huh. I helped my father in the royal archives, before I joined the army. I remember my father saying, I guess this was the year before last, him saying the old king made a bad deal when he let the wizard use that land, because Lord Salva was making so much money from the farm there. The reason my father wasn't happy is that, because the farm is on land owned by the royal family, Lord Salva doesn't have to pay taxes on his income from that farm. The wizard doesn't pay any taxes at all, so he must not own property anywhere in Tarador."

Koren fell silent, unable to speak.

"Sorry." Lenner said, after a few minutes. Koren's sunny morning had been crushed by the news from Lenner. "Maybe, uh, maybe he meant land in, where's he from, Stade, some place like that?"

Koren nodded gloomily. "Sure, sure, that must be it." He said, without believing his own words. Why would Paedris have lied to him? Although, Koren was sure the wizard had lied to him before, at least several times. Paedris was a powerful wizard, Koren only a poor servant boy without a family. Why bother-

"Sometimes, my parents would tell me whatever I wanted to hear, just so they could shut me up for a while." Lenner said, but Koren wasn't listening.

Koren's wonderful, brief dream, of owning a farm, was crushed. It had all been a lie, only a lie. And an obvious lie, one that Koren could have discovered by asking almost anyone around the palace. Did Paedris care so little about Koren, that he couldn't even bother to come up with a decent lie? Koren nudged Thunderbolt into an easy gallop. "Come on, if we hurry, we can be at the palace before nightfall." Be at the palace, and confront the wizard about his lies. Being in battle had changed Koren, changed him in ways he wasn't even aware of. Having faced death, he was no longer willing to be the servant boy that people tried to kick around. He had saved the crown princess, not once but three times. He had found the Cornerstone, found it after centuries of the best minds in Tarador searching in vain. He had rescued the wizard, all by himself. What had he gotten from it? A cramped cubbyhole in a dark, drafty tower, a job working for a wizard who lied to him, and denied him credit for his accomplishments.

Lenner spurred his horse onward, catching up to Thunderbolt. Koren wasn't speaking, but the young soldier could see from the expression on the servant's face that he was angry, very angry. Lenner had left the palace before Koren arrived, so he didn't know the boy. From Koren's tale of the battle of Longshire, the wizard's servant was either a good storyteller, or extraordinarily brave. If Koren had lied about saving the wizard, why would he now be riding to help his master? And if Koren truly was as brave as he said, and as angry as he looked, well, Lenner wouldn't want to get in his way.

Ariana left her personal guard at the entrance to the hospital, and went straight for the court wizard's bedside. Lord Salva, usually with fire, or a twinkle, in his eyes even at his most weary, now looked sunken into the bed. His skin was gray, ashen, thin, like old paper. A vein in his neck showed his pulse was rapid and erratic. Ariana gestured for the Chief Physician to attend her. "What ails Lord Salva?"

The man snatched off his official white cap in respect for the crown princess, "For the most part, exhaustion, Your Highness, deep, draining and unnatural exhaustion, though simple exhaustion nonetheless. In an ordinary man, who experienced ordinary combat, I would prescribe rest, and nutritious, plain, simple foods such as broth, and bread, and fruit to regain his strength. For a wizard, of his unnatural age," Ariana thought she saw the man make a superstitious sign behind his back, "who was attacked by forces beyond this world," he shuddered slightly, "the best course of treatment is beyond my skills. It may take a wizard, to heal this wizard."

Ariana bent close to examine the court wizard. He smelled faintly of brimstone, though he had been bathed carefully and was dressed in clean robes. Whatever had happened to the court wizard, it had been bad enough to test even his powers to the limit. "Has he been awake at all?"

"Lord Salva has been talking in his sleep, it was difficult to understand at first. He mentioned your name, Highness, and his servant, you may have met the boy, Koren, I think is his name? And he spoke of several other wizards. Mostly, he kept repeating one word, over and over; he said 'ascendant'. He has been most agitated when saying that word. Does it mean anything to you?"

"No, it doesn't." She frowned. "Ascendant," she pronounced the word slowly. "It must be important. You sent for a wizard?"

"Yes, Lord Feany should have received word by now. He is a skilled healer."

Ariana straightened Paedris' robe, and brushed a stray lock of hair from his eyes. "When Shomas gets here, ask him what 'ascendant' means. Unless Lord Salva awakens first, then ask him. And when Lord Salva awakens, send for me, please."

As she left the hospital, Ariana saw that her personal guards were speaking with some of the palace guards, they were all looking grim, shaking their heads. "Princess," her guard captain bowed slightly, "how fares the wizard?"

"Weak, and he needs to rest. Lord Feany is on is way; he will surely heal Lord Salva. Our wizard will be back on his feet in no time," she said with a smile. The smile didn't work, all the men looked grim, staring at the stone floor, shuffling their feet, muttering under their breath. "What is the matter, captain?"

"Well, it's like this, Your Highness, I spoke with a soldier this afternoon, he'd come in from the west, General Magrane sent him back with dispatches. He said all the soldiers are worried, by how bold the enemy has been, attacking Lord Salva on our own territory. It," he glanced at the floor, embarrassed, "it shows the enemy's strength, Your Highness." And, he did not say, Tarador's weakness.

"Does it?" Ariana asked. "Strength, or fear?" She thought back to something her military tutor Captain Raddick has told her. "The enemy took a great risk, sending three powerful wizards to attack Lord Salva, a terrible risk. Perhaps the enemy took such a risk because they fear our court wizard's growing power. There are few wizards in the world, and few of them can handle power, I'm told. The enemy sent three of their precious wizards into our territory, to kill Lord Salva. And they failed. I think that tell us of the enemy's desperation, not strength. But, I am after all only a girl, and I do not know of military matters as you men do."

She had shamed the men, shamed them, and opened their eyes. Her guard captain nodded. "Her Highness speaks the truth. The enemy fears us. My apologies, Your Highness, I should not have let fear enter my heart."

Ariana thought of another thing Raddick had said. "There is nothing wrong with fear, Captain, unless it leads to despair. I think it best that we leave fear and despair to our enemy?" She said with a smile.

The captain bowed. "Yes, Your Highness." This young girl was going to be a formidable queen someday. If she lived that long. And if her mother didn't stand by while the enemy conquered the realm while Ariana awaited her crown.

Lenner and Koren did hurry, to the point where Lenner's horse was wobbly on its legs and even Thunderbolt was laboring to gallop, but it was still after nightfall when they arrived at the castle gate. The roads toward Linden had been choked with wagons, with people from the border counties looking for safety in case of further invasion by Acedor, and by wagons loaded with grain, in case Acedor raided or burned the storehouses near the border. News of the battle in Longshire had everyone spooked, particularly news that the raiders included three wizards, who had been bold enough to challenge Lord Salva. The court wizard's near-mythical powers, in the minds of the citizens of Tarador, were such that for an enemy to feel confident enough to attack their wizard, the situation for Tarador must be dire indeed.

When they finally reached the castle gate, with much shouting, cursing and pushing by Lenner, the young soldier pulled out the pass signed by Captain MacKurt, and the oilskin pouch of dispatches. "Trooper Lenner Smith, with dispatches from Captain MacKurt to General Magrane."

The lead guard, tired from long hours of mostly turning people away from the gate, held Lenner's pass up to the torchlight. "Looks real, but if you've been in the field, you won't know today's password."

"Lenner! I recognize you," said another guard. "Your father is a scribe here. He's all right, let him through."

"Wait!" The lead guard snapped. "Who's this with you?"

"The wizard's servant, Koren Bladewell, come here from the battle at Longshire." Lenner answered.

"Koren Bladewell?" The lead guard held the lantern up to shine light on Koren's face. "Why, it is you!" This caused surprised muttering amongst the guards. "Didn't expect to see *you* here." What the guard said next shocked both Koren and Lenner. "Seize the prisoner," the man said, almost reluctantly.

"What?" Koren gulped, and Thunderbolt danced backwards, away from the approaching guards. Koren's hand reflexively went to the hilt of his sword, which caused the guards to draw their swords.

"Whoa, whoa! What are you talking about?" Lenner moved his horse between Koren and the guards, keeping his own sword in its sheath.

"Captain Raddick sent back word from Longshire, about the battle, and his dispatches said Koren here is a coward and a deserter. That he left the wizard at the start of the battle, and later left his post, to run off. Sorry about this, Koren, lad."

"*What*? I am not a coward, and I didn't desert, I went to *rescue*-" Koren stopped, seething with anger. No words from him were going to convince the guards, who had orders. He looked behind him, then at the guards, at the open gate behind them. Koren knew, and so did the guards who had watched him riding, and sparring with the weapons master, that if Koren rode away, they couldn't catch him, and if he fought, it would be a bloody battle.

"Where is the wizard?" Lenner asked sharply. "What has he said?"

"In the hospital, delirious with fever. He hasn't spoken about Koren, or the battle, or much of anything." The lead guard admitted. "Koren, lad, I have to take you in. Don't make this difficult on everyone."

"*I'll* take him in," Lenner offered the break the stalemate, "but first Koren is going to attend to the wizard. Koren knows where Lord Salva keeps his potions and things, he may be able to help the healers."

The lead guard considered for a moment. "All right, then, it's on you to watch him, Lenner. But Koren, you can't keep your sword. Can't bring it into the hospital, anyway. We'll see to your horses."

Koren silently handed his precious, dwarf-made short sword to Lenner. *Prisoner.* He was to be locked in the dungeon, unless Paedris could tell the truth to the guards. Koren felt a chill go down his spine. If the wizard *would* tell the truth. He'd lied about so many things, why should Koren expect the wizard to tell the truth now? There was nothing else he could do, so he let Lenner lead the way through the gate. Instead of ducking his head in shame, Koren met the guard's eyes with anger and defiance. Anger and determination.

Her Highness Ariana Trehayme, crown princess of Tarador, soon to be queen of the realm, maitress of the church, protector of the weak, commander-in-chief of the royal army and navy, and etcetera, also was quite angry that very moment. Furious, in fact. Since word reached the palace of the wholly unexpected battle in Longshire, followed by the arrival of the seriously ill court wizard, she had been consumed with preparing her country against invasion. Or, rather, watching her mother frantically make one decision after another, sometimes changing her mind twice in the space of an hour. Carlana was doing the best she could, but she was in a panic over the raid and near death of her court wizard, and she wasn't thinking clearly. She was driving her army commanders crazy, to the point where General Magrane in a weak moment confessed to Ariana that, as soon as Captain Raddick returned to the palace, Magrane was going into the field to assume command of the defense forces on the eastern border. At the very least, in the field, he would not get contradictory orders from the Regent every hour.

What had made Ariana absolutely furious is that she just learned, a few minutes before, that Captain Raddick's hurriedly written account of the battle had declared Koren Bladewell to be a coward and a deserter, and that the servant boy was to be arrested on sight. That her mother had not known of the army's orders didn't matter, what mattered was that Ariana insisted her mother come with her, as soon as they were done reviewing the evening changing of the guard, to see General Magrane, and rescind the awful, untrue charges against Koren. And that Magrane immediately send out a patrol of soldiers to find Koren. When the wizard had come back, delirious with fever and without Koren, Ariana had assumed Koren was still with Captain Raddick. Safe, with Raddick's men. Now, apparently, no one knew where he was!

Ariana burst out of the doorway into the courtyard, her mother and guards trailing behind. Carlana was forced to hike up her skirts to keep up, an uncomfortable and undignified action that had her red in the face. "Young lady, you slow down-"

Ariana spun on her heels, oblivious to the royal guards who were lined up, waiting for the Regent and crown princess to watch their ceremonial evening changing of the guard, as they did most evenings. "*No*, mother." She said in a harsh whisper, loud enough to scandalize the servants. "Koren has been missing for days, and the army has orders to *arrest* him, as a *coward*? And no one thought it was important to tell me?" She stomped over the raised dais where she usually stood to review the guards, and was about to signal for the ceremony to begin without her mother, when she saw a familiar person emerge from a doorway on the opposite side of the courtyard. "Koren!" She shouted in delight.

Koren had been biting his lip, looking at the ground, lost in thought about what he would say to Paedris, if the wizard were capable of listening. As he and Lenner came into the torchlit courtyard, he heard a familiar girl's voice cry out "Koren!" He was so startled that he stumbled, and bumped into Lenner.

And right then, it happened. As Ariana shouted in delight, she dashed forward, and a heavy stone gargoyle crashed to the dais right where she had been only an eyeblink before. A large piece of stone that had been the gargoyle's right arm broke off, and struck the crown princess hard on her back, smashing her to the hard flagstones of the courtyard.

She lay stunned, the breath knocked out of her, stars swimming in her eyes, her ears ringing.

Koren's feet got tangled up with Lenner's, and the two fell hard to the stone surface of the courtyard, with Koren bumping his head on the flagstones. He was on his knees, shaking his head, when he saw, heard, and felt the stone strike Ariana.

Carlana had been behind her daughter, far enough that she was only pelted with a few pebbles broken off the gargoyle, close enough that she was at her daughter's side, cradling her bloodied head, before Koren had run more than a few steps toward Ariana. Guards had moved to surround the stricken princess, to protect her against further danger, with swords drawn, eyes peering up at the roof where the gargoyle had come from. The Regent was not looking upward. Her weapon was the daggers in her eyes, eyes fixed on the unexpected, and unwelcome, sight of Koren Bladewell. The boy had been gone for weeks, and the instant Carlana saw him again, her daughter was struck down? Koren had been in LeVanne when that province was invaded. Koren was at the river when a bear attacked her daughter. Koren was at Longshire with Paedris when the wizard was attacked by the enemy. Carlana had sent Paedris there because that area of Tarador was one of the *least* likely places the wizard could find trouble! But, oh, no, every time Koren is there, terrible trouble follows! She knew it was a bad idea to let the boy into the castle, she knew it!

"Get away from my daughter, you *jinx*!" The Regent screamed, pointing at Koren, and he stopped in his tracks. "Look what you did to my daughter, you cursed jinx, get out!" Ariana groaned and Carlana cradled her daughter's head. "Get out of here, and don't ever come back! *Get out*!"

Koren froze, hands up to show he had no weapons, listening to the Regent's voice echoing off the stone walls of the courtyard, burning into his ears. One of the guards, assuming the Regent meant that Koren had somehow caused the gargoyle to fall, took a hesitant step forward, and Koren ran. Ran, blindly, pushing the stunned Lenner out of his way, down a corridor, up another, around a corner, running, running, running until he was out of breath and out of places to run. He stopped, huffing and puffing, bent over, hands on his knees, trying to catch his breath. And trying to collect his wits.

Jinx.

He was a jinx, he knew it. Bad luck to everyone around him. With Paedris ill, the wizard had been unable to counter the power of Koren's curse. Now his curse had hurt Ariana, hurt her badly. His curse struck everyone he cared about.

The wizard abruptly sat upright in his hospital bed, startling the healer who had been sitting by his side, cooling his feverish forehead with damp cloths. Something had awakened him from his fitful sleep. Magic! Dark, foul magic, here in the castle! "What is happening?" Paedris demanded.

"I, uh, uh, I don't-" The healer stammered.

"Find someone who does, then!" His head swimming, Paedris' initial burst of energy was fading quickly. Knowing he would soon be slipping back into feverish delirium, he reached into the spirit realm and pulled power into himself. It was a temporary surge of power, a dangerous surge he would pay terribly for later, especially in his weakened condition. If he did not feel the need so dire, he would not have done it.

Impatient, the wizard swept aside the bed sheet, looking in dismay at the thin, sweat-soaked robe he was wearing. "A robe! Get me a decent robe! Oh, forget it." Sweeping past the paralyzed healer, Paedris grabbed a cloak off a hook and threw it around him, storming out past the guards. He strode quickly down the hallway and out of the hospital building, where he saw the chief guard rushing across the courtyard. "Temmas! Temmas!" He shouted in a powerful voice to get the man's attention. "Come here! What has happened?"

The man named Temmas hurried over to the wizard, out of breath. "Begging your pardon, my lord, a gargoyle fell off the roof, and struck the princess, she may have broken ribs. The Regent blamed your servant-"

"My servant?" Paedris grabbed the man's shoulders and shook him. "Koren is here? When did he get here?"

"I think he just got here recently, my lord." The chief guard actually didn't know, the comings and goings of servants was not something his guards were instructed to inform him about. "He was in the courtyard when the gargoyle fell, the Regent believes he had something to do with it, she said he is a jinx? I suspect this was an accident-"

"Fool! That idiot woman!" Paedris raged, not caring who heard him railing against the Regent. "Koren had nothing to do it with it, and this was no accident, this was the act of an assassin. I can sense the foulness of dark magic; this is the work of the enemy. There is an assassin in the castle, perhaps more than one!"

The chief guard, who was responsible for the safety of the royal family within the confines of the castle walls, tried to swallow with a throat that suddenly was dry as a desert. He had already been dealing with increased security because of the battle at Longshire, dealing with the constant demands of the Regent, and on this perfectly ordinary evening, with an old piece of masonry falling off the roof. An unfortunate accident, that was. He would, he had thought, have a long night making sure the princess had the best of medical care, calming down her mother, and sending a crew onto the roof to inspect the hundreds of other gargoyles and other decorative stone objects attached to the top of the walls.

But, an assassin? An assassin, that he had let inside the walls of the castle, the capital of Tarador, the very seat of power? Such a failure could not be borne; he would have to resign in disgrace. If he survived the night. He knew better than to question the court wizard's pronouncement; if Lord Salva said he felt dark magic, then foul deeds were afoot tonight. And Temmas would trust the judgment of a feverish wizard over the flighty and emotional Regent any day. Especially this day. "What are your orders, my lord?"

"Seal off the castle, no one in or out." Paedris paused; for that order was so obvious it didn't warrant speaking aloud. Think, he told himself. What was most important? "Koren! My servant," he said, as his right hand squeezed the chief guard's shoulder in a magic-powered crushing grip, and the man grunted in pain, "you *must* get my servant to safety. Bring him to the fortress, and post guards there, do it now! You must protect him. Oh, and bring the princess there also," Paedris said it as an afterthought, "I will be there as soon as I can to tend to her injuries."

Temmas thought he should ask the wizard to tend to his shoulder, which he rotated to make sure it still worked, after the wizard released his iron grip. Why did the wizard care so much about a lowly servant, who no assassin would think twice about? It wasn't his place to question the mighty, not on a night when dark magic stalked the castle walls. "Yes, my lord. Do you need assistance, to deal with the assassin?"

Paedris blinked slowly to clear his vision. He was already feeling the effects of the artificial energy coursing throughout his mortal body. "Yes, lend me two of your guards. I need to go up on the roof."

The chief guard turned to bark orders at his men, and that was where the night truly began to spiral out of control, and the future path of Koren's life was decided. Because, when an unwritten order is repeated enough times, from one person to the next, the original intent is often lost in a confusion of misunderstandings, rumors and embellishments. That explains how '*protect* Koren' and 'bring him to the *fortress*' changed into what guards throughout the castle heard.

CHAPTER THIRTEEN

When Koren recovered his wits, he angrily wiped away his tears, and considered what he should do. Nothing, he thought, had changed from his original purpose of coming to the castle. He needed to attend to the wizard, although now it seemed best that he first go to the tower and collect a sample of healing potions to bring to the hospital with him. The courtyard was in an uproar, with guards running this way and that, although no one seemed to know what they were doing, and no one yet called out for him to stop. He ran up into the tower, and pressed the locked door to the potion room in exactly the place Paedris had instructed him to, to avoid the wards from releasing banshees and blasting his ears. He had collected a sample of healing potions in a leather satchel, when he heard several sets of boots tramping across the courtyard to stop at the doorway below. Koren froze in place to listen, holding his breath.

"What're we here for?" One guard's voice asked.
"The wizard's brat, we're to take him to the dungeon, is my orders."
"The dungeon?" The first guard exclaimed, surprised. "I didn't even know he'd returned. He's a coward and a deserter, but-"
"And he made that gargoyle fall on the princess, I heard the Regent say it myself. The wizard told the captain of the guards, find Koren Bladewell, and bring the boy to the dungeon."
"The wizard is up from his sickbed?"
"Aye, an attack on the princess is enough to make the dead rise."

Koren's ears didn't register the next words of the guards, for all he could hear was that the wizard ordered the guards to bring Koren to the dungeon. The *dungeon*. The word sent chills down Koren's spine, for the dungeon held only the worst of Linden's criminals.

Slowly, he set the leather satchel on the floor. He would not need potions this night. This was the moment Kyre Falco had predicted. Koren needed to run, to run far away, and never come back. Sought by the army as a coward and a deserter. Declared by the Regent to be a dangerous jinx who had injured the crown princess. He was not a coward, not a deserter. But he was a jinx, he knew it. He would always be a jinx, always bring nothing but trouble to the people around him, and the worst trouble was for the people he cared about most, for the people-

A horrible thought struck Koren like a lightning bolt. He had not rescued Ariana from the bear after all! She had been attacked by the bear *because* Koren was there. Koren the jinx, who brought misfortune and disaster everywhere he went, to everyone around him. Ariana's life had been in danger because of him. He was no hero, far from it. He was a curse. If there had not been a bear in the forest, Ariana would have fallen from the boat and drowned, or sat down in the forest and been bitten by a serpent, or maybe been struck by lightning. As long as Koren was nearby, something bad was bound to happen to the princess. And he had not rescued Paedris from the enemy; the enemy had attacked the wizard in a peaceful village, because Koren was there. Koren had brought the attack down on the wizard and Raddick's men! That was why Paedris had ordered him thrown into the dungeon, and why the wizard would use the charges of cowardice and desertion as an excuse to get rid of Koren Bladewell. Because Koren's curse was so strong, so dangerous, that Paedris realized by now that even a powerful wizard could not stop it. For the security of the nation, Koren Bladewell belonged in a dungeon.

Or in a grave.

Koren sat on the floor of the potion room back against the stone wall of the tower, hearing guards' feet pounding on the stairs, up, then down. No one had tried the door to the potion rooms, they must have recognized the ward symbols. From the window, he heard the second guard's voice say "he's not here. Leave two men at the door, and follow me, we'll search the west wing of the palace next."

A few minutes later, Koren risked a glance out the window; there were only two guards, waiting by the door. No matter, Koren knew a secret way out of the tower. The trouble would not be getting out of the tower; the trouble would be getting out of the castle walls. And he might know how to do that, too.

Moving slowly and carefully, he stepped out of the potion room, and down the stairs to his bedchamber. The guards had searched his small room, things were strewn all over the floor and his bed was laying on its side. Quickly, Koren went directly to a particular stone in the wall behind the bed, and wriggled it out of the wall. Behind the stone was a hole, with a cloth-wrapped package, which Koren pulled out. Inside there were two knives, fishing line and hooks, string, flint and steel for starting fires, the money he had saved from his pay, and most importantly, the money Kyre Falco gave him. Koren had changed those gold coins for smaller coins, for servants running away should not attract attention by trying to use gold coins. He paused to look around the small room that had been his home. He realized that he would miss it, even though it could be cold, damp and drafty. Heading out the door, he stepped over items the guards had scattered on the floor, and saw one of the items was a quill pen and inkpot that Paedris had given to him. Back when the wizard was pretending to care about his servant. A note. He couldn't leave without writing a note, at least to apologize to Ariana for nearly killing her; he would never get another chance. It was important that Ariana know he hadn't meant for his curse to hurt her, and that he was leaving so his curse couldn't hurt anyone else.

It was surprisingly hard to put his thoughts on paper, and not just because the quill pen kept running out of ink. He had too much to say, too much anger and regret, and not enough time to write it all down. When he finished scribbling the note, he read it, and almost tore it up. It was a mess, full of smudges and misspellings, as a result of his haste. "Oh, to hell with it," he said aloud. Almost too loud, for the guards were only two floors below him, and left the note on top of the bed.

What the guards outside didn't know was that firewood for the tower originally used to be stacked in a room under the ground floor, to keep it dry, and so occupants of the tower did not have to go outside in nasty weather when more wood was needed. There was a room in the foundation of the tower, accessed by a trap door under a closet on the ground floor. And a hatch leading outside, up against the wall of the castle, hidden behind overgrown bushes. When Paedris moved in years ago, he had the firewood moved outside, because he didn't want bugs like termites inside the tower. But the trap door and the hatch still worked, Koren had oiled their hinges only two months ago. The moment of greatest danger was moving the cleaning supplies that were stored on top of the trapdoor, with the guards just outside the heavy wood door of the tower. Koren's heart nearly stopped when a mop toppled over, he managed to catch it with a foot just before the handle hit the floor. The trapdoor opened quietly, Koren slipped through, and carefully let it close behind him. Now he was in darkness, complete darkness. Fortunately, since he could not light a torch, he knew every step on the ladder, and the chamber was empty. When he reached the floor, he felt his way along the wall until he came to the hatch, which he unlocked by sliding aside the bar. Cracking open the hatch only an inch, he listened for voices, but no one sounded nearby. Careful to open the hatch only enough to squeeze through, he stepped into the night, and closed the hatch, crouching behind the bushes that screened the hatch from the castle courtyard. The courtyard still rang with shouts and commotion; it must be that the guards, soldiers and palace staff were frantically searching for him. He felt safe for now; the bushes were thick, and extended almost all the way to the castle wall. The wall was in darkness behind the wizard's tower, and there Koren knew another secret; a possible way under and through the wall. A storm drain, which let rainwater cascading off the wizard's tower drain away, without flooding the courtyard. This particular drain had an iron cover that had rusted over the years, the castle maintenance crew knew about the rusty cover, but none of them was eager to be near the wizard's tower, so the cover rarely got attention. Koren had discovered a couple months ago that the cover was loose, the rusted iron was not only weak, the rust also had eaten away at the stone the iron cover pins were set into. He had brought an iron bar with him for the purpose of popping the cover out of its setting. It was surprisingly easy to break the rusted pins, but the cover was also surprisingly heavy! Koren nearly lost a couple fingers getting the cover out of the hole, moving slowly so the sound of heavy, rusted iron scraping on stone didn't alert guards. He dropped his pack in ahead of him, and considered whether to crawl in headfirst or feet first. Head first. He might need his hands if there was a cover at the other end.

There was a cover, which Koren found after perhaps half an hour of crawling and squeezing his way along the storm drain. It was disgusting, but still better than the last time he'd been stuck in a wet, smelly, slimy drainage channel. The opening at the far end was barred with an iron gate, above a stream, in the shadow of a grain mill. This gate was well maintained, and sturdy, with a lock, for the gate was periodically cleaned of leaves and other storm debris to keep it from clogging. There was no way Koren could break this gate open. But, he didn't need to. With his thick, short knife, he picked away at the mortar around the stones the gate was set into. Soon, enough stones were loose that he was able to push them out, out, out, until the stones tumbled into the stream, and the gate fell away. He was free, away from the castle, in the city of Linden! Now where was he going to go?

Captain Raddick nodded to the guards at the entrance to the royal hospital. Visiting the wizard was his first stop in the castle since arriving only an hour before; as the Regent was busy. General Magrane he had met on the road, the general was so anxious to take command of the eastern borderlands that he arranged to meet Raddick along the way. Raddick hated going to hospitals, even more than he hated being a patient in hospitals. Twice in his life, he had lain weak and sick in a hospital bed, suffering from fever, nausea and terrible pain. In his long military career, which began when he was only sixteen, he had never been actually wounded in combat seriously enough to require being sent to a hospital. Once, a sword cut to his leg, shallow as to be shrugged off as a mere scratch, had become infected within a week, and he had come near to death as he had ever been. Potions, herbs and poultices had served only to keep him barely alive until a minor wizard, by chance passing through the town, healed him with a single spell. The second time, he had been bitten by a snake, and potions had served to save his life, although he had been so sick that he had almost felt dying would be better.

"Halt!" One of the guards called out, blocking the entrance to the hospital with his pike. The three other guards, Raddick noted, had hands on the hilts of their swords. "What is the password?"

"I'm Captain Raddick, you oaf, get out of my way." Raddick said with a deliberately haughty sneer, and moved to brush aside the pike.

The pike didn't move, being held in a grip like iron, and three swords came out of their scabbards. "You look like Captain Raddick, I served under him last year on patrol in Holdeness. Maybe you're him, and maybe not. But whoever you are, you're not getting through that door alive without the password."

Raddick fairly beamed with pride. These men had been trained well, and took their jobs seriously. They guarded not just a door, not just a hospital; they guarded the court wizard, who lay on his sickbed within. "I know you, Tom Bestin, and you served well in Holdeness with me. The password for today is 'red wolf'." The three other guards, Raddick noted with satisfaction, did not relax until Bestin lifted his pike, and saluted the Captain. "How is the wizard?"

Bestin held his hand out, and waggled it side to side. "Some good, and some bad, the healers say. Don't think they rightly know what to do with a wizard, sir, leastwise, a wizard who isn't in hospital to heal the sick. Lord Salva is driving the nurses to distraction, the few times when he is awake."

Raddick nodded grimly. "General Magrane sent for Shomas Feany, or any other wizard, but likely they won't arrive in time to matter. Lord Salva will have to fight this battle himself, I fear. Bad enough that he had to fight three wizards, but having to rise from his sickbed to deal with that assassin may have been too much, even for him."

Raddick found the court wizard in a private chamber that had been set up within the large, high-ceilinged space of the hospital. The hastily built chamber had wooden walls, but no roof, to let in air and light. Eight guards surrounded the chamber, four of them archers positioned behind screens, and four in full armor with swords drawn. Raddick had to repeat the password, and get permission from the healer, before he could even peek his head in the chamber's door. The wizard appeared to be asleep, his face grey and damp with sweat, until Raddick approached, and the wizard's eyes opened.

"Ah, Captain Raddick." Paedris struggled to focus his vision, the man's face kept fading in and out. "The castle, secure? The nurses here won't tell me anything; they want me to rest, and not to worry. Not knowing what is going on is making me worry!"

"Yes, my lord. We have swept every inch of these old stones, and found no trace of the enemy, other than the assassin you killed. The princess is well, her mother is insisting she rest also, but you healed her remarkably well, my lord."

"Take care, Raddick, be watchful. It is not like the enemy to send only one assassin for such an important task. It would be best to keep the princess securely within the fortress, until I am able to search the castle myself."

"Yes, Lord Salva."

The wizard reached out a shaky hand to get a drink of water, Raddick helped him hold the mug steady as he drank, then looked discretely away as Paedris wiped up the water he had spilled on himself. Raddick knew that no man, especially no powerful man like Paedris, wanted others to see his weakness. After Paedris had found and killed the assassin, he had collapsed, and lain almost dead in his sickbed for two full days. Even now, he was terribly weak. "Thank you, Raddick." Paedris said, laying his head back on the pillow. "Now, I have a dispute with you. I am told that when my servant came back to the castle, you had ordered the guards to hold him, as a coward and a deserter?"

Raddick's eyebrows lifted in surprise. He certainly hadn't expected the court wizard to ask about his servant boy, not with so many other important matters to occupy the wizard's attention. "Not exactly, my lord. My dispatches about the battle mentioned Koren only briefly. In the battle, he hid amongst my men, instead of staying by your side, and later, he left us, against my specific orders that he stay and help with our wounded."

Paedris' eyelids shut tightly, overcome with great weariness. "Raddick," he said in a voice so soft that the army captain had to kneel by the bed and put his ear to the wizard's lips to hear, "you are a damned fool. If not for that young man, that extraordinarily *brave* young man, we would all be lost. It was not I, with my wizard senses, who saw the enemy had laid a trap for us, it was an alert young man who knew that no farmer would leave his sheep alone in a field. Koren saw we were riding straight into trouble, while I was looking at the pretty flowers growing in the fields. He didn't hide amongst your men, I sent him away. I *ordered* two soldiers, Arteman, and another, I can't remember her name, she had long black hair, Darton, Datman-"

"Dartenon, my lord?" Raddick suggested.

"Yes, that's her. A good woman. I ordered them to get my servant to safety; he could do me no good in a wizard fight, and could be a distraction. Your saying he is a coward is an insult to him, and to me."

Raddick bowed his head in shame. "I am sad to report, my lord, that Dartenon did not survive the battle, and Arteman was injured badly enough that I feared he would not survive the journey back here. I left Arteman in the care of a village near the battle, I had no occasion to speak with him, for he was weak with fever, the last I saw of him. I meant no insult to you, or to the boy."

"To the young *man*, Captain, Koren Bladewell is no boy. Not any more."

"Forgive me, my lord." Raddick looked up, and waved away the nurses who were approaching, out of concern that the wizard was exerting himself too much. This needed to be a private conversation. "I would not have said he was a coward, for many men find themselves sorely tested in their first battle, but, after the battle, he went against my orders, and he did desert us."

Paedris summoned his energy, and grasped the front of the army captain's shirt with surprising strength. "*Fool* you are again! He left you to *rescue* me, when you and your men twiddled your thumbs and did nothing while my need was dire. If not for Koren, I would be dead now, a pile of scorched ash, as the enemy intended. It was not for you and your soldiers that the enemy sent three wizards into Tarador, nor for plunder. They laid that trap to kill *me*, and they could have succeeded, if Koren had not disobeyed your inept orders and ridden off to rescue me, all by himself! He found me, sorely beset by the last two wizards, and distracted the foul sorcerers so I could kill them. At great risk to himself, he faced wizards, and a squad of enemy soldiers. The only reason I am alive today is that Koren Bladewell, who you falsely named a coward and deserter, risked his life to save mine. He got me on his horse, and sent me to safety, while he faced the enemy's soldiers, trapped in a ruined castle in the darkness, alone. That he survived, and made his way here, is some kind of miracle. If you seek men your soldiers should look to for inspiration, you need look no further than my most faithful servant."

"I, I am," Raddick stammered, "I regret accusing him, my lord." Raddick had proven himself in battle many times; no one who knew him would question his bravery. Faced with the wizard's wrath, however, he found himself shaking. As an army commander, Raddick had authority. The Regent who commanded him had authority. Paedris had *power*, before which all sane men quivered.

"You can't help being a fool, Raddick. Now, bring Koren to me."

Raddick swallowed hard, his throat dry as dust. "I, I, I beg your pardon, my lord, I thought you knew. Koren fled the castle, while you were hunting the assassin."

"*What*? Why? I ordered guards to take him to the fortress, to protect him! Where did he go?" Paedris struggled to sit upright in bed.

"We don't know, my lord. I regret to say, the guards had orders for him to be considered a deserter. And, and potentially, an assassin, he injured the princess?" Alarmed by the angry look in the wizard's eyes, Raddick hastened to add "At the time, my lord, the Regent feared the boy, the uh, young man, had somehow caused that gargoyle to fall on Ariana. This was before you discovered the assassin."

Paedris threw off the covers and swung his feet to the floor, shouting an impressive string of curses in his native language. "The Regent! Another fool I am forced to deal with." Nurses who ran over to protest that the wizard needed to rest, stopped in their tracks when the wizard's eyes blazed. "Raddick," Paedris demanded as he reached for the army man's shoulder for support, "help me up. I need to get to my tower immediately. Send a runner to fetch the Regent, I want her to meet us there."

"Uh, my lord," Raddick stammered again, conflicted because Carlana was his commander, "the Regent is with her daughter, and left orders not to be disturbed."

"Ariana," Paedris said slowly with smoldering anger, "is fine and will recover completely, she doesn't need her mother fussing over her. You send word that the Regent is," Paedris' jaw worked side to side as if he had swallowed something distasteful, "strongly *requested* to join me at my tower to discuss an extremely urgent matter. Or I will grab that silly woman by the throat and drag her there myself."

"Yes, my lord." Raddick answered as he helped the wizard to his feet, while gesturing for a guard to carry a message. In the future, Raddick thought to himself, he would request to always be in the field with the army, for he would rather face all the hosts of the enemy in battle, than deal with wizards and Regents.

It was a very annoyed Regent who found her court wizard, sitting on top of a chest in his former servant's bedchamber, head bowed, shoulders slumped, staring down at a single scroll of paper. Carlana was annoyed because Paedris should have been resting in bed, she was annoyed because she had been *fetched*, however diplomatically the guard had phrased the wizard's demand, she was annoyed because she wanted to be by her daughter's side instead of roaming around the castle, she was annoyed that her daughter had been asking, more strongly every day, to get out of the cramped and gloomy fortress.

And, mostly, she was annoyed that she had to be the Regent, instead of letting someone else worry about assassins, war, and death. "Captain Raddick." Carlana acknowledged the soldier curtly, and turned to the wizard, about to vent her fury. She was stopped by Raddick making a cutting motion across his throat with his hand and shaking his head. Whatever had caused the wizard to summon her, this was absolutely not the time for her to voice her complaints. Carlana had not been raised and trained to command a nation, or an army, but she had been raised and trained to deal carefully with powerful men. She had met no man more powerful than Paedris. "Lord Salva?" She asked softly. "You wished to see me?"

When the court wizard looked slowly up to meet her gaze, she was completely unprepared to see tears in his eyes. Without a word, he handed the scroll to her.

At first she found the scroll difficult to read, her being used to documents written carefully by expert scribes. This scroll was written hurriedly, in poor handwriting, with many words misspelled and crossed out. Only when she skipped to the bottom, and learned who had signed the letter, did she understand. She started over at the top, reading slowly and carefully, correcting the spelling and grammar mistakes in her mind.

To who is concerned (crossed out)
Ariana (crossed out)
To her Highness the Crown Princess Ariana
I am very sorry my jinx curse caused you injury, I did not mean to hurt you
I am leaving so that I can never hurt you again, please forgive me

Then there were numerous lines crossed out and smudged, but Carlana could see it originally said *I love you*, then he had tried to write *I greatly esteem you*, then it simply said *Thank you for being kind to me, your friend always and forever*

The letter continued, and the pen strokes were more forceful, angry

My Lord Salva, I heard guards saying you ordered me brought to the dungeon, and when I arrived at the castle, the guards said I was a coward and a deserter. I am not a coward, when I tried to follow you as the enemy attacked, two soldiers told me they had orders from you to bring me away. Later, I disobeyed Captain Raddick's orders, because I went to rescue you. I am only a servant, and you owe me nothing but my pay, but I am not a coward and not a deserter. You should tell people that. You lied when you told me you would give me land, I know now you don't own that land so you can't give it to anyone. A powerful man like you should not need to lie to little people like me
The priest told me God cursed me to be a jinx because I was a bad son, and I can't do anything to change God's judgment on me. Keeping me around so you could stop my jinx curse from hurting people must take a lot of energy, I thank you for that, but now I am leaving and going far away so I can't hurt people

Then the pen strokes became lighter, and the paper was smudged with spots that Carlana guessed were tears.

Thanks to everyone who was nice to me -Koren Bladewell

P.S. Please take good care of Thunderbolt. He is a good and brave-hearted horse and should not pay for my sins

P.P.S. Please tell her Highness the lady Carlana that I never meant to hurt her daughter, and she was right to not want a jinx around the castle

P.P.P.S. If you ever find my parents, please tell them I am very sorry for being selfish, and not leaving on my own, instead of making them leave their own home

Carlana's knees weakened, she swooned back against the wall. Captain Raddick appeared at her side, helping her to sit on the edge of Koren's bed. He also dismissed her guards and maids with a curt gesture; the Regent needed privacy. She looked up at the wizard, wiping away her own tears with the sleeve of her dress, paying no heed to proper manners. "I don't understand. You ordered guards to take him to the dungeon? Why?"

"This is, this is all a terrible, terrible series of misunderstandings. Not the dungeon." Paedris said slowly. "The *fortress*. I ordered the guards to take him to the *fortress*; the safest, most secure part of the castle. To *protect* him, from the assassin. Other than your daughter, Koren most needs to be protected." And Paedris was not sure that the princess was not less important that the young, unknowing wizard.

"But, I don't understand."

Raddick cleared his throat. "I explained to Lord Salva that, because the lower level of the old fortress is now used as a dungeon, and that is where guards work in that building, they call the entire structure the 'dungeon'. If one guard was repeating his orders to another guard, he likely would have said *dungeon*, and not *fortress*. Any boy, I mean, young man, who heard he was to be brought to the dungeon, would be fearful. Especially a young man who had been falsely accused by his captain of cowardice and desertion. Falsely, and most grievously, accused. By me, I am ashamed to say."

"And falsely accused by his Regent of hurting her daughter." Carlana added miserably. "He has left? He is gone?"

"Yes," reported Raddick, "he left, soon after Lord Salva ordered the guards to find him. He must have written that note very quickly." Seeing the effect the letter had on the court wizard and the Regent, Raddick was burning with curiosity to know what the letter said. And how a mere servant boy could affect powerful people so much.

Although, anyone who rode off against orders and alone, to rescue his master from three enemy wizards, could not be a *mere* anything. If Raddick ever met Koren Bladewell again, he would look at the boy very differently, And very closely.

"Three days ago!" Carlana said in a hollow voice. "Why wasn't I told? Has anyone searched for him?"

Raddick cleared his throat nervously. "At the time, with the castle being searched for more assassins, the guards did not think to bring it to your attention. And, as you wanted the boy away from your daughter, his leaving was in keeping with your wishes. Your Highness, I apologize. I did not think, with the country invaded, and assassins about, that this Koren boy was important?" Raddick hoped his question would lead to an answer, but he was frustrated.

"You did your duty, Captain." Carlana said. "Have you searched for him?"

"No, your Highness. My soldiers still have orders to arrest him as a deserter, if they see him, but no one is out searching for him."

"We should search for him." The wizard spoke for the first time. "We must!"

Raddick burned with curiosity to know what that letter said, what could be so important that the Regent of the realm and the court wizard, were so concerned about a lowly servant boy. A brave boy, but still a boy. "Ahem, uh, begging your leave, your Highness, my lord, but we have been invaded, and assassins could still be lurking in or around the castle. The army is needed here. Until we have recalled units from the field, I won't have the men to spare, to follow this boy."

The Regent and the wizard shared a long look. Carlana turned to Raddick. "Captain, you don't need to know-"

"He does." Paedris said, pushing himself upright on the chest. "There have been too many secrets. It is *deception* that has brought us to this point. Deception, and half-truths, and misunderstandings. Oh, this is a disaster. No, a tragedy."

"I did warn you about deceiving Koren." Carlana reminded the wizard. "And what is this he said, you lying about giving him land?"

Paedris gave a long sigh and rubbed his face. "Ah, I should have been more clear with him. The farm that is my country retreat, it used to be your husband's hunting reserve? I've only been to the place once or twice. Well, I told Koren that if he remained as my servant until he was sixteen, I would give him fifty acres. I thought the prospect of land would keep him with me, until he needed to leave the castle, to begin his training."

Carlana tapped her chin with a finger, while she thought. "If I remember correctly, Adric granted you use of that land, and the income from it, but I don't think he gave it to you outright?"

"He didn't," Paedris responded irritably, "but I intended to ask you to give me the land, as a boon, or I would buy fifty acres of land somewhere. I did not lie to Koren, I simply didn't bother to explain all the details. At the time, I didn't think it mattered! How he discovered that I didn't own the land, I can't imagine. This is all," Paedris pulled at his beard in frustration, "a distraction anyway. We *must* find him!"

"Can't you use your wizard senses, to find him?"

"No, magic doesn't work like that, I would need to first have a rough idea of where he is. And even then, the blocking spell we cast on him would hide him from me. This is a disaster. How could I have been so blind? So stupid?"

Raddick had been silent, while his mind was racing. Secrets. Deception. Lies. A disaster? Losing a servant was, at most, an inconvenience. And, begin his training? What training did Koren Bladewell need? He was already training with the weapons master, and surely Koren knew how to scrub floors. Blocking spell? Blocking Koren from doing what? Suddenly, the captain gasped as the only possible truth dawned on him, and he blurted out his thoughts. "The boy is *wizard*?"

Paedris looked at Raddick sharply, then sighed. The captain was not, after all, an idiot. Any intelligent person, having heard what Raddick had heard, could figure out the truth. "Koren is not only a wizard, he is the most powerful wizard I have ever known. Those three enemy wizards I struggled mightily against? Koren could have crushed them as you would swatting flies," Paedris emphasized his words with a casual flick of his wrist, "if he were properly trained, and ready to use his enormous power. Captain, I could cast a spell, to make you forget everything that has been said here today, but I am going to rely on your loyalty, and more important, your discretion. Only the Regent, myself, a few other wizards, and now you, know about this great secret. This terrible secret. Koren himself does not know he is a wizard! He is too old to have his power guided by another wizard, and too young to control it himself. And too young not to be tempted by such power, if he knew it. The enemy, you see, the enemy would stop at nothing to capture Koren, and use his immense power against us, if they knew about him. So, we have kept his power hidden, even from him, until such time as he is ready to begin training. If the enemy could use Koren's power, all, all would be lost."

Raddick could not imagine how a wizard, a powerful wizard, could not *know* he was a wizard, but then, Raddick knew little of wizards. He put a hand to his forehead and closed his eyes briefly, trying to make sense of what he had heard. He was beginning to feel a headache. Truly, dealing with wizards and Regents was no job for a soldier! "My lord, your Highness, I understand now why we must search for this b- this young man. But, if I send out army patrols, particularly now when we are understrength here, will that not catch the enemy's eye, and cause him to wonder what is so important about a mere servant boy?"

"You speak the truth, Captain. As much as I detest it, your orders to arrest Koren as a deserter, and perhaps for causing harm to the princess, are all your soldiers need to know. And I agree we need to keep our strength here. Instead of sending out patrols to look for him, could you send riders to carry messages to our units in the field? It would be more effective to have units in the field keeping watch for him, a search patrol may only spook Koren and drive him into hiding. If you agree, your Highness?"

Carlana nodded, she typically left such matters to her army captains.

Raddick gazed out the window for a moment, while he formed his thoughts. "And if-" He stopped, trying to think of a better way to ask a delicate question. "Lord Salva, it would be a disaster if the enemy were to capture Koren?"

"Unthinkable. Unimaginable." Paedris said, before his tired mind realized what Raddick was truly saying. "The end of all things."

"Then, what are my orders," Raddick spoke slowly, "if he has been captured, and we are unable to-"

"To get him back alive?" Paedris asked angrily.

"Forgive me, my lord, but I must ask the question."

"And I must answer. By all that is holy, I hate this war!" Paedris gave out a heavy sigh. "If Koren has been captured by the enemy, and only if we have no hope of rescuing him, then, then he must be killed. We must. His power is too great."

CHAPTER FOURTEEN

The night that Captain Raddick learned the truth about Koren, the young man himself was hiding between bales of hay in a stable. Getting out of Linden had been easy, he had hopped aboard an empty wagon that was trundling slowly westward, hiding under the wagon's canvas cover. None of the guards at checkpoints on the road had orders to search wagons that were headed away from the capital, so he was not discovered that night. Before daylight, he had dropped to the ground and dashed away into a field, then made his way to a wooded area to sleep.

The next night, he walked west on the road for several miles, alone, before a group of wagons passed by, but he had no opportunity to hitch a ride, for these wagons were loaded, and armed guards on horseback patrolled alongside. From a comment he overheard one of the guards make, Koren guessed the wagons were only going a short way down the road, before stopping for the night in a village. He let the wagons pass by, and followed, walking down the road in the dark. His stomach rumbled, for he had nothing to eat since the afternoon of the day he had returned to the castle. In a way, he had come full circle in one year; once again forced to leave a home, tired and hungry, on his own, with few supplies, and no particular destination in mind. When he neared the village, he burrowed into a haystack to sleep a few hours, rising with the dawn. In the village, he bought a rough loaf of bread, a wedge of hard cheese, dried meat and dried fruit. When the shopkeeper asked whether Koren was with the wagons, Koren merely grunted, and let the man think what he wanted. Best if the man did not later remember a boy on his own, passing through the village. He left the village before the wagons, and hid in a grove of trees as they passed by later. In a field, he found a discarded, broken hay rake, and he bound it back together with twine. With the hay rake over his shoulder, he no longer needed to hide every time a wagon passed by, for to anyone seeing him, he was a farmhand walking to work. That day was a long, foot-aching walk for a young man, who had grown used to riding a fast horse, but his belly was full and he had enough food to last the next day. Late in the afternoon, he saw ahead of him a substantial town, on the banks of a river, with a pair of bridges soaring high above the river. It looked like a place a young man alone would not be noticed, and could buy more supplies, although he would need to stash the hay rake somewhere.

And then an instinct, perhaps a faint vibration, a sound, maybe a change in the wind, made Koren look back east behind him. Riders, coming fast. A group of men on horseback, moving at speed, one of them carrying a royal army banner. Koren tossed the hay rake aside and simply ran, until he was around a bend in the road, where he dashed across a field and lay down behind bushes. The soldiers rode straight by, their horses' hooves pounding the road. After they were gone, he left the road and entered the town from the north, where he snuck into a stable near the river. There seemed to be many soldiers in the town, and Koren could see both bridges were well guarded, with travelers in both directions being stopped and searched. He could not go further west. He was pondering what to do, when he heard voices, and two men came into the stable. Scrunching himself up as small as possible, Koren hid and listened.

"With all these soldiers and wagon trains, you'd think we'd have more business." The first man grumbled. "Two horses in here! That barely pays for the hay they eat."

"Calm down, Lan, we had eighteen horses last night." The second man responded, as he settled down with his back against the low wall Koren was hiding behind. "Comes and goes, it does, comes and goes. Ricker will be back tomorrow, and we'll be busier than we can handle, so rest yourself tonight."

The two men were silent, while Koren fought to suppress a sneeze from hay dust, then the second man spoke again, and made Koren forget all about his itchy nose. "You hear about the wizard's servant?"

"What's he to me?" The first man asked, sounded uninterested.

"Tried to kill the princess, he did."

"What?" The first man was now interested. "The hell you say."

"It's true, that's why there are so many soldiers in town. I overheard a group who arrived this very afternoon talking at the guard post. The wizard's servant is an enemy assassin, he tried to kill the princess."

"You and your stories." The first man said, and spat onto the ground.

"I'm telling you, I heard the new soldiers repeat their orders! This boy is charged with cowardice, and desertion, and their orders are to capture him if they can, or kill him if they must. Dead or alive, it's all the same to them. And an assassin tried to kill the princess, so it can't be a coincidence they're hunting this boy now, can it?"

"The princess? You telling the truth?"

"I swear. Look, these two horses are bedded down for the night, what say we slip across to the Happy Dragon for a pint? There's always a couple soldiers there, you can hear it for yourself."

"A pint? When did you ever stop at one pint?" The first man scoffed, but he was curious to hear more. An attempt to kill the princess was big news, bad news. News that could lead towards more war, which was bad for business. "All right, but we come back in half a glass, mind you, and check on the horses again."

As soon as the two men were gone, Koren scrambled out of his hiding place and ran into the night. Capture him if they can, *or kill him*. He was no longer running only for his freedom, he was running for his very life. Dead or alive? Probably dead was better, the soldiers would think. Where Koren had been worried before, now he was terrified. Every shadow seemed like it could be a soldier seeking him, every sound could be a sword slipping from a scabbard, or a bowstring being drawn back. The alley behind the stables was dark even to Koren's eyes, he stumbled over discarded junk while trying to walk quietly, and lay flat on the ground, sure someone had heard the noise. While he lay on the ground, two soldiers walked by the street at the end of the alleyway. As the soldiers were not holding lanterns, and didn't even glance down the alley, maybe they were off duty, and not looking for a runaway servant? Koren hoped. There were more voices, and a half dozen men walked by in the opposite direction, these men were carrying crates or sacks on their shoulders. That gave Koren an idea. From his pocket, he pulled a handkerchief, and tied it around his head like some of the men had, tucking his hair up under. From the alley, he picked up a broken crate, the very item he had tripped over. If he held the broken part next to his head, no one would likely notice the crate was empty in the darkness. Hurrying down the alley and onto the street, he caught up to the men and stayed behind them, just another laborer carrying trade goods. They walked towards the river, the men ahead of him talking loudly, until they came to another street, and Koren's heart almost stopped. Two soldiers were standing under a torch, at the intersection. These soldiers were on duty, both of them watching everyone who walked by them, hands resting on the hilts of their swords. Koren reached down to his pant leg, which was muddy, he scraped away mud with his fingernails, and rubbed it across his cheeks, to make his face less visible. Imitating the men ahead of him, he leaned to one side, as if the crate he was carrying was heavy. When the man in the lead approached the soldiers, he called out a greeting, asking something that Koren couldn't quite hear. The soldiers laughed, and one of them said something about rain. For a frightening moment, it looked like the man in the lead was going to stop and chat with the soldiers, then he laughed loudly, and continued on down the street. Koren kept his head down as he passed by, the soldiers not paying him much attention. Either these two soldiers had not yet received orders to capture, or kill, Koren Bladewell, or they were looking for a boy alone, not part of a group of laborers. Two blocks later, he could smell the river, and then they were at the docks. Here, barges loaded and unloaded their cargo at a long series of warehouses. Further down the docks, there was another group of soldiers, clearly on patrol, for they all held lanterns, and held them up to the faces of everyone who passed by. As soon as he could, Koren ducked into an alley, and set the crate down. He waited a moment for even his excellent night vision to recover from the torchlight, then walked quietly along the alley until he found windows, he tried several before finding one that was not locked. Climbing in the window, he stepped into deeper darkness, and slid the window closed behind him. The warehouse must hold barrels of liquor somewhere, for there was a smell of whiskey in the air. Setting his pack down, he was about to get comfortable, then a whisper made him freeze. "Hey, this is my spot."

Koren's hand flew to a knife, then he relaxed. The voice was a man's, the words somewhat slurred. Now Koren knew where the smell of whiskey had come from. "Sorry. Did I step on you?" He whispered back.

"No. You not here to steal anything, are you? Don't want any trouble."

"I'm not here to steal anything." Koren said she settled down against the wall. "I'm only, taking a rest."

The man laughed softly. "Those soldiers outside wouldn't have anything to do with it, would they? Don't worry about me, I won't say anything. You look like a young feller, I headed out on my own too, when I was about your age."

Koren wasn't sure what to say, but somehow he trusted this man, whose face he still couldn't see. "I just don't want any trouble. I've caused enough trouble already." He added, without meaning to speak the words aloud.

"Aye, know what you mean, I been there myself. Been there myself." The man repeated his words, and there was a slurping sound, with a strong scent of whiskey. "Long time ago, that was, long time ago. Caused a lot of trouble, hurt about everyone close to me. I was in the army, I was, had a wife, and a little girl. But, I took to drink, and can't shake it. They're better off without me." Another slurping sound. "Better off without me around, they are."

Sitting in the dark, dusty warehouse, listening to the drunken man tell his sad tale, Koren pulled his knees up to his chest, and thought he had never felt so low in his life. Where was he going to go? And why? To run away forever? His curse would follow him wherever he went, hurt anyone around him. What kind of life was he running toward?

"A good soldier I was, back then." The man said, as if he needed to fill the silence with words. Maybe he felt as lonely and hopeless as Koren did right then. "Was a sergeant in Grand General Daruck's personal guard, under the old king, way back that was. Too many battles, too many friends lost. Seen," his voice trailed off, "seen, seen too much. Too much death. So, I found comfort in the bottle. What about you? You hurt someone, you didn't mean to hurt?"

"Sort of. Yes." Koren found himself answering. It was easier to tell a stranger in the darkness about his sins, easier to tell a man whose face he couldn't see, a man he didn't know, a man he probably would never meet again. "My parents, first. They're-" there was a catch in his throat, "they're good people. They deserved better than me."

In the darkness, the man reached over and patted Koren's shoulder. "Don't you worry about it, lad. They're your parents, they love you. They have forgiven you, whatever you think you did. Anyone else? A girl? I'll bet there was a girl."

Koren let out a long sigh. Tried to kill the princess, the guards had said about him. *Tried*, meant Ariana was alive, his curse had not killed her. Koren was relieved to hear that. "There was a girl, not *my* girl. She's too good for the likes of me." Did Ariana know now that his curse had brought the bear to attack her, made her almost drown in the river, made a stone knock her down, almost kill her? Was she now regretting the day she invited him to live in the castle? Better that Duke Yarron had locked him in the dungeon as a poacher and a bandit, than that he be set free, to cause her nothing but trouble?

"You're young, whatever you did, you can learn from it, and make it up to them."

Koren choked on a laugh. He was cursed by God. There would be no making up for that, no way, as the priest had told him, to make it go away. "It's too late for that."

The two sat silent for a while, listening to the sounds on the docks outside; lots of shouting and cursing from sailors, sounds of things banging and knocking into each other as the sailors loaded a barge for a trip downriver.

"Where you going from here?" The man broke the silence.

"I don't know. I really don't." He truly had no idea where to go. Glumly, he considered traveling west, if he could get across the river without being caught or killed by the army. West, toward the Acedor border and war? Change his name, cut his hair, hire on with the army of some local baron? Try to do something useful with his life even if it meant constant war? No, that was a terrible idea. With his curse, the last thing Tarador's army needed was a jinx fighting on their side.

"Hmm. If I were a young feller like you, running away from my troubles, why, I'd head out to sea, to seek my fortune. Get on a barge downriver, to the sea, and sign on aboard a ship bound for other lands. Go to the exotic South Islands, if you like, where fruit hangs from every tree, and all the girls are pretty!" He chuckled to himself.

"Really?" Going to sea wasn't something Koren had considered. Could he do that? A ship could take him far, far away from Tarador, far away to lands where no one was hunting him, no one knew him, no one knew about his jinx.

"Well, I don't know as to myself, never been there, but-"

"No, not the South Islands, I mean, I could go aboard a ship, as a sailor? I've never been to sea before."

"Why, sure you could. Merchant ship're always looking for able-bodied men, lots of sailors jump ship when they get to port and get their pay." And too many of them spent their pay on drink, the man thought to himself. "You got any skills?"

Koren thought for a minute. "I'm good with a blade, and a bow." As he said the words, he suddenly wondered if his magical skills would go away, now that he was no longer servant to the wizard. "And, and, I'm good with horses."

"Huh. Well, not much use for any of that on a ship, unless you're in pirate territory, and I suggest you avoid that. Good pay, not worth the coin, if you ask me. Anything else you can do?"

"Uh, well, I lived on a farm. I, uh, I don't know." What kind of work did sailors do aboard a ship? "Um, I can cook?"

"You can? Where'd you learn that?"

"I, uh," Koren hesitated to say too much, "I was a servant for a rich man, a, uh, a merchant, and he liked foods from his homeland, Stade? So I learned to cook the kind of foods he liked. But, I can cook regular food, too. Taradoran food, I mean."

"That's good, that's good, a good cook makes for a happy crew, that's for sure. If you go, look for a ship flying the Estadan flag, it's red with a white circle and a black star. You speak any of their lingo?"

Koren shrugged. "A few words, not much."

"Can't speak a word of it, myself. Don't hold with strange foreign talk."

"How, uh, how would I get there, to the sea?"

"I'd duck aboard a barge, if I was going. Plenty of barges headed downriver out there," he pointed toward the docks, "sneak aboard one. This time of year, with the spring flood, they're overloaded with cargo, because the water's deep. And with the moonlight tonight, they'll be leaving soon as they're loaded, not wait till morning. The next stop is about a day downriver, so you need to get off and swim to shore, before they start messing with the cargo again. You can swim?"

"Yes." Koren was reminded that the last time he went swimming was in the river with Ariana. The more the man talked, the more the idea of going downriver sounded like a good idea. Down the river, find a ship, and leave Tarador behind. Leave his life behind. Start over, somewhere new. Somewhere so far away that people could not have heard of his jinx. Maybe, so far away that he could leave his curse behind? Why not? "Yes. I'll do that, thank you." Peeking out the window, he saw only a few people at the docks, and the clanging, banging and cursing noises of a barge being loaded had died down. Was a barge getting ready to leave, soon? "Any advice on how to get aboard one of these barges?"

The man snorted. "If I did something like that, I'd go up to the front of this warehouse, the front of the building is on the dock, over the water. There's a couple floorboards loose, if you know where to look, you can climb down under the pier, get into the water, and up the side of a barge. Loaded the way they are, they're low in the water, and there's netting on the sides." The man raised a bottle to his lips, then looked at the bottle, put the cork back in it, and set it down. "Aaah, I've had too much of that tonight already." He spat on the floor, then rose unsteadily to his feet. "You seem like a good feller, I'll show you where it is. Stay behind me and move real quiet like, and keep your head down."

They had to squeeze between stacked crates and piles of grain sacks to get to the middle of the warehouse, the man had to lean on crates, and then on Koren, to keep from falling down. Koren wasn't sure which smell was stronger; the musty, dusty warehouse, or the whiskey on the man's breath. With the only light coming from one half-closed door facing the river, Koren slid his feet along the floor, feeling for objects they might trip over. When they got near the door, the man put a finger to his lips, so Koren would be extra quiet, then pointed to the right with a shaky hand. When the floorboard squeaked under Koren's foot, the man gripped his arm, and they both froze. "Quiet! It's right here." He whispered. As the man tried to get down on his knees, he fell and rolled clumsily onto his right side. "Ah, don't you ever start drinking, young man, it'll be the death of me yet." He pushed himself onto his knees, and felt around the edges of the boards, until he was able to get fingernails caught on one, and lift it up. The other three boards were easy to remove, and Koren peered down to see dark water splashing around thick log pilings that supported the floor of the warehouse. Boards had been attached to the piling next to the gap in the floor, forming a rough ladder.

"That's how I get in here, to keep out of the weather." The man said, pride in his voice. "Hurry now, if that barge is done loading, a guard will be coming by to check this place soon."

Koren stared at the water below, at the uneven boards nailed to the piling, at the darkness. That way lay his future; to run, to hide, to leave his country behind, to forever deny who he is. "I don't-"

The man patted him on the shoulder. "The first step is always the hardest, is what I've found. After that, it gets easier."

That was something Koren's father had often said. Especially when he wanted Koren to do something hard, something that would take all day, like plowing a field. Something hard, like leaving everything he had ever known behind. Hard, because it was the right thing to do, the best way to protect the people he cared about. "All right." He heard himself saying, and stepped carefully down onto the first board of the ladder, before he could change his mind. The board wobbled a bit, but held his weight. When he climbed down enough that only his head was above the floor, he looked up at the man, whose face he could barely see, except for the man's scraggly beard. Pulling a silver coin out of his pocket, Koren pressed it between his finger and thumb, *wishing* it would bring the man some good luck, to turn his life around. The coin seemed to grow warm. "Here, take this."

"Oh, I can't take your money." The man protested.

"It was given to me, I can give it to you."

The man held the coin up to the poor light, Koren could just see his eyes open wide as the man realized he had been given a gold coin, not a common copper piece. "Well, bless you, young man. And, good luck to you, wherever you may go."

"Yes, Your Highness?" Paedris asked, standing at the door to his tower, more than slightly flustered at finding the crown princess waiting for him. He was still feeling very weak, even walking down the stairs to answer the call at the door was an effort that had left him slightly out of breath.

"I wanted to thank you for healing me," Ariana answered, unconsciously moving her right shoulder blade, where the stone had hit her and knocked her to the flagstones of the courtyard. "I brought chicken soup," she said as she held up a large silver tureen, her arms shaking. The tureen was solid silver, part of the royal dinnerware, and it was heavy by itself. Filled with soup, Ariana had to hug it to her chest to keep from dropping it.

Paedris saw her distress, and tactfully said "why, thank you, Your Highness. Perhaps your guard could carry the soup, while you help an old man up the stairs."

Ariana blushed, and silently mouthed 'thank you', with a wink to the wizard.

Paedris held onto her arm lightly, he truly did need help climbing the two flights of stairs up to the chamber that had been built for a wizard to receive guests. In the years Paedris had been living there, he had few guests other than other wizards, and the occasional army captain or general. The chamber had never been fancy, and now it was quite simply a mess. Rather than climb more stairs, Paedris had requested his bed be moved down here, and with Koren gone, the chamber was not being cleaned regularly. Servants from the palace were sent every couple days, but none of them liked being in the forbidding tower, and left as quickly as they could, after hurriedly tidying up. Paedris sat down in an over-stuffed chair, and waved toward the table. "Set it down there, good man."

The guard frowned when he saw the table, already overloaded with old plates, bowls, mugs, scrolls and cutlery. Ariana scooped up an armful of dirty dishes, and set them on the floor. When the guard had placed the soup tureen on the table, she dismissed him. "You may leave us, wait in the courtyard."

The guard lifted an eyebrow in surprise. The crown princess was never supposed to be alone with a man; she always was accompanied by a guard, or a maid. Always. "Your Highness-" The guard began to protest.

"You may leave us, *now*." Ariana insisted, in a voice of command that belonged only to a crown princess, with no trace of the young girl. Paedris rose halfway out of his chair, and gave the guard his best intimidating wizardly glare. The guard might have stood his ground against a fourteen year old girl, princess or not, but wizards were not to be trifled with. The guard had seen the charred remains of the assassin, after Paedris had risen from his sickbed to chase the assassin across the rooftops, and blast the man from Acedor into a crispy cinder. Bowing deeply to both princess and wizard, the guard backed out of the room, and from the sound his boots made, fairly ran down the stairs.

Ariana found two clean bowls and spoons, and served the soup, before sitting in a chair across from the wizard. Paedris, although he had been around the royal Trehaymes since Ariana's father was a little boy, couldn't remember ever having a royal person act as a dinner servant. He wasn't really in the mood for chicken soup, but so as not to offend the princess, he took a spoonful, and exclaimed in surprise "This is chicken fortana soup! How did you, where-"

"I had the kitchens make it for you, there is a man from Stade who works in the stables, his wife gave the cooks her recipe. Is it good?" Ariana had feared the cooks in the royal kitchens, who had been skeptical about making exotic foreign food, had gotten it wrong. To her, the soup tasted good, a bit too spicy for a girl raised on bland Taradoran food, but good.

"Good! It's good. The peppers should be roasted a bit, and it's a bit bland, but that's probably better for me right now. Thank you, Your Highness."

A bit bland? Ariana wondered how the wizard could say that, as she sipped water to cool the burning in her mouth. "I thought that, Koren said he used to cook special food for you, and, since he's not here-" She stopped to wipe a tear away with her handkerchief.

Paedris remained silent for a moment, to let the princess recover her composure. It had been four weeks since Koren ran away, four weeks that had seen the wizard deathly ill, until Shomas Feany had arrived to heal him. Even now, Paedris was still weak and tired.

"Have you heard anything, any word?" Ariana asked. Paedris had sent word to those other wizards who were on the way to Linden to tend to the stricken court wizard, that he needed them instead to do whatever they could to find Koren Bladewell. If Paedris died, that would certainly be bad, but Tarador would likely survive. If Koren was captured by the enemy, Tarador and the rest of the free world, would certainly fall to the Dark One of Acedor.

"News of Koren? No, no, nothing. You?"

"Nothing from the army."Ariana twisted the handkerchief in her hands, then used it to wipe away the tears that welled up in her eyes. "I never really told him I was sorry that he didn't get credit for finding the Cornerstone. And that I should not have made him leave the Regency Council meeting. I never told him how I feel."

Paedris looked away, to give the young princess time to compose herself. "It is early yet. Plenty of time for a young man alone to realize where he belongs, and return home." He added, unconvincingly.

"Home? This isn't his home, not any more!" Ariana's voice fluttered with anguish. "He believes people here consider him a coward, a deserter, an assassin, that you wanted him thrown into the dungeon? And he believes that he's a terrible jinx who almost killed me. Why would he ever come back here?" Carlana had tried to keep Koren's letter secret from her daughter, but that had not lasted. As soon as Ariana heard a rumor that Koren had left a letter, addressed to Ariana, the crown princess had summoned the royal chancellor, to consult the law. The chancellor had informed her that, as Koren's letter was addressed to Ariana, it was her property. Further, the elderly chancellor said gravely, that interfering with delivery of mail to the royal family was a crime against the state, a *serious* crime. Ariana had never seen her mother so mad at her as when she had been forced, in front of her own chancellor, to deliver Koren's letter to Ariana. Whatever anger Carlana felt paled in comparison to Ariana's own anger, and then bitter sorrow, when she read the note. Her mother trying to explain that Koren's woes were caused by terrible misunderstandings only made Ariana feel worse. "He saved my life again. If I hadn't seen him across the courtyard, that gargoyle would have fallen right on top of me."

"What?" Paedris asked, astounded. He had not heard this part of the story. "What do you mean?"

"My mother still thinks Koren is a jinx, no matter what you tell her. I was standing on the dais in the courtyard, and when I saw Koren, I called out and started to run toward him. Then the gargoyle fell, right where I would have been if I hadn't run. I would have been standing there, if Koren had not come into the courtyard. He was on his way to see you, with a soldier escorting him, because he was a *prisoner*."

"Yes, that was, an, um, unfortunate misunderstanding. Which I have since corrected, by explaining to Captain Raddick." Captain Raddick, who learned that he had earned the displeasure of the crown princess, and left the castle as soon as he was able. Carlana had told Paedris that, so far, Ariana didn't know the army was officially searching for Koren as a deserter, Ariana only knew people were searching for the young man. And she certainly didn't know the secret order for Koren to be killed, if he had been captured by the enemy.

"And if I find which priest told Koren he was cursed-"

"Mother Furliss says it wasn't her, and I believe her." Paedris hastened to say. The priestess had been furious, and had told the wizard her suspicion that a certain worthless priest named Emil Gruch may be the culprit. Father Gruch was soon going to find himself reassigned to a miserable church in the Fethid swamp, where he would be too busy swatting mosquitos and worrying about snakes to do any more damage to the faithful. Which was still a better fate than what Paedris, in his anger, had wanted to do the wretched man.

"Koren is not a jinx! He was there to save me, when the bear attacked. And he was there to make me move, exactly when the gargoyle fell. He is the *opposite* of a jinx."

"I agree, Your Highness. While he has been good luck for you, and for me, and for Tarador, his own luck has been rather bad." Much of which is my own fault, Paedris added to himself, if I hadn't kept the truth from him. "Is this what you wished to talk about in private?"

Ariana dabbed at her eyes with her handkerchief, not caring if the wizard saw her tears. "Partly, yes. I know you care about Koren, and I need to talk with someone else who does. Mother thinks he is nothing but trouble."

"Your mother-"

"Is sometimes a silly woman." Ariana declared forcefully. "I know she loves me, and thinks she's doing what is best for me, but she has no idea what she's doing. She was raised to be a wife, and a mother, she never expected to rule a country. She's driving General Magrane to distraction, and he's too loyal to say it, but she's a terrible Regent." After initially ordering the royal army to the capital after she heard about the raid in Longshire, she changed her mind and ordered General Magrane to the western border. Then after the discovery of an assassin in the castle, she had ordered the army back, even to the point of recalling royal troops that had been sent to reinforce the provinces, and allies in other countries, that were most threatened by Acedor. Even Duke Yarron, who had always been a strong supporter of the royal family, was grumbling about Carlana leaving LeVanne province to fend for itself on the border. "If she keeps doing this, we're going to lose the few allies we have left. And the Regency Council could shift votes to making Duke Falco my Regent." Ariana shuddered at that thought. With Regin Falco as her Regent, a position that Duke had wanted since her father died, Ariana feared it would not be long before an unfortunate 'accident' happened to her.

Paedris shifted uncomfortably in his chair. As court wizard, and a foreigner, he was forbidden from taking sides in any internal Taradoran politics, including matters of the Regency Council. Perhaps, especially decisions of the Regency Council, for that was where the Dukes and Duchesses most jealously guarded their power. Paedris had remained scrupulously neutral, but if Regin Falco was named Regent, Paedris did not see how he could remain silent. He did not trust the man, not at all. Until such a thing was about to happen, however, Paedris felt he needed to remain silent on the matter. For Paedris to interfere in the Regency Council would be to thrust Tarador into an outright civil war. "Your mother does what she thinks best." He responded carefully.

"By trying to protect me, my mother is risking me never becoming queen, or not having much of a country left once I take the throne."

"Hmm, well, I can't speak against-"

"Yes, you can. You can speak against the Regent, to me alone. I checked with the royal chancellor about the law on this. Mother is *my* Regent."

Whatever the written law stated, Paedris knew the law mostly was whatever those in power said it was, and Carlana had the power. At the moment. This conversation was getting into dangerous territory, at a time when Tarador was threatened, and the wizard himself was not at full strength. Before Paedris could respond, Ariana continued her argument. "Lord Salva, I need to become queen, *now*. If I wait until my sixteenth birthday, that will be too late. Too late for me, and too late for Tarador. Our enemy will not sit idly by for another two years, while we argue and my mother does nothing."

"The law-"

"The law is whatever the Regency Council agrees to. Enough of the Dukes are afraid we're going to lose the war, soon, that I think I can push my mother aside. But, I will need your help. Can I count on your support and advice, Lord Salva?"

Paedris should have taken some time to consider the crown princess' stunning proposal. He didn't need to. Ariana was ready, far more qualified at her young age to rule Tarador than her mother ever was. Seeing the young girl making such a momentous decision on her own, and acting so forcefully, to take the reins of great responsibility, swept away any doubts he may have had. He had been waiting for Ariana to take power, planning, wishing and hoping for that day, hoping it did not happen too late. Now, he could do something about it, and together, they could thwart the plans for the enemy. He cleared his throat, and announced "Your Highness, I have been waiting for this day, ever since your father died. Yes, you have my complete support. And, the gratitude of an old man. I should have suggested this to you, before we came to such a crisis."

"Thank you, Lord Salva." Ariana said gravely, then the young girl in her broke through, and she leaped out of her chair to fling her arms around him and kiss his cheek. "Thank you, thank you, thank you."

Paedris could feel the wetness of her tears on his cheek. He gently unwrapped her arms from around her, and looked her in the eyes. "And now, Your Highness, if you are going to be our queen, there is a very important secret you need to learn, about Koren Bladewell."

That very same night, Koren held onto the ropes that led up to the mainmast of the ship, and looked down at the angrily foaming black water. Not actually *down*, for the ship was healing over so far that the crests of the waves were above him, and as he tried to make his way to the railing, a wave smashed him full in the face, he lost his grip on the rope, and was washed across the deck to be bashed against a stack of crates. As the ship healed over the other way, the water cascading off the deck pulled him along with it, and he tumbled, out of control, up against one of the holes the sailors called 'scuppers' where the water poured out over the side. Coughing and choking on seawater, Koren decided that nothing aboard a ship was easy, not even throwing yourself overboard.

The ship rolled the other way again, and Koren let himself slide across the deck, splinters from the rough wood deck scratching his skin. He bumped against the rail, and scrambled up the railing, determined to dive overboard, before a wave threw him back, or he lost his nerve. A black wave loomed above him, gray foam curling to strike him down, as he pulled himself up onto the top of the railing, and took a deep breath.

A breath that was knocked out of him, when a rough hand took hold of his shirt collar and yanked him back onto the deck, just as the wave broke over the railing and knocked him down. Once he recovered from being battered into the deck by the water, Koren was hauled to his feet by a large sailor named Alfonze. "What in the hell are you doing, you young fool? You could have fallen overboard!"

"I was trying to!" Koren choked out the words, which only made him realize how very much he wanted to live.

"Trying to-" Alfonze was dumbfounded, as he pulled the young man he knew as 'Kedrun' up next to the mast, where they were safer from the waves breaking over the side. "Why would you want to go over the side, at night? You seasick?"

Koren shook his head. Unlike the five other new crewmen, he had not gotten seasick during the week the ship had been sailing due south across the open sea, not even in the storm. "Jofer said this storm is going to sink the ship, and that one of us new men brought bad luck with us. It's me, I'm a jinx! I brought this storm on us, and we're *all* going to die as long as I'm aboard!"

To Koren's surprise, he saw Alfonze's teeth shining with a broad smile. "A storm? You call this a *storm*, you stupid landlubber?" Alfonze roared with laughter. "This ain't even a blow, nor not a squall. When we get into a *storm*, I'll let you know, and there won't be no mistaking it. And never listen to Jofer, that useless old idiot hasn't learned a darned thing about sailing in all his long years. He sees mermaids around every shore, and there ain't no such thing, mark my words." Seeing Koren was not yet convinced, Alfonze pointed toward the bow of the ship. "Lookee there, you wooly-head. See the sky yonder is lighter? That's moonlight, where this little cloudburst ends. We'll be out of this in half a glass, and then you'll be called on deck to clean up some of this mess. So no sense going below now to get out of these wet clothes, you come with me." Koren held onto the big man as they climbed the stairs up to where two sailors were wrestling with the big wheel that steered the ship. "You see? If this were a *storm*, the cap'n hisself would be up here, instead of snoring away in his cabin. Storm?" Alfonze shook his head and laughed, and truly Koren could see that, although the ship still bobbed alarmingly on the waves, the crew had everything under control. "Yussaf, Renten, this young fool Kedrun here thinks this is a fearsome *storm*!"

The two sailors laughed along with Alfonze. As Koren held tightly onto the railing at the top of the stairs, and squinted to see in the stinging sea spray, he peered ahead, to where he could now see the night sky truly was distinctly lighter. He may still be a jinx, trouble and doom for everyone around him, but not this night. Not this one night. And that gave him hope.

THE END

Turn to the next page for a preview of Transcendent; Book 2 of the Ascendant trilogy

Transcendent
Chapter 1

The evening breeze blew a stray lock of hair into Nurelka's eyes, and she brushed it away in irritation. The light, swirling breeze danced the lock of hair straight up, then back into her eyes. Huffing in frustration, she took firm hold of it and tucked the end up under her scarf, tugging the scarf down to secure the hair in place.

The guard next to her leaned over in his saddle to whisper. "You missed a-"

"I know," she whispered back, more loudly than she intended, and ignored the stray hairs as best she could.

The man looked stung, and turned away.

"Sorry, Duston," she said to the man, "I didn't mean to snap at you. I am only, oh, how many nights are we going to do this?" She nodded toward the setting sun, toward the silhouette of the young crown princess, sitting still and silent on her horse, with another riderless horse beside her. The crown princess of Tarador was gazing sadly into yet another sunset.

"Until it's enough," Duston announced with the wisdom of his many years. "Until she decides it is enough."

"It will never be enough," Nurelka declared, "not until that boy returns."

"He's no boy," Duston replied, twisting in the saddle to ease his stiff back. "Not anymore. Not after all that has happened to him. Not if he is out there, on his own."

"He is out there?" Nurelka asked, not expecting an answer.

"Most likely. The wizard says he would know if Koren were dead. I don't know how he would know, he seemed pretty sure of it, I tell you. Best to stay out of the affairs of wizards."

"It's best," she agreed. "Still, I don't know as to why Lord Salva is so concerned about one servant running away. He's had many, over the years."

"Any of them ever been accused of injuring the princess?" Duston asked. "Or being a jinx?"

"No, but-"

"That's why the wizard cares. Something's going on with that Koren. I don't know whether the wizard feels guilty that he is somehow at fault for Koren leaving," Duston frowned. Someone in the castle knew the full story, and whoever they were, they weren't talking. "Or that he didn't stop the Lady," he meant the Regent Carlana Trehayme, "from accusing Koren of being a dangerous jinx."

"Is he?" Nurelka asked.

"A jinx?" Duston rubbed his beard. "Talking to the soldiers who were with him and the wizard, when they were attacked, most of them think Koren's quick action saved them. He certainly saved the wizard, all by hisself. Others, ah, they're not sure. It was certainly very odd bad luck to be attacked, deep inside Tarador, on a fine, clear spring morning. That was bad luck; you could say they were jinxed. So, I don't know. The wizard says there is no such thing as a jinx-"

"You'd expect a wizard to say something like that, wouldn't you?"

"I suppose. Yes, they would have to say something like that."

The two, the former royal guard who now watched over the young crown princess, and the woman who had been Ariana's maid since the girl was little, sat silently on their horses a moment, looking into the setting sun. Looking at the princess, who was alone. Alone, except for two trusted personal servants just out of earshot. And a hundred members of the royal guard, mostly staying out of sight but forming a secure perimeter around their precious charge, the future leader of Tarador.

"She never smiles anymore," Nurelka sighed. "She used to smile all the time. It was such a joy to see her happy."

"She didn't smile for a long time after her father died," Duston observed. Her father. The man Duston knew as the king of Tarador, back then. Duston reached over to the maid and gave her shoulder a reassuring squeeze. "She will smile again, someday. Someday, you'll see, Nurelka," he added with a smile that he didn't feel.

"It had best be soon, Duston, before the enemy falls upon us. None of us will be smiling then."

Duston nodded grimly. After the enemy attack on the court wizard, the whole nation seemed to be holding their breath, waiting for the enemy to strike again. "Soon," he said, "it will be soon."

As the sun touched the horizon, Ariana almost held her breath. She had done that, holding her breath, the first time she watched a sunset after Koren had fled. At the time, she had told herself that Koren would return, if only she could hold her breath from the moment the bottom of the sun kissed the horizon until it disappeared entirely. That first time, she had gasped for breath in panic before the orb had sunk halfway, alarmed at how long it took for the sun to set. Usually, it happened within seconds, it seemed! Perhaps time slowed when you held your breath. Knowing she was likely being silly but desperate to do *something*, the next time she was able to view a sunset, she had timed it with a glass. Over three minutes! Could she hold her breath that long? No matter, it was silly anyway, something she did for herself and not to help Koren in any real way. The time for her to indulge in silly things was long past. She needed to put little girl things aside and lead her nation to victory. Or, survival. Survival first, then perhaps they could begin thinking of eventual victory. Survival, in her lifetime, might be the best she could hope for.

Not taking her eyes off the setting sun, she reached out with her left hand, and Thunderbolt stepped close enough for her to pet the horse's head. After Koren left, the horse had been frantic, nearly breaking out of his stall. The stable master had not known what to do, he had been almost in tears the day Ariana visited the stables. Ariana had ordered that the great horse be released from the stables into the high-walled paddock, and allowed to wander in and out as he pleased. No one, Ariana decreed, would ever put a saddle or bridle on Thunderbolt, until Koren returned to do that by himself. Ariana leaned over to scratch the horse's mane, which was tangled and needed brushing. Thunderbolt only allowed two people to groom him; Ariana and Lord Salva, both of whom were extremely busy, and both of whom came to the stables several times each week anyway. Ariana enjoyed spending time with Thunderbolt, she felt close to Koren while she was grooming the great horse. As she tussled the horse's mane, and he leaned in close to her, the last rays of the sun fell behind the western hills; the sun had set on another day. Another day when Koren Bladewell had not returned. "What do you think he's doing right now?" She asked the horse. "Is he watching the sun set?"

Thunderbolt tossed his head, looked at her with one eye, and snorted sadly.

Lord Paedris Don Salva came back to awareness with a gasp, pulling himself from deeply within the spirit world. His eyes not focusing properly, he blinked and looked around, wondering where he was. Then realized with a shock, and looked to the west. He was at the platform on top of his tower, and the sun was almost touching the horizon. "Cecil!" He tried to shout; all that came out was a thin croak. How long had they been there? They had begun the spell after mid-day. Hours? They must have been there, unaware, for hours.

"Cecil!" He swallowed to soothe his raw throat. "Mwazo! Lord Mwazo!" He shook the other wizard, who lay slumped on the platform, having fallen off the bench they had been on. The man did not respond, even when Paedris shook him. Glancing at the sun, which had now slid down so that its bottom edge was below the horizon, Paedris felt fear. The darkness of night was the province of the enemy; Paedris knew that Mwazo was in grave danger. He gathered his strength, thinly stretched as it was, touched a palm to the man's forehead, and delivered a shock. Strong enough that Paedris felt the shock up his own arm to his shoulder and neck.

It worked. Mwazo gasped, his eyes fluttering, as he was rudely pulled from the spirit world. "Wha-" he choked, rose onto one elbow, and collapsed.

"Rest, my friend," Paedris managed to say, and pulled Mwazo's head into his lap. "Drink," he said, as he pulled the cork from a flask of water and held it to Mwazo's lips. The other man drank sloppily, most of the water pouring down into the platform. No matter, Paedris had plenty of water. "We were gone for far too long. That was foolish of me."

"S-sorry," Mwazo stammered, his mouth still parched.

"Sorry? For what?" Paedris asked, as he opened another flask of water and drained the whole flask. His hands shook so much that half the water spilled out onto his clothes. He was weary, weary deeply into his bones; he knew that he and Mwazo would be weak and exhausted for many days.

"I failed," Mwazo explained. "Even with you lending your power, I could not discern the enemy's mind." The wizard had traveled the spirit world, seeking to penetrate the enemy's mind, to learn the thoughts and plans of their ancient enemy. "All I can tell you is that I received an impression of great eagerness, a terrible impatience, a longing. The enemy will strike soon. Beyond that, I cannot tell you anything. I'm sorry."

"Cecil, you tried to enter the mind of a demon from the underworld. You could have been lost to us, forever. You did not fail, my friend," Paedris assured the other wizard, and he watched the last rays of the setting sun. "I lack the ability to see into the enemy's mind, only you can do that. It is perhaps past the point where even my power can make any difference."

"Perhaps," Mwazo agreed. Lord Salva's power was truly impressive, beyond anything Mwazo could imagine. But the enemy's power was greater still, great enough to evade even Mwazo's skill. To penetrate the shield the enemy had around its mind would take the power of a wizard more powerful, far more powerful than Paedris Don Salva. There was only one such wizard Mwazo knew of who had that much power, and that young wizard had fled Tarador. "I am certain of one very important thing, Paedris," Mwazo said quietly.

"What is that?"

"The enemy has not captured Koren Bladewell."

"No," Carlana Trehayme, Regent of Tarador, said. Then she sighed. "Must we have this argument every time we talk, General?"

Grand General Magrane was as weary of the argument as Carlana was. "Every time you seek my advice in military matters, yes. The enemy is poised for attack along our border. Our scouts, and wizards," he glanced out the window to Lord Salva's tower, "report that the enemy is massing forces in three areas, and that wagon trains of supplies extend back at least thirty miles. They will attack this summer; such a large force cannot be sustained in the field indefinitely. So, again, Your Highness, when you seek my advice I will tell you that we must attack. We must strike before the enemy is ready, if only to conduct a raid for the purpose of throwing off the enemy's timing. To remain on the defensive, especially pulling back our main force to defend the capital, is certain to fail. We must go on the offensive, we must seize the initiative, take the fight to the enemy. Then we can dictate the terms of the fighting. All my years of military experience tell me this; yet when you seek my advice, you ignore my council."

"Seeking advice does not mean always agreeing. I have many advisors, General," Carlana looked out the window to where the sun was approaching the horizon. "The decision ultimately rests with me."

"Then, again, I offer my resignation."

"And again," Carlana managed a hint of smile at their little dance, "I refuse. Your nation needs you, General. An old soldier like you would not shirk your duty in time of war."

Magrane nodded curtly. As long as there was a chance, any chance, that he could prevail in his ongoing argument, he would remain in command of Tarador's army. "If we are done, Your Highness, I will take my leave of you?"

Carlana nodded, and turned her attention to a pile of scrolls on her desk. Magrane bowed slightly, strode purposefully out of the room, walked down a long hallway, and stepped through a door onto a battlement. The guards there saluted stiffly, and backed away, to give the general privacy. With hands scarred from many battles, and calloused from years of hard toil, he gripped the edge of the stone that was also worn smooth from years of use. Looking into the setting sun, he knew that same sun would soon be setting on the enemy's forces to the west, just across the border.

The enemy would be coming, soon. And Tarador was not ready.

Kyre Falco was also standing on a battlement watching the sun setting on a bitter day; only Kyre was atop the outer wall of his family's keep, not the royal castle in Linden. After the attack on Lord Salva, Ducal families had been allowed to bring their eldest children home from Linden, to make preparations for war. Kyre's younger brother Talen remained in Linden, as hostage against his father attempting to use the Falco's ducal army to overthrow the Trehaymes; it had always been that way. The fact that the royal family needed hostages to avoid a civil war, Kyre thought sourly, was a sign of the divisions within Tarador that made the realm weaker in the face of the enemy. In the case of his father, he had to admit, the Trehaymes were wise to require a hostage; his father burned inside to take back the throne that he thought rightfully belonged to the Falcos.

"Don't you worry about it, young sire," The soldier said quietly enough so that only Kyre Falco could hear him. "Your father will see your qualities soon."

Kyre turned away from gazing at the sun, which had just touched the hills to the west. "Jonas," he addressed the man by name, something that his father would never have done. Regin Falco would consider knowing the names of the common soldiers in his army to be beneath him. "Thank you. How is your son doing?"

Jonas brightened. "Much better, thank you, Your Grace." His son had been injured when a farm cart fell against his leg; Kyre had sent the Falco's personal surgeon to look after the young boy. That was another reason Regin Falco was not happy with his son, and had spent much of the afternoon railing against Kyre's weakness and lack of focus. "He was walking this morning, he will be healing right soon, thanks to you."

"Thank our surgeon, Jonas not me. I am only sorry that he was called away on an urgent matter." There had been no urgent matter, and Kyre and Jonas both knew that. When Regin Falco learned that the family's personal surgeon had been sent to care for the son of a lowly foot soldier, the Duke had called the man back to the keep, and angrily instructed both Kyre and the surgeon never to do such a thing again.

Jonas coughed. "Yes, Your Grace. No matter, my boy will be fine, up and around in a week, the surgeon told us." The man glanced quickly left and right, assuring they were still safely out of earshot. "There are others who," he hesitated, seeking to choose his words carefully, "appreciate when a leader sees that loyalty runs two ways, not one."

Kyre looked at the man sharply, thinking he was being baited. Seeing the almost pleading look on the man's face, Kyre relaxed slightly, and nodded. Jonas had been with Kyre on the night that Kyre had given up his tent, to let a sick soldier get a comfortable night's rest. Regin had not been happy about that either, but the majority of the soldiers had heartily approved, and word had spread quickly within the ducal army. "With war coming," Kyre responded, choosing his own words carefully, "we will need to rely on loyalty more than ever."

Jonas nodded silently, and stepped back to give the ducal heir privacy, as they watched the last rays of the sun disappear behind the hills.

Inside the secure walls of his keep, Regin Falco stepped back from a balcony, and closed the door behind him. He stood facing the window, watching the sun set over hills that defined the border of his ancestral lands.

Once, all of Tarador belonged to the Falcos, before the upstart Trehaymes used a crisis to greedily seize power, and they had held the throne ever since. Seeing the shrunken border of his land only made Regin angry, he sought to use that anger as energy to feed his resolve. Regin was in a foul mood, having once again having to correct his eldest son and heir. Kyre, who had as a young boy been so promising, had grown soft during his years in Linden. The boy had fallen under the influence of those people in the capital who sought to curry favor from the Trehaymes; weak people who had no minds of their own. Regin himself had experienced such influence when he was a boy in Linden; he had resisted the usurper Trehayme family's attempts to make him betray his legacy. Regin had stood fast and remained true to the Falcos, never wavering from the family's cause that had consumed every duke and duchess for hundreds of years; recapturing the throne. Now, Regin feared that Kyre, because of weakness and self-doubt, preferred the false comfort of popularity to the hard path of power. Regin knew his son was popular with some soldiers in the ducal army, popular for the wrong reasons. Popular because Kyre was soft on the men, because he took the easy path of popularity, rather than maintaining the distance a commander needed. What did Kyre think would happen, Regin asked himself bitterly, the first time the boy led men into battle, the first time he had to order men forward to their deaths? How popular would he be then, when the soldiers saw their fellows laying dead on a battlefield, knowing Kyre's actions led to their deaths?

Not so long ago, Regin had high hopes for Kyre, that the boy could gain the favor of princess Ariana, and the Falcos could regain the throne through marriage. Now, Regin concluded bitterly, his heir might someday catch the eye of the princess, but it would be due to Kyre's softness and weakness, and he would no longer truly be a Falco. Any alliance between Kyre and Ariana, Regin saw, would be the Trehaymes seeing a way to absorb and corrupt the Falcos. The opposite of what the Falcos had sought for centuries.

As the blazing sun touched the horizon, Regin spoke. "Forne. Tarador will not survive this coming war, with Carlana as Regent."

Niles Forne could not argue with his duke. He could not argue, both because he agreed with Regin on the issue, and because he knew Regin blamed Niles Forne for the growing softness of Kyre. "Yes, Your Grace."

"We must act." Regin's hands clasped tightly behind his back. "For the good of the nation, it is our patriotic duty. We cannot stand by while Carlana does nothing."

Forne cleared his throat quietly. "The Regency Council may be in the mood to replace the current Regent, but not, I judge, to accept you as her replacement. The political stars are not aligned for you to become Regent, Your Grace."

"Forne," Regin smiled for the first time that day. Occasionally, he was able to surprise his own adept political advisor. "You must think more subtly. The time is not right for me to assume the Regency," and effectively the throne, "but there is another candidate we can put forward."

"Who, Sire?" Forne asked, with curiosity and dread. Whatever plan Regin intended, the Duke would expect Niles Forne to make it happen.

"Ariana's uncle."

"Her uncle?" Forne almost laughed in surprise and horror. Leese Trehayme was a drunkard, a man who had never taken responsibility for anything in his life. Given a monthly stipend by the royal family, the man had left Linden to live a life of leisure and debauchery, surrounded by people who plied him with drink and, it was rumored, stronger substances. "That would be," Forne considered what to say to avoid insulting his Duke, "rather surprising, Your Grace."

"The man can be controlled, Forne. All we need is a figurehead, a symbol for the nation to rally around. He would not be expected to bear the burden of making the hard decisions, for that, we would provide guidance."

"It might be difficult to persuade him to return to Linden, Sire. He left because he could not stand the thought of his young niece being ahead of him, in line for the throne."

"Inducements can be provided, Forne. Flattery. If there is a strong call for Leese to return, to lead us in such dire times, how could any man not respond to such a summons?" Regin smiled wryly. "He should be reminded, also," the Falco Duke added darkly, "that these are dangerous times. How many attempts have there been on the life of our crown princess already?"

Forne sucked in a breath. The doors and windows were closed, no one was listening to them. Still, he was surprised to hear his Duke even broadly hint at such treason. "Many, Sire. Our crown princess is in great danger at all times."

"And in greater danger, as long as her mother holds the Regency. To protect our crown princess," Regin could not prevent his lip from curling, "we must act. Although," he shook his head sadly, "there is only so much we can do. If Ariana were to suffer a terrible fate," he looked into the fading sun, "someone must be ready to lead this nation."

Chu Wing stood in the stirrups to stretch her legs, and to relieve the pain in her aching backside. After living in a comfortable cabin on a sailing ship, during the journey from Tarador to Ching-Do, with a stop at Indus, she was unused to riding a horse. When the message from Lord Salva reached her, she had concluded her official visit to Indus, and had been about to board a ship for the final leg of her journey home. Immediately, her hosts had turned the coach around, and she had raced, day after day, through the landscape of Indus. That time of year, the winds blew strongly in the wrong direction for a sea voyage from Indus to Tarador. A ship would have to slowly beat back and forth all day to progress a few miles, and on some days all the skill of captain and crew could only hold the ship in place. It was faster to make the long, arduous journey overland. When hills turned into mountains, and roads narrowed then disappeared, she had left the bouncing, coach behind to ride a series of horses. The Indus Empire had a series of stations across the remote mountainous area, where imperial couriers could change horses, in their swift race across the sparsely populated wilderness.

"Halt!" The captain of her escort shouted in warning, holding up a fist. Wing pulled her horse to a stop, and stood again to peer into the setting sun. They were in a broad mountain valley between two towering mountain ranges; peaks thickly covered in snow and ice even this far into the springtime. The mountains here were referred to by the Indus as the Roof of the World, and Wing could understand why. Even where they were, in a valley, the air was thin and cold; the horses huffed loudly to fill their lungs even when merely walking.

Banners flew atop staffs to the west, almost within the disk of the lowering sun, and Wing squinted to see what lay ahead of them. Even with her wizard-enhanced senses, she could only discern it was a party of people on horses, perhaps a dozen. Banners were carried by two of the horsemen, the cloth flailing in the brisk wind making it impossible to tell what the banners signified.

The captain of her Indus escort drew his sword, and shouted commands to his men. The captain's orders, written directly by the Raj himself, were to deliver Madame Chu to Tarador safely, even at the cost of the men's lives. This remote part of the Empire, lands only loosely controlled by the Raj, held vicious bandits who preyed upon travelers and merchant caravans.

Wing closed her eyes, and let her senses fly on before her. Concentrating, she swayed a bit in the saddle, the balance of her body wavered as her consciousness was briefly projected elsewhere. Smiling, she opened her eye and spoke. "Captain, you may rest easy. Ahead of us are Rangers of Tarador. They have come a great distance to meet us."

Her escort remained on alert, though swords were sheathed. The sun had slid halfway down behind the horizon by the time the Rangers arrived; their leader came on ahead, hands up in peaceful greeting. Seeing the wizard, he dismounted from his horse and got down on one knee, bowing to the powerful wizard from Ching-Do. "Chu Wing? Madame Chu, Her Highness the Regent of Tarador, and the wizard Lord Salva, thank you for answering their call in our time of great need."

"You are?" Wing asked.

"Lieutenant Tems of the Ranger Corps, ma'am. We are here to escort you to Linden. There is a full complement of Rangers several leagues back, we could not bring our full strength, due to lack of fodder for our horses in these parts," he nodded back to his men. Behind the saddle of every horse were bags of grain to feed the horse; the sparse springtime grasses in the high mountain meadows meant the horses would otherwise have to spend most of each day eating, rather than traveling.

"Thank you, Lieutenant Tems. Captain Rashesh of Indus will accompany us to Linden," she announced. Seeing the look of surprise and not a little wariness on Tems' face, she hastened to add "the Raj has ordered them to see to my safety. His Imperial Majesty the Raj will be sending an army of five thousand soldiers to defend Tarador, but they will be arriving by sea, and the winds this time of year are not favorable."

Five thousand skilled imperial soldiers could make a great difference on behalf of Tarador. If they arrived in time. "The winds?" He was familiar with the seasonal winds and ocean currents between Tarador and Indus, having served on a Taradoran naval ship early in his career. "When does the Raj expect his troops to arrive in Tarador?"

"Likely not until the leaves are falling," Wing said sadly.

Tems looked grim. "I fear to say, that might be too late, ma'am. With your strength and skill, and that of Lord Salva, we may yet prevail."

"We may," Wing looked at the last flash of the day's sunlight. "It is two miles, I believe, to the way station, and it grows dark. Lead on, Mr. Tems. We have a long way to go, and no time to tarry."

Captain Raddick winced as thorns scraped his face and snagged in his hair. He pushed the rose canes aside slowly, carefully, lest the movement catch the eye of the enemy below. They were in a bad position, for the setting sun to the west illuminated the slope they were on, while looking into the glare made it difficult for Raddick to see his quarry. Against the orders of the Regent, and following the hinted desires of Grand General Magrane, Raddick had crossed the border into Acedor with only four men. Traveling light and swiftly, they were now on a rock-strewn slope, wrestling with thorn bushes that provided their only concealment. To get into position had taken all day, stealthily crawling up the hill, avoiding poisonous serpents that were sunning themselves on the warm rocks. Only now were they in position to view the enemy, and what Raddick saw dismayed him.

Campfires. Many campfires, filling the valley below him. Campfires stretching along both sides of the river; orcs on one side, foul men on the other. Two armies, building up strength to invade Tarador. The last light of day fell on a train of wagons coming from the east, bringing more supplies for the enemy's forces.

Raddick turned his head and looked at his lieutenant, catching sunlight barely glinting off the man's eyes.

Soon. The enemy would attack soon. The coming summer could be the last for Tarador.

And for the world.

Shomas Feany was on his own long voyage, although he was able to travel in relative comfort aboard a ship, instead of a bone-jolting ride on horseback. Relative comfort was a relative term; sleeping in a swaying hammock, trying to walk on a heaving deck, and eating what sailors considered good food had made Shomas yearn for the ship to get into port as quickly as possible. Yet, there he was, back aboard the ship, with sailors climbing the masts to unfurl more sails. Beginning a voyage as the sun was setting did not seem wise to Shomas, but the sailors explained they must take advantage of the tides, and sailing at night was nothing unusual. The ship was barely making way at the moment, under half sail and still within the main harbor of LeMonde. The main harbor was a fine anchorage; wide, deep enough that heavily laden ships need not fear running aground, shallow enough to securely anchor. Hills ringing the harbor and a reef offshore, protected it from summer storms that sometimes raged with little warning. It was the safe anchorage of the harbor, and its location in the main shipping lanes off the coast of Tarador, which had made the little Duchy of LeMonde a wealthy and prosperous nation. Despite her title of ancient origin, the Duchess of LeMonde was a queen in all but name; she answered to no one but her subjects.

Although that was not quite true, and that was the reason Lord Feany had made the uncomfortable sea voyage. The Duchess of LeMonde allowed two small offshore islands to be used as bases for pirate ships, pirates supported by Acedor. Not allowed, exactly; the Duchess did not encourage Acedor to use two of her islands, and she did not allow ships flying the flag of Acedor to enter the main harbor. She had also done nothing to remove the pirates from the islands. Tarador, in years past, had for centuries maintained a strong naval presence in LeMonde, at the invitation of that Duchy's rulers. No more did Tarador protect its smaller neighbor; ships and troops had been pulled back to the mainland, leaving the Duchy to defend itself. And so, the current Duchess turned a blind eye to piracy, even to Acedoran ships flying false flags using her fine harbor. Those ships paid an anchorage fee, and their crews knew to keep their visits ashore brief and quiet.

The purpose of Shomas paying a visit to the Duchess was to discretely inquire what support from Tarador she would need, in order to act against the pirates. The answer he received, from a chilly and skeptical Duchess, was not encouraging. Unless Tarador could station a substantial force in LeMonde; a half dozen ships, perhaps five hundred soldiers, the Duchess would not do anything to risk an open invasion of her little country by Acedor. As Tarador appeared to be unable, or unwilling, to protect even itself, the Duchess was not optimistic of a renewed alliance between her Duchy and her once-powerful neighbor across the sea to the north.

The problem, thought Shomas as he watched the sun settle into the sea to the west, was Tarador's current Regent. As long as Carlana Trehayme refused to risk her armed forces in battle, the outcome was inevitable. When he returned to Linden, he needed to discuss a taboo subject with Paedris; the Wizard Council may need to take action, lest Tarador be defeated before the battle had begun.

Koren or, as he now called himself, Kedrun, was also on a ship, though his ship was gliding slowly into a harbor far to the south of LeMonde. That same island had been Koren's first landfall after departing from Tarador. It was the northernmost of the South Islands, and a popular trading port. The harbor held a half dozen ships at that moment; two weeks ago Koren had counted fourteen ships anchored in the warm, clear water.

He stood at the rail and looked down; even in the golden light of sunset, he could see the white sandy bottom of the harbor. As he watched, a school of multi-colored fish flashed by and under the ship. He inhaled deeply, breathing in the scent of something still that was still new to him. New, and wonderful and delightful, and so invigorating that every time the scent wafted past his nose, he smiled. It was the scent of what sailors called the tropics, and so indescribably wonderful that Koren could never have imagined it. The scent was a combination of things called pineapples, and coconuts, and papayas, and guava fruits, and sand baked by the midday sun, and of sunlight glinting off crystal clear waters. The balmy evening breeze caressed his bare arms, he had followed the advice of fellow sailors, and cut sleeves off one of his shirts as the air grew warmer on their sea voyage south. The tropical breeze also carried from land the dry rustling of palm fronds, so unlike the sound of wind through the pines that Koren remembered from his childhood.

"Beautiful, isn't it?" Alfonze asked as he came to stand by the rail next to the young man he knew as Kedrun. With the ship gliding into the harbor on almost bare poles, with all sails furled but one, there was not much for the sailors to do right then. The ship's momentum was carrying it slowly to its selected anchorage. In a few minutes, the captain would call for the sailors to back the single sail, then furl it, and the ship would come to a stop for the night.

"It is," Koren admitted enthusiastically. "Alfonze, when you told me about the South Islands, I didn't believe you, not all of it. I could never have imagined this."

Alfonze breathed in deeply, filling his lungs with the enticing scent of land, welcome after many days at sea. "A man could be happy here, Kedrun."

Koren nodded silently in agreement. He could be happy here. He *was* happy here. Aboard the ship, he had found a home; his fellow sailors were a band of men who knew nothing of his past, knew not that he was a jinx, did not think him a coward and a deserter. Indeed, his jinx had not arisen since he had been aboard the ship; nothing bad or even odd had happened. As each day passed without incident, Koren was beginning to dare hope that he had left his curse behind in Tarador. This, maybe, was where he belonged; far from those he had injured, far from his curse, far from his home. This place, this tropical paradise, could become his new home, if he embraced it.

Then he frowned, a shadow passing across his face. There was a ship, between his ship and the land, the shifting breeze had just lofted that ship's flag. Koren could now see it was the flag of Tarador. The last time Koren had been in this port, rumors had flown that many sailors from his homeland were answering the call to come home. The taverns had been filled with men from Tarador, some of who had not seen home shores for many years; they were now leaving to take passage north. To serve in their homeland's navy, in their nation's time of dire need.

Alfonze saw the look on Koren's face, saw the young man was looking at the flag that fluttered lazily from the stern of the other ship, glowing in the golden light of the setting sun. Alfonze knew what the young man was thinking, and the sailor clasped a calloused hand on Koren's shoulder reassuringly. "Don't you worry about them, Kedrun. The war between Tarador and Acedor has been raging for a thousand years, if tales be true. Oh, they will tell you about duty, and honor, and noble causes, and none of it puts food in your belly, or coin in your pocket. I've seen war, Kedrun. I've seen war, and it's all only spoiled kings and queens who have too much, and lust for more. They live in their castles, surrounded by every luxury, and all the land they can see belongs to them. And they are not happy, because lands they cannot see do not belong to them. So, they send men like you and me to fight and die." He spat in the sea. "What do royalty think of their duty to us? Nothing, that's what. I tell you, the troubles up north amount to nothing down here. Tarador has been fighting for a thousand years, this dust-up is nothing new, mark my words. Whatever happened up there, whatever you did, whatever happened to you, put it behind you."

The young man did not appear convinced, so Alfonze continued, looking at the sky where stars had begun to shine. "Tell me this, Kedrun, what do they owe you?"

"Nothing," Koren said quietly.

"That's right. And that's what you owe them. You're a young man, you need to make your way in the world. Leave strife and glorious quests to others, eh? The South Islands are peaceful. Tell you what, we won't be paid until the day after tomorrow, but I have coins in my pocket. When we get to shore, I'll buy you one of those drinks you like, served in a coconut and all."

"No rum in it, please," Koren grinned at the thought. Alfonze was right. He had left his homeland to protect the people he cared about from his jinx; he owed nothing more to Tarador. He could be happy here.

And he would.

Contact the author at craigalanson@gmail.com

Made in the USA
Middletown, DE
13 April 2018